THE SUMMER AWAY

Sometimes hope is found in the most unexpected places.

AIESSA HOLLAND

This is a work of fiction. Names, characters, places, and incidents either are the product of the author's imagination or are used fictitiously. Any resemblance to actual persons, living or dead, events, or locales is entirely coincidental.

Copyright © 2024 by Aiessa Holland

All rights reserved. No part of this book may be reproduced or transmitted in any form or by any means, electronic or mechanical, including photocopying, recording or any information storage and retrieval system now known or to be invented, without permission in writing from the author, except by a reviewer who wishes to use brief passages in connection with a review or an article.

Scripture taken from the New King James Version®. Copyright © 1982 by Thomas Nelson. Used by permission. All rights reserved.

First paperback edition July 2024

Book design by Jackie Dras

ISBN 979-8-218-45940-6 (paperback)

ISBN 979-8-218-45941-3 (ebook)

Dedication

For my husband and every single person who valued my soul enough to share the gospel with me. I'm eternally grateful to each of you.

Lastly, for Frank and Jane, because you had evidence in me.

The Summer Away

Aiessa Holland

1

Sweat trickled from my palms as I brushed my damp, sandy hair away from my face. The night's salty sea air provided a gentle breeze I desperately needed. I climbed higher into the tree in Lacey Lockhart's front yard. Every move had to be deliberate; one unsteady shift and I could plummet to the ground at any moment.

"That's it," Ronni coached me from the ground below. She had far more experience than I did with rolling someone's front yard. "Lena, look at me!"

I took a deep breath, peeked down, and saw her staring back up at me. Ronni's long blonde and pink locks were blowing in the night breeze beneath the black hoodie she wore. She held a roll of toilet paper in her hand. I wasn't sure if it was my current position in the tree or the fear of getting caught, but my heart was racing faster than it ever had before.

"Catch!" Ronni exclaimed as she hurled the roll up to me. I swiftly grasped the branch above my head with my left hand, steadying myself as I stretched out to catch the roll with my right.

"Nice!" Ronni cheered me on from the ground. "Now roll as much of the tree as you can."

I leaned against the tree trunk, breathing deeply, and unraveled the paper from the roll, letting it unfurl above my head.

"Lena, move faster!" Ronni called up to me again, keeping her voice low. "We're trying to get back at Lacey, not get caught!"

My hands trembled as I unwound the toilet paper more quickly. A rustling below caught my attention, and I peered down to see Ronni launching another roll into the tree. The paper clung to a branch before unraveling back to the ground.

The longer I remained crouched in the tree, the more I second-guessed this decision. I had witnessed other acts of Ronni's vandalism, like using her fake ID to buy beer while underage or shoplifting, even though money was no object to her. Tonight, I was proving to be the amateur between the two of us.

When the surrounding branches were coated with toilet paper, I tucked what little remained on the roll inside the front pocket of my black hoodie. I reached for the branch above my head and heaved myself upward, positioning my feet carefully below me as I climbed higher. I reminded myself to breathe slowly and stay calm to avoid falling or getting caught.

I leaned back against the tree, shifting my weight to navigate the branch, balancing carefully. I worked to finish quickly, driven by the need to get us out of here. Ronni used to be the last person in the world I could have expected to be in this situation with, but Lacey had left the two of us with no choice. We had to take a stand against her once and for all.

Ronni threw another roll into the tree, but it stopped short in a branch just below me, tangled in the leaves. I grasped the tree trunk, focusing on the present, and pulled the toilet paper roll free. Holding it tight, I hauled myself back up the tree and began my last climb.

As I pulled myself up, I stopped when the window's light hit my arm, clinging to the trunk with all my might. A sudden motion caught my attention, causing me to freeze. I pulled my black hood over my face, trying to blend into the tree.

"Lena! What's happening?" Ronni urgently whispered from the ground. Stuck in a tense silence, I couldn't move or warn her to keep quiet as I gazed through the window. Lacey's curtains were partially open, and I spotted her seated at her desk with her back to the window.

I felt a wave of nostalgia when I saw the bookshelf, filled with books I'd helped her collect. The bedroom remained unchanged, like a time capsule from our friendship that felt like a lifetime ago. I had spent almost as much time at her house as I had my own. The only change was the new cheerleading trophies on the top shelf.

***

Lacey and I met in our middle school gym class. I had just moved to Freeport, courtesy of my dad's Coast Guard career. The transition to middle school provided a sense of normalcy. For the first time, I wasn't the only newcomer, as everyone in the surrounding area was navigating the challenges of a new school. The first week, our class had to run around the school's track, and Lacey had forgotten to bring a pair of socks. I wasn't feeling very well. My stomach had been in knots after a pop quiz in math class, and I had asked to sit out. Mr. Miles seemed to understand, but when I overheard Lacey asking if she could sit out too, he had said no. Who could run a few laps with no socks? That would cause horrible blisters. I could tell she was dreading the laps, so I let her borrow mine.

"Can you believe Mr. Miles said no?" she exclaimed.

"I knew he was strict, but that was kind of harsh," I responded.

"Thanks for these," Lacey expressed, pulling on the borrowed socks. "I'll make sure to return them."

I wrinkled my nose at the idea of receiving sweaty socks back, even if she washed them. "Don't worry about it. You can keep them or use them as a backup pair in your gym bag if you have to."

Lacey grinned and then sprinted off. Afterward, she joined me on the bleachers, and from then on, our friendship blossomed. We joined the cheerleading team and met Worthy and Camille, forging a tight-knit group. During the spring, we created a step team to practice our moves in the off-season. On Fridays, we would spend the night at the Lockharts' for girls' night.

Over the next three years, we all became the best of friends, though Lacey and I remained inseparable. If one of us missed a day of school for being sick, the other got asked how the other was. People knew we were a package deal. Soon enough, we styled our hair the same way and would even borrow each other's clothes. Sometimes, I found more of Lacey's clothes in my closet than my own. I had no siblings, but Lacey was the closest thing to a sister I had ever had.

Once Lacey and I started high school, our friendship felt unbreakable. We attended Freeport High's cheerleading tryouts in the fall and dreamed of making it to the state competition in the spring. When cheer tryouts were over, we anxiously awaited the results to see if we made the team.

By the end of the first week of school, our world shifted. Lacey, Camille, and Worthy made the varsity squad. I was the only one who had made the junior varsity team. I felt crushed, as my friends joined the upperclassmen and left me behind. Lacey assured me we could still see each other at the games, but I knew it wouldn't be the same. Varsity games took place on different days and the teams traveled to away games on separate buses.

I wanted to hold on to my friends, so I walked away from cheering to support them. That year, I attended all their practices and home games, cheering on my friends from the stands.

For a while, I still felt included, until relationships formed. Halfway through the season, Lacey started dating Javier Diaz. He was a freshman student who had made the varsity football team and was well on his way to leading the team to victory. As Javier rose to become one of the school's star players, he and Lacey became a Freeport High freshman power couple.

Even when I started dating Chase Conway, Javier's best friend, things kept changing. Varsity game after-parties took over Friday night sleepovers, and soon enough, I drifted away from everyone. Whenever I attempted to make plans with Lacey, she was always busy with the varsity cheer squad or Javier. Even though she assured me she'd make it up to me, as time passed, we grew more distant.

The summer after freshman year, I started noticing the fractures in my family. Over the next year, I watched my mom completely lose her way. She had kept her drinking a secret for a while before Dad and I noticed she was struggling. When Mom lost her job, she began her first of several failed attempts at joining Alcoholics Anonymous. She never stuck with it, though she always promised us she was fine. The night I realized my mom was truly sick was at the end of sophomore year, and Lacey abandoned me when I needed her the most.

That night, I dialed Lacey's number, her name illuminated in my favorites. The photo of us in our cheer uniforms served as a poignant reminder of happier times as I waited for her response. The phone rang, my legs trembling with anticipation, and when Lacey finally answered, there was no greeting from her end.

"Lena, hang on!" she shouted on the other end of the line. The music blared until I heard a door slam and the sound died down. "Are you there?"

"I'm here," I choked out, my voice growing unsteady with each moment that passed.

"Lena, I can't hear you. Can you speak up?" she yelled once more. "It's really loud at Javi's house."

Of course, she was at Javier's house. She stayed glued to his side, but this was serious and I needed her.

"My mom's going through some things and, um, something happened today." I managed before my voice broke once again.

"What?" Lacey shouted. "Lena, I can't hear you. Can we talk tomorrow?"

Her disregard shook me, and I couldn't believe what I was hearing. "No, I need you now. My mom is sick!"

"Oh gosh, I'm so sorry Lena!" she responded, but her voice was hollow.

Her reaction took me by surprise, but I still pressed, "Do you think you can come over?" I noticed I was still shaking and finally realized it wasn't from the chilly evening breeze I felt standing on my front porch.

"I can't. I'm at Javi's house and don't have my car. Can I call you tomorrow?"

Before I could respond, I heard a crash on the other side of the line and Lacey squealed, "Javi, stop!"

I listened as she giggled loudly before the line finally clicked and she hung up on me. For a moment, I stared at the *Call Ended* display before my normal wallpaper reappeared. "Don't bother," I whispered to the night air.

The following weeks blurred together as my family unraveled. My mom ended up in the hospital for alcohol poisoning, facing a long road to recovery. I succumbed to the fear of losing her, missing several days of school as the year concluded, unwilling to leave my mom's side. Because of everything going on at home, the school granted me a chance to make up the finals I missed.

On the day of my last makeup final, I bumped into Chase in the hallway at school. To say things were awkward between us was an understatement. Chase, along with everyone else in Freeport, caught wind of Mom's hospitalization and the rumors swirled. With no notice, he broke up with me over text. I thought our breakup would hurt more than it had, but the worst part was Camille's betrayal when the two of them began dating just a week later. Not only had I felt the first sting of heartbreak with Chase, but Camille's complete disregard for my feelings ended our friendship.

Chase scoffed when our shoulders collided, but behind him, I noticed Javier and Lacey. When her eyes met mine, she slid her arm from Javier's waist and tiptoed over to me.

"Hey, I'm sorry about last week. We were having an end-of-year party, and—"

"Yeah, I heard," I snapped, looking down.

Lacey flinched, and her cheeks flushed. I watched as she glanced back at Javier, who was impatiently tapping his foot, before turning back to me. "How are you doing?"

I eyed her closely, sensing a stark change in just a few months. The friend I once shared secrets with had become a girl who viewed me from the rearview mirror.

"You don't have to pretend like you care," I murmured.

Lacey's eyes widened and she glanced back at Javier once more. When she faced me, I was shaking my head and grinning at her in disbelief. She cared more about pleasing Javier than ensuring I was okay. At that moment, knew our friendship would never be the same.

"Have a good summer with your boyfriend," I erupted, brushing past her.

I heard Javier and Chase chuckle behind me, murmuring something about how crazy I was as I stormed off. Little did I know losing Lacey was just the beginning of the trouble coming my way.

To get out of the house and away from everything going on with my mom, I got a job at the Movieplex in town. I began working almost every night until the early hours of the morning, when the last movie would end. As the summer pressed on, I slept in later and later, waking just in time to get a few chores done around the house before going to work.

Around mid-summer, Lacey, Javier, and some of the other varsity crowd came in on a weeknight to see the latest horror flick. I stood behind the counter, taking ticket and concession orders as their gang approached.

"How can I help you?" I greeted, treating them like any other customer.

Lacey's bright smile dimmed with my lack of recognition.

"Two tickets for Evil Dead, a large popcorn, and one large Coke," Javier requested, throwing a sly grin in Lacey's direction. Her face flushed before she sheepishly peered back at me. I retrieved their popcorn and filled their large cup before passing the items across the counter. Javier swiped the items away and headed into the theater, but Lacey lingered back. I could tell she wanted to say something, but was hesitating. When I met her gaze, I found her staring at me before Javier called after her. Without further pause, she headed after him.

I let out a deep sigh when Lacey was out of sight as the line carried on. Once the line had cleared, I busied myself restocking popcorn bags and cups. As I moved past the counter to the far wall where condiments and napkins were stacked, I noticed someone's footsteps approaching from behind. I was expecting to help a random customer, but was startled to see Lacey standing there.

She began picking at her nails before saying, "He's not bad, you know."

My brows furrowed in confusion. "What?"

Lacey's gaze swept up from her feet to meet mine. "Javier. He's not bad, he's actually a good guy."

This didn't clear things up for me. "Why are you telling me this?"

She chuckled, treating my skepticism like a silly joke. "Because you don't like him and I'm not sure what to do."

I eyed her, and she seemed genuinely baffled, as if I were being ridiculous for not being as obsessed with her boyfriend as she was. "You're right, I don't like him."

Lacey deflated. "You just have to give him a chance, Lena."

"No," I replied firmly. "I don't like him, and I haven't liked the person you've turned into for a while now either."

Once my words were out, her face fell. For a moment, she seemed wounded, struck by my words. Suddenly, her lips pursed and her nostrils flared. "Fine, I guess we're not friends then."

"Fine," I echoed. My heart sank knowing she finally chose Javier over me.

"Have a great summer buttering popcorn," Lacey spat. "We'll miss seeing you in the stands."

I said nothing as Lacey spun on her heel and walked away.

Movement from the bedroom alerted me as Lacey's mom entered her room. A wave of discomfort hit me as I watched Lacey stand, her lengthy black hair gathered in a bun atop her head, dressed in pajamas. Lacey's mom hugged her, her identical black hair styled in a pixie cut.

The sight of the two of them talking brought back a flood of memories. Mr. Lockhart never missed a game and was always there to support Lacey, often driving us back to their house for sleepovers. Mrs. Lockhart had always been a wonderful host during Friday night sleepovers. She always had tons of snacks ready for us to dig into when we arrived. I always admired their family, and when my mom got sick, I often wished they were mine.

"Lena!" came Ronni's whispered scream again. I snapped out of my thoughts and gazed down at her from my position. My stomach lurched as I realized how far up I had climbed.

"If you don't hurry, we're going to get caught! What are you doing up there?" she demanded.

Before I could move or even warn her, Ronni began hurling multiple rolls at me. One roll, then another, and by the time the third roll came, I tried to catch it but completely lost my balance. I accidentally struck the side of the roll, causing it to fly and ricochet off Lacey's bedroom window.

My pulse pounded in my temples, and sweat dripped down my forehead as I leered wide-eyed through the window to see two sets of eyes staring back at me.

"Run!" I screamed, abandoning all attempts to conceal myself. Down below, Ronni raced across the yard, heading towards her parked car half a block away. Panic seized me, rendering me frozen as Lacey threw her curtains open and spotted us.

I quickly began my descent. With sweaty hands, I clung to the tree but struggled to keep my grip while lowering myself. I peered down, realizing the ground was closer than before, and in a panic, jumped. The impact on the ground proved more painful than I anticipated. My left ankle took the full force of my landing, causing a sudden wave of pain to shoot through my leg. As I attempted to stand, my ankle gave way, and I cried out.

I leaned against the tree searching for Ronni, but she was now just a distant figure, disappearing from view. Hopping as quickly as I could across the yard, I had reached the mailbox when the front door creaked open behind me. Lacey emerged onto the porch, clad in a robe, while her father stumbled out after her.

"There! Dad, look what they've done!" Lacey's cry pierced the night, drawing attention to the blanket of white strewn across their yard. Clenching my teeth, I collapsed in Lacey's driveway, unable to support my weight with my injured leg.

Mr. Lockhart rushed down his driveway, towering over me. "You're not going anywhere, you little brat!" he spat. Unable to hide my identity any longer, I peered up at him beneath my hood.

After more than a year, I finally crossed paths with Mr. Lockhart again. Shorter and rounder than my dad, he glowered at the mess Ronni and I had made. When his gaze flicked back to me, the recognition dawned on him and his eyes softened. "Lena Harris?"

Filled with shame, I stayed silent and lowered my gaze.

"Lacey, honey. Go get me my phone and the first aid kit," he ordered.

While Lacey darted inside, I stared up at the man who was looming above me, wincing from the ache in my leg and shaken by his unexpected mercy.

Lacey quickly reappeared with her father's requested supplies. Stripped of her usual flawlessly made-up face, the look of disdain she shot my way was all too familiar. "Daddy, we have to call the cops! Ronni Dice was with her."

"Hush, honey. We'll work it all out. Now, hand me the phone," he instructed. Lacey passed him the phone, and he peered down at me.

Dread filled the pit of my stomach when I wondered who Mr. Lockhart would be calling at this hour. *Was he going to have me arrested?*

"Alright, Lena, I'm going to have to call your father, so he knows what kind of stunt you pulled tonight. I need a number," he commanded.

All the color drained from my face. At that moment, I wished he had opted to call the cops—a far lesser punishment. "I'm assuming there's no chance of changing your mind, right?"

I heard Lacey scoff.

"Not a chance. Give me his number," her father insisted, before he glared back at Lacey. "You can go inside."

She glowered at her father. "But dad—"

"Inside now," he demanded. Lacey spun on her heel, but not before sneering at me.

I waited until their front door slammed before I summoned the courage to recite my dad's cell phone number. The familiar beep of phone buttons echoed as Mr. Lockhart dialed. While awaiting my dad's response, he gently cradled my injured leg, placing it carefully on the pavement.

"Hi there, is this Tom?" he inquired. "Great, yes, sir. This is Aaron Lockhart. Lena has had an accident at my house. I believe she's badly twisted her ankle; would you mind picking her up?"

A brief silence ensued. "Okay, great. We'll be here waiting for you."

My dad's voice filtered through the line, but his words were inaudible.

"Yes sir, she's fine, but we can discuss the rest of the situation as soon as you get here," Mr. Lockhart continued.

I felt a wave of dread wash over me. The past year brought its fair share of disappointments for me. My dad was never happy about me spending time with Ronni, and getting fired from the Movieplex a few weeks ago for pretending to be sick just to hang out with her only made things worse. I lost my job when my colleague exposed the fact that I had lied about being sick. As peeved as I was, I couldn't blame him; I deserved it.

Getting fired was just one part of the difficult junior year that I barely survived. I had skipped enough of my algebra class, ducking out early on most school days with Ronni to go shopping or just hang out at the beach. My Dad had gone before the school's administration to plead for me to have a second chance. Just three weeks ago, I could take the final and secure my spot as a senior for the upcoming school year.

Freeport High's administration was made aware of our challenging home situation by my dad, who described how it was affecting me. He blamed himself for not being a stronger influence and attributed my struggles to falling in with the wrong crowd, namely Ronni, who wore her bad reputation with pride.

Now, amid this mess, I'd be fortunate if my dad allowed me to remain under his roof.

"This might sting a bit," Mr. Lockhart began, wrapping a bandage around my swelling ankle. "Your dad should take you to the hospital, but for now, I'll help you get the shoe off and onto the porch. Ready?"

I stared at him, questioning why he was being unexpectedly kind. "Why are you being so nice to me?"

"This is how adults act," Mr. Lockhart spat. "Children vandalize like you've done. Since you're not mature enough to know how to act like an adult, I'll be sure to demonstrate for you."

As he assisted me, bearing most of my weight, my gratitude waned from his mini-lecture. I vowed to stay silent until my dad arrived. We approached the doorstep, and I noticed Lacey glaring at me through her front window. Our eyes locked uncomfortably, and she forcefully shut the curtains. Mr. Lockhart helped me crouch on the front stairs, straightening my leg to finish the wrapping.

"So, I'm guessing you were the one who did the fine work in the tree there," he motioned where I had fallen.

"Yes, sir," I grunted.

"I'll give you the opportunity to tell me the truth." He peered up at me, still working on my ankle.

I nodded, silently.

"Why roll my yard? Are you girls fighting again?" he questioned.

"No," I answered, my eyes fixed on my feet. Mr. Lockhart's interest in my friendship with Lacey revealed his lack of understanding. I wasn't about to reveal that I now considered her to be my arch-nemesis.

His eyes narrowed, confused by my response. "So, is this how you're spending your time these days?"

"No," I repeated flatly. He didn't realize just how much I hated the idea of rolling his house. How I had begged Ronni to get our revenge on Lacey this way instead of whatever heinous plan she would have come up with.

Mr. Lockhart's voice dripped with irritation as he froze mid-wrap. "Then why would you do this, Lena?"

My thoughts spun like a merry-go-round as I debated revealing the truth to Mr. Lockhart. Did I let him know about the way Lacey had been tormenting me all school year? Should I confess how Ronni was the one to stick up for me when everyone else had turned their back on me? Or how about how Lacey had thrown tea on Ronni in the cafeteria, starting the war between all of us? I knew I couldn't say anything, especially not about how Javier had cheated with Ronni behind Lacey's back.

I knew he'd be stunned if he knew Lacey was still dating Javier even though she knew he had cheated on her. Mr. Lockhart still believed she was his innocent little girl. I wouldn't be the one to tell him Lacey had keyed Ronni's car and egged mine just a few nights before. Ronni wanted to get back at Lacey, but with all she had already done to humiliate her, I intervened before Ronni could go overboard.

Headlights flashed, and my dad's beaten-up truck pulled into the driveway. Dad emerged, a tan, slim figure with buzzed hair and chronically tired eyes. "Lena, what's going on?"

"Dad, I can explain—" I started, but was interrupted.

"Tom, I'd like to explain if I could," Mr. Lockhart interjected. "Lacey saw someone in our yard. When we ran out to see who was here, I found Lena had fallen out of the tree—" he motioned to my fine toiletry work.

The lights dimmed in my father's eyes, and he rubbed his face, unable to hide his disappointment. "Lena, I can't believe you would do something like this. Aaron, I apologize. She will clean up every bit of this."

"Is this something your daughter makes a habit of?" Aaron asked, prying unnecessarily. "If this happens again..."

His voice trailed off as Dad interjected. "I promise, Aaron. This won't be a problem again."

I couldn't bear to hear him apologize for my behavior. His face grew weary, and I knew this stunt was the icing on the cake of an already long, challenging year. Being here, directly witnessing my actions affecting him, was painful.

"I'm sorry, Mr. Lockhart," I spoke up. "I shouldn't have done this, and I promise to be here first thing in the morning to clean this mess up. It won't happen again."

Dad reached out to take my hand, and I leaned on him as he wrapped his arm around my shoulders for support. "Can you even walk?"

The fire in his voice struck me and I winced, my voice coming out a low whisper. "No."

"Aaron, I will have her here in the morning to clean this up. She won't leave until every last speck is gone."

Mr. Lockhart seemed relieved, but still angry. He sighed heavily. "I suppose I'll see you both in the morning."

"Yes, sir," Dad affirmed, taking a glimpse at me to do the same.

"Yes, sir," I answered, unable to meet Aaron's stare.

We wasted no time. Once the words left my lips, Dad guided me to the truck. His silent support was torture. Sweat coated my skin as my nerves continued to rattle. I dreaded seeing his faith in me grow dimmer. There was no way to disappoint him more than I had already.

As he opened the passenger door for me to climb in, approaching headlights grabbed my attention. My gaze followed, and I realized—I was staring at the black beetle with checkered dice hanging from the mirror. The car moved so slowly I could see Ronni's face as she watched me too.

"Please tell me that's not who I think it is..." Dad groaned.

"Dad—" I attempted.

"Lena Michele Harris." He used my full name, and at that moment, I knew I was in deep trouble. "Was that Veronica Dice's car?"

"Dad, please—"

"Lena, was that Ronni?!" he shouted, cutting me off.

I could only stare up at him, my eyes wide with guilt. He wouldn't drop it until I answered him. "Yes, sir."

He released my weight so abruptly I lost my balance, and my weight shifted to my injured ankle. Wincing, I knew he was unrelenting by now.

"Get. In. The. Truck. Now." He gritted his teeth. He marched around to the driver's side, slamming the door so hard the noise echoed down the street. I heaved a heavy sigh, knowing it would be a long night.

2

"What was it this time, Lena?" Dad seethed as we drove through town after leaving Urgent Care.

My new set of crutches leaned against the passenger door beside me. The cracked windows allowed the cool night air into Dad's truck, in need of several repairs, including air conditioning. I wished I was in my air-conditioned beater, driving anywhere but home.

Dad impatiently tapped his fingers on the steering wheel. "Did Ronni promise to buy you booze with her fake ID or get you into a club?"

"I don't drink, Dad, you know how I feel about that, and I would never go clubbing. I'm only seventeen," I retorted, my voice meek, wanting to shrink away from this lecture.

"So what was it?" His voice grew shrill as we drove further. My throbbing ankle made me more uncomfortable. Pressing the window button, I tried to lean out for more air.

"Oh, no you don't," Dad demanded, pressing the button on his side.

I whipped my head back inside to avoid the window hitting me as he raised it.

"You had better have some sort of explanation for why you rolled Aaron Lockhart's yard. I'm sick of worrying about where you are at all hours, going to school to bail you out of trouble, and fighting to keep you enrolled. I've gone to the Movieplex to apologize after you so irresponsibly lied and got yourself fired, and now this. Lena, I've had it up to here with you this year!" His free hand moved from the steering wheel to hover high above his head.

"You don't know what she's done," I tried to speak up. Dad's wide-eyed glance between me and the road told me there was nothing I could say to curb his wrath. Leaning my head on my hand, elbow on the armrest, I stared blankly out the window. The memory resurfaced before I could suppress it any longer.

"You're right, I don't know, but I'm sure it didn't warrant this kind of stunt," Dad lectured.

He was wrong.

I wished Dad had stayed in the Coast Guard so we could get orders out of Freeport. He had no idea just how awful this past school year had been for me. On the first day, I had been called to the guidance counselor's office. Freeport was a small town. The news of my mom's addiction spread faster than I could blink. Even a trip to the local grocery store brought stares from those aware of my dad leaving his military career just a few years before he could have retired with full benefits.

Dad hadn't made the decision lightly, but he was the type of man who put his family and marriage first, especially since my mom was struggling. Supporting her in this battle became his first and only priority. All year I had fallen by the wayside while he cared for her. Staying out of their way became my mission.

When Dad took a job with the City of Freeport, doing maintenance, he took a huge cut in pay and the comfort of life as we knew it faded away. Before my junior year began, the school administration checked in with Dad since they heard how tense things had been at home with Mom being sick.

Dad, the principal, and the guidance counselor—Mrs. Jones—decided I would have "talk time" during the school day to help process our home issues. Mrs. Jones was a young counselor. I guessed she was just out of college since she seemed inexperienced. Her meticulous note-taking and the variety of pamphlets she handed out after every session annoyed me.

The war between Lacey and Ronni began after the first week of school, and I ended up caught in the middle. After exiting Mrs. Jones' office from one of our sessions, I made my way to class, filled with dread at the thought of passing by Lacey's locker on the way.

"Happy junior year, Pickle!" Lacey exclaimed when our eyes met. The remark baffled me until I realized it was a dig at my mom's alcoholism. After she uttered those words, some of Javier's friends nearby burst into laughter. Without a word, I sprinted to the bathroom, barricading myself in the largest stall in the corner to cry.

In a matter of weeks, the nickname Lacey gave me gained traction. Whispers of it echoed through the halls and I wished I could get out of Freeport for good.

Things only grew worse when Mrs. Jones mentioned the nickname during one of our sessions. She empathized, hoping I could rise above the cruelty of my peers, assuring me that high school wouldn't last forever. Despite her efforts to comfort me, I heard the moniker every day.

One afternoon, as I was leaving Mrs. Jones' office, I heard the name calling again. "Pickle!" the voice rang out.

Turning on my heel, I saw Veronica Dice, or as she preferred to be called, Ronni, squatting outside Mrs. Jones' office. She had on a bleached band tee, too-short shorts for the school dress code with fishnet tights underneath, and worn-out combat boots. Her blonde hair was black underneath, yet behind the thick eyeliner rimming her eyes, Ronni was beautiful.

Everyone knew Ronni thanks to her father owning nearly every hotel along the Carolina Coast. To say they were wealthy was an understatement. Though her father's business sense and her mother's socialite status brought them recognition, Ronni was the black sheep of the Dice family.

"Don't call me that," I warned. Her grin only widened, and as she stood, she clapped me on the back.

"Don't worry about Jonesy," she reassured me, motioning to the guidance counselor's office. "Once you can make her happy and follow her advice, you can ditch these stupid talk times."

Her advice caught me off guard. "What do you mean?"

Ronni grinned slyly. "I have to see Jonesy, too. Apparently, the Administration thinks that my behavior is a cry for help. I guess people think rich kids don't have actual problems."

I remained silent, and Ronni gently patted my shoulder. "When you convince Jonesy you're into her advice, she'll let you go. Just fake it 'til you make it."

As Ronni turned from me, she strolled confidently into Mrs. Jones's office.

"Close the door, Miss Dice," our guidance counselor instructed her.

After that, I took Ronni's advice. I presented a more upbeat demeanor during my sessions with Mrs. Jones, and she was right. My grades were good and remained that way during the first semester. When Mrs. Jones approved of my progress, she finally released me from our talk times.

While leaving my last session with Mrs. Jones, I bumped into Ronni in the hallway. "Heard you were free," she stated, leaning against the row of lockers.

"I am," I agreed.

She grinned with a pen in her mouth. "You're welcome."

I chuckled sardonically. "Were you waiting for me to thank you?"

Ronni shrugged, crossing her arms. "It's the least you could do."

Her sarcasm amused me, but my smile vanished when I saw Lacey at her locker.

"Pickle!" she called out in a sing-song voice. Javier and Chase smirked. I rolled my eyes before refocusing on Ronni.

Ronni eyed Lacey over my shoulder with disgust. "Who are you calling 'Pickle'?"

Lacey tried to ignore her, but Javier and Chase tuned into the standoff.

"Stay out of it, Veronica," Lacey retorted.

Ronni laughed, "Pickle? You have no imagination, 'My Little Pony'." Turning to face Javier, she smirked. "You know her name sounds like a My Little Pony figurine from the nineties, right? *Lacey Lockhart*, I mean just think about it."

The hall roared with laughter, and Ronni winked at Javier before motioning for me to follow her. She wrapped her arm around me, taking me under her wing. I was happy to accept the lifeline I was being thrown.

As we strolled off, I told her, "You didn't have to do that. I could've handled Lacey myself."

Rolling her eyes, Ronni wrapped an arm around me, leaning in with a coy smile. "You're welcome, *again*."

From that day on, I actively sought Ronni out at school, and surprisingly, Lacey left me alone. Though I still heard the taunting of *Pickle*, it wasn't as prevalent. Unfortunately for her, Lacey's *My Little Pony* moniker had spread like wildfire. Even Javier didn't intervene when others taunted her with the name-calling.

Come fall, Ronni and I were inseparable. At school, she acted as a protective barrier, shielding me from the mockery. The whispers died down, and soon, so did my nickname. Ronni emerged unexpectedly as my new best friend. Football Fridays faded into the background as Ronni introduced me to beach bonfires with the locals. Although the parties weren't my typical scene, Ronni's presence brought me comfort. College guys brought six-packs or occasionally a keg, while others took drags of various illegal substances.

"Don't feel pressured to do anything you don't want to. Just hang out," Ronni would reassure me whenever I felt out of place.

On those beach nights, I sat with the group, observing Ronni effortlessly mingling. She was a chameleon with her carefree demeanor, adapting seamlessly to any environment she was in.

The first house party I attended with her was at Carl Boyd's. Ronni promised we'd spend the night dancing to the live band. In the crowded living room filled with college students, the pulsating rock music enveloped us. I excused myself for the bathroom and found a line of strangers, feeling like a wallflower among them.

After a twenty-minute wait, I returned to the dance floor, but Ronni was nowhere to be found. I navigated through the crowd several times before moving to the kitchen keg stand, but I still couldn't spot her. Heading up the stairs, I hesitated outside a door, knocking and calling for her.

"Ronni, are you in there?" I shouted over the blaring music.

After a brief silence, she replied, "Yeah?"

"Can we leave?" I asked.

"Just a minute!" a male voice responded. I felt a heat rush to my cheeks having interrupted. Unable to endure the discomfort, I went outside.

From the curb, I sent Ronni a text: *When you're done, I'm outside and ready to go.*

Half an hour later, Ronni finally appeared. She was disheveled, her once-high ponytail hanging low and her shirt inside out.

Annoyed with her obvious indiscretions, I snapped, "Having fun?"

Unfazed, Ronni retorted, "I was. What's your problem?"

"My problem? This isn't like you, hooking up at parties," I protested.

"Relax, you little saint, I'll get you out of here," she dismissed me.

A week passed before Ronni and I spoke again.

"We're going to the football game this weekend," she declared, as if it were non-negotiable.

"No," I asserted firmly. She had ignored me since the house party and I had no idea if we had been in a fight or if she had grown tired of my inability to keep up with her partying.

Ignoring my objection, she feverishly texted on her phone, refusing to acknowledge me. "We're going, end of story."

Before I could continue my protest, she walked away. That Friday, we found ourselves at the next home game. It struck me as odd that Ronni had opted for seats so close to the field, on the third row, directly in Lacey's line of sight. Ronni, exuberant, cheered wildly every time Javier scored, catching the attention of both me and Lacey.

The following Monday at school, Ronni and I stood in the lunch line, awaiting our turn to pay. "Ready for the game this Friday?" she asked again with a sly smile.

I gawked, remembering just how obnoxious she had been while attending the game last week. I felt even more surprised she preferred the upcoming game over Carl's house party. "No, are you?"

As we approached the lunch lady, Ronni's coy smile persisted. "It'll be fun." She settled her bill, and as I stepped forward, gasps and clattering ice interrupted the routine. Lacey stood, holding an empty cup, its contents now decorating Ronni's front.

"Stay away from my boyfriend!" Lacey shouted.

"Then you stay away from me!" Ronni retorted. Before they could carry on, two teachers intervened, separating them. We were all sent to the principal's office and when they questioned us, I admitted to Lacey's tea-throwing, but kept quiet about Ronni's flirting with Javier that had obviously egged her on.

Our punishment was being sent home for the day instead of detention. When our parents arrived to take us home, I stayed close by as Dad apologized to Mr. Lockhart for my involvement, though I had only been an innocent bystander. While they talked, I noticed Ronni and Lacey exchanging silent warnings at one another on the way to the parking lot.

In Dad's truck, he questioned our severed friendship. "Since when are you and Lacey having issues at school?" he inquired.

"Since she chose her boyfriend over me," I sighed, turning to stare out the window.

Dad placed a hand on my shoulder. "Honey, that's no reason to associate with the wrong people."

Silently, I reflected on Dad's obliviousness to everything that had been going on with me at school, his unawareness of Ronni's support or Lacey's mistreatment. I knew he had enough to deal with as Mom relapsed again, and I refused to involve him in my high school drama.

Things had a way of working themselves out, though. Ronni's true colors shone through as I realized she and Javier had sneaked around after the next football game. She had finally gotten back at Lacey in the worst way possible. That was my wake-up call to walk away from her like my dad had warned before she pulled me down any further.

I buckled down after my dad vouched for me to retake my algebra final and tried to lie low. Ronni remained relentless in reaching out to me despite my attempts to distance myself from her.

Once summer had officially begun a few weeks ago, I tracked down Ronni at the beach and confronted her. When I found her down at the beach bonfire, she took me by surprise, giving me a wave with a vape in hand. She seemed happy to see me and I knew she was buzzed.

"Look what the tide rolled in!" she exclaimed, pulling me into an unexpected hug. I tensed. The smell of alcohol on her breath made me want to gag.

Ronni picked up on my body language. "What's up with you?"

Placing my hands on my hips, I let out a sigh. "Stop contacting me. You've finally gotten back at Lacey, and if you're still sneaking around with Javier, I want to be left out of it."

Ronni grinned, exhaling a cloud of vapor from her e-cigarette. "Not that it's any of your business who I am or am not hooking up with, but don't pretend like you're innocent in all of this. What would this past year have been like for you had I not stood up to My Little Pony for you?"

I folded my arms over my chest, but this only made her laugh. "Look, I just came down here to let you know I don't want any more trouble, okay?"

Ronni blew out another cloud of smoke. "You think you're such a little saint, Lena? You're not. Everything that has happened this year is on you, too."

"Don't you think I know that?" I narrowed my eyes at her. "But isn't this enough trouble for one year?"

She crossed her arms, eyeing me narrowly. "So, what are you, Team Lockhart now, Pickle?"

Hearing her use the nickname to hurt me caused my blood to boil. This wasn't the Ronni I knew anymore. This version of her was the one Lacey had encountered all school year. I'd lost my best friend before, but this was different. I was choosing to let go of whatever superficial friendship Ronni and I had.

"Don't involve me in whatever it is you're doing."

Ronni laughed, completely unfazed. Applauding me, she exhaled the last of her vape. "It's about time you stand up for yourself, so I don't have to feel sorry for you anymore."

As soon as those words hung in the night air, I knew I was done with the conversation. I motioned between the two of us, "Let me do you a favor then. Consider us done here."

I spun on my heel, and Ronni laughed, her footsteps following mine across the crunchy sand. "Sweetie, you started this. If anything, I should be mad at you."

I picked up my pace while Ronni's taunts motivated me to move faster across the sandy terrain. When I reached my car, I gasped at the sight of it. Ronni bumped into me and I bounced forward. When she realized what I saw, she cursed loudly.

"I can't believe this!" I shouted, kicking sand. Someone egged both our cars in the parking lot. My windshield read: PICKLE, while Ronni's was more explicit.

"You can't?" Ronni asked, glaring at the sight before us. "My Little Pony is insane!"

She marched over to her car, removed her flannel shirt, and began wiping off the eggs with it. "I hate her!"

I used my sandal to start scraping the egg off the front hood of my car. I was eager to find a car wash before driving home so my dad wouldn't know. I knew Lacey was behind this, but when had she been here?

Ronni's flannel shirt landed on my hood suddenly, and when I looked up she stood at my side. "Hate me all you want, but you're not done with me yet."

Taking her ruined, sticky shirt in hand, I worked to wipe the remaining egg from my car. Ronni glared at me. "This isn't over, you know. Lacey will not do this to me and get away with it."

Silently, I let her words sink in and agreed. Lacey couldn't get away with this. As I met Ronni's blazing eyes, filled with determination, I knew she was determined to seek vengeance. Passing the egg-soaked shirt back to her, I felt the same fire inside me.

"It's not over, but this time, we'll do it my way."

***

Tonight had been the night Ronni and I made our stand against Lacey. We hadn't reached the point of writing on her car, and I felt relieved, especially now with an ankle injury, while my dad awaited my response.

Dad pulled us into the driveway and slammed the truck into park. "Lena, we can't keep going on like this. You can't keep acting this way. You're so much better than this."

Thinking about everything that had transpired with Lacey, Ronni, and especially Mom, I couldn't hold back the tears any longer. My ankle throbbed painfully, but even worse, my heart ached.

I was trying to survive the worst summer of my life, but I felt like I was living in slow motion. My mom had left to go to a treatment facility right after school had let out for the summer. She was gone before I made it home on my last day and all she had left was a note explaining how sorry she was. In the letter, Mom said she wouldn't be back until she was herself again. I knew Dad believed she could change, but after everything she put us through, I had stopped believing her a long time ago. That day, everything about life as I knew it had changed.

"Lena?" Dad asked, his voice softening. I felt his hand on my shoulder and another sob escaped me.

"You'll never understand," I cried. I didn't want him to see me like this so I did the only thing I could think of. I climbed out of the truck, grabbing my crutches, and marched through the front door to my room and cried myself to sleep.

***

The next day passed by in a blur. I spent the morning at the Lockharts', attempting to tidy up the front yard despite my throbbing ankle. My dad arrived at lunch, though I hadn't finished, to pick me up. The sight of me trying to maneuver on crutches was punishment enough for Mr. Lockhart, and he decided I had served my time. While I climbed into Dad's truck, I observed Lacey emerging from the front door with a trash bag in hand, intending to finish the job. As I settled into the passenger's seat, I heard her utter, "Pickle."

Swiftly, I shut the door, hoping Dad hadn't overheard, but he did. Puzzled, he asked, "What did she say?"

I shrugged and requested he take me home, eager to change the subject. Dad didn't hesitate.

Once we were home, I limped into the kitchen, desperate to quench my thirst from the largest glass of water available. Spotting a well-worn, oversized plastic cup—the kind I often snagged for free from the Movieplex—I filled it all the way up. My thirst was so intense I gulped down half of it while the other half cascaded down the front of my shirt.

Dad stood there, an eyebrow raised, observing me as if I were some sort of extraterrestrial.

"I have cottonmouth," I explained, glowering back at him.

He chuckled and strolled across the kitchen to position himself in front of the sink. Leaning against it, he folded his arms across his chest. I felt a sudden need to brace myself, familiar with the stance he took.

"I've spoken with your Aunt Lou," he informed me. Her name lingered, creating a palpable rift in the air between the two of us. Neither of us had spoken to Aunt Lou in years, especially not after what happened between her and my mom. "She still volunteers at the Bible camp during the summer, the one where she and your mother grew up going. There is still space available for campers, and I think you should go this summer."

His words sliced through me like a knife. "Dad, I don't understand."

"The camp is four weeks," he continued explaining, while I stood there, utterly stunned. "There are kids you know from going to church in Meadowbrook with your mom when we used to visit. Lou says it might be a great change for you."

"Dad, no. I can't go there," I protested, horror flashing in my eyes. "Since when are you and Lou so chummy again? You know what she did—"

He sighed, his hands gliding wearily down his face, causing me to pause mid-sentence. "Lena, you're acting like I'm sending you away to boarding school or something. It's New Hope Bible Camp—somewhere with familiar faces, positive influences, and a chance to escape Freeport for a while, just like you've been wanting."

"That's not what I meant, Dad," I retorted. "I'm not that kind of girl anymore. I haven't been to church in a long time."

Dad shrugged and the determined look in his eyes remained. "Maybe it's time you go back."

"You don't understand," I tried to defend, but Dad raised his hand, not letting me finish.

"This isn't about me." His eyes turned serious as he stood tall, a demeanor I hadn't seen since he left the Coast Guard. His military stance was unmistakable as he narrowed his gaze at me. "Enough is enough, Lena. You used to be a straight-A student, a dependable employee, faithful to your beliefs, and I never used to have to worry about where you were, who you were spending time with, or what you were doing."

"Dad, I promise, I won't let you down anymore. I'll block Ronni's number and I'll stay out of Lacey's way."

His eyes met mine and with that one look, I knew there would be no arguing my way out. "This discussion ends here. We leave at the end of the week for Meadowbrook to meet Lou. From there, you're going to church camp. That's final."

I held my tongue, though I wanted to scream for him to just listen to me. But if there was one thing I could trust about my dad, it was that he meant business. There was no changing his mind once it was made up. After years away, I was headed back to Meadowbrook to be reunited with my estranged Aunt Lou.

3

My heart pounded when I saw the giant green sign on the highway. Its bold white letters read: MEADOWBROOK. Seeing the sign instantly brought back a flood of memories from our last trip here for Gramps' funeral. In the years prior, Meadowbrook had been the one constant place I felt like I could call home. My mom and I had often made an annual trip to visit my grandparents and Aunt Lou growing up. When my Grams passed, we still visited, but not as often. Something had changed in my mom after we lost my grandmother, but after Gramps passed, she had never been the same.

The distant trees on the ridge had a mystical blue glow as we gained elevation, making it feel like a different world from Freeport. The air became more dense and even grew cooler despite the early July sun. I leaned out the window and felt the exhilarating rush of wind on my face.

As Dad exited the freeway, we merged onto the main road leading into the heart of Meadowbrook. The majestic water tower appeared, reminding me of my childhood dreams of climbing to the top.

The weathered Welcome sign became visible as we approached, adorned with faded cursive and floral designs against a mountainous background. We caught sight of familiar landmarks as we drove through the town square. Max's Place, our favorite diner, had undergone refurbishment, and the Cupcake

Cottage, a past favorite spot for girls' nights with Mom and Aunt Lou, stood next door. The Peaks and Paperbacks bookstore and old Mercantile were still standing, but a new addition was The Ridge Roast coffee shop.

"The place almost looks the same, huh?" Dad asked, breaking the silence. Neither of us had spoken much during the ride up.

"Yeah, almost," I sighed. Without my mom or grandparents, nothing about Meadowbrook would ever be the same to me.

From the town square, Lou's house was just a short drive away. The faster we approached, the quicker my heart pounded in my chest. After my family's last visit, I never thought I would see Lou or step foot in Meadowbrook again.

***

The day of Gramps' funeral was the last time we had set foot in Meadowbrook. Upon reaching Lou's house, we discovered she had already left for the church to prepare for the service. But Mom insisted on taking a moment to freshen up and knew the location of Lou's hidden spare key beneath a discreet brick to get inside. When we finally arrived at the church after an hour, we saw that a large crowd had already gathered. Mom straightened her black skirt and nervously stepped out of the car. Without uttering a single word, I could feel her anxiety and see the pain written on her face.

Friends from church and around Meadowbrook warmly hugged us as we entered the church. A sea of loved ones surrounded Mom at once, all there to celebrate my grandfather's life. We made our way through the crowd and Mom spotted Lou. When they locked eyes, Mom rushed forward and threw her arms around her sister. Lou's stiff initial response softened as they held each other, tears streaming down her face as she buried her head in the sleeve of Mom's dress.

"Are you hungry, kiddo?" Dad asked as he pointed to a table lined with food nearby. I said yes to steer clear of everyone's repeated condolences. Dad and I grabbed a small plate and settled in the corner, though we continued to be bombarded and receive small talk from strangers. I sensed Dad felt just as out of place as I did.

Later, when the funeral was over, I asked Dad if I could slink back to the corner we found earlier, and he agreed. He excused himself to check on Mom, assuring me he would be right back. I sat there, trying to remain polite to those who continued to greet me. When the small talk became too much, I stepped into the hallway. Suddenly, shouts erupted from down the hall. I froze, watching Mom storm out, followed by Lou.

"I'm not doing this here," Mom cried, trying to scurry away.

"Why? Are you just going to leave and not come back again?" Lou hissed. "I needed your help, Natalie, but you couldn't even bother to take your bereavement leave from work?" Lou hissed.

"I have a life of my own, Lou!" Mom shouted. "I'm sorry you're too busy living in Mom and Dad's shadow to see it."

"A life?" Lou balked at her. "Is that what you call staring into the bottom of a bottle and falling away from God?"

My mom stopped mid-stride, noticing a crowd had gathered to watch. Her eyes widened with horror, and her chin quivered.

"You can say all you want about me living in their shadow, but at least I'm not living in *the shadows*!" Lou bellowed.

Tears fell down my mom's cheeks when her eyes landed on me. The horror in her eyes intensified, and I watched as my dad pushed his way through the crowd, pulling her under his arm.

"Come on, Nat, we're leaving," he said, throwing his coat around Mom as if shielding her from Lou's further backlash. "Let's go, Lena."

Obediently, I followed them out of the church. That was the last time any of us had seen Lou, almost two years ago.

***

I found it strange that Dad contacted Lou, given the circumstances. Once Mom was hospitalized, I realized he had been attempting to reach out to Lou, or at least it had appeared that way. None of that mattered now, because here we were.

Lou's U-shaped driveway led to her massive log cabin-style home, which she had built with her ex-husband, Ryan, when they were first married. After their divorce, she kept the property while he left town. Beneath two gables, one of which featured large second-story windows, the house had a cozy front porch. Encircling the entire house, the porch ended at a ramp that led to a swing and a pond behind the house.

Aunt Lou emerged just as we arrived. She looked the same, wearing linen overalls and sandals, her long sandy hair tied back with side-swept bangs blowing gently in her face. Lou greeted us with a wave as though no time had passed. Still, I felt uneasy. The memory of her explosive reaction towards my mother still haunted me, and now I was obligated to spend the summer with her.

Just as I was getting out of the car, Lou moved towards me and swiftly wrapped me in a tight hug. She pulled away before I could figure out where to put my hands, but kept her hands on my arms as she examined me. Lou gave me a thorough once-over before admitting, "My favorite niece is all grown up."

As my dad appeared by my side, she shifted her gaze from me to him. "I'm sorry it's been so long," Lou apologized. When Lou embraced him, it was less warm and more strained, mainly from Dad's side. "You haven't changed a bit, Tommy."

Dad responded, "Lou, I could say the same about you." Quickly changing the subject, he added, "The house looks great. Heard you guys had a bad winter this year?"

Lou shifted her gaze towards the roof, where Dad was gazing, and leisurely took a sip of her coffee. "The good thing about small towns is there are lots of good people who will help."

Dad agreed.

Lou gestured for us to follow her. "Should we go inside and get out of the sun?"

Dad glanced back at me as if silently asking, *How are you holding up?* I flashed my eyes at him, hoping he would know my attitude hadn't changed in the slightest.

The moment I stepped into Lou's home, the scent of pine, orange, and clove immediately brought back memories from my childhood. Despite being untouched, the open-concept living area with its pristine white furniture continued to be inviting. The kitchen's spacious island and seating area seemed frozen in time. A flight of stairs, adorned with family photographs, connected to the second level.

"Are either of you hungry? I was thinking of grilling steaks on the deck for dinner," Lou asked as she opened her refrigerator and pulled out two water bottles, handing one to each of us. Out of an old habit, I took a seat on a stool around the island. Once I noticed I had done so, I went to jump up, but they both regarded me strangely and I quickly settled back down.

"Steak sounds great," Dad answered, and I was thankful for his diversion. "But I might just swing by a drive-thru and pick something up on the way home."

My eyes widened, and so did Lou's. "Tom, there's no way you're going to drive back tonight. You just spent almost five hours getting here."

Dad's flushed neck and awkward head rub told me he was feeling as uncomfortable as I was. "I don't want to impose, and I didn't take off work tomorrow."

Lou leaned over the counter, challenging him. "Tom, get some sleep here and take off as early as you need in the morning. The guest rooms are ready for you and Lena, and I can have coffee ready for you to be on your way first thing."

He cast a quick glance in my direction before giving his answer. The moment he saw my pleading eyes, he immediately agreed. "As long as we're not imposing."

She scoffed. "You're family. You're not a bother."

While Lou was busy searching the freezer, I stared out the window at the pond, desperately wishing to escape the tension of the afternoon. "Do you guys mind if I go check out the pond?" I asked.

Lou's warm smile made me feel at ease, but my reserve soon took over. I slid off the stool and headed for the back door, eager to escape. As I stepped onto the deck, the warm summer air enveloped me. I settled into the shaded patio area, where I saw solar-powered lights strung above. The gentle breeze rippled the pond's surface, and the sun's reflection danced across the water. Being near the water always calmed me, making me feel more myself when I was feeling off.

Before I lost my faith, I believed God created the ocean just for me. The water served as a refuge where I could submerge myself, experiencing a sense of weightlessness and freedom from the worries of the world. It had been ages since I had felt that sense of connection and peace. As I was about to step off the deck, Lou opened the back door and glanced outside.

"Hey Lenny Lee, can you come help me chop some veggies for dinner?" My mom's nickname tumbled from her mouth, sending a shiver through me. She was acting as if we had been the best of friends all along and no time had passed. Did she even care about what she did to my mom? I stared down, wringing my hands, and her smile faded a bit. "But if you don't want to, there's no pressure at all. I just thought I'd ask." Lou flashed me a sheepish smile and swiftly retreated indoors without giving me a chance to respond. I looked back at the pond and then followed her inside after taking a deep breath. When I entered the kitchen again, I saw Dad on the phone in the living room, and Lou had returned to chopping a mound of veggies.

"So, Dad's on the phone with work again, huh?" I asked, attempting to make small talk.

Lou grinned at me, but the gesture didn't reach her eyes. "Duty calls. Isn't that what everyone always says?"

"How is River Ridge doing?" I asked politely.

Keeping her eyes on the chopping board, she swiftly responded, "Blessed. How is work for you? Are you still at the Movieplex?"

I took a deep breath, uncertain of how much Lou knew about recent events. In response, I simply shook my head.

"Oh," Lou muttered. "That's okay. There will be other jobs."

Hopefully, I thought to myself. Like the crackling of static in the air, the tension between Lou and me grew more palpable. Sensing the tension, Lou began placing the colorful vegetables in a large bowl on the counter.

"Sorry ladies, where were we?" Dad came back into the kitchen at the perfect time.

Holding the bowl, Lou glanced at him and motioned towards the defrosted steaks. "We're ready to grill."

***

When dinner was over, I asked to be excused and found my way to the guest room where I had always stayed when visiting.

I found a transformed space with a more mature aesthetic. A queen-size bed had replaced the old bed and frilly canopy in soft pink and beige. A white desk now sat in front of the large window, and the closet had been neatly organized.

A picture frame on the desk captured my attention. The photo held my grandparents, my mom, and a much younger me. I crossed the room to open the French doors leading to a small balcony overlooking the pond. The familiar view had been a comfort during my childhood, especially when I missed the ocean. I remembered Lou's dream of this balcony belonging to her own daughter, but it had become a space for me during visits. Her dream had faded with the end of her marriage.

Feeling fatigued even though it was only 7:30 p.m., I opted to take a shower and change into comfier clothes. Lou popped her head in just as I was going through my bag.

"Did you need anything?" she asked. "There should be shampoo and soap in the bathroom, but no toothpaste. If you need that, I can grab a tube for you."

With a polite grin, I responded, "I'm okay. I've got some in here somewhere."

I could tell from her sheepish smile that she knew I still had some doubts.

"Thank you, though, Lou," I said, meeting her gaze. "For allowing me to come up here despite everything..."

Lou's grin faded, and she crossed her arms. She sighed before locking eyes with me. "I'm glad you're here, Lena."

Just as she said good night, Dad appeared in the hallway behind her. Lou quietly passed him as he stood in the doorway. "Get some sleep, Len; I'll see you bright and early."

I nodded and resumed sorting through my bag. Dad didn't move. Pulling out clothes in the hope he would leave me alone, I knew better; that had never been his style.

"Hey, Len?" he asked, drawing my attention back. "I love you, okay?"

His voice was barely audible, as if he didn't want Lou to hear. My resolve wavered, but I couldn't stay silent.

"I love you too."

With an unspoken understanding, we left the issue lingering between us for the rest of the night.

4

I couldn't sleep that night. Memories of the past flooded my mind and kept me awake. At 3 a.m. I took the quilt from the bed and wrapped it around myself, surrendering to its comforting warmth. Running my fingers across the gentle, weathered cloth, I felt a comforting connection to my Grams, a gifted seamstress who had taught me the art of sewing. Quietly, I made my way across the room and settled on the balcony outside the French doors. As I stood beneath the crescent moon, I looked out at the serene pond, and my mind quieted as I breathed out a calming sigh.

Hours later, I awoke leaning against the door as the sun rose. With Grams' quilt bundled around me, I realized I had fallen asleep while still out on the balcony. Though groggy, I found my footing and climbed back into bed. Before I could close my eyes, I heard the door gently creak open.

"Hey honey, I have to get on the road," Dad greeted me. He sat beside me on the bed, ruffling my hair as I sat up. Though my face was all Mom, my sweet smile was a dead giveaway of my father.

"Drive safe," I said, stifling a yawn.

Dad enveloped me in a warm bear hug, a rare treat since my recent behavior didn't exactly warrant it. He usually reserved his hugs for goodbyes, like when he left for deployment or sea duty. But now, I was the one leaving him.

"Len," he whispered, kissing my forehead, "I love you. I know you think this is the end of the world, but it's not. Camp is going to be great for you."

Despite everything, a strange calm washed over me when I met my father's gaze. I didn't like it, but as I looked into his eyes I accepted his decision for me to spend my summer at Bible camp. I had made my bed and now I had to lie in it. *Literally.*

"I love you too, Dad. Don't worry about me." I wiped my tired eyes and tried to give him a reassuring smile.

For the briefest of seconds, I saw him falter, but he quickly regained his composure. Ruffling my hair again, he climbed to his feet and walked towards the door. "Try to get some sleep, kiddo. It might be a long day."

***

Dad hadn't lied; it was a long day, and my lack of sleep wasn't helping. By the time I got up and got dressed, it was 8 a.m., and Lou was busy loading her black SUV with boxes of supplies when I went downstairs. Lou pulled her hair back, just like she had the day before, and she wore a maroon New Hope Bible Camp t-shirt with hiking capris.

"Good morning," she greeted me warmly. "Did you sleep okay?"

Lou gracefully moved around me, pouring a mug of coffee and sliding it across the island to me. "Cream or sugar?"

"Both, please," I answered the coffee part of her question. She placed two small white porcelain containers in front of me, each labeled to reveal its contents. I took a sip of the warm liquid and watched as Lou continued to bustle around. I didn't have it in me to sit still, uselessly, no matter how awkward I felt.

"Need help loading up?" I asked.

Lou turned from the cooler she was filling with water bottles and took a sip from her mug. "I've got most everything loaded up already. Whenever you're ready, we can put your things in the back and grab some supplies before we head out."

"What supplies?" I wondered, taking another warm sip.

Lou, hesitant to answer, scrunched her nose. "I think your dad thought all you needed to bring were some clothes and toiletries, but we're just going to go pick up a few more things."

"Like what?" I eyed her as I tossed my hair back into a high ponytail, using the tie on my wrist. The warmth of the coffee spread through me, heating my neck.

"Just a few essentials," Lou brushed the idea off casually. "No need to worry. Are you ready to go?"

I nodded and took one more sip from the mug. *As ready as I'll ever be*, I thought silently to myself.

A few hours later, we wrapped up a trip to the Meadowbrook Mercantile, securing a sleeping bag, a pillow, a laundry bag, a shower caddy for the cabin, and a few colorful towels Lou picked out for me. She spared no expense, and when I attempted to pay, the cashier retrieved Lou's card with a quick reach past me.

"You really didn't have to do all of this," I remarked as we drove towards camp.

"It's my treat," she said, moving her right hand from the steering wheel to adjust the air. Her vehicle was massive, the back nearly filled to the brim with cases of water, breakfast bars, juice, and other snacks. The back seat housed both our luggage and all the items we had just purchased. "Besides, this is your first time at camp. I've been coming here for twice as long as you have, so I know what essentials you'll need."

I made a conscious effort not to balk at her words. Spending most of my summer at Bible camp was the last place I wanted to be. I remembered overhearing Mom and Lou's stories about their childhood camp experiences. They enthusiastically described it as a sanctuary, a place free from the troubles of the world. But I knew no amount of hiding could shield me from the harsh realities of my life.

"So, what can I expect from camp this summer?" I questioned, hoping to mentally prepare myself.

Lou signaled and changed lanes on the highway. "Camp has changed a lot since I was your age, but the important things have remained the same. You will have separate breakout sessions for small group Bible study based on age groups. Then, in the afternoon, campers team up for sports and activities. The best part is, you'll have free time before and after dinner to grab snacks, do crafts, or hang out with friends."

The closer we got to camp, the more my sense of dread grew. The thought of being surrounded by Bible thumpers and cliques of tight-knit friends dampened my mood.

"After camp worship, older teens, including yourself, take part in Teen Devotional in the evenings. The younger campers, who are in middle school or below, head back to their cabins for their own devotional time," Lou continued.

"What is that?" I peered over at her.

With two hands on the wheel, Lou grinned, lighting up as she spoke about camp. "Teen Devo is what everyone calls it. We tailor the topics to the issues older kids deal with. Your age deals with a lot, so it's important to address the struggles you face."

Lou wasn't lying. I had been dealing with a lot. As I struggled with my faith, I dreaded the upcoming lessons. At church in Freeport, our preacher often discussed topics like worldliness, sin, and sexual immorality. Despite being raised in a conservative Christian home, my mom's love for drinking compelled her to stop going to church. I had watched her slowly fade away from our faith over the past few years. I couldn't imagine the lessons at camp would stray far from everything I had already heard before, none of which could explain how a parent could love alcohol more than their own children, or how a loving God could let that kind of neglect happen.

As soon as Lou veered onto a gravel path, I suddenly snapped back to reality. The winding road led us deeper into the heart of the woods. A sizable navy sign emerged, adorned with the words WELCOME TO NEW HOPE BIBLE CAMP etched in bold, white letters. Below the words, a cheerful green banner declared, WE'RE HAPPY YOU'RE HERE! radiating a bright and inviting warmth that instead filled me with even more dread.

As we drove, a charming log cabin called THE LODGE came into view, its wraparound porch and rustic roof nestled in a clearing. A man at a small stand waved us on, and soon the camp came into view. On the right, a sign marked BOYS CAMP led to cabins with screened porches and handicap ramps, a welcome sight for me and my injured ankle.

As we continued, a softball field with bleachers and dugouts came into view, with a serene lake shimmering through the trees in the distance. Nearby, a sand volleyball court and playground added to the scenic landscape. Across the road, tennis and basketball courts stood alongside picnic tables, with a substantial cabin and towering gazebo rounding out the scenery. As we turned left, Girls Camp came into view and a sign reading DINING HALL marked a spacious cabin on the front lawn.

Without warning, Lou slammed on the brakes, causing us to jerk forward in our seats. "Sorry, I was about to head to your cabin, but we should probably check in first."

She took a right turn at the fork and parked by the ramp leading to the Dining Hall's front porch. "Let's get you signed in. I'll grab your crutches."

As soon as I unbuckled and opened my door, Lou appeared with crutches for me to hop onto and secure under my arms. "Thank you."

I walked up the ramp behind her, with wooden beams clattering beneath. The lengthy gravel path stretched out before me, and I dreaded the idea of navigating camp on crutches. With a sense of helplessness, I entered through the door Lou was holding open, limping ahead of her. Two lines formed on the far right, with campers and parents patiently waiting. A prominent brick fireplace stood behind the sign-in tables, flanked by a small stage and a cleared area for supply boxes. To the left, a large opening offered a view into the commercial kitchen, where aluminum refrigerators and metal food prep tables filled the space.

A girl with blonde hair tied back and an array of beaded bracelets on her wrists waved us over and greeted my aunt with a cheerful "Hey, Lou!" As I looked at her, I instantly recognized her, and she motioned for Lou and me to come over, saying, "I'll take care of your sign-ins."

"Hey, Hannah," Lou greeted as I hobbled behind her. "Is everything going smoothly so far?"

Hannah beamed. "So far, so good." Peering over Lou's shoulder at me, I watched as recognition dawned on Hannah's face. "Lena Harris? Is that you?"

"In the flesh," I affirmed. It had been years since I'd seen Hannah. Memories of our encounters at the church in Meadowbrook during my family's visits came flooding back. I admired her classy style and kindness, especially since she was always so welcoming to us younger kids, unlike others her age. She always passed out candy to kids my age and would let us sit with her during worship and color. For a long time, I wanted to be just like her.

"It's great to see you!" She smiled before looking down, noticing my ankle boot. "Oh no, what did you do to your leg?"

"I, uh, it was an accident," I answered elusively, suddenly feeling self-conscious of what she would think if she knew the truth. "Just a bad sprain. My ankle should be better in a week or two."

Hannah studied Lou with wide eyes. "Should I page for one of the golf carts?"

Lou nodded, motioning for me to come closer. "Can you please? I need to show Lena around and get her settled, and that will make things much easier."

I was suddenly grateful to Lou for not saying anything about what really happened.

"Of course," Hannah agreed. Picking up the walkie-talkie from the tabletop, she spoke into the speaker, calling for a staff cart to the Dining Hall.

Lou handed me a drawstring bag with the camp name and logo on the front. "This has a t-shirt, water bottle, and some other things to get you started this week."

She gave me the bag and quickly placed a lanyard with my name around my neck. I picked up the tag and read the words KITCHEN STAFF and let out a deep breath, peering down at my sealed fate.

"I've got you both checked in. You can just hang tight. They're coming to pick you both up," Hannah informed Lou, signaling campers behind us to move forward. Lou gestured for me to follow her outside, but before we could take more than a few steps, two girls rushed up to her. I quickly halted, trying not to bump into Lou or trip her with my crutches.

"Hey Lou, there's an issue with Kelsey's assignment," one of the girls said rapidly, gesturing to her tall friend on her right. She wore a tank top and knee-length shorts, her braids framing a face with perfectly lined eyes and ruby-red lips. The other stood taller, with deep gray eyes, tanned skin, and bright blonde hair collected in a thick messy bun on top of her head.

"What's the problem?" Lou scrutinized.

"She's not in my cabin," the girl sulked. "We have to room together because that's what we put on our application, and we both packed things to share. It would be kind of tough to go between cabins just to give each other stuff. Can you fix it?"

"Riley, you'll have to talk to Hannah. See if she has an empty bunk, and then she can try to fit you together," Lou instructed.

"Thanks, Lou!" Riley gushed. Before they could wander off, Lou stopped them.

"Girls," she warned, "if there isn't space for you to stay in the same room, then you'll have to settle for staying in the same cabin. We cannot move room assignments all willy-nilly when they're already in place."

Riley nodded, but I got the sense she wasn't paying much attention to Lou. Both girls turned abruptly and cut in line. Neither Riley nor Kelsey acknowledged the scowling young camper who reluctantly stepped back while they barged in front of her. Their selfishness struck me as odd, considering we were at church camp and they acted like they were anywhere else.

Outside, Lou guided me towards a golf cart waiting by the porch ramp. I carefully got into the passenger seat, securing my crutches, while Lou started the engine. "We're going to go for a quick tour and then I'll show you to your cabin, where you can start setting up."

Lou hit the gas, and the summer breeze whipped past us, providing a welcome cooling off as beads of sweat instantly formed all over me. Lou navigated the gravel path, gesturing towards the Craft Cabin and tennis court. On our way down, she made sure I saw the Med Cabin on the first level. I knew I'd be visiting the camp nurse daily for my ankle for a while as my sprain healed.

Lou then gestured to an enclosed fence as we continued forward, locating the pool. "Boys and girls have different swim times in the afternoon, just so you know those rules."

I smirked in acknowledgment. The heat was oppressive, but with my sprained ankle, I wasn't sure I'd be able to do much more than sit by the pool to cool off.

"During team activities, you'll likely be sitting out until your ankle improves. The Sports Staff is in charge of activities and will be notified of injured campers," Lou explained. As we reached Boys Camp, she veered right, driving up another path until we arrived at a beautiful clearing by the lake.

Lou pointed out, "You might find yourself here quite often since this is where the teens spend a lot of their free time." *I doubted it.*

On the way back to Girls Camp, Lou pointed out a small laundry shelter and a weathered outdoor pavilion sitting vacant. "Down the hill from the Dining Hall, a new amphitheater was constructed a few years ago. We use that space for worship and larger gatherings now instead of the pavilion we just passed. The amphitheater offers the best view of Cobalt Bluff."

Turning left near the Dining Hall, we entered the Girls Camp. Lou stopped at the first cabin on the left, surrounded by others on both sides of the path.

"Here we are," she announced, sliding off the seat.

I leaned on my crutches as I followed Lou up the ramp to the cabin's screened porch. She pushed open the creaking door and we entered the spacious common room, with lawn chairs and a card table to the left. The walls were covered in signs with various messages, like "Unplug from your devices and recharge with your Bible" and "You are the light of the world, a city set upon a hill cannot be hidden."

Lou opened a door and inside were two bunk beds on both sides. The front of the room had roomy shelves that looked like closets, and there were two big drawers under the lower bunks for more storage. "This is your room. You can choose the bunk you want."

I glanced at the bunk on the left and right, realizing they were my only choices in this situation. Lowering myself onto the left bunk, I sank into the small cushion that barely qualified as a mattress.

"I'll go get the car so you can start setting up your things," Lou said, and then spun on her heel heading back outside. I hopped to the window, using the top bunk for balance, and peeked out at the gentle stream of sunlight shining through. Several young girls emerged from a parked car, talking with their friends while their parents assisted with luggage. I imagined Lou and my mom arriving alongside my grandparents as children and I wondered if anyone would remember my mom or recognize me.

While I was deep in thought, the screen door opened with a creak, diverting my attention. Rather than finding Lou, I was taken aback by the sight of a girl wrestling with her bags and a massive suitcase. With a sigh, she released the weight of the two duffle bags from her shoulders. She was a petite Asian-American girl with big red glasses and smooth black pigtails. She had on short overalls paired with a vibrant tie-dye shirt. Her brown eyes appeared larger behind her lenses as if recognizing me. "Lena Harris?"

As soon as she uttered my name with her sweet southern drawl, I knew exactly who stood before me. During family visits, I spent a lot of time at the church in Meadowbrook where my mom and Lou grew up. I used to enjoy playing on the sandy playground after church, while the grown-ups chatted. During one visit, a few of the boys were throwing sand at me while I shouted for them to stop. They finally stopped when a little girl with a black overall dress and cropped black hair threw sand back.

"Joanna Wright?" I asked, staring back at her in disbelief. I hadn't seen her since middle school, when her hair was frizzy and she was still growing into her limbs. Now, she stood tall, stunning, and still unapologetically herself.

With a shrug and a beaming smile, she told me, "Nowadays, everyone calls me Jojo. But, Lena, how have you been? It feels like it's been forever."

"It has been," I agreed. "Maybe since we were in sixth or seventh grade."

"Wow, really?" She began dragging her duffle bags into the room only to toss them into the corner. "I can't believe it's been that long."

"Hopefully, the boys stopped throwing sand at you?"

Jojo giggled, leaning against the bunk with her hand on her hip. "For the most part, but I always throw it back."

"I'm guessing you also outgrew the cooties," I teased, recalling why the boys had thrown sand at us in the first place.

She laughed once more, and theatrically dusted off her hands. "I promise, no more cooties. You, on the other hand, look like you've got a nice boo-boo there."

Jojo pointed to my ankle, as I grabbed the bunk to steady myself. "I like to keep things interesting."

As she set up her bunk, I noticed her take the mattress from the top bunk, creating a makeshift double bed.

"Don't you think someone else may want their mattress?" I argued.

Jojo shook her head. "Not at all, we won't have any other roomies. It's just me and you."

The idea of not having a room filled with other campers was music to my ears. Jojo continued setting up her bunk before turning back to me. "Here, let me help you."

Leaning against the bunk, I watched as Jojo brought down the top bunk mattress and put it on the bottom. The sound of tires on gravel caught my attention, and I glanced out the window to see Lou getting out of her SUV. "It looks like my stuff is out front."

Jojo quickly sprang up and signaled for me to follow. "Then let's go grab your things." We bounded to the front door and Jojo helped me onto the porch before bouncing down the stairs. She rushed over to embrace Lou warmly, and they began talking like old friends. Jojo was my first surprise so far. A stark contrast from the past week, Jojo felt like a small beacon of light offering hope for the summer ahead.

5

"We should sit over here." Jojo led me to the back row of chairs in the Dining Hall, gesturing for me to sit beside her. We'd barely started unpacking when Lou arrived to escort us to staff orientation. Lou had clarified my role on the ride back to the Dining Hall. I would be working as a staff camper, which meant I would receive a reduced fee for my stay instead of being a regular camper. *No wonder Dad thought this would be good for me, I was here to work.*

Hobbling into the Dining Hall behind Jojo, I noticed others trickling in. Adults and teens alike chatted excitedly while others hugged, reuniting after a long separation.

"How can I tell the difference between a staff member and a camper?" I asked Jojo, leaning over after we sat down. "And what's the difference?"

She lowered her head as though we were exchanging secrets. "Campers don't have badges, only staff members do. Campers typically attend either on a church scholarship or by paying their own way and don't have responsibilities. The discount is why some of us choose to work here, otherwise we have to pay full price."

I glanced at my Kitchen Staff badge as I processed this. "So, you would rather come to camp and work than just come as a camper?"

Jojo laughed. "Of course, all of my friends are on staff." I watched as she pointed over to where Hannah stood with another older girl who seemed her age. "Hannah and Nellie are Junior Counselors who are in charge of the girls in their assigned cabin. The women you see are actually parents of the campers here, volunteering as Adult Counselors."

Scanning the area, I noticed a couple of women she gestured towards, chatting by the entrance.

"Likewise, Boys Camp has male counselors. According to Hannah, finding staff to fill those spots was difficult this summer and some counselors have to monitor multiple cabins."

Unsure of what to say, I observed Jojo's gaze darting around the room, as if searching for someone.

"The guys aren't here yet," she noted, looking around behind us. "They're always late."

"What guys?" I asked, wondering if Jojo was trying to find her boyfriend. At first, I felt intrigued by the possibility of cute boys, but then I snapped back to reality. Dating wasn't possible for me here, especially since I had nothing in common with anyone and lived four hours away.

Jojo rolled her eyes and blinked down at her smartwatch. A picture of a cat lit up the background as she glanced at the time. "My friends from church. They're all on the Sports Staff and they're never on time for anything except activities."

The rest of the people in the room swiftly took their seats near us, drawing our attention to the front suddenly. From the sign-in table emerged a tall, slender man wearing a polo shirt and tan pants.

"Welcome back to NHBC, everyone!"

There was cheering from some of the adults and campers as the man smiled. He couldn't have been any older than his mid-thirties, with thick curly brown hair trimmed to a professional look. He had a smile that could dazzle the ladies but a natural modesty about him to ward them off.

"Some of you I know," he pointed to a young man in the front row. "Looking at you, Landon."

A few staff members laughed at what I could only guess was an inside joke.

"Some of you I don't know," the speaker continued as he further scanned the crowd. "I'm Adam Taylor. Some of you prefer to call me Preacher Adam, but I'm fine with going by Adam."

More cheers erupted as I examined the audience, who seemed entertained by Preacher Adam.

"This is my second year as Director here after my dad decided to step down after serving the camp for thirty years." More cheers and claps sounded, and things began to click. Adam must have been a part of some New Hope dynasty, making him a legend here.

"I'll keep this short and sweet since I know you're all eager to reunite with friends you haven't seen in a while," Adam's voice bellowed from the front of the room. "All staff members have your schedules. If you haven't received one yet, there is one by the front door of all cabins."

To my right, I watched as Jojo pulled a piece of paper from the front pocket of her overalls, unfolding it. I leaned closer, glancing over her shoulder. The early 6 a.m. wake-up on the top of the page made my stomach clench. The schedule noted mealtimes, breakout sessions, free time, and a breakdown of afternoon team activities, followed by more events into the night.

"What exactly do the team activities involve?" I whispered over to Jojo again.

Jojo leaned in, keeping her voice to a minimum. "The Sports Staff hosts team competitions every afternoon during the week, but during Field Day, there are lots of activities, and each team competes to win the Best Team Award. The last Friday of camp is when friends and family can come for the day, and that evening is the Award Ceremony at the End of Summer Banquet."

I glanced back at the schedule, but there was no mention of an Awards Ceremony. Winning any kind of trophy this summer would be out of reach for me with an ankle boot holding me down.

"What is the Banquet?" I asked again, keeping my voice low. "Is it like a formal thing?"

Jojo subtly shook her head. "It's not formal, but most of us dress up."

Her eyes lit up while she talked about the event. "There are staff, camper, cabin, and team types of awards handed out, but everyone really wants to win the Mister and Miss NHBC awards."

"Is that for married people or something?" I kept pressing.

Jojo stifled her chuckle. "No, they're the trophies given for the male and female campers who have the best character during camp. The counselors and directors pick the award winners, but the best part about the Banquet is getting asked to go with a date."

Now it was my turn to hide my laughter. I had no hope of finding a date anywhere, especially not at Bible camp. I just had to survive my time here and then I could go home and back to my normal life. Noting the schedule in Jojo's hands, I saw that Teen Devotional was the final activity before lights out at 10 p.m. I could feel the onset of exhaustion. The only break I seemed to have during my stay here was on the weekends, when I could look forward to free time. How was I supposed to do all of this on crutches?

"Kitchen Staff!" Adam called, grabbing my attention. Jojo became part of the hooting crowd, acknowledging all the Kitchen Staff in attendance.

"You'll report early before mealtimes to prepare and set up shop." Adam explained, glancing down at the schedule in his hands. "Counselors, you'll be early risers to ensure all of your campers are ready and report on time."

A few adults in the crowd cheered and hollered, revealing their positions within the staff. I spotted Hannah in the midst of the counselors cheering.

"Med Staff!" Adam called again, and his eyes fell on a corner behind the group. I peered back to see a tall woman with bright auburn hair and heart-shaped lips pumping her fist into the air. My focus was immediately captivated by the guy on her right.

His deep chocolate eyes were framed by his tousled caramel hair. I estimated he was about my age, but his serious demeanor was out of the ordinary. The guy wore a bold red soccer jersey with a fiery Viking logo, and a playful smirk as he waved at Adam. I was captivated by his magnetic presence, unable to look away.

"Please be sure to have the campers' medicines ready and available at all mealtimes," Adam instructed them. "Be sure you maintain a presence during team activities too."

I glanced from Adam back to the boy. He leaned down to the redhead and whispered something to her. She nodded before whispering back a response.

"Are there just two of them?" I spun back to Jojo. She seemed preoccupied and kept looking back at the door expectantly. For the duration of camp, two people seemed like a small crowd given the number of campers. Jojo's gaze swept back to me, following where I pointed back to the Medical Team.

"Yep," she whispered back. "Angie is the Head Nurse and oversees their team. She's some kind of travel nurse though, so she gets a lot of time off in the summer. Her kids are small, so they don't stay here but come during the day. There's a separate time for kids who are too young to be campers to visit and participate."

I turned back again to see the boy had disappeared from the corner. I couldn't spot him anywhere, though I found myself searching the room. All of a sudden, the front door flung open, and four guys entered, letting the door slam shut behind them. They unexpectedly captured the attention of all the staff.

Beside me, Jojo scoffed and rolled her eyes. "Here comes the cavalry."

My gaze shifted back to the group of guys filing in. The tall, stocky one stood out, with broad shoulders and a youthful face. The two behind him were slightly shorter, one slender and the other athletic. The last boy, with shaggy blonde hair tucked behind his ears, had gray, moody eyes that seemed familiar, yet I couldn't quite place him.

"Welcome, gentlemen!" Adam called out to them. "Ladies and gentlemen, our better-late-than-never Sports Staff!"

The audience erupted into cheers, making me jump unexpectedly. I observed the larger boy, who entered first, sit down in the chair next to Jojo, leaning back with a toothpick in his mouth. He removed it and flashed her a sly smile, which she met with a glare.

Jojo turned her attention back to me. "These are the *friends* I was telling you about."

A mischievous boy slyly pulled the chair out from under the tall blond. The blonde gave him a cautionary look, as the two boys next to him giggled silently. I watched as the blonde mouthed the words *You just wait* in a warning for them to watch their backs.

The boys were cutting up beside us as Adam finished his speech, none of us catching a word he said. Just as I was picking up my crutches and getting up after being dismissed, I was taken aback by a completely unexpected bear hug. Caught off-guard, I stumbled backwards, attempting to regain my balance.

"Whoa! Whoa!" the voice said, balancing me in place. "Watch yourself there, Lena."

I peered up to see the toothpick bearer as the culprit. His warm blue eyes and charming, dimpled smile peered down at me. Grasping my crutches, I backed away from him quickly.

When I caught his mischievous chuckle, I quickly turned my head to meet his gaze, his laughter was strangely familiar. When I had first heard him laugh, he was a young boy throwing sand into my eyes. The next time was when he beat me in Bible Bowl during a visit to church in Meadowbrook. Even without being part of the youth group, I managed to hold my own.

"Denny Mayhew?" I asked, peering up at him in shock.

He popped his collar, still wearing his same smile. "Like you could forget me." Without warning, Denny raised his arm to ruffle my hair. He looked completely different compared to the last time I saw him. I couldn't believe it. Denny now stood at least at six foot and my guess was close to 200 pounds.

"Lou said her favorite niece was coming to camp, and I almost didn't recognize you!" Denny exclaimed. "Lena Harris is all grown up."

With my left hand, I brushed my ruffled hair back out of my face. "It was sort of a last-minute decision."

"I'd say," Denny agreed, motioning to my ankle. "You're going to have a heck of a time getting around the campgrounds with your weak bones."

"Denny, leave her alone." Jojo nudged him. Standing at his side, she was several inches shorter than him. I saw him wrapping her in a hug that was much softer than the one he gave me, pulling her towards his side. I noticed a gentle connection between them, making me question if they were more than friends.

"Come on, Jo, I haven't seen the girl in forever. I had to give her a hard time, otherwise what kind of impression do I make?" he asked, staring down into Jojo's dazzling eyes.

"You've always made quite the impression," I tried to affirm him, remembering all the teasing I endured at his expense.

"Speaking of impression," Denny added, releasing his hold on Jojo. "You need a warm camp welcome."

I raised an eyebrow in silent response.

"You girls have to come to the lake after dinner. We're going to have a bonfire tonight."

"Is that why you guys were late?" Jojo wondered, jabbing a finger in his chest.

Denny feigned injury beneath her touch. "That's for me to know and you to find out." He raised a large hand to bop her nose and a noticeable blush covered her cheeks.

"Count us in," Jojo said, as Denny swiftly turned and followed the others who were starting to leave.

"See y'all!" he called behind him, flinging his arm in the air.

When Jojo turned to face me, I couldn't hold back my smirk. "So, I'm guessing he knows you don't have cooties anymore, huh?"

Jojo's face reddened. "We're not... I mean, we're just friends. Like best friends and that's it."

I couldn't help but laugh, unable to hide my scrutiny. Sighing, Jojo, twirled one of her pigtails and pointed to the kitchen behind me. "Should we go check out the kitchen and see where our stations will be?"

Holding my crutches under my arms, I followed her while she changed the subject. Pushing through a pair of lightweight aluminum double doors, Jojo skillfully maneuvered between prep tables to reach the center of the room. Positioned on the far wall were two large commercial ovens.

"This is where I work," she informed me, standing by the ovens. "I'm like the resident baker here since I work at the Cupcake Cottage in town."

The quaint bakery in Meadowbrook flashed in my mind as I remembered all the trips I had taken with Mom and Lou. "You work there? I love that place!"

Jojo nodded excitedly. "Me too, it's even better to work there. I get to take unsold cupcakes home after my shift since we can't sell the ones that are day old."

The thought of cupcakes made my stomach rumble, reminding me of how hungry I was. A long adjustable hose accompanied a large faucet on the far-right wall's massive sink. There was a sizeable opening to the left, containing stacked trays and two large trash cans. Pots and pans for cooking were suspended above the prep tables, with metal mixing bowls placed below. By Jojo, there was a row of refrigerators beside a commercial freezer, which led to an open pantry room.

"Oh, there you two are." Lou's voice appeared behind me. As I turned, she silently approached me, already busy with a clipboard in hand. "Jojo showing you around?"

I nodded and Jojo beamed. "I was just giving her a kitchen tour."

Lou grinned and looked around, reminiscing. "It's good that some things never change."

"Isn't it?" Jojo agreed. "Speaking of Lena though, can she bake with me?"

Lou slowly winced. "I wish I could girls, but I think the best situation for Lena will be dishwashing while she's on crutches."

She took a step back to slide a wooden stool my way. "The sink is the most stationary place in the kitchen."

As I glanced at her, I felt like she expected me to protest. When she looked at me, my stomach instantly sank. After the awkwardness of the night before, I could easily recognize worry in Lou's eyes. I wasn't certain if it was due to my ankle or her concern about my behavior under her watch.

Without saying a word, I shrugged off the thought and moved away from Lou. I embraced the cards life dealt me this morning. With almost one day behind me and a jam-packed schedule ahead, it felt like the next four weeks would zoom by.

"Maybe when you're more mobile," Jojo piped up, trying to lighten the mood.

Lou grinned at her. "Well, girls, you should both try to set the rest of your stuff up in your cabin. Tomorrow will be here before you know it."

Jojo squealed excitedly, running around the table back over to me. Lou turned to face us, "I can give you both a ride back to your cabin."

Thinking about the tension still lingering between us, I turned her down. "I'm okay, I need some fresh air."

Lou's eyebrows shot up in surprise as she glanced at Jojo, who nonchalantly shrugged. "Works for me."

The two of us disappeared back through the Dining Hall and out the front door. Jojo graciously kept the door open while I propelled myself forward, my crutches clunking on the wooden deck. "So, what now?"

With a mischievous grin, Jojo skipped past me and zoomed down the ramp before spinning around to face me. "We can go finish setting up our room and then grab dinner."

"Where?" I eyed her curiously.

She pointed behind me, motioning to the door we just exited. "The first night is bagged dinner that the adults hand out. After, we'll head down to the lake."

Flashing yet another grin, she skipped with excitement towards our cabin, and I followed quickly behind her.

6

Just as I finished setting up my sleeping bag, Jojo appeared again, looking fresh with her makeup done. Her eyeliner accentuated her striking eyes, and she'd changed into a striped top and tights with shorts. With her pigtails cascading down her back and a beret atop her head, she rocked a style that was uniquely her own.

"How's it going in here?" She happily placed her makeup bag on the available top bunk, preparing her pajamas and outfit for tomorrow.

"Good, my bed is made, so whenever we get back, I'll officially be ready to tuck in."

Jojo checked the watch on her wrist. "Denny should be out front any moment to take us down to the lake. You ready to head outside?"

I witnessed her swipe her index finger on her watch, clearly texting someone. She had found a clever way around the cell phone policy I reviewed once we got back to the cabin. To my surprise, the camp rules weren't as bad as I had expected.

New Hope Bible Camp Rules and Expectations:
1. *No cell phones. (Staff exceptions apply for emergency use or for those without a walkie-talkie.)*

2. *No medications allowed on campers at any time. All*

required medications must be given to the Medical Staff for daily distribution.

3. *Shorts must be at least mid-thigh or below and tank tops must be three fingers wide.*

4. *Bullying or harassment (physical or otherwise) will not be tolerated. Campers reprimanded will be sent home.*

5. *No weapons, lighters, knives, tobacco products, alcohol, or destruction of property will be tolerated.*

6. *Boys are not allowed in Girl's Camp. Girls are not allowed in Boys Camp. Staff exemptions may apply with an accompanying adult.*

7. *Pre-K campers must be accompanied by their counselor(s) at all times during their allotted morning time on the grounds.*

8. *No inappropriate public displays of affection, including kissing, cuddling or excessive hugging, and/or touching or caressing.*

I agreed, stashing my phone in the back pocket of my cutoff shorts. For a moment, I contemplated leaving it in my bunk. I knew no one would contact me except my dad, but I left the device in my back pocket anyway.

Following Jojo outside, I quickly heard the revving of a four-wheeler. Denny came to a sudden stop in front of us after successfully jumping over the ditch by the cabin. His sudden appearance left me both shocked and amused. With unbelievable confidence, Denny wore a shirt with the American flag and cargo shorts.

"What's shaking, ladies?" he greeted with a wide grin.

The Denny before me was a stark contrast from the Denny I remembered growing up. Although he had always been charismatic, he had recently grown even more charming.

Jojo wasted no time and eagerly hopped onto the back of the four-wheeler, signaling for me to sit beside her, and reached out for my crutches. Denny assisted me in steadying myself as I hopped over and smoothly slid onto the back of the ATV next to her. I glanced at Jojo to gauge her response to his chivalry. She didn't bat an eye as she grabbed my crutches to help me hold. Using one hand, I grasped the back rail while clutching my crutches with the other.

"We ready?" Denny called over his shoulder. Before we could respond, he turned and grabbed his handlebars, and we sped away. "It's going to be a bumpy ride!"

The cool night wind whipped through my hair as I let down my ponytail. Racing along the gravel path in the woods, my t-shirt billowed behind me. We traveled on the bumpy road until we arrived at a clearing and the path vanished suddenly as the tires spun on the sand.

A small bonfire was whirring several feet from the lake as the moon cast its elegant reflection along the surface. Down near the water's edge, fireflies caught my eye, glowing along the shore.

"Vamos!" Denny shouted, throwing his beefy legs over the seat. Offering his hand to Jojo once more, he watched as she took hold and gracefully hopped down. They hurried down the shore, racing each other without turning back. I glanced further down the shore and noticed a small crowd of girls huddled by the dock. A little further down, there were others by the shore skipping rocks.

On a log beside the fire, I spotted the blonde boy from orientation earlier. With a dark hoodie on, he skillfully strummed an acoustic guitar. I slid down from the four-wheeler and found my footing in the sand. While I approached the bonfire, I had the impression that the boy didn't see me, or so I thought.

"You should take a picture, it will last longer," he murmured, placing his pick between his teeth and plucking a marshmallow from the large, open bag beside him. At his feet was a bag of chocolate and graham crackers for s'mores.

My mouth dropped open a little as I turned my eyes away. Had I been staring at him for too long? I quickly scanned the shore, anticipating Jojo's return to save me.

"I'm kidding," he insisted. I turned to face him and was met with his devious smile. "It's always fun to give the new kids a hard time."

My brow furrowed. *Was I the new kid? Why couldn't I remember this guy?*

"Are you sure you're not the new kid?" I asked, retaliating. "I don't see you hanging out with the others."

While a breeze swept by, he took the pick out of his mouth and ruffled his hair with his hand. "I'm definitely not the new kid, but you would remember me if you saw me every week like the rest of them."

Attempting to get a better view of him in the light, I inched closer to the fire, but it was too hot for my face. When he chuckled and I saw his smile, it suddenly dawned on me. Although his face and hair had lengthened since the last time I laid eyes on him, I could easily recall those striking gray eyes and mischievous grin. The day I met Jojo and Denny on the playground, he was one of the sand-throwing accomplices.

"Caleb?" I asked.

He laughed but disagreed. "I'm Theo Lockwood. Caleb is down by the shore with Josh."

I followed where he pointed to the other two boys who had almost pulled his chair from under him. "Caleb is the taller one, right?"

Theo nodded and narrowed his eyes at me. "I can't believe you thought I was Caleb, that hurts."

I shrugged innocently. "It's only been forever since I've seen *any* of you. And when I did, it was only in brief visits."

He rolled his eyes and continued strumming his guitar. "That's strike one for you, Lou's niece."

I scoffed and leaned over to grab a marshmallow from his bag. As I stuffed the marshmallow in my mouth, I reminded him, "I have a name too, you know."

Theo stopped strumming his guitar and placed his right hand over the strings to stop their vibration. He pondered for a moment, trying to remember me too. "Yeah, I got nothing."

I chuckled and made an effort to reposition my ankle for a more comfortable position in the sand. "It's Lena."

He snapped his fingers once I said it. "That's right. For some reason, I was thinking Lily."

It was my turn to roll my eyes. "So, you've exchanged sand throwing for guitar playing now?"

Theo winced as if recalling the memory. "You remember that?"

With a laugh, I flipped my hair back and felt the warmth of the flames. Suddenly, I wanted to dip my toes in the water to cool down. "Of course, I remember everyone who has ever wronged me."

"It all depends on if you still have cooties," Theo joked.

Shrugging, I replied, "The jury's still out on that one."

He winced again and slid closer to me, offering his marshmallows. "Consider these a truce then?"

I plucked one out of the bag and popped the sweet foamy substance into my mouth. "I'll consider it."

Riley emerged from behind me, accompanied by her friend Kelsey from before. Kelsey leaned down beside Theo to swipe the bag of marshmallows from him, but he was too fast. She crossed her arms and frowned. "Give them to me, little brother. I brought them to share with everyone, not so you can sit here by yourself and eat the whole bag."

Theo frowned and motioned towards me. "Kelsey, obviously I'm not alone, I'm sharing them with Lena."

Kelsey peered down at me with a sneer. "They're mine, Theo. Hand them over."

"Or you'll do what?" Theo opened the bag and started eating a few. Kelsey groaned as he chewed with his mouth open, unable to close it. Before she could threaten him, a loud outburst of laughter erupted behind us, and suddenly we were all sprayed with sand. Both Riley and Kelsey gasped as Denny and Jojo slid across the shore, landing at their feet. Denny was face first with Jojo trying to pull herself off his back.

"You guys!" Kelsey and Riley roared in unison. I watched as they both tried brushing sand off their fronts and out of their hair. When I peered over at Theo, he was wiping his eyes and searching for the marshmallows.

A horrid groan erupted from Kelsey as she swiped the marshmallow bag from the ground. "I can't believe you, Denny, you got sand in the bag!"

Denny stood up and brushed off the sand from his front and arms, then noticed the sandy marshmallows. I watched as he peered over Kelsey's shoulders before reaching his hand in. He snatched a marshmallow, blew on it, and ate it. "They're fine, Kels. Now they have the perfect crunch."

Laughing uncontrollably, Jojo threw her head back as Kelsey and Riley glared at both of them. Riley wasted no time. Reaching into the bag, she grabbed a handful of marshmallows and flung them directly in Denny's face.

Jojo gasped as Theo rushed to cover his face. Acting quickly, Denny snatched the bag from Riley's grasp and swiftly poured its contents over her head. Expecting her anger, I was taken aback when Kelsey bent down to pick up the bag by Theo's feet. She tore open the packages of graham crackers, candy, and chocolate and began hurling them at Denny.

Theo groaned and tucked his guitar away. "You guys are ruining a perfect s'mores night!"

"I don't think they care!" I pointed out as I watched the commotion unfold. I was glad, for once, that I wasn't in the middle of it. Jojo almost collapsed from laughing so hard as Kelsey and Riley began to use Theo as a human shield.

"Just don't hurt the guitar!" he shrieked as Denny pelted him with candy pieces. With his eyes closed, Theo tried to catch them in his mouth, turning the tables on them. Riley, grinning deviously, picked up a handful of candy and hurled them behind me. Darting my eyes, I spotted her target.

The guy who captured my attention in orientation appeared. With a fierce look, he threw his arms in front of his face and stared at Riley. Her smile wavered a bit, catching his reaction. "Can you not?" he asked her, clearly offended.

"Sorry, I thought you were joining us," Riley apologized, looking genuinely remorseful.

Jojo danced over to his side, chewing on a piece of candy she plucked from her hat. "Carter, you have to meet Lena. She's Lou's niece."

She gestured towards me, and Carter briefly looked in my direction. Once again, an inexplicable force seemed to seize me in his presence, our eyes locking momentarily. Our introduction didn't seem to relax his furrowed brows.

"Hey." He spoke flatly, before brushing something off his sleeve. Carter strolled up the shore without saying another word, then vanished into the dark clearing.

I peered up at Jojo and spotted her faltering smile.

"What's with him?" I whispered.

With a sheepish grin and a shrug, she acted as though his reaction was predictable. "He's just Carter Rose."

It was clear that Jojo didn't hold this in high regard, but his disrespect deeply affected me. For the first time in a few hours, I felt like I was once again the outsider and didn't belong.

A loud beep sounded ahead of us through the clearing and a golf cart arrived with Lou in the driver's seat. Her expression was unreadable until she cruised closer to the firelight. "Alright everyone, it's time for Devo!"

A few moans sounded from others down the shore and Lou threw up her arms innocently. "It's not my rule! And remember, growing in your faith is what you're here for!"

She caught my gaze and came over to me. Holding out her hand, she offered to give me a hand up, but I refused her grasp. "I can get it."

Lou took a step back to give me space. "I actually have one more stop for you before lights out. I need you to meet one other team, and then I can get you to Devo."

"Sure," I agreed, following her to the cart.

Lou helped me secure my crutches before she turned her attention back to the others. "Make sure the fire is completely out. You'll start a wildfire out here if you don't."

"Already on it, Lou!" Denny called, pouring out his large water bottle over the fire.

"Good boy!" Lou cheered as she began to drive off. We hurriedly raced back up the sandy beach and onto the shadowy gravel pathway. Beyond the lights from the golf cart, the clearing was so dark the stars beamed through the trees far above us.

"Beautiful night," Lou pointed out, following my gaze. "Did you have a good time with the others?"

I wanted to tell her I was surprisingly shocked that I did, but the last thing I wanted her to think was that I was enjoying myself. This was still not the place I wanted to spend my summer. "They're nice."

I could feel Lou's eyes dart over to me as she took this in. Thankfully, she didn't press. Driving through the woods, we finally arrived at the other end of the clearing, where we proceeded along the lengthy pathway leading to the grand cabin adjacent to the Dining Hall. We pulled onto a paved path to the second story where another cart sat. To my right was a glass door that read MED CABIN in large white letters. Lou put the cart in park and hopped out. "I'm just going to check to make sure they're here and then I'll come back for you. Just sit tight."

While she moved towards the entrance, I witnessed her open the door and confidently enter. Without pause, I gathered my crutches and followed her to save her the trip. I could manage to walk a few feet to the door without needing help. Once at the door, I shifted my weight onto my strong leg and maneuvered inside.

"Lou, I've got plans for camp this summer," a familiar voice groaned. "I don't want to have to drive her around."

Lou and Carter were talking by an exam bed. He squeezed the space above his nose with his hand, as if her question was causing him pain. With hands outstretched, Lou stood before him, pleading. "Carter, you are a part of this team. Lena needs your help. She can't hobble around camp while she's on crutches and Angie will have her hands full. I really need you for this."

Before he could answer, he glanced up and finally caught sight of me standing there. His eyes widened and I saw his perfect complexion redden. A strange sensation washed over me as I eavesdropped on a conversation that wasn't meant for me to hear. I felt foolish for being intrigued by him earlier, only to be met with his unjustified scorn.

Lou noticed his expression and turned to see me standing there as well. "Lena, honey, I didn't hear you come in."

I suddenly wished I had the ability to teleport and escape. "I didn't mean to interrupt."

Carter brushed an uneasy hand down his face and eyed Lou as if seeking her help. Without waiting to hear more, I spun around and hobbled away. Accepting anything from Carter was the last thing I would do. I'd be willing to limp around camp all summer if it meant staying as far away from him as possible.

7

I fumbled out the door as quickly as I could muster on one good leg. The idea of escaping back to my cabin on crutches seemed daunting, but far less than having to face Carter or Lou again. The look on his face when he saw me standing in the doorway made me want to run away all the way back to Freeport. After spending an entire school year feeling shame and embarrassment, my summer was supposed to be different. Yet, here I was, already facing another jerk who didn't even know me.

I heard the door squeak open behind me as Lou filed out. Her feet pounded the pavement as she crossed the walkway. "Lena, I'm so sorry you had to hear that but—"

"It's fine, Lou," I replied with a sardonic laugh. With her eyes downcast, she gestured towards the golf cart and offered a helping hand as I settled into the passenger seat with my crutches.

During the school year, I had quickly learned that teenagers were cruel, and I couldn't wait for high school to be over. *Just one more year.* Carter could see I was clearly struggling to walk and his role on the Med Staff made him the perfect candidate to help. But no, after witnessing his poor attitude twice in an hour, I was not going to stick around for a third time. If he didn't want to deal with me, I would make things easy for him.

"Some boys clearly haven't gotten over their fear of cooties," I joked, attempting to ease Lou's mortification. My smile helped her relax a little, but I could tell Carter's complaints still bothered her.

"Teen Devo is a really great time, I think you will enjoy it," she quickly changed the subject.

I raised my eyebrow and glanced behind us, questioning if she was actually referring to me. It had been over two years since Lou and I had last spoken or caught up. She knew nothing about me.

"If it's okay with you, I think I'll just go back to my cabin," I told her as the wind picked up, blowing my hair into my face. In the darkness, I could see Lou's grimace as I plucked a loose strand from my mouth.

"Not happening," she denied, veering away from Girls Camp towards the Dining Hall. "Camp rules are that you are to be at Devo."

"You can't make an exception?" I asked, waving my arm over my injured leg. "It's been a long day, Lou."

She remained silent as we slid around an extended brick corner and down a small hill where a large amphitheater stood. Campers were gathered just beneath a sweeping pergola where a projector displayed a hymn across a massive screen. When we arrived, the bright lights made me squint until my eyes adjusted. Once they did, I saw a small hand waving at me in mid-air as Jojo motioned for me to join her.

Lou and I made eye contact, but her expression quickly turned serious. Within the last twenty-four hours, she seemed more like my mother than ever before. Before Mom left, I couldn't remember the last time she had smiled. She had become a shell of herself, and a completely different person. Now, seeing Lou beside me with my mother's shared expression made me want to flee.

My eagerness to escape the memories of my mother overshadowed my initial reluctance to join Devo. I quickly adjusted my crutches under my arms and propelled myself forward until I stood above Jojo seated on the concrete below.

"Where did you go?" she asked, reaching out a hand as if to steady me. I positioned my crutches next to each other and carefully lowered myself down, making space to extend my injured leg in front of me.

Before I could answer, though, Adam shouted from the front of the crowd, "Alright, everyone sing out!"

Suddenly, all eyes were on Adam as he led us in song.

How do you explain
How do you describe
A love that goes from East to West
And runs as deep as it is wide

The lyrics enveloped the crowd, swirling into the night around us. As I looked from left to right, I saw everyone around me raising their voices in praise. The melody came back to me, having sung the lyrics myself in church on multiple occasions growing up.

So listen to our hearts
O Lord, please listen
Hear our spirits sing
A song of praise
From those you have redeemed

I suddenly felt transported back to the last time my family was all together and happy while my Grams was still alive. She used to sing all the time, even if it was just humming while she baked in the kitchen. This song had been one of her favorite hymns. I remembered sitting in the kitchen, coloring at the table with my mom during a visit to my grandparents' house. My Gramps came in from outside and hugged Grams tenderly from behind as he always did.

"I love that song," he had exclaimed before he joined in. "*We can use the words we know to tell you what an awesome God you are, but words are not enough to tell us of your love so listen to our hearts."*

The two of them had continued singing, and then my mom joined in, all of their voices harmonizing beautifully together. The memory of that day was still so vivid, with everyone closing their eyes as their words of praise filled the air. Singing together became so common for them that whenever one initiated a song, the others effortlessly joined in. It wasn't long before I too, found my voice, and fell in love with singing.

Chill bumps crawled up my arms, bringing me back to the present as Adam led us in song after song. With each hymn they sang, I felt as though I were being pummeled with memories of my past. When my mom left, I promised myself I would bury all thoughts of her so my broken heart could heal. The memories of her were overwhelming me here, making me want to forget.

When the singing ended, I felt a small wave of relief wash over me. Adam stood in front of all of us, choked up from the music that was just created. He took a deep breath, fighting to suppress his emotion. "Our God is awesome, amen?"

"Amen!" the crowd cried out. The sudden shout took me by surprise. Looking to my right, I saw Jojo's watery eyes, sharing Adam's emotion. Leaning in next to her, Denny's elbows rested on his knees as he attentively watched the speaker.

"The singing always helps me prepare my mind," Adam spoke. "After all, we are here to learn more about our awesome God and to grow in our faith."

Some whoops and cheers sounded as he continued. "We all typically refer to this place as Heaven on Earth. I love that we all make fellowship and growing our faith a priority, especially when the world offers all kinds of distractions."

As Adam went on, I began to notice how out of place I felt again. The last time I had been to church, I was all on my own. After my Grams passed, my mom still made the same effort she always had to take me on Sunday mornings. She had always made that time a priority, even when we moved around while Dad was in the service. But when my Gramps passed, something shifted in my her. Mom began to make excuses for plans that suddenly came up. Sunday morning worship had become a habit for me, though. With my new driver's license, Mom allowed me to take her car to the small white church by the sound, even though she had stopped going.

In the beginning, it felt awkward to go alone, especially when my mom just decided to stay home. Worthy Clarke, one of my close friends at the time, was always there, though. Both she and her grandmother, Miss Pearl, always saved me a seat on their family pew, and for a while, I didn't feel so alone. As other members asked about Mom's whereabouts, I realized I had inherited her talent for making excuses. At first, I let them know she was sick, which felt like the truth. *Didn't spiritual sickness count?* Little did I know, she was truly making herself sick when the drinking started.

As news of Mom's illness spread, the questions about her absence at church turned into sympathetic smiles, largely due to Miss Pearl. After worship, she would always give me a hug and say, "Tell your mama we missed her." At first, it was a sweet sentiment, but the longer I heard it, the more I felt exposed. Not long after, Worthy made the Varsity cheer team with Lacey and Camille. When Worthy and I drifted apart, I lost the will to go back to church, knowing I would feel completely alone.

I heard Adam raise his voice and felt carried back to the present. "One of the greatest blessings of camp is that we have a safe place to encourage one another when it feels like the world pulls us down. But God's church will always stand," Adam declared. "He promises that he will never leave us or forsake us no matter what we face. And when we come together to lift each other up, we become that much stronger!"

More whoops and cheers echoed around me, and I felt the powerful urge to shrink away. These people believed that being together here could magically solve all their problems. I saw campers who were likely only freshmen, and the only problem they had probably faced was making a C on their report cards. There was no way these kids had faced true hardships. I had to agree with Adam on one point, though. The world did pull us down.

"As we begin the summer," Adam wrapped up, "I want you all to remember your 'why.' Remember why you're here. Remember that each person here has their own 'why.' And finally, remember that we all have a shared goal of helping each other get to Heaven."

The others began turning to their friends, taking Adam literally with his instructions.

"This summer, remember, if there's a need you have to make it known. No matter if you want us to pray for you or if something is on your heart. If the world has been knocking you around and you need our prayers of encouragement, please lean on your family here, and we will pray with you."

Suddenly, the projector lit up with another hymn as Adam finished. The campers near me stood up again, and another song filled the night.

Humble yourself in sight of the Lord
And He will lift you up

I maneuvered my crutches into place while balancing on my good leg. Despite Jojo's piercing stare, I was intent on breaking free from the melody and making my way back to the cabin. Adam's words were echoing through my mind at rapid speed.

Who was he fooling? Pray? Where had that gotten me? Lean on your friends? What happened when they stabbed you in the back?

I picked up speed, deciding this place was a joke. While rushing through the crowd, I suddenly stopped in front of a steep slope. I exhaled in frustration as I contemplated how to move without slipping down the hill. Just as I was about to start climbing, a warning voice sounded behind me, "I wouldn't try it if I were you."

Suddenly, Carter materialized next to me, running his hands thoughtfully over his face. He stared from my crutches and back to the hill with a puzzled look.

Filled with eagerness, I stepped forward to create distance between us. In an instant, he hurried in front of me, blocking my path. "Don't even try it. Do you want to ruin both legs, or possibly an arm?"

Carter hovered a few inches above me and I felt his hand come over my right shoulder, holding me back. I felt betrayed as my stomach flip-flopped beneath his touch. *How could I feel both disdain and a magnetic pull to some guy I barely knew?* Remembering how rude he was, I immediately refused to listen to my impulses as I stepped around him.

Carter sighed behind me. "Fine then, suit yourself. But just so you know, I'm not going to catch you since you were warned."

Hearing his retort, I immediately began to rank him among the biggest jerks I knew.

1. Chase Conway

2. Carter Rose

Lou came around the corner on the golf cart and headed straight towards me, causing me to freeze. She wore the same stern expression from earlier. "Lena, don't you dare. Get in this cart right now."

I threw my crutches in the back without any argument and forcefully hopped to the passenger's side. "Fine, I'm getting in."

Lou backed up so quickly that I had to grip the handle above me to ensure I stayed in my seat. I stared daggers at her as she drove up the hill, weaving down the gravel path. Her presence was revealed in short bursts of light from passing street lamps.

"You have to follow the rules, Lena." Turning at the fork, I saw the sign for Girls Camp come into view. "I get that that may be a foreign concept to you, but here you *will* follow them."

I could feel my blood begin to boil beneath my skin. *Who did Lou think she was?* Racing through the trees on the path, I averted my eyes from her, wishing I could escape this place. Lou came to a stop and turned to me, but before she could say anything else, I hopped out. With my weight balanced on one leg, I swiftly retrieved my crutches and hurriedly moved away from her.

"Lena, I'm not finished talking to you," Lou called out. I kept going, and almost as quickly as I opened the cabin's front door, I slammed it shut. Only when I leaned on the closed door did I hear the golf cart beep, indicating Lou's departure. At last, I found myself alone, the familiar territory I had grown accustomed to.

8

Despite a few mishaps, I managed to survive my first breakfast shift the next morning. My neck and back were stiff, and my hands turned into prunes after hovering over a never-ending pile of dirty dishes. Not getting enough sleep didn't make things any better. Last night, I had tossed and turned, unable to sleep soundly as I ruminated on my past and replayed the night's devotional songs over and over in my head. My early morning confrontation with Lou hadn't helped things, either.

At six o'clock, Jojo's phone buzzed and she instantly jumped up and began grabbing the supplies she laid out the night before to get ready. Right as I was about to doze off, she barged in and shook me awake. "Lena, we have to get going, we have to be at the Dining Hall in ten minutes!"

"And what happens if I don't?" I retorted, wiping my sleepy eyes. "Are they going to kick me out?"

Once the words were out of my mouth, I cackled at the thought of it. Being sent home felt like the perfect consolation prize, and I rolled back over. Jojo groaned before turning to grab her belongings to go get ready.

In just a matter of moments, the bedroom lights started flashing and my pillow was abruptly pulled from beneath me.

"Get. Up. Now," Lou demanded sternly, appearing out of nowhere. Glancing upwards, I saw her eyes flash and immediately sat up, narrowly avoiding hitting my head on the top bunk.

"I mean it, Lena," she demanded, beginning to unzip my sleeping bag.

"Alright!" I gave in, brushing her hand away. "I'm getting up, hold your horses!"

She stood, arms crossed, staring daggers at me. "You're not going to behave this way while you're at camp, Lena. I won't allow it."

Grabbing my unpacked bag from beside my bunk, I couldn't help but roll my eyes. While she continued lecturing, I started going through my clothes, searching for something that wasn't wrinkled.

"You may be able to get away with whatever you want while you're at home, but you will not do that here."

My hand stilled in my bag as I returned her fiery gaze. It was far too early for this type of lecture and completely uncalled for. "Since when was it a crime to sleep in a few extra minutes?"

Lou's eyes narrowed as she let out a sardonic chuckle. "That's not how things work around here."

"Then why don't you tell me how things work? Do I just show up for duty and do dishes? Then I can just go through the motions pretending to be fine when I don't want to be here?"

Her demeanor shifted, yet she stood her ground, crossing her arms more tightly.

"I'm not some sheep, Lou," I told her.

Despite the fire in her eyes, her expression wavered. "You're right, you're not." I watched as she sat across from me on Jojo's bed and tucked her hands between her knees. "But I know that you're better than this." Lou sighed and tried to level with me. "I know that the circumstances that brought you here were less than ideal, but believe it or not, this is *not* the worst place you could be."

I scoffed and returned my focus to retrieving a partially folded shirt and shorts from my bag.

"When your dad called me, he mentioned you were having trouble at school and that you stopped going to church a while ago. I hated hearing that," she explained. "You used to talk about your faith so openly."

My stomach sank at the thought of who I used to be. I hated to hear her disappointment, but I wasn't that girl anymore. How could I be, when God let bad things happen to good people?

Before retreating to the bathroom to change and have some solitude, I simply stated, "Lou, people change."

Church had fallen by the wayside, as had my relationship with God. Being at camp, surrounded by the very people I tried to avoid, brought back all the emotions I tried to suppress. I found myself recalling the Sunday I last tried to wake my mom for. The Sandy Shores church we attended in Freeport was hosting a Friends and Family Day with a potluck lunch after. My dad had left early that morning, and when I tried waking my mom, I immediately noticed the smell of alcohol on her breath. She turned away, still in a daze.

Alone, I drove to church and quietly took my place in the back pew, our usual spot. After the service, while making my way to the doors, people were kind enough to approach me, though most of them kept asking about my mom.

"She's sick," I answered, thinking I had lied. Not realizing it at the time, I had actually told the truth. Despite having Worthy and Miss Pearl for support, I started feeling anxious about people's opinions of my family.

I remembered the anxiousness of going to services alone after Worthy and I drifted apart. As summer approached, I found myself slowly giving in to my thoughts. I vividly remembered the first Sunday I decided not to attend church. I discovered an online streaming service and soon it became my way of worshiping at home.

When school started back, my circumstances completely changed. As our family began to fall apart and I hid in the confines of my shifts at the Movieplex, worshipping became a thing of the past. The further I witnessed Mom fall, the more I prayed. The more Mom's condition deteriorated, the more apparent it became that God wasn't answering my prayers. *If God wasn't going to hear me, why should I be listening to Him?*

Lou's reminder of my past as a believer made me feel vulnerable once more. I worked hard to build my armor, hiding the scars of my past and rejecting the shame of my mother's addiction and the daily toll it took on my father and me. Nevertheless, after only a single day, I once again felt the weight of it all.

I felt tortured by my racing thoughts as I sat on a stool at the sink during breakfast. By the time I finished all the dishes, the others had cleaned up their stations and were leaving. There was a throbbing ache in my neck for which I longed to ask Angie, the head nurse, for something to dull the pain. When I peered through the open window in front of me, I spotted her handing out morning medications with Carter. The last thing I wanted was a run-in with him, so I decided to just bear it.

"Need a hand?" Jojo asked, appearing as she finished cleaning her station. With her tote slung over her shoulder, she looked prepared for school, as a tall notebook poked out from the top.

"Just finished," I answered. "But you don't have to wait for me. I don't want you to be late."

Jojo flashed a smile before glancing down at her watch. "One of the downfalls of being on the Kitchen Staff is being chronically late. While we clean up the Dining Hall, everyone else adheres to the schedule." She spun on her heel, grabbing an apple from the leftover stack from breakfast and dropping it into her bag.

"Stealing food now?" I questioned.

Jojo chuckled as though she disagreed. "One of the perks of being Kitchen Staff is access to the best snacks."

I laughed as she tossed an apple to me that I barely managed to catch. "Once you're done, you can find Carter. I think Lou said he was going to be your camp escort."

The last thing I would do is seek out Carter for anything. "I don't need to, I can manage. Where is our first session?"

Jojo whipped out her schedule from her bag before answering, "Yours is at the gazebo with Adam."

"Are we not in the same session?" I wondered.

"No, the teens normally have a few different groups since there are so many of us," she explained, folding her schedule back into her bag. "While you enjoy the shade, I'll be out in the amphitheater getting roasted by the sun."

I knew the gazebo wasn't too far across the field, but I wondered if I could catch Lou for a ride instead. "Have you seen Lou?"

Jojo shook her head. "Not since earlier. She normally comes and goes during the day if she has to be at her office, but she's typically back in the evening."

After Gramps' death, Lou took over the family's real estate business. Despite knowing she had a lot on her plate, I found it strange that she didn't mention she wouldn't be at camp during the day. She wasn't my keeper, though, no matter what she thought, and I wasn't hers.

Jojo clapped her hand on my shoulder. "I'm off to my session, but I'll see you at lunch."

I waved as she disappeared through the double doors. With each step towards the front door, I pondered whether anyone would notice if I didn't attend my session. Though I knew Lou wasn't here now, I still felt as though there were eyes on me. Following two sleepless nights, I realized I lacked the energy for outright disobedience today. Consequently, I hobbled out of the

Dining Hall and onto the front porch. My heart stopped as I saw the golf cart parked at the end of the ramp.

Carter was leaning against the side of the golf cart, wearing an olive green t-shirt with tan shorts and comfortable shoes. At first, he didn't see me, but when the door slammed shut, he spotted me. His hair was just as perfectly messy as it was yesterday. The green of his shirt contrasted sharply with the forest behind us, and I felt a familiar jolt in my stomach as his eyes, the color of coffee, connected with mine.

"It's about time," he greeted me with his familiar attitude.

Limping down the ramp, I paused when I reached him. "I think I'm going to do us both a favor and find my own way to my session."

Before he started running his hand through his brown hair, I noticed his flared nostrils. "Look, I don't know what you think you heard last night—"

"We don't have to do this," I interrupted, gripping my crutches tighter, ensuring I had a good grasp on the handles. "You obviously have much better things to do than help a crippled girl hitch a ride, so I'll see you around."

"Lena," he grunted as I began to hustle past him. Walking across the lawn, the sound of my footsteps echoed with the crunch of the dry summer grass. The spacious gazebo was conveniently located just on the other side of the field. I could take a hint, and I hoped he could too.

***

Within minutes, I made it to the gazebo where about ten campers, along with a few Kitchen Staff, were already seated. As soon as I approached the stairs, Adam noticed me and paused his lesson. "Hey there, you're Lena, right?"

"Only for my whole life," I responded, my sarcasm coming out like a reflex. I heard a few chuckles from the campers and even Adam himself.

"A great sense of humor," Adam pointed out. "I like it."

A smirk played in the corner of my mouth as I took a seat on the end of the bench. A few pairs of eyes met mine as I surveyed the others. Some campers had Bibles on their laps and were taking notes on paper, as if they were in a classroom.

"Lena, we're doing an introduction session this afternoon and discussing personal faiths," Adam informed me, trying to get me up to speed. "Now, where was I?"

I watched as Adam flipped through his Bible until he found his place. "As I was saying, Jonah ran from the Lord, though he was commanded to preach to the sinful people of Nineveh. We can imagine how intimidated and scared he must have been, right? His fear led him to disobey.

"Then we see that the Apostles, the very disciples who followed Jesus, and those who were in His inner circle, were uneducated and simple tradesmen," Adam preached. Gazing around, I noticed how he captivated the attention of those around me. "These are the very men who helped turn the world upside down. The Lord's church was established as these men preached the Gospel to the point where it even cost them their lives."

Even though I was an outsider, I could see the others were hanging onto his every word. Adam believed in exactly what he was saying. He had faith in the cause of those who had traveled the earth with Jesus and shared His same beliefs. Still, I couldn't help but question the cause. Those men had sacrificed and given up their lives to follow Jesus. They were mocked, tortured, and murdered for their faith. *And what for?* The world never changed.

"I know the Gospel can sound intimidating and sometimes not worth it for some," Adam confessed. "I know because I used to be one of those people. I was completely unqualified and still am."

His joke caused a ripple of brief laughter through the circle of campers. "When I was in high school, I hung with all the wrong people. I spent time with the druggies at school and went to wild parties with my friends," he told us. "I lived like that until I found out my grandmother had cancer when I was seventeen."

The sudden silence was palpable, and I felt a lump form in my throat as emotion welled up inside me.

"My parents were both killed in a car accident driving home from a work party for my dad's company," Adam further explained. "They hydroplaned off the road during a bad storm and never made it home. My grandmother took me in and raised me. She knew all that time that I was partying, drinking, and just living for myself. I didn't care about anyone else, or really even myself."

His words had a profound effect on me, pulling at my heartstrings. I began to think about my own actions. Especially the choices that landed me here in the first place. My decisions almost mirrored those of Adam's former life.

Adam continued, "When I found out my grandmother had cancer, it was like a switch flipped. All of a sudden, my world seemed to come crashing down around me. My grandmother never condemned me or told me she thought I was a failure, though that's how I felt. She asked me to go to church with her for as long as she was able. That was all she ever asked of me."

Tears threatened to spill as I felt a burning sensation behind my eyes.

"I went to church with her every time those doors opened. I quickly made friends with others in our congregation and those friends became my family. Those people brought us dinner when the chemo and radiation drained all of Grandma's strength. They mowed our lawn. They cleaned our house. They took Grandma to her doctor's appointments so I didn't miss school. When my grandmother was on her deathbed, those people never left my side," Adam described before he paused.

Tears welled up in his eyes as he tried to hold them back with a deep breath. "One night while I was with my grandma, I thought she was asleep, so I prayed. I took her wrinkled hand in mine, and I prayed while she slept. I thought I could bargain with God, asked for Him to heal her, and promised to turn my life around.

"I cried at my grandmother's bedside for a while before a friend joined me. That man sat and prayed that God would give me the strength to endure. That God would give me the courage to make it through whatever came our way. He prayed that I would put God first in my life and that I would trust in God to bring me through the pain." He wiped a tear away and smiled at us, his sudden happiness taking me by surprise.

"When he left, I slept by my grandmother's bed, and the next morning my grandmother told me that she heard me, and she thanked me. She asked if I was happy with how I was living my life. I wasn't, but after that talk, my grandma had her last best day. We strolled around the hospital and played cards in the dayroom of the cancer unit. Then, around dinner time, we had visitors bring dinner and sing songs with us.

"That evening, the man that had come to pray with me the night before stayed with me after the singing was over. I talked with him, and once we were alone, I told him I wanted to live for Jesus. I had watched for over a year as our church family showed me what being a Christian was all about. It was about bearing each other's burdens and being there for each other. I didn't want to keep living the same way, so I vowed to give my life to Christ that night. I wanted to join the family that so graciously took care of me and my grandmother. I wanted to have the hope of seeing my grandmother again at the end of my life."

Resting against the railing, Adam disclosed that the man who stayed and prayed with him sought the help of church members. Adam went to the parking lot, where a truck bed filled with water awaited, visible from his grandmother's hospital window. A few available members quickly arrived and filled the parking lot with songs of praise to God. Upon confessing his faith in Jesus as the Son of the living God, Adam was baptized and emerged as a new person in Christ. When he finally arrived at his grandmother's room, she prayed with him and admitted she could die happily now that Adam had devoted his life to God.

"Before the next morning, my grandmother passed. Her body gave up, but her spirit soared," he grinned through happy tears. "The Lord turned my life upside down that night when I surrendered to Him. I finished high school and went on to preaching school."

"I have a beautiful wife who is my best friend. We serve our church together, and together we'll help each other get to Heaven. That is what being a Christian is all about. No matter what you've done in life, you are never too far from God."

Once he finished, I couldn't shake the feeling that his lesson was specifically for me. It was like someone peering into my soul and calling me out, though no one else around me had any idea.

When the lesson ended, Adam asked if anyone had experiences to share about the influence of Christ in our lives. One by one, campers answered how Christ had been working. Some said they could only join the camp as staff because they couldn't attend otherwise. Others shared more common examples, like prayers being answered for their ill loved ones or their siblings' safe return from military duty overseas.

Adam finally moved over to me, giving me the chance to share. I could contribute like everyone else, but when I pondered the state of my life lately, the only thing I viewed as a blessing was the air filling my lungs.

"I'll pass," I answered, folding my hands in my lap.

Adam uncrossed his arms and stuffed a hand in his pocket, tucking his worn-out Bible under his opposite arm. "That's no problem, Lena."

Not until I let it go did I realize I had been holding my breath. Adam pointed to a guy on the middle of the bench and asked for him to close out our session in prayer. As everyone lowered their heads, the young man guided us in a prayer, requesting help in our journey to become better servants.

Once he said "Amen," all heads rose up, Adam released us, and then he turned to me. "Lena, it was great to have you in session today. Like I said, it can be intimidating to be somewhere new, but I'm glad you're here with us this summer."

Adam signaled for me to go in front, his arms ready to support me. Smiling politely, I made my way down the stairs. As soon as I caught sight of Carter sitting on the golf cart nearby, I paused. *When did he get here?*

He locked his gaze with mine and leaned in, as if expecting me to join him. I heard Adam behind me say, "It looks like you're in good hands."

When Adam walked past me, I spun around and saw that Carter was still waiting. He wore the same look of contemplation as the first time I saw him at Staff Orientation. As I stared at him too long, he leaned back, draping an arm over the back of the seat. With an expectant arch of his eyebrow, he motioned for me to come over. The arrogance of this boy was shocking. When I turned and began going the other way, I heard him sigh once more. Maybe now he would take a hint.

9

The glaring afternoon sun felt unforgiving while I sat on the bleachers during team activities. Teams were chosen based on the age of the players, with each team being represented by a distinct color. Thanks to me, the Red Team was down one player. So far, I had spent the afternoon sitting out while Theo and Asher, a shorter, red-haired boy, carried our team in a game of kickball.

I attempted to fan myself with the neck of my t-shirt, but it was no use. On the softball field, there was no shade, and I was dying of thirst, desperate for any other activity.

Theo was up to kick next. Though he was part of the Sports Staff, which meant he normally led the activities, he had agreed to stand in for me to make both teams even. I watched while he tried three times, to kick the ball, but each time resulted in a foul. On his final kick, the ball came my way, and I had to duck to miss it. The First Baseman made an incredible catch, flying backwards to get the ball. Theo was out.

Rather than going back to the lineup, Theo jogged over and slowly made his way up the bleachers to stand in front of me. He tucked his blonde hair behind his ears as sweat beaded down the sides of his face. "I think you're faking that injury just to get out of playing."

I cocked an eyebrow up at him, squinting beneath the sun. "Trust me, if I could move this game along, I would have joined in a long time ago."

Theo scrunched his face in disgust all of a sudden. "Is that what that smell is? Man, Lena, when's the last time you showered?"

I raised my crutch to strike him, but he deflected it with his hand. Theo seized the crutch from my hand and began inching down the bleachers.

"You can borrow it, but you'll have to bring it back. There's no way I'm getting back to the kitchen with just one."

"Nonsense, you can make it, but it may be in the form of a Denny piggyback ride," Theo jeered.

I began fanning myself with my shirt again and scoffed. "I think Jojo is the only one who gets piggyback rides."

A chuckle escaped Theo as his eyes widened. "You've only been here for a day and noticed it too, huh?"

"What's the deal with those two anyway?" I wondered.

Theo wiped the sweat from his brow with the back of his wrist. "They've been best friends since I could remember, and I think they're scared if they date and break up, it will ruin our group dynamic."

"That's sad, but I can understand," I admitted. "So, what about you? Is there a girl you have your eye on here?"

Theo leaped up to his feet, suddenly holding his ear. "You know, I think I just heard my name, I should really get back out there."

I chuckled as he successfully evaded my question. "That's fine! You can keep your secrets!"

He jogged back onto the field to join the team, not once glancing back, while I noticed movement in the corner of my eye. Peering down, I saw my crutches slipping out of sight. As

I started sliding across the bleachers, I noticed Carter stashing my crutches in the golf cart nearby.

"What do you think you're doing?" I cried, glaring at him. "Are you crazy?"

He turned to face me, wearing his arrogant smirk. He tilted his head and shrugged, crossing his arms as he leaned against the cart. "Are you done being difficult?"

Leaning on my good leg, I slid off the bleachers with determination to retrieve my crutches. The moment I stood, though, I felt a little dizzy from the midday heat and wiped at the sweat beading over my forehead.

"I'm not being difficult," I rebutted. "I'm trying to help you help me by not helping me."

Carter raised an eyebrow and I was almost certain I caught a glimpse of a smile. I started leaping towards the cart, attempting to snatch my crutches back, and came very close to succeeding until I failed to notice a small, uneven dip in the field and started to fall.

Before I could hit the ground, Carter quickly sprang into action. With a sudden movement, he lunged towards me and held me tightly in his arms. My heart rate quickened in anticipation of falling, and once I realized he was holding me, my pulse showed no signs of slowing down.

Carter shook his head, murmuring something to himself. Hoisting me up, he bore most of my weight before firmly planting me in the passenger's seat. While he walked away, I quickly turned to retrieve my crutches, but our eyes met.

"Don't even think about it."

I grimaced at him, and then noticed the orange water jug in the back and remembered how parched I felt. "I'm not trying to run. Obviously that plan didn't work like I thought it would."

His mouth turned up at the corner, and I could have sworn he almost smiled again.

"Can you just give me some water?" I asked, trying to shield my eyes from the sun.

Carter crossed his arms. "Can you say please?"

I wasn't planning on giving him the satisfaction, so I quipped, "No, but thank you."

He was still muttering something under his breath when I swiveled in my seat, and I finally heard the steady stream of water. Carter came over to the driver's side and handed me the water cup without getting in. I grabbed the paper cone from his hand and downed its contents in two large gulps before the icy liquid hit my stomach with a gurgle.

Carter finally climbed in beside me, placing a bag in his lap as he rummaged through it. Without saying a word, I held the cup back over to him, silently asking for more. He frowned and flared his nostrils before leaping back up to refill my cup. When he finished, he plunked down so hard into the cart that the whole thing shifted beneath his weight, and some water slipped from the side of the cup onto my hand as I took it back.

"Wait, don't drink any yet," he demanded, rifling through his bag once more. I sighed loudly, hoping to make my impatience clear. Finally, finding what he needed, Carter commanded, "Hold out your hand."

I stared at him in confusion. "Why?"

"Just hold out your hand," he groaned. Carter's warm cocoa eyes locked with mine, momentarily erasing any ill feelings between us. With a sigh, he took hold of my hand and poured the contents into my palm. I stared down at two pain relievers as he instructed, "Take those."

Without further protest, I popped the medicine into my mouth and washed it down with the ice-cold water in my cup. A sigh of relief escaped me as the cool water glided the medicine down my throat. Relief was on its way.

Carter started the golf cart by turning the key and drove us slowly back towards the gravel path. "You can hate me all you want, but we have to establish some ground rules here."

"Great, more rules," I balked, glancing at the trees as we sped through camp.

"I take my responsibility seriously—" he tried to lecture.

"Clearly," I muttered.

Carter huffed, "So, that means I need you to be ready for me to pick you up between activities as soon as possible. We both have responsibilities we can't be late for."

To my surprise, he appeared to be earnestly begging me as I glanced at him. Was he worried that I was going to cause problems for him?

"Fine," I spat, giving in. As soon as I said it, I could see something resembling relief wash over him. "Can you at least drive faster, though? As much as I appreciate the lecture, I have to be back in the kitchen, and you're going to make me late."

Carter scowled. "Maybe if you weren't so busy trying to hop everywhere I wouldn't have to explain simple camp rules to you."

A loud groan escaped me as I drummed my fingers on the side of the golf cart. "Just get me to the kitchen, please, Scooter Man."

Skeptically, he narrowed his eyes. "This is a golf cart."

"But you drive it like it's a scooter, Captain Obvious. Now floor it!"

Granting my wish, he pushed down on the gas pedal, propelling us forward with such force that I had to grasp the handle to avoid being catapulted out. I was astonished to see him laughing at me as I peeked over.

"Very impressive, 'Fast and Furious'."

Racing ahead, we passed the tennis courts where other teams were still in action, although not for much longer. When we arrived at the Dining Hall, Carter roughly came to a complete stop. He briskly made his way to my side and returned my crutches. "Here you are, your *Highness.*"

With a snort, I grabbed them away from him and muttered, "Whatever." Despite not wanting to be around Carter, there was no denying the immediate relief I felt with having a ride.

While I was making my way up the ramp, I heard him call from behind, "Or, maybe I should call you, Duchess. That has a much better ring to it with all this royal treatment you're receiving."

Out of the corner of my eye, I noticed him stroking his chin, wearing the same pensive look as before. He was clearly trying to get a rise out of me.

"Whatever you say, Scooter!" I dismissed him.

For the first time, I saw a bright smile come over Carter's face as he slid his sunglasses back down over his eyes. "See you soon, Duchess!"

10

Dishwashing was meant for more than one person, I thought, while all the other staff seemed to work in pairs. During dinner, I ended up with soaked elbows as the dishes kept piling up. Was it really so hard to buy disposable dinnerware and utensils? When I wasn't scrubbing large dishes clean or stacking plates, cups, and utensils in the dishwasher, I was scraping off half-eaten meals into the trash can. Campers were supposed to scrape their plates clean, but I quickly realized they rarely did.

Tonight's menu was sloppy joes, slaw, and fries. I felt grateful that the Kitchen Staff had time to scarf down a quick dinner before everyone else until now. With each dish I scraped, my dinner threatened to make a reappearance. The dirty dishes in the large window piled up so high that I had to work three times faster to stay on top of them.

I glanced around the kitchen after loading the dishwasher again. Others were busy with their own duties. While one boy was changing trash bags, a girl who worked as a server kept going to the back to grab milk boxes from the large fridges. Jojo was stacking cookies onto platters for the servers to deliver to the Dining Hall. I sighed when I saw the table crowded with big mixing bowls and baking utensils, and went back to dish washing. I would be scrubbing the bowls soon enough.

From the corner of my eye, someone caught my attention as they approached the window. The sound of dishes crashing was immediately followed by a large splash that covered my front. I gasped and looked down at my shirt, which was now drenched in what looked like chocolate milk. Looking up, I saw Riley standing there, eyes wide. She clasped her hand over her mouth and began to stifle a giggle.

"Oops!"

A milk carton lay empty on its side and I felt the uncomfortable chill of the beverage. I pulled my shirt away from my chest, looking around for something to sop it up with. Kelsey came around the corner and pulled Riley away from the window, not bothering to offer an apology.

The image of Lacey throwing tea on Ronni in the school cafeteria popped into my mind. The revenge-filled sneer on her face was one of the catalysts for me ending up at camp in the first place. There were bullies everywhere, no matter where I seemed to turn. Someone was always trying to get the best of me.

"Here." Jojo came to my side, holding out a large dish towel. "Try to dry off with this."

Pressing the towel to my front, I couldn't help but wince at the feeling of the cold liquid. Jojo then pulled off her apron, handing it over.

"Take this, too. You can cover up your shirt. At least until you can get back to the cabin to change."

"She is just like these girls at my school," I huffed as I tied the apron around my waist.

With a gentle expression, Jojo leaned against the countertop. "What girls?"

I briefly considered confiding in her about Lacey and Ronni, but decided against it. Jojo seemed like the only lifeline I had this summer. I wasn't going to jeopardize that.

"Just these girls I haven't exactly gotten along with." I shrugged it off and rolled my eyes. "High school, am I right?"

Jojo agreed, "Riley and I aren't exactly close, and this doesn't excuse her behavior, but I have to admit, she's had a rough year."

I leaned in closer with piqued interest as Jojo began scraping plates beside me. As she leaned over the sink and washed, I shifted to create space for her while I rinsed.

"So, what kind of hardships could a girl like Riley have?" I asked sarcastically. I found her troubles a little unbelievable. The girl was dressed in name-brand clothes and had makeup smooth enough it seemed airbrushed. I bought my clothes second-hand and hardly ever wore makeup, except for mascara.

Jojo lowered her voice. "She and Carter broke up in the spring and it was not on good terms."

My eyes widen in surprise. *Carter and Riley?* "How long did they date?"

She bobbed her head back and forth, trying to remember. "Not long, maybe five or six months?"

"What happened?" I pressed, suddenly needing to know all the details.

Jojo winced, keeping her voice just above a whisper. "We were at a youth cookout, and I'm not sure if they were taking a break or in a fight, but she was pretty upset."

I leaned in, soaking in every word.

"I didn't witness anything myself except for Carter leaving with his parents right away. Denny told me that he heard that Carter suggested they break up, and Riley slapped him."

My mouth hit the floor. That was the last thing I expected to hear from two youth group kids. *What happened to turning the other cheek?*

I suddenly thought of Lacey. I never had a chance to pass her in the hallways at school without experiencing some form of ridicule. My stomach sank at the thought of Riley being the camp version of my ex-best friend.

"What else happened?"

Jojo simply shrugged. "I'm honestly not sure. She was a crying mess after their breakup, I think Kelsey took her home that day. After their fight, we all just helped clean up and left. It seems like the youth group has been divided since then. Carter even took a step back from youth activities for a little while."

"You would think they would want Carter and Riley to be more involved in church activities," I quipped.

The more that I thought about Carter and Riley dating, the more things made sense. In my opinion, they made a great pair. Both of them seemed to hold a high opinion of themselves. Each focused on getting their own way, as I had witnessed first-hand.

Jojo nodded in agreement. "Carter's been focused on school this summer. He has a lot to overcome..."

I noticed her voice trail off. "What does that mean?"

Jojo seemed to mull this over before saying, "Carter is complicated."

With amusement, I scoffed. "Complicated? Or do you just mean he's rude?"

Jojo quickly shook her head. "No, Carter has a colorful past."

She began to wipe up the countertop while I piled the last of the dishes to dry. I stopped and held my gaze on her, urging her to continue.

Jojo caved. "Fine, but I'm only telling you what everyone else knows. His business isn't mine to share."

"Go on," I chided her.

Grinning, Jojo placed her hand on her hip. "I can't get into the specifics of his life, but all I know is he has a rough past. Carter moved to Meadowbrook a few years ago, after the Roses adopted him. He and Denny became best friends pretty quickly, since we all go to school and church together. It took a little while, but then he finally joined the youth group."

"I would have never guessed," I admitted. Carter seemed like the type of rude, pushy, arrogant guy that lived a privileged life.

He was one of the best-dressed guys at camp and always seemed put together.

"Everyone's got their stuff, Lena," Jojo pointed out. As we finished cleaning up, I got the feeling that there was a lot more to the story than Jojo told me.

The new information about Carter intrigued me. He had all the makings of being a simple jock who thought he was the king of the world. Sure, he was rude and needed to improve his bedside manner, but I would have never imagined he was adopted.

Jojo suddenly slapped her knee, as if remembering something she forgot. "Your shirt, you need to get changed!"

Despite my damp shirt, I found myself unexpectedly captivated by the drama of Carter and Riley's breakup. "You're right, I'll go get changed."

"Just bring the apron back when you're done and we may catch some evening free time before worship starts," Jojo ordered.

On my way back to the cabin, I struggled with the decision to confront Riley or brush it off as a mere accident. The last thing I needed for the summer was to walk away from one drama only to start another. I decided to put my ill feelings aside and be the bigger person. It was bad enough to go to school with an enemy, I didn't want to spend a summer at camp living with one, too.

Hurrying, I rushed back to the cabin, found a New Hope Bible Camp t-shirt in my goodie bag, and threw it on. Free time was over once I returned the apron back to the kitchen and I found Jojo snacking on a leftover cookie.

"Ready for worship?" she asked, wiping her hands on her shorts.

"Lead the way."

Together, Jojo and I made our way down to the amphitheater and found a seat with the boys in the back row. Denny and Theo appeared as tired as I was. From the looks of the dirt on their legs and shoes, they had been unable to clean up before dinner.

I leaned over to Theo and asked, "What happened to you guys?"

Denny answered before Theo had the chance, "We decided to take the four-wheeler for a joy ride through some mud after setting up water activities this afternoon."

Jojo rolled her eyes as Denny and Theo high-fived each other.

"It was epic!" Theo grinned.

"Boys." Jojo shook her head before turning her attention to the front as Adam took his place before the crowd. After we sang a few songs, the projector displayed the lesson topic on full display: FRIENDSHIP.

"Raise your hand if you have a best friend," Adam instructed us. Hands everywhere shot up with no hesitation. Beside Jojo, Denny and Theo were smacking each other's hands down, which resulted in a sort of arm-wrestling match.

"Sometimes they can be Neanderthals," Jojo whispered, hiding her face as if ashamed to be seen with them. I laughed. They may be Neanderthals, but at least they had each other. For the past year, the only friendship I had was based on mutual vengeance.

"Raise your hand if your best friend is the person you can count on for anything," Adam commanded once more. Hands immediately flew back up. I had the sudden urge to shrink away. *If all things were possible with God, couldn't he make me invisible?*

Adam went on, "Okay, now raise your hand if your best friend has ever gotten you into trouble."

A wave of murmurs spread as people started glancing around. Fewer hands were raised this time, but I managed to join in finally.

Jojo eyed me with a grin. "I can't even tell you the things these guys have gotten me into."

Denny and Theo's arm wrestling still continued as the two of them bumped and nudged each other hard enough to send Jojo rocking into me. As I leaned into her, she leaned against Denny, who in turn fell against Theo, like a series of falling dominoes. Immediately, Denny shifted, unaware I had started it, and began tickling Jojo. She covered her stomach, trying to push his hands away as she did her best to stifle her laughter.

"Denny, stop! We're going to get in trouble!"

"Tonight, we're going to talk about two friends in the Bible that were each other's ride or die," Adam announced. As soon as he did, Denny and Jojo settled down.

"We all have three types of friends," Adam preached. "The first type of friend is an acquaintance. They're the type of friendship that stays at a surface level.

"The second type of friend," he went on, "they're our best friends, our inner circle who we enjoy hanging out with and getting to know."

To my right, I glanced over to see an inner circle of friends: Jojo, Denny, and Theo. The three of them always found each other and had a good time. The thought of their friendship made my heart sink. I used to know how it felt to have an inner circle.

"Then there is the third type of friend," Adam announced, pausing, his face turning serious. "This friend is our ride or die."

The group erupted in cheers, and the girls in front of me exchanged a quick squeeze. I felt my stomach clench, as if suffering hit by hit from Adam's lesson.

"Our ride or die is the friend that truly knows us," Adam exclaimed. "They're the one person in this world who knows you like you know yourself."

To my right, Denny coyly leaned his shoulder against Jojo's. The gesture brought a large smile to her face and her cheeks reddened.

"Our ride or dies are the friends that can tell how we're feeling just with a look," Adam said, emphasizing each point he made. "Our ride or dies are the friends who tell us the truth, even when it hurts. They're ones we can always count on to be there, no matter what."

Adam began flipping pages in his Bible before finding his place. "God's word tells us about two best friends in the book of First Samuel. Does anyone know who I'm referring to?"

Dozens of hands went up in the air at once before Adam called on a young man in the crowd.

"David and Jonathan?"

"Yes!" Adam confirmed. "Through David and Jonathan's example, we can learn a lot about how to be Godly friends."

My focus was particularly drawn to something in this lesson. I couldn't shake the feeling of being an outsider, even with people all around me. But as the lesson continued, my thoughts raced.

Adam described Jonathan as a loyal servant to both God and David. He painted the picture of how Jonathan grew up with every need in life being met and how he wanted for nothing as the son of a king. But Jonathan wasn't a typical prince, he was a man who had a heart after God. Just like David. Jonathan's unity set him apart as both a remarkable servant and friend.

"There are five things to know about Jonathan." Adam held up his hand as he counted. "One, he was likable. Two, he was courageous because he put his faith in the Lord. Three, he discerned who he could trust. Four, he was loyal even when that loyalty put him in the middle of the fight. And five, he was willing to lay down his life for his friends."

Adam further explained how Jonathan was there for David when he needed him the most. Even when it meant Jonathan needed to go against his own father, who tried to murder David. He recognized the plans God had for David.

"Jonathan's example mirrors the friend Jesus is to us. Jonathan's loyalty, humility, and love led him to the battlefield where he laid down his life. Jesus did the same for every one of us here." Glancing back at his Bible, Adam read, "Greater love has no one than this, that someone lay down his life for his friends.

"There is a beauty to being a ride or die," Adam began to close. "We have the opportunity to be a Jonathan for our friends. To be the type of people who encourage, pray for, and strengthen our friends. The more that we treat others like this, the more we show the love of Jesus. What better way to live our lives?"

When he finished, Adam led the crowd in a song. Campers climbed to their feet to sing about the steadfast love of God. The lesson made me ache, not for Lacey or Ronni to come back into my life, but for what they once meant to me. I used to be able to tell Lacey anything, and her house once felt like my second home. At one point, her parents referred to me as their other daughter. Worthy and Camille were part of our close-knit group of friends, and we were always together.

With Ronni, it was different. She defended me when I needed it most. She never said a word against my mother and never judged me. Yet, none of them stuck around. *Why was it so easy for others to leave me behind?*

As the song ended, Denny and Jojo's poke war brought me back to the present. After the closing prayer, Denny leaped to his feet and Jojo lunged after him. Without a second thought, Theo joined in, and the three of them chased each other up the hill.

I grabbed my crutches and climbed to my feet. Groups of campers joined their friends, chatting as everyone headed back to the heart of camp. Following behind, I noticed a group of girls skipping together, their wrists adorned with beaded letter bracelets. A few guys passed by next, teasing each other about who was their ride or die, while I felt adrift.

A sea of campers bustled around me, and though I hoped to blend in, I just felt like I stuck out. I was an island, unseen and undiscovered. With each step, the crutches I leaned on caused a deep ache beneath my arms. I began searching high and low for the Med Cart that Carter drove, hoping for some relief.

I paused once I saw him. Still sporting the same green shirt from earlier, he leaned against the cart, moving his hands as he spoke. I spotted Riley standing in front of him and felt a wave of shock at the sight of them. As I watched them interact, they seemed casual. I was taken aback when Riley even smiled at something he said.

The two of them seemed to be deep in conversation. Carter spoke with his hands, and despite what I had found out about their break up, I couldn't help but notice how much more relaxed he seemed than when he was with me. I thought about the Banquet at the end of the summer and wondered if they would end up rekindling their relationship by then. The thought made my stomach churn. I didn't come to camp to make enemies, but I couldn't shake the feeling that the two of them were approaching my enemy territory.

I spun on my heel, deciding to leave the two of them to their conversation. I chose to take a brief detour along a dirt path to avoid going uphill near the amphitheater. With each swing of my crutches, the soreness spread until I felt a stinging pain. I took two breaks to rest my arms on the way back to the cabin before I finally made it.

I abandoned my crutches and promptly hopped to the shower. With my hand pressed against the wall, I let the steaming water rain down on me. The sound of laughter and scattered footsteps echoed from just outside the thin cabin walls. Peeking past the shower curtain, I noticed that the small window above the sinks was open, and I could hear the campers returning to their cabins.

Since Jojo was nowhere to be found, I got ready for bed and slipped into my sleeping bag. All I wanted was to fall into a long uninterrupted sleep. Just as I relaxed, though, Adam's words drifted back to me. *The more we treat others this way, the more we are showing the love of Jesus.*

The first time I heard this, I was just a little girl. I had run crying to my mother because Denny and Theo had thrown sand at Jojo and me on the playground. When I found my mother on the front porch of the Meadowbrook church, she bent down and held my face in her hands.

"Lenny Lee, what's the matter?"

I stared into her eyes, which were just like mine, and whimpered that the mean boys had put sand in my hair. Mom had given me a pouty face as she took my hand and led me down the stairs to face my playground bullies. When we found Denny and Theo on the playground, there was no sign of Jojo. My mother requested that they stand before her while she conveyed that throwing sand at people was not kind, and questioned how they would feel if I were to throw sand at them.

Both Denny and Theo agreed they wouldn't want to be hit with sand as my mother crouched in front of them. Gently, she explained, "We need to treat others how we want to be treated, okay?"

Both boys nodded eagerly, their eyes filled with fear.

"Can you say you're sorry to my little girl?" she asked them, her tone gentle, yet firm.

Denny and Theo both apologized, and as soon as my mom thanked them, they bolted back to the church. With a smile on her face, Mom lovingly moved my hair from my face. "We can be sweet to others even when they hurt our feelings. That's how we love them like Jesus."

I thought about those words as I grew up. Treat others how you want to be treated, and love others like Jesus. How come it was effortless for her to do the complete opposite? How was it so easy for her to choose alcohol over her love for our family? Why did she turn her back on her faith?

Living by this rule felt like an empty promise, as the person who taught me couldn't even live up to her own advice. I wasn't sure if I would ever shake off the feeling of being left behind by the person I loved the most. I felt lost, alone, and more out of place than ever. My thoughts engulfed me as I lay in the dark, making my throat feel tight. I could feel the warmth of tears behind my eyes and I pressed the top of my sleeping bag over my face to hold them off.

Just breathe. I thought to myself. *Breathe in. Breathe out.* I lay like that, breathing slowly until I found a rhythm that guided me into a deep sleep.

11

As the first week drew to a close, I felt a sense of emptiness, as if I was simply going through the motions at camp. I mentally started a countdown. Only three more weeks, and I would be homebound. Until then, I could get up, go to my kitchen shifts, sit in my breakout sessions, hang out on the bleachers during team activities, make it through free time, and survive Teen Devotional. The only great advice I ever took from Ronni was "Fake it 'til you make it," and that's what I committed myself to.

Being at church camp was tough because I was always surrounded by people who felt the need to tell me how to live my life and become a better person, which was already difficult given the problems at home. Not a single person here had walked a day in my shoes and had no ability to relate to what I had been through over the last year. Sure, it seemed easy enough. *Treat others like I want to be treated. Follow Jesus and He will bear my burdens. Pray and the Lord will handle everything.*

Did people believe it was really that simple? Every time I listened to that advice in the past, where had it gotten me? I had prayed day in and day out that my mom would get better, and she got worse. I prayed that my family could heal for months on end, and we were ripped apart. The longer I stayed here the worse I felt. The memories of the life I used to have and the faith I once clung to served as a reminder of all that I had lost.

"Hey, you okay?" Jojo asked during breakfast. Her dark hair was pulled perfectly into a sock bun as she sported a cute top, jeans, and rain boots. The rain was pouring outside and would linger for most of the day.

"Yeah, all good here," I fibbed, returning to the dishes.

"I saved you a cinnamon roll," Jojo mentioned. "Whenever we're done, it's yours."

I thanked her as she moved back to her station to finish cleaning up. The breakfast spread included cereal in large containers and a fresh fruit à la carte stand. Jojo had even cooked a large batch of cinnamon rolls that campers were likely to want for the duration of camp.

When I arrived for duty, there was an apron dangling over the side of the sink. I knew it had to be from Jojo. Tying it behind my back, I went to work. Almost thirty minutes into breakfast, Riley showed back up to the window, sliding her dirty dishes to me. She had a half-eaten cinnamon roll left on her plate and a bowl full of milk from her cereal.

Before she disappeared, I asked, "Can you please clear your plate next time?"

Riley was no rookie at this, she knew the rules. There was a bucket just below the window for liquids and a small trash can for food scraps. Riley seemed unfazed by my question and pointed to the door.

"I'm sorry, it's just that I'm in a hurry this morning. Do you mind?"

Without bothering to let me answer, she stalked away. I shook my head in disbelief. It must be nice to be in her shoes where the rules don't apply to her. From day one, I had witnessed Riley getting her way without any consideration for other people, and I was over it. Among many reasons, this was just another one that intensified my desire to leave this place.

Once I finished the dishes, I left the cups on the counter to dry and looked out the window at the Med Table. I hoped to spot Angie or Carter for some pain reliever but there was no sign of them. After a good night's sleep, my arms felt better, but the non-padded crutches weren't doing me any favors.

Taking off my apron, I tossed it back over the sink as Jojo approached me. Throwing her bag over her shoulder, she was ready for her breakout session.

"Hey, thanks for that by the way." I motioned to the apron.

Jojo grinned but seemed oblivious. "It wasn't me, but I'm glad you had one today. But you'll need something to keep you dry from this downpour outside."

I followed her out of the Dining Hall, and she stopped by the entrance to grab her raincoat off the coat rack. I kicked myself, metaphorically speaking, as that was the one thing I hadn't packed. Although I had my umbrella, it was too difficult to carry while I limped around.

Heading outside, I watched for Carter and spotted him by the stairs, talking to Riley again as a crowd of campers filed past Jojo and me. As usual, Carter looked polished in a black raincoat and jeans. Riley peered up at him in almost the same way Jojo gazed at Denny. As if there was nothing else moving in the world around her. Riley had braided her hair back into two buns while still sporting bright red lips. Carter didn't seem as entranced in the conversation, as he held a walkie-talkie expectantly.

I knew he had been waiting on me, but I felt like he had more important things to attend to at that moment. He began speaking into his walkie-talkie as Riley listened. She squinted her eyes as though trying to make sense of the conversation, and when he finally lowered the device from his mouth, he smiled. Riley snickered at whatever they had heard and touched the top of his arm.

The sight of her touch caused me to look away. I felt like I had observed far too much of a private moment between the two of them. Clearly, they had unfinished business, and as much as I wanted to not use my crutches, I wanted to stay out of their way even more. As I followed the pack of campers shuffling off the front porch, I strode right past them. Carter took no notice as they continued chatting, and I made my way to my breakout session in the pouring rain.

***

Underneath the gazebo roof, I listened to Adam preach as the raindrops tapped rhythmically. The sky was a canvas of muted grays and the fragrance of damp earth mingled with the scent of pine. The landscape enhanced the image Adam was portraying. Today's lesson was about Saul of Tarsus, a Roman who persecuted Christians in the first century.

The more I heard about Saul, the more it intrigued me. Adam read from the Book of Acts as he described the state of the world at that time. As Jesus and His disciples spread the Gospel, the Roman society became increasingly paranoid that yet another false teacher was gaining popularity.

"Jesus came claiming to be the Messiah," Adam informed us. "The government officials didn't want someone disrupting their laws and creating a religious uproar." He described how the disciples continued teaching and preaching despite being imprisoned and even beaten. Nothing seemed to stop their efforts, not even death.

"Then entered Saul of Tarsus. He was not your ordinary Jew, he was a Pharisee, a devout one at that," Adam pointed out. "He set off imprisoning and killing Christians, including women."

Adam addressed the religious leaders' role in covering up Saul's Christian genocide, allowing him to carry on. He not only imprisoned the followers of Jesus, but tortured them before putting them to death.

"Finally, Jesus was the one to stop Saul in his tracks," Adam declared. "This is the beauty of a life with Jesus, let's read on." With his nose in his Bible, Adam read aloud about how Saul was confronted by Jesus. "In the presence of the Lord, Saul could not deny Jesus. He was blinded and sent to Damascus where he immediately obeyed the Lord."

Adam snapped his Bible shut and held it to his chest. "Saul was baptized by a man named Ananias, and he then went on to become one of the greatest Christians in history. He wrote most of the New Testament as he worked to spread the Gospel."

What intrigued me about Paul's life was the persecution he carried out against the early church before becoming a Christian. I had always heard about God calling the simplest men who were unqualified and uneducated. But hearing how Paul joined the cause of the Christians he murdered began to pique my interest.

"Let's go around and share some thoughts on Paul," Adam instructed. To my surprise, he chose me first.

"I think, maybe," I choked out, "I can relate to Paul because he had his whole life turned upside down." The words tumbled out of my mouth.

I looked up as Adam pursed his lips and stroked his chin, his expression thoughtful.

"How so, Lena?"

The other campers stole glances from me to Adam, awaiting my response. I gulped. There was no way I was going to open up to a bunch of strangers about my family issues, nor about how I struggled to share their faith. I shrugged, wringing my hands in my lap.

"I just know how it feels."

Adam held my gaze for a few seconds before moving on. Taking a deep breath, I quietly let it out, not noticing how my heart had quickened being put on the spot. The only time I felt even remotely close to this level of panic was when I took a daring leap from the enormous tree in Lacey's front yard.

Sitting there, my right leg began to shake with anticipation of wrapping the session up. My t-shirt had finally had a chance to dry to a slightly damp level after my hustling through the pouring rain on my way to this session. Dreading the trek to afternoon activities, I looked around. Carter had disappeared since breakfast, and I wondered if he had finally quit trying to be my chauffeur.

Once the closing prayer was over, everyone started packing up and heading to their afternoon activities. The raindrops started to softly hit my head and exposed arms the moment I hopped down the steps. I discreetly pulled out my phone to check the time. Before team activities, I had a few minutes to spare, so I decided to go back to my room to change my shirt. Right when I was about to leave, I heard tires crunching on the gravel from behind. Throwing a glance over my shoulder, I spotted Lou seated on one of the camp's golf carts.

"Hey there."

"Hi," I greeted in return. She donned a hat from New Hope Bible Camp and a raincoat that showcased her real estate business logo on the front left shoulder. Her name was displayed below the logo in small capital letters: Lou Rivers.

"Where you headed?" she asked, eyeing me suspiciously.

My jaw clenched as my teeth tightly ground together. Would the rest of camp be like this, with her all over my case?

"I'm not skipping out on anything if that's what you're asking, Lou," I replied with a glare.

Her mouth twisted and her eyes furrowed. "Lena, I wasn't trying to accuse you of anything, I was just asking a question."

I leaned my weight forward on my crutches and fully turned to face her, the rain transitioning to a sprinkling.

"Since activities are outside, I thought I might need to go grab some kind of cover from the rain," I admitted, holding out my hand as if to catch a drop. "But it seems like I may not need one after all."

Lou relaxed and glanced up at the sky for a brief moment. "I think you're right," she agreed, observing the clearing skies overhead. "Come on and I'll give you a ride."

I didn't want to be in the small vehicle with her, but I also didn't want to argue today. Without bothering to change my damp shirt, I quickly scurried over to climb in next to Lou.

"So, how are things?" she questioned, raising her voice as the wind whipped past us. I felt goosebumps as the humid mountain air mingled with my damp shirt, and I wished I had changed.

"They're fine," I answered.

A moment of silence passed before she announced, "I spoke with Adam."

My eyes flicked to her face. "You did?"

Lou nodded, keeping her focus straight ahead. "He mentioned you've been quiet in your breakout sessions."

She was giving me the same amount of information I gave her. Shrugging, I replied, "I'm the new girl, I don't have a lot of people to talk to."

I could feel her gaze on me as I looked away. *What did she want me to say? That I was having the time of my life and this place felt like Disneyland?*

"He just said that you typically pass on answering questions or participating in discussions," Lou confessed.

I sighed. It wasn't enough that I was stuck here for the next three weeks, but I had been right. Lou *was* keeping tabs on me. What had my dad told her about me? She was beginning to treat me like I was some sort of escaped convict who needed constant surveillance. With my mood as damp as my shirt, I remained silent. The moment she parked at the tennis court, I didn't hesitate and quickly jumped out.

"Lena, it was just a question!" she tried to explain.

My temper flared and I suddenly turned around. "I'm here doing exactly what's expected of me. I didn't realize I was getting a participation grade, too."

Lou's face fell. I felt a shred of regret once I saw the change in her expression, but it was quickly replaced with satisfaction. Lou wasn't my mother, no matter how much they looked alike.

The remaining part of the afternoon was spent in utter boredom as I watched my team play volleyball. We were on the tennis court in an attempt to avoid the washed-out sand court on the other side of camp. The air hung heavy with the scent of damp earth, and the humidity clung to everything. As the day progressed, the sun came out and the temperature climbed again.

My team seemed to be having the time of their lives. The court was alive with the rhythmic squeaks of athletic shoes against the pavement and their laughter and cheers filled the air. Theo and Asher, in an unexpected turn of events, became the unofficial team captains.

The longer I had to sit there while watching everyone else enjoy themselves, the worse my mood became. If I had two good legs, I would have already marched back to my cabin to isolate myself for the rest of the afternoon. When the whistle finally blew, the teams split in different directions for a water break.

Hustling over, Theo plopped down with a small paper cup in his hands, gulping it down right in front of me. As he gulped the water down, I noticed how parched I felt. I wished more than anything a huge downpour would erupt from the atmosphere at any point so I could just tilt my head back and drink it in.

"You know, we can't hear you," Theo pointed out, staring up at me expectantly. "If you're going for a silent cheering section, then mission accomplished. I wonder if there is a Benchwarmer award you might win at the Banquet."

I glared at him, but Theo didn't seem to care. He took another step up the bleachers and plopped down in front of me, tapping my ankle boot. "Does that hurt?"

Although I couldn't feel pain, I suddenly wanted to tap him on the forehead to see how he liked it. Instead, I remained silent.

"I like it better when we can exchange some sort of witty banter," Theo confessed, "What's with you?"

He took one last swig from the paper cup before crushing it in the palm of his hand.

"I thought we were merely acquaintances who kept their secrets," I quipped.

Theo's face twisted in a grimace, as if my words had stung him. "Someone's a moody little mermaid today."

With a glare, I pulled my legs in tightly, hugging them against my chest. Theo looked up at me with a grin, as if he thought I would get his joke.

"Get it?" He pressed. "Mermaid? Because you're from the beach."

I continued with my silence and he finally got the hint. Scoffing, he climbed down the bleachers, murmuring, "Tough crowd."

Theo threw away his cup in the trash can a few feet away. As if playing follow the leader, others began to rise to their feet and follow suit, like they were on autopilot. Why did no one ever talk about being a leader instead of preaching about being a follower all the time?

I took out my phone and checked the time. I had almost an hour and a half before dinner would begin, and roughly thirty minutes before I needed to show up for duty. As both teams began to head in separate directions for afternoon free time, I took my own path back to the Dining Hall.

***

I kept to myself for the rest of the day. The dinner rush was busier than usual, crashed by unexpected visitors. According to Jojo, family and friends usually visited on Friday nights to spend time with their campers or bring them home for the weekend. Due to the sizable crowd, the schedule was slightly modified to include a singing session before Teen Devo began.

Jojo invited me to go down to sing with her and some of the others, but I declined, trying my best to fade into the background. The event brought to mind the last time I had sung with my family. During one of our last visits to Meadowbrook before my Gramps died, we had surrounded a small fire by the pond at Lou's. My mom and Lou were reminiscing, teasing each other about their antics growing up.

Grateful for his family to be together again, Gramps asked to sing. Mom was reluctant at first, pointing out how we would be missing Grams' harmony. Gramps looked at me with warm blue eyes, saying I was the perfect third harmony to fill Grams' place.

That night, I sang the words to "I'll Fly Away" with my family. Our voices rang out, filling the night air, connecting our hearts. In that moment, I felt this sense of belonging that I had never experienced before. Mom and Lou had always been the "Singing Rivers Girls," but just like that, Gramps embraced my voice too, bringing me into the fold. When my grandfather passed away and our family started to crumble, I hid my talent in the same way that I hid my faith.

When Jojo left to join the singing, I lagged behind. I dedicated my time to working as slowly as possible. I had no desire to be in the midst of families and friends, especially not at Devo. By the time I finished finding things around the kitchen that could use some extra polishing, I glanced at the clock to see Devo had already started.

Tonight, I arrived slightly late and noticed that the speaker was new. The man had a round middle, white hair, and a voice that conveyed a sense of urgency.

"The world has seen so many senseless attacks on innocents," the man's voice boomed. "From genocides to racial persecution, the hatred of others has always inflicted evil in our world."

This man had a fire in his eyes that I hadn't seen before. He talked about the injustices of the world as though they caused him physical pain. For once, I agreed with someone this week. The world was full of hatred and there were always others suffering at the hands of another.

"The Christians who followed Jesus experienced their own forms of persecution!" he shouted. "They were hated for spreading the Gospel, and if they weren't imprisoned, they were tortured, and even martyred because of their faith!"

"Hate is a disease," he said, lowering his voice to just above a whisper. Gazing over the crowd, he held up his index finger as if having an epiphany. "There is only one cure for hate, and it's love."

Immediately, I frowned. Overcoming hate with love was a farce. Where did it get anyone? In my experience, no matter how much you loved someone, it wasn't enough.

"Raise your hand if you feel like you've been unfairly attacked by someone," he commanded us. Hands shot up in all directions.

"Now, raise your hand if you've ever been hurt by someone you're close to," the man asked again. "Maybe it was a best friend or even a family member."

Hands continued shooting up as I gaped around. My neck began to grow hot despite the dewy chill in the night air around me. I wondered what kind of hurt those with raised hands had experienced. Were they betrayed by their closest and most trusted friends? Had one of their parents succumbed to their substance abuse? *I doubted it.*

My eyes searched the crowd, and I noticed Riley seated by the front, nestled between her friends. Her hand was raised, and I wondered if she was thinking about her breakup with Carter. I scoffed, remembering what Jojo had confided in me about the two of them.

"We've all been hurt, whether it's by those we love most or those we consider our enemies," the speaker continued. "The only way we overcome hate is to drive it out with love."

I felt deflated, remembering how love had failed me when my thoughts turned to my mother. The sicker she became, the less she tried to hide it. She started out sneaking vodka in her morning coffee or orange juice before carrying it openly in her water bottle throughout the day. Eventually, she stopped trying to hide it altogether. Either Dad or I would find her passed out in the middle of the day or sleeping into the early afternoon.

The more we tried to hold onto her, the faster she slipped away from us. She was the woman who taught me how to count to ten and tie my shoes. She taught me to respect my elders and mind my manners. She was the woman who taught me about the omniscient God in the sky. She taught me to pray and took me to church. Eventually, she became the person who taught me heartbreak and how it felt to be left behind.

I wanted to let go of everything that reminded me of her, including the faith we once shared. Being here made me feel closer to her, as if I was sharing all of her childhood experiences and walking in her shoes. Wasn't God supposed to carry me through this pain? Where was he when my mother was sick? Why did he leave me when I needed him the most?

The speaker revealed that love has the power to transform our enemies into allies. Everyone around me seemed to be eating this up. A girl in the crowd to the left was busy jotting down notes, clinging to his every word. I scoffed, feeling the emotion rise inside me. No matter how many weeks they spent here, the Bible couldn't protect us. The only protection any of us had was not letting people close enough to hurt us.

"If we don't win them over with our love," the man leveled with us, "those who are not in Christ are enemies of God."

I couldn't help but scoff again, drawing the attention of those in front of me. Their gazes filled with both curiosity and concern. I felt my stomach sink as I processed this man's message. For so long, I felt as though God had turned his back on me. As my prayers went unanswered, I was convinced he was no longer listening to me. Letting go of the faith I clung to was the only thing that made sense. *Had I become an enemy of God?*

The man continued reading Bible passages, explaining how those outside of Christ were lost. He mentioned the horrors that a life without God brought an eternal life in hell. I could feel hot tears pooling as I fought to suppress them. I didn't understand how God could do something like that to those who He created. Did the Bible not say that we were created in His likeness? For His glory? *Those who were outside of Christ were enemies of God.*

This whole Christian journey seemed impossible. No matter how hard I could try, I would never be good enough to deserve Heaven, and if I gave up, I would only be deserving of hell. As heartbreaking as it felt at first to walk away, the more convinced I felt this was all wrong for me. I was done faking it.

Unable to endure any more of this, I grabbed my crutches and began making my way back to my cabin. I didn't care if this was against the rules anymore. This was all too much for me. The preaching, breakout sessions, fake smiles, sleepless nights, and memories were the absolute worst. I couldn't do this anymore.

"Hey honey." A woman in the back approached me as I shuffled along. "You need to have a seat."

She was a small woman with long dark hair, and her badge named her a counselor. Ignoring her, I continued my stride to the shortcut I found, avoiding the hill. My arms ached so badly, leaning my weight on my crutches, that I now felt sharp jolts of pain. The pain and frustration in my shoulders became too much, and tears started flowing down my cheeks. Behind me, I heard my name being called as I crossed the field by the Dining Hall.

"Lena! You can't just leave!" Lou called, catching up to me.

I picked up my pace, trying to distance myself from her. I felt the crunch of the gravel beneath me as I crossed over the path winding through camp.

"Just leave me alone, please!"

Finally, she caught up to me and I felt her hand pulling on my arm to stop me. When she did, her arm caught me off-guard and one of my crutches slipped from under me. Falling forward, I hit the ground with my knees before landing on my side. Pain rippled through my forearms and my knees as they took the brunt of my fall.

Lou reached out, trying to help me up. "Lena, I'm sorry. I didn't mean—"

"Just don't!" I yanked myself away from her touch and worked to help myself. "You've done enough. Please, just leave me alone!"

"I can't do that," she cried, standing with her hands on her hips. Another wave of tears came over me as I noticed the striking resemblance to my mom she bore. "Lena, I know this is hard on you but if you would just give things a chance..."

I scoffed as more tears fell. "You have no idea what I've been through, Lou. I'm sick of being here! I'm not the same girl you used to know."

Lou's eyes began to well up. Slowly, she crossed her arms as if to hug herself. "That's not true—"

"You know what's not true? Everything I've heard here this week. This camp is the worst possible place my father could have sent me! Life will beat us down and people will hurt us and there is nothing any of us can do about it!" I couldn't face her any longer.

As I stormed off, I heard her behind me, though her voice was distant.

"You're right!"

In an instant, her words stopped me dead in my tracks. *Lou was agreeing with me?* When I looked at her, I saw her cheeks shining in the moonlight.

"People will always hurt us or let us down. But Jesus doesn't, Lena! He will never fail us!"

For a split second, I had felt a shred of hope that she finally understood me, but I was wrong. Her efforts to bridge the gap between us were evident, even in the darkness. She believed in everything this camp stood for, she trusted in the faith she held so tightly to. But I didn't, not anymore. I wiped my tears and turned, leaving her standing in the dark.

12

The first hint of dawn was painting the sky in delicate pastels as I navigated the hushed paths of the summer camp. I felt a mixture of determination and apprehension as my heart thumped. The time was just past 5 a.m., and the camp was engulfed in a serene stillness. My crutches were beating along the gravel path that wound in different directions throughout camp. I moved swiftly but cautiously, dressed in a relaxed t-shirt and frayed shorts, my focus set on making a quiet escape.

Over my shoulder hung the lightweight drawstring bag I had been gifted on my first day at camp. Sneaking out of the cabin without disturbing Jojo, I brought along a recycled plastic bottle for hydration, a stick of deodorant, an extra t-shirt, and my wallet. All I wanted was to make my way to the bus stop in town and head back to Freeport. Last night, I turned the decision over in my mind. I knew making the trek on crutches would be strenuous, but if I could just make it up to the main road, maybe I could find someone to give me a ride.

Camp was just outside of Meadowbrook, and since it was a small town, I hoped I would find someone who recognized me to take me to the bus stop. Meadowbrook was filled with kind people, and I had no doubts about finding safe passage. Worst case scenario, I would just use my crutches to get me all the way to town, even if it took all day.

I needed to move as swiftly as possible to remain undetected. Jojo would soon wake up and realize I was gone. The last thing I wanted was for Lou to be notified and come to find me. As long as I moved quickly, I had the best chance of getting out of camp and finding a ride.

The longer I stared out at the long dirt road in front of me, the more I anticipated seeing the paved asphalt of freedom. Word of my running away would likely get to my dad before I did, but I could explain everything once I was back home. I could explain to him that I needed to take matters into my own hands because camp just wasn't working out for me. As long as I got a job and focused on school, he would see that I was determined to change.

Maybe instead of going back to school, I could just convince him to let me transfer. Normally, transferring schools seemed like the worst possible form of torture for a senior, but for me, it felt right. I would drive to school every day, show up on time, and maybe even join a social club to help build up my extracurriculars. Or, with a fresh start, I could try something new.

Plan B was to convince my dad to let me go get my GED and start classes at the local community college in the fall. Of course, that wasn't the plan we had always had, but come to think of it, the past year had gone completely off the rails for all of us. Though I dreaded facing Dad's wrath, I knew in time he would be able to move past another indiscretion once I made serious changes. He just needed to give me a chance.

The further I traveled away from the heart of the camp, the faster my heart quickened. Every few minutes, I found myself looking back in case someone had woken up early and spotted me. I had made it through the main areas and worked on passing Boys' Camp. Typically, Denny, Theo, and the rest of the Sports

Staff were up early to set up activities before breakfast, but not on a Saturday.

Jojo, Denny, and Theo were the only reasons camp had been tolerable. I felt my heart sink a bit at the thought of them discovering I had left without saying goodbye. I knew they had each other, though, and that before long they would forget about me. *Everyone always did.*

Efficiently passing Boys' Camp, I felt a newfound sense of hope as I neared the main road. The subtle glow of dawn began to paint the sky in hues of soft pinks and purples, signaling the approaching sunrise. As I continued to put weight on my crutches, I started to feel the familiar ache resurface beneath my arms. Pushing the pain down, I focused on the sense of liberation awakening within me. Just as I began to smile to myself at the thought of being free, I saw a figure emerge from the line of trees ahead of me. The unexpected person made my heart race as I shielded my eyes from the first rays of sunlight.

Carter's gaze fixed on me in a mixture of shock and concern. The joy I felt quickly transformed into guilt. Adorned in a short-sleeved shirt and workout shorts, Carter approached me.

"You headed somewhere, Duchess?" he asked, taking his headphones out of his ears. Sweat covered his face and neck, and he breathed heavily, as if he had just finished running.

I tried to remain inconspicuous. "Just going for a morning walk, Scooter. I wanted to watch the sunrise."

Tilting his head at me, he gave me a coy smile, scrutinizing my crutches. "Oh yeah? You wanted to watch the sunrise all the way out here? In your condition?"

Without hesitation, I agreed. "I know it seems bizarre, but back home I got up early in the morning often to take a walk down the beach. For fresh air. You get it, right?"

Carter nodded, agreeing, flashing a brief smile at me. My heart was pitter-pattering in my chest, but so far he seemed to buy it.

"I'm going to finish my walk before I have to head to breakfast," I said, trying to move past him. As I crept along, I heaved out a deep breath at the close call. Failing to create enough distance, I heard footsteps behind me once again. In an effort to remain composed, I gripped the crutch handles tightly and tried to act nonchalant. *Would he offer to help me?* I didn't need or want his help, I just wanted him to get back to his jog and forget about me.

Carter appeared, falling in step beside me. I noticed his hair didn't look perfect for once. Sweat rolled off his forehead onto his rosy, stubble-covered cheeks. He was still catching his breath as he kept in stride with me.

"I think I'll walk with you if you don't mind. I could use a good cool-off."

Feeling my stomach clench, I held my façade. "I actually like to walk by myself, it gives me time to think and process things, if you don't mind."

Carter clenched his jaw. Coming to a stop, he wiped his forehead with his sleeve and glared at me. "What are you doing, Lena?"

I gazed at him innocently. "I told you, I'm taking a walk."

"To where?" He narrowed his eyes. "Timbuktu?"

I laughed, trying to keep things light so he was none the wiser. "Just to the end of the road and back."

Carter wasn't laughing, in fact, he was doing the complete opposite. Moving closer to me, he stroked his stubbly face. The last thing I wanted to notice at the moment was every move he made. I couldn't resist the magnetic pull I felt whenever he was near, and now I felt it stronger than ever before.

"You can't do this," he said, his tone coming out strong and steady. I felt trapped as his chocolate eyes bore into me, and realized there was no avoiding him. Without a second thought, I wheeled-around and picked up my quick pace, trying to hurry back away from him. The moment I did, his footsteps echoed behind me until he was right beside me again.

"Lena!" Carter pleaded. "You can't leave! Where do you think you're going to go?"

Battling to maintain my lead, I pushed myself steadily forward, feeling shooting pains from my crutches with every step. "I'm leaving, I can't be here anymore!"

"How do you expect to do that? Are you just going to hitchhike back home?" he pressed, keeping up with me.

Frustrated, I groaned and attempted to create distance between us. "I'm going to the bus stop and I'm getting out of here. I'll find someone to give me a ride. Now, please just leave me alone."

Quick on his feet, Carter stopped in front of me, grabbing my shoulders to still me. I tried to move away from him, but it was no use. Between his steady grip and the crutches, I couldn't maneuver well enough. I gazed up at him, seeing the concern in his eyes as he searched mine.

"I can't let you leave," he steadied his voice. Once I stopped fighting to break away from him, he let me go. "This will destroy Lou."

"I don't care," I replied, trying to move past him once more.

"I think you do care," Carter confessed, lowering his voice. His words lingered in the air between us as I turned to face him. The moment our eyes met, he swallowed anxiously and extended his hands, ready to present his case.

"I don't!" I proclaimed, my voice shaking. Unconvinced, Carter crept closer to me, as if trying to talk me off a ledge.

"I know you care about not getting into trouble. But if you don't come back to camp with me, I'm going to have to tell Lou and you're going to get in even more trouble."

Narrowing my eyes, my mind began to race. "You don't know anything about me."

Carter looked deeply into my eyes, his brows furrowing. "You're right, I don't know a lot about you, but I do know this week hasn't been a walk in the park for you." Proceeding with caution, he continued, "I know that coming to camp hasn't been easy on you. And I know coming here wasn't exactly your idea, considering how mad at the world you are."

With each word, he stepped on my toes. There was just something in his voice that made me think that he knew more about me than he was letting on. I had never met him before in my life. *Had Lou told him what brought me here?*

I could feel his pleading eyes as he stood right in front of me.

"Can you stay right here? I'll run to get my cart and come back for you."

This version of Carter standing before me appeared to be from an alternate universe. All week he had been cold and snarky, acting as if my mere presence was ruining his camp experience. Now, here he was begging for me to return back to camp with him. The most shocking part was that some vulnerable part of me felt like I could trust him.

Carter raised his eyebrows expectantly. "I'm going to run now and grab it. I'll be right back for you, okay?"

Though I stood silently before him, I knew he wouldn't leave unless I agreed. I had been so determined to free myself from this place. Still, I had a nagging suspicion that Carter was hiding something, and some twisted part of me wanted to know what that was.

I nodded and watched as he turned to run back up the gravel path. Taking slow strides, he looked back over his shoulders a few times, checking to make sure I was still there before he broke into a sprint. As he disappeared into the line of trees, I felt myself let out a deep breath. Peering down the gravel drive I had almost traversed, I wondered how much distance I could cover before he returned. It was pointless. Now that Carter knew my plans, he wouldn't let up, even if that meant following me all the way to Meadowbrook.

Warm tears prickled behind my eyes as a lump formed in my throat. I had been so close to getting out of here. So close to going back to normal. I hung my head to avoid the rising sun as the tear slid from my cheek onto the rocks at my feet.

In mere minutes, I heard the familiar approach of the cart as Carter made his way over to me. Quickly, I wiped at my cheeks, trying to hide my despair. As he stopped in front of me, Carter hopped out and his brown eyes searched mine carefully, as if I were a fragile glass object. Studying me, he offered me his hand.

"Come with me."

With a gentle hand, he helped me into the passenger's seat before sliding behind the wheel and turning the key over. I saw a tenderness in his eyes among a mixture of emotions, but found him difficult to read.

"I'm going to take you somewhere, okay?"

"Where?" I wondered, my voice coming out thick.

"Somewhere to talk." His eyes met mine. "I'm a good listener and you look like you could use one."

I didn't remember saying yes, but I must have because Carter whirled us around and headed for a hidden path in the woods.

***

Carter slid the cart into park on the shore by the lake. Initially, I thought he would just take me back to my cabin or straight to the Dining Hall, but he surprised me with his choice. I watched him while he downed his water bottle in one breath before wiping the sweat off his face with a small towel. The early sun's golden rays painted the surface of the waters a warm apricot and rose.

Sitting by the water filled me with a stillness amidst the emotional chaos of the last twenty-four hours. My plan had failed, and here I was, back in the heart of camp with Carter Rose, who I knew wasn't about to let me leave anytime soon.

"Breakfast bar?" he asked, cutting through our silence. I stared down at the packaged fruit-filled bar he offered and felt my stomach growl in response. Accepting it, I unwrapped the package and took a large bite. The burst of strawberry woke my taste buds, satisfying my hunger.

Carter, unwrapping another bar, casually asked, "So, what sent you over the edge?"

The question sounded ridiculous, as if I were some crazed person who had unraveled. Carter's eyes met mine and there was a warmth to them. After knowing him for a week now, this was the first day I had witnessed his grace. I knew he felt obligated to escort me around the camp, but I couldn't figure out why he felt the need to talk with me.

"It's a long story," I responded, finishing the last of the breakfast bar.

Carter smirked, his face bright with intrigue. I watched as he glanced down at the fitness watch he wore before adding, "We've got plenty of time."

I shook my head. "I beg to differ. I'm supposed to be at breakfast soon."

The corner of his mouth curved up once more. "I'll get you out of this one, trust me."

Trust him? I barely recognized this one-eighty version of him. For all I knew, he could have a case of Dr. Jekyll/Mr. Hyde going on. With a steady gaze, he waited for me to answer. Once again, I stared out at the lake and felt a sense of calm.

"I don't want to talk about it."

"If you don't talk about it with me, your next option is Lou, and I'm sure you don't want her finding out about your little morning getaway plan."

There was the Carter I recognized.

"So what, you're going to narc on me unless I spill my guts to you?"

He turned to face me, surprised by my tone, his eyes sharp. "For the record, I'm literally telling you I'm not going to spread your business. But what kind of person tries to run away from church camp?"

"You wouldn't understand," I sighed, feeling my blood begin to boil.

Carter turned, propping his leg on the seat, his calf muscle bulging with the movement. "Then *help* me understand, Dutch."

"Do you expect me to confide in you while you call me names?"

Carter shrugged, nodding as if the answer were obvious. I crossed my arms, glancing away when I heard him chuckle.

"Isn't this what we do?" Glancing back, I saw that he was motioning between the two of us. "We give each other a hard time. You annoy me, I annoy you. It's an interesting acquaintanceship, but it works, right?"

I thought back to one of the first lessons we had received here at camp about the types of friends. *Did he consider me a type of acquaintance?* Although we were aware of each other's existence, he showed no interest in truly getting to know me, so why should I bother?

"That doesn't sound like any kind of relationship I want to have," I replied.

Carter wiped his hand over his face, his frustration growing. "Look, I don't know what I did to make you hate me but—"

I sneered with laughter. "You don't know what you did?"

Carter's deep brown eyes grew wide with my outburst.

"How about on night one, after saying like one word to me, you decided that you're some holier-than-thou dude who can't be bothered by my mere existence?!" I raised my voice. "And don't get me started on your ex-girlfriend, who is just as self-righteous as you are."

"Oh!" I continued, the truth erupting from inside me like a volcano. "And then there's this whole stupid camp that I don't want to be at! The lessons are so extra. Kitchen duty is exhausting, I mean, who decided to put the injured girl on such an extensive duty? I literally only have three limbs right now!"

From the corner of my eye, I swore I saw a slight grin on his face as my irritation finally reached the surface.

"It's so hot here, and all I do is sit in the sun all afternoon and then work the rest of the time. This place is boring and there is nothing for me here!"

My peripheral vision did not deceive me, as Carter began to chuckle. His smile placed a wrench in my angry monologue.

"Why are you laughing?" I demanded. "Oh, and my shoulders are killing me from these stupid crutches!" Massaging my underarm area, I crossed my arms over my chest and looked back out to the lake. I could never admit it to him, but finally getting everything off my chest did make me feel somewhat lighter.

"Now are you done?" he questioned, clearly amused.

I shrugged, not bothering to meet his gaze. Carter seemed completely unfazed by me and further angled himself to face me.

"Can we go back to the part about your existence bothering me?"

He was grinning from ear to ear. I had no idea why he felt so amused by my anguish.

"What about it?"

"I don't know what you're talking about." He cracked up again.

Throwing my hands up, I spoke as if he could not understand my big words. "The first night I was here, remember? You told Lou that you didn't want to be bothered by me."

Carter's brows furrowed and his smile turned to confusion, as if he were trying to recall the conversation.

I scoffed once more. The conversation clearly had not impacted him in the same way. "Just forget it."

Carter snapped, as if having an epiphany. "Are you talking about when you stormed out of the Med Cabin when Lou and I were talking?"

I scowled but said nothing.

"Wow!" Carter's eyes grew wide. "Dutch, I was trying to tell her that I didn't want to just be some camp taxi. I want to be where the action is, you know? Like if a camper breaks an arm or experiences a concussion. The more medical exposure I have, the more experience I gain for school."

I raised an eyebrow. Was he serious? This whole time I felt like he hated me just because.

"So that's it?"

Carter nodded, grinning in disbelief. "Was that it?"

Shaking my head, I scoffed once more. "No, it still doesn't explain why you're so rude. Well, you and Riley are so rude."

As soon as I said her name, he threw his head back and groaned, "Don't even get me started on Riley."

Now it was my turn to laugh at his expense. Twenty minutes ago, I was ready to head for the hills, and now, here I sat with Carter Rose of all people, and we were... laughing.

"So, what's with you?" I retorted.

Carter straightened, shaking his finger at me. "No, no. We did not come here to talk about me. We're here to talk about you."

"There's nothing to talk about," I protested. "Besides, you should know that I didn't initially crash your camp medical experience."

Carter cocked an eyebrow at me, smirking. "Is that your way of apologizing?"

"No, not at all."

He snickered, "Good, because you're actually helping me with my bedside manner."

"I love that for me," I replied sarcastically.

Carter chuckled. "So, why don't you stop deflecting and tell me why you were trying to escape already?"

Grasping my ponytail in my hand, I twirled the locks through my fingers as my thoughts raced. "I promise there's nothing to tell."

He eyed me suspiciously. "I don't buy that. No one runs from something the way you did unless there is something going on. I would know."

Now it was my turn to wonder about what he had to run from. "Are you talking about Riley?"

Carter narrowed his eyes at me, playfully. "Not at all." I watched as he gazed out at the lake thoughtfully.

"We're not going to bond over shared trauma now, are we?" I teased. Somehow, the tables seemed to be turning, and as curious as I was about what he had to say, I had no intention of confiding in him about my own family issues.

He shrugged, smirking. "That depends, I mean, I'm an open book. You, on the other hand, are like a diary that's been locked and the key thrown away."

I shifted in my seat, suddenly feeling exposed. Carter held out his hands as he spoke, as if trying to bargain for a peace treaty.

"Look, Dutch, we got off on the wrong foot. You can hate me or the world all you want, but honestly, you just seem like you could use a friend."

My gaze met his and I felt stunned by how deep and sincere his amber eyes reflected the warmth he radiated. *Had I been wrong about him? Had I retaliated for no reason?* Carter was throwing me a lifeline, but once he knew what happened, he would just yank it back and disappear like everyone else. I wasn't going to let myself feel the sting of rejection again.

"You couldn't handle the truth," I told him, wringing my hands in my lap.

"Want to bet?" Carter dared. "Do you have a biological family that didn't want you and left you behind?"

I cocked an eyebrow, hearing his words dangle in the air between us. *He couldn't be serious.* Waiting impatiently for my reply, he nudged my shoulder with his hand. "Well?"

"Close," I replied, pinching my fingers as if holding a small object. "Not too far off."

Carter threw his head back, heaving a deep sigh. "Come on, Lena, just tell me."

"Okay! Okay!" I finally felt myself give in. I didn't have to tell him the whole truth, I could easily just scrape the surface to get him off my case. "I have a mother who did leave me behind and a father who sent me off to camp just so he no longer had to deal with me."

I watched as he opened his mouth to say something, but then he stopped himself.

"What?" I asked, curious about the sudden change in his mood. "Was I right? You actually can't handle it?"

Carter quickly shook his head. He licked his lips as if carefully choosing the right words. When he looked into my eyes once more, he winced slightly. "It's just, I know a little about your mom."

My brows furrowed in confusion and I remembered how vulnerable he made me feel earlier, as if he could see through me. "What do you know?"

I watched as he held his hands back out in caution as if I were some sort of flight risk, given this morning's events. "Lou is best friends with my mom. Occasionally, she comes over to my house to talk with my mom or I may overhear them talking at church or on the phone."

I crossed my arms back over my chest, wishing I could disappear or burrow myself into a deep, deep hole. "Oh, um, I don't know what you think you've heard—"

Before I could finish, Carter cut me off. "Not a lot." He seemed genuine, but also as if he were trying to convince me not to bolt again.

"I only overheard them talking when Lou came over one night last week," Carter went on, leaning back over the steering wheel, more relaxed as he explained. "Lou seemed pretty upset."

I tilted my head as I listened carefully, needing to hear more. "What do you mean she seemed upset? Was she mad?"

Carter shook his head. "No, she seemed like she was trying not to cry."

This took me off-guard, and I suddenly felt as if I had lost my balance sitting down. *Had Lou been crying about me?* It was strange how much she had seemed like herself when I saw her at her doorstep after years of not seeing her. Lou behaved just like her usual cheerful and easygoing self.

"Do you know what they talked about?" I pressed him for answers.

"I don't," Carter answered, his eyes soft. "The only thing I remember hearing is her mentioning how disappointed she was."

My own disappointment grew as I felt my stomach sink. Of course Lou was disappointed in having me show up at her door after so long. *If she didn't want to be involved with my mother, why would she want to be involved with me?*

As if he were reading my mind, Carter sat up taller in his seat, his eyes focused on me. "She said she was disappointed in your mom and everything that had happened between your family."

I watched him closer, wondering if I had actually just heard him correctly. Carter surveyed my face intently, searching for his own answers.

"Do you care to tell me?" he asked once again.

For so long, I felt as if Lou just decided to walk away from all of us because of her issues with my mom. Sitting with Carter, I was taken aback to learn that she also felt completely devastated. I felt a mix of anger, sadness, and even relief. In an instant, it finally felt as if I wasn't completely alone in this anymore. The more Carter pressed for information, the more I felt my guard going down. No one had mentioned anything to me yet, even those who actually knew me and my mom. Carter must not have said anything to anyone.

Staring down at my hands, picking at my nails one by one, I sighed. "A few years ago, my grandfather passed away."

Without looking at Carter, I knew I had his full attention.

Continuing, I explained, "My mom and I used to come up to Meadowbrook all the time to see my family, growing up. But after my Grams passed away we made fewer trips. When my Gramps got sick, I didn't know until it was too late."

"I'm sorry," Carter apologized. His sincerity reached inside my chest, tugging on my heartstrings.

"It had been a long time since we had been back to Meadowbrook when we went up for his funeral," I explained further. "But, at the funeral, Lou had a fight with my mom. My parents left and after, we went our separate ways from Lou."

Carter ran a hand down his face while processing my family drama. It didn't take long before he added, "I know it's not my place, but I think Lou deserves a chance to be heard."

Without looking in his direction, I finished pulling a piece of nail from my left thumb. "Maybe."

My thoughts suddenly felt like a jumbled mess as I pictured Lou at Gramps' funeral once again. The disdain I saw in her eyes had altered my entire perception of her in that moment. Still, I never realized the way it must have affected her. There are two sides to every story, and being on my mom's side for so long, I never really considered Lou's.

Carter clapped his hands and rubbed them together, pulling me from buried memories. He was peering over at me expectantly. "Is it my turn?"

I smiled and motioned for him to open up. "Give me your worst."

He chuckled, a dimple popping in his cheek. "The short version is that my biological family is tumultuous. Gazing over at me, he shrugged helplessly before continuing, "Let's just say my mom's family drama led me to develop my own colorful way of living."

"Oh yeah?" I wondered. "Define colorful."

Carter smirked and waved me off. "I'll save that story for another time, but my colorful past led me to an alternative school for troubled youth, to say the least."

Carter surprised me as he opened up about meeting his now-adoptive mother, who had become his summer school teacher while he attended the alternative school during his probation. "Eventually, after some unfortunate circumstances with my biological father, the Roses took me in."

"Wow," was all I could manage, hearing his truth.

Carter smiled, clearly used to sharing his background with others. "It's not the easiest past to have, but it's led to a much better future for me."

Still trying to gather the right words to say, I replied, "I would have never guessed any of that about you."

He was so light-hearted about everything. "God has done a lot for me."

As soon as he brought up his faith, I turned to stare back at my hands again. Nearly all of my nails were picked apart by now, and I had nothing more to tear off. The two of us felt like we were finally finding common ground, but I felt my walls go back up.

"What about you?" Carter nudged my shoulder again.

I shied away from him, redirecting my focus to the water. "I don't really do the whole church thing anymore."

"And why is that?" Carter pressed, his tone surprising me. He seemed unfazed by my confession of doubt. I watched as he opened another breakfast bar, as if this were any other casual conversation.

I shrugged. "Having faith never really got me anywhere."

Carter grinned as he chewed his last bite. I watched him gulp down his bar and my truth. He sat up a little taller again, crumpling the wrapper. "I used to feel that way, too."

Feeling shocked, I pressed back. "You're joking."

He shook his head. "Not at all. I couldn't see God working in my life until I looked in the rearview mirror, but once I did, it was clear to me that everything I've gone through has led me to where I am now. It's *all* because of Him."

Trying to remain as sincere as he was with me, I grinned politely but remained silent.

"If you give Him a chance, I bet you'll be able to do the same," Carter challenged.

I didn't say anything, but watched as he turned the key over in the ignition, starting up the cart again. "I need to get you to the kitchen so I can go shower and get ready for the day."

I agreed, sliding my palms down the front of my shorts. This whole unexpected soul-bearing session had caused my palms to sweat. Whipping the cart around, Carter quickly drove us along the familiar gravel path through the woods, returning to camp. The wind whipped past us as we headed through the line of trees. The sun was up, and the closer we got to the heart of camp, the more I noticed the grounds had finally awakened.

As we approached the Dining Hall, I could already hear the clattering of dishes as breakfast was ready to be served. Throwing the cart in park, Carter eyed me, his hands still on the wheel as I hopped up. I no longer felt the same disdain for him, but more as if we could possibly be friends. Just talking to someone about my past brought more relief than I thought possible. I never would have imagined sharing such a moment with Carter.

Stabilizing my weight back on my crutches, I caught Carter staring. He was searching me as if I were a puzzle he was working to solve.

"So, I'll see you around?"

He flashed me a coy grin, "Oh, you'll be seeing me."

I couldn't help but smirk as I started up the ramp. I stopped halfway and glanced back one final time. "Thanks for…"

Carter caught my drift, helping me save face. "Don't worry about it, Dutch."

I rolled my eyes at the nickname, and just like that, we were back to normal.

13

Compared to the weekday hustle and bustle, the Dining Hall felt eerie during the weekend. The normal rhythmic clattering of pots and pans now fell into a few chairs scraping and quiet morning chatter. According to the camp schedule, weekends were different. After an à-la-carte breakfast, one breakout session stood between me and some much-needed free time. There were strings attached, though, as I pulled the wrinkled copy of the schedule from my pocket to review.

For most of the morning, family pickup was at the top of the agenda. Jojo had explained earlier this week that some campers lived close to camp and went home on the weekends. After the morning's breakout session, we were all given the opportunity to clean up our cabins or do laundry, followed by a bagged lunch option, and then free time. As with everything at camp, free time came with rules. For any activity campers participated in, we were required to check in with an adult or stay with a group so no two campers were left alone to their own devices. After an already emotional morning, I craved alone time, but according to the sheet of paper in my hands, it would have to wait.

"Hey!" Jojo called out to me, a stack of packaged cereal in her hands. With campers leaving, the Kitchen Staff seemed as sparse as the crowd in the Dining Hall this morning. When I looked, I saw trash accumulated at the window, where dirty dishes were usually stacked for washing. "Where did you go this morning?"

Setting down the stack in her arms, Jojo watched me expectantly as she straightened her apron out. I chewed my lower lip and tucked a strand of hair that had fallen loose from my ponytail behind my ear.

"I, uh, wasn't able to sleep." Thinking further, I didn't want to lie. The truth was, the time I shared with Carter this morning had proved to be a much-needed breather. Almost a week had passed and I had all of these emotions bubbling to the surface ready to break free. "So I just went for some fresh air."

"Oh!" Jojo's eyes widened beneath her large frames. "Was it because of me? Was I snoring?"

"No, not—" I tried, but before I could finish, Jojo pinched her lips together with her hands for a moment, lost in thought.

"I do snore, though," she informed me, her embarrassment showing in her ruddy cheeks. "I wish I didn't, but I've been told that I do. With all of the heat and the busy days, it can really take it out of me. When I'm tired, I can just conk out."

Amused by her rambling, a small chuckle escaped me while I brushed her thoughts away. "You didn't snore, there's just been a lot on my mind…"

I let my sentence drift off and Jojo stood straighter, as if regaining her confidence.

"I've been collecting trash and setting it on the window there. I think most of the Kitchen Staff are leaving for the weekend, so I'm trying to keep the packaged breakfast options stocked with some of the others," Jojo informed me, motioning to the staff that remained. "There are breakfast bars, cereal, and fruit and yogurt set out on the chilled prep table out in the Dining Hall."

"Are there no dishes for me to wash?" I asked, still trying to figure out how I could pitch in.

"Not yet," she answered. "But when we dismantle the prep table there will be. Otherwise, you can take over throwing out any trash we bring to you."

While Jojo continued stacking cereal in her arms, I hopped over to the window to begin getting rid of the trash.

"Since the weekend is here, are you going to go home?" I asked her, curious to know if I would know anyone on the grounds for the next couple of days.

She shook her head, balancing a large stack in her arms to carry out as many cereal containers as she could. "No, I'm sticking around. It's your first weekend here, after all, and I can't just leave my roomie all alone."

Jojo burst through the double doors to deliver the armload of cereal she carried while the words she spoke replayed on a loop in my mind. *I can't just leave my roomie all alone.* With only eight words, Jojo shattered my heart's icy barrier. After coming back into my life, after only one week, she managed to make me feel seen with only a few words.

She didn't want to leave me alone.

I spied out the window to see her setting more food out while another line of campers formed behind her. Jojo and some of the other staff showed up this morning on time for the same duty without complaint. While I stood in the kitchen, I finally grasped the importance of my role as I saw others filling in for me. When I tried to escape earlier, my last thought was about how my disappearance would have affected the people who were depending on me.

Now, standing here seeing Jojo bustling around the Dining Hall doing twice the work gripped me. Lou came to mind next. I had no idea what kind of strings she pulled to get me here, but I could imagine the last-minute arrangements weren't easy. This morning, I had been ready to throw away every ounce of effort

Lou had made to get me here. Then, it finally dawned on me just how easily my dad could feel so frustrated with me.

The thought of my ungrateful behavior made me want to run away just from sheer embarrassment. When a camper delivered trash to the window, I took the waste and dropped it in the trash can by the sink. I took a seat on the stool and stewed on the fact that, over an hour ago, I was ready to forget this place and everyone here. Yet, hearing Jojo want to stick by my side and remembering what Carter said about Lou sent me into a spiral.

She mentioned how disappointed she was, Carter's words echoed through my head. *She was disappointed in your mom and with what happened with your family.* This whole time I thought Lou hated my mom and wanted nothing more to do with any of us. I wondered how she was feeling about all the distance that had come between our family.

"Lena, are you okay?" Jojo questioned, leaning against the counter beside me. I hadn't noticed her, lost in my own thoughts. Now, I could see a mix of concern and bewilderment in her eyes.

"Yeah, I'm okay." I tried to shake myself from my thoughts. "I'm just tired. It's been a long day already."

"Understandable," Jojo leveled with me. She began grabbing clean cups from the drying rack and stacking them back into place below the window. "The first week can be tough to adjust to. Especially with the mattresses here."

Murmuring under my breath, I chuckled, "Or lack thereof."

Jojo grinned. "Exactly." She filed away a stack of paper plates before she untied her apron and breathed a deep sigh. "I could use a coffee."

"Are we allowed to have coffee here?" I cocked an eyebrow. "Can you imagine all of us running around camp with all that caffeine? We would never be able to sit still and focus."

She laughed as she let out a yawn. "You're right, I only get my coffee from the Ridge Roast Cafe in town anyway."

"So, what's next?" I wondered, as campers began to file out of the hall. I looked down, pulling out my phone to view the time. It was almost 9 a.m. and breakfast was wrapping up.

Stifling another yawn, Jojo motioned to another stack of trash piling up at the window. "I'll go help clean up out in the Dining Hall, and we'll start bringing you dishes to wash. Once we're done and finished with our breakout session, maybe you and I can find the boys or do some crafts?"

"Sure," I agreed, willing to accompany any plans she made for the day. "How does free time work today? The schedule says we have to check in and stay in groups."

Jojo waved her hand like the schedule was no big deal. "When we go to different activities like crafts or down to the archery range, we just need to sign in or check in with the adult staff so they can easily find us."

"But isn't hiking an option?" I asked, recalling acceptable free time activities on the weekend.

"Not for you," Jojo teased. "But if anyone decides to hike, they have to go in a group or with a staff member. The same goes for the pool or the lake. No one can be on their own for obvious reasons."

The news made me feel surprisingly excited. Camp was suddenly beginning to sound fun for once.

***

The kitchen clean-up was surprisingly quick, and when I glanced at my phone again as we went outside, I was amazed to see that we were actually on schedule. Jojo and I moved through the Dining Hall in sync, without even thinking. Jojo made way for me, holding the door, and I was immediately captivated by a rare sight.

Carter was seated in the golf cart, but this time, a small girl was seated in his lap. She wore a crown braid in her golden hair, a flowing dress with a wildflower pattern, and a tiny denim vest. The girl had the brightest smile as she peeked up at Carter, the two of them giggling together. I watched as he plucked at her nose, pretending to hold it in his fist, and I felt my stomach flip-flop at the sight of them. A wave of homesickness washed over me as I remembered playing this game with my dad when I was the same age as the little girl.

"I thought only camp patients were allowed to ride in the Med Cart?" Jojo teased, as we made our way down the front porch. At the sound of her voice, the little girl in Carter's lap jumped up eagerly. "Joey!"

As the child jumped into Jojo's arms, she playfully twirled her around, causing the girl to burst into a delightful fit of laughter.

"There's always a chance to bend the rules when Sadie comes for a visit," Carter answered. He was finally freshened up, wearing a white henley tee paired with dark khaki shorts. I couldn't ignore the radiant glow on his cheeks or how his shirt accentuated his well-defined arms. Carter caught my eye, motioning to the girl in Jojo's arms. "This is my little sister, Sadie."

With a smile, Sadie looked up at me and waved, not meeting a stranger. "She's pretty," I heard her whisper unsuccessfully into Jojo's ear. I felt myself blush as Carter laughed, glancing at me briefly before his gaze drifted back over to Sadie.

"I think you're pretty," I responded to her sweetly. Sadie's face turned red and she quickly moved away from Jojo, wanting to be put down.

"What happened to your leg?" she asked, standing in front of me, nearly touching my ankle boot.

"Believe it or not, I fell out of a tree," I confessed. Something about this little girl had me admitting secrets I swore I wouldn't release. Out of the corner of my eye, I saw Carter tilt his head, eyeing me curiously.

"You did?" I heard Jojo ask, sharing the same curiosity.

Sadie crossed her legs, suddenly distracted by her own thoughts, twirling a small loose hair in her little fingers. "Sometimes me and Carter climb trees at our house and play monkeys together."

"Do you?" I asked, chuckling. Without pause, Carter swiftly picked her up and placed her on his hip, showering her cheek with a big kiss. Sadie made a face as she wiped it off, but she still clung to him tightly, wrapping her arms around his neck. The sight of the two of them made me feel like the Grinch at the end of the book as his heart grew two sizes. Seeing Carter with Sadie once again proved that there was a whole different side to him I had yet to discover.

A couple emerged behind them, appearing too well-dressed to be staff. The woman, with her dark auburn hair and piercing green eyes, was slim and shorter than the man. The man had a skin fade haircut and a neat graying beard. His sea blue eyes took in the adorable sight of Carter and Sadie.

"Hey, y'all!" Jojo greeted them with a sweet southern drawl. "Is Sadie going to be hanging out at camp today?"

"No, I'm going to ride with Carter!" Sadie piped up.

The woman, who I was guessing was Carter and Sadie's mother, motioned for Sadie to hop down. "Not today, Sade. Carter's working."

Sadie hopped into the woman's arms, pouting and sticking out her bottom lip. The sight of the two of them sent an ache through me as I pictured myself at Sadie's age with my mom, always glued to her side in the same way.

"Sorry, Sade," Carter apologized. "I have to help Lena since she has trouble walking, but I promise to come find you later."

When he said my name, their mom shifted her focus to me. She widened her eyes and adjusted Sadie in her arms, extending a stretched hand towards me. "Lena, I'm Amy Rose, Carter's mom."

Accepting her hand, I shook it, feeling the warmth of her small and soft hand in mine. "It's nice to meet you."

Behind her, the man who I guessed was her husband, offered his hand to me too. "And I'm Jack, Carter's dad." His hand was large and a bit moist, almost engulfing mine, but his eyes were soft and full of kindness.

Thinking back to what Carter had said earlier in the day about his mom being best friends with Lou, I felt myself flush in the Rose family's presence. I had no idea what they knew about me or my family, but according to the strange drop I began to feel in the pit of my stomach, a hunch told me everything. Amy's grin and the excitement in her gaze caught me off guard.

"I should get going." Jojo motioned as if to move forward.

"Me too," I agreed, moving to follow along without hopping on the golf cart.

Jojo whirled to face me, her brows furrowing. "Haven't you been saying your crutches are making your arms sore?"

Feeling my face flush, I glared at her while trying to dismiss her point. "It's nothing I can't handle."

"You're a trouper for using those things to get around here," Amy cheered me on.

"What are those?" Sadie's small voice wondered.

"Crutches," Carter answered. "Lena has an ankle boo-boo and needs them to help her walk."

Sadie leaned over, her little eyes growing wide with worry. "Do I need them too?"

Amy chuckled, shaking her head no. "No, honey, your legs are working perfectly fine."

Carter chuckled at Sadie and I noticed him watching me expectantly. "We should get going too."

Amy and Sadie waved as Carter turned the key to the cart over and took my crutches so I could settle in beside him.

"I'll see you in a little bit, Sade!" he called out to her.

Sadie beamed in their mother's arms and waved with excitement. A moment later, we were speeding off across the grassy knoll. Carter effortlessly caught my attention. In the presence of his family, he had a massive smile on his face that made my heart flutter.

He had confessed to me that they had adopted him, and I could imagine how he felt to have a family. A nice warm bed to sleep in at night. Parents to make sure he felt safe and loved. Three square, warm meals on the table. A father's gentle guidance. A mother's warm embrace. The little things that make family so huge. I could understand because I had those things. I still did since my father stretched himself too thin trying to make up for all the missing pieces.

As Carter pulled up to the familiar gazebo, I felt a sense of warmth in his presence. I counted myself as someone with good judgment, who could read others easily. Yet, here I had been completely wrong about Carter.

"I'll be back to get you in just a bit," he promised.

"Sounds good," I replied, climbing out. Sliding my crutches under my arms, I leaned down to peer at him as his cocoa eyes met mine. "Enjoy some time with your family."

I saw his smile reflected in his eyes as he promised, "I'll see you soon."

***

The morning sun was already beaming down while I sat beneath the shade of the gazebo during today's only breakout session. While Adam was discussing Paul's missionary travels, I found myself lost in my own thoughts.

My distraction was intensified by the sound of wheels rolling on gravel. I expected to see Carter, but my stomach dropped when I saw Lou instead. Initially, I hesitated, thinking of our last interaction, but quickly decided against my doubt and waved. To my dismay, she offered a gentle wave but continued to speed by without stopping.

The last time we saw each other, she was desperately trying to make me stay. I could still see her wide eyes and the heart she wore on her sleeve, trying her best to reach out to me. Remembering what Carter said to me by the lake, I wondered again about Lou's side of the story. *I think she deserves a chance to be heard*, Carter's voice echoed through my thoughts once more. *Could we even have a conversation after our last one had gone so horribly wrong?*

I didn't have a chance to mull it over anymore as the familiar sound of wheels sounded behind me again. Expecting to see Lou again, I watched as Carter hopped from the driver's seat. Joining our session, he sat right beside me.

"Thanks for joining us, Carter," Adam smiled. He turned his Bible so Carter could see the page he was on. "We have dived into Saul's transition to Paul."

Focusing on the Bible in Carter's lap, I was shocked to see him flip straight to the Book of Acts with no hesitation. The only Bible I had was a worn-out hardback copy from camp, with yellowed pages and a musty odor.

"What are you doing here?" I whispered to him.

He turned his head just slightly, revealing an *isn't it obvious?* expression before whispering back, "I'm trying to learn about Paul."

I nudged his elbow. "Aren't you supposed to be somewhere? Your family is here."

Carter moved closer so I could hear him better. "My parents are with Sadie, and she's at water sports, so I'll catch them later. I don't want to be soaking wet and have to go help a camper."

He refocused his attention on Adam once more while I sat still unable to concentrate. I felt all too aware of Carter's presence beside me. I caught sight of nearly every move he made, like flipping straight to every verse Adam called out, or wiping his brow with the back of his wrist.

"Can you think of a time when you have been guilty of something?" Adam asked the group. This question pulled me back to attention as I surveyed the room. There was no way I was going to answer this question. If I confessed how guilty I felt just over the past year of my life, I could start a podcast with multiple seasons just to get it all off my chest.

"Anyone?" Adam pressed, scanning the silent crowd. He seemed as if he were trying not to laugh at the crowd's reluctance to confess our consciences to him.

"I'll go," Carter piped up.

Adam grinned. "Finally, a brave soul."

Carter wiped his hand down his stubbly face, a gesture I was becoming familiar with. "I've been guilty of breaking the law before."

Adam seemed intrigued and probed for more information. "What was the result of your doing so?"

Carter sat up straighter. "I was punished, which was well deserved."

His confidence in confessing his past sins was so unexpected. Carter seemed so confident, I could even sense the humor in his voice as he and Adam carried on their conversation.

"How did other people take the news?" Adam questioned. "Did you feel supported or rejected?"

Carter chuckled and I noticed how he talked with his hands. "I was continuously rejected by the people who I thought were supposed to love me. They had every right to be disappointed in me, but the reaction I got then was not the reaction my family today would have."

"What do you mean?" Adam asked, attempting to understand.

Carter closed his Bible. The faces all around us homed in on him, taking in his every word. "Some of you know me, but most of you probably don't. I'm adopted."

Some offered sad sighs while the others continued listening as he spoke.

"I was a troubled kid growing up and didn't really have a family until I met Amy and Jack Rose."

He glanced at Adam as if he should carry on, and Adam motioned for him to do so with a wave of his hand.

"I likely would have continued down a destructive path without them," Carter said. "I relate to Paul's story because God intervened in my life in a similar way."

"How so?" Adam pressed.

Carter grinned. "God has a plan for me. Looking back on my life, I finally noticed it. I was on a troubled path, doing some illegal things, and I got caught. It's evident that God intervened and brought other Christians into my life to lead me. I'm living proof that God can use his enemies for his purpose."

"That's amazing," Adam concurred. "Anyone else?"

I couldn't even pay attention to others who were speaking up. My heart had been beating fast with the fear of being called on to share my own shortcomings. Not Carter, though. He was fully aware of his past mistakes and comfortable sharing them with others. I couldn't believe how unashamed he appeared and that no one else seemed to judge him over his past.

As I spent more time with Carter, I began to realize my initial impression of him was completely off. He was a guy focused on walking firmly in his faith and loving the people who loved him back. The part that surprised me most was how I was beginning to doubt my own judgment. Having been so wrong about Carter, I began to think maybe he wasn't the only person or circumstance I had been wrong about.

14

Weekends at camp were quickly growing on me. Jojo and I were finally set free after lunch and had some time to do something just for us. Saturday afternoon was wide open until dinner. The best part was there was additional free time following dinner, with an optional evening singing session.

"So, you don't sing anymore?" Jojo asked, though her focus was on looping another bead through the fifth bracelet she had made so far. This particular bracelet in her hands spelled out the word HOPE alongside other colorful beads. With each one completed, she tied it and added it to the stack that was climbing up her wrist.

"Only if you like the sounds of nails on a chalkboard," I joked. I didn't want to delve into the reasons why I chose not to sing anymore. We were having a relaxing afternoon, and I didn't want to ruin it by adding, *Yeah, Jojo, I stopped singing after my Gramps died because it reminded me of him. Oh, and it was something I used to do with my mom. Now that she's out of the picture too, I've sworn off music.*

Jojo scoffed. "I remember you having a beautiful voice. Your whole family could sing, so you can't be that bad."

I shrugged, refocusing on the fabric headband I was crafting. When Jojo and I had arrived, I found a large tote filled with old fabric scraps and decided to do something different. Some girls were using them to make bandanas, but I wanted to go in a different direction.

"Probably not," I answered. "It's just been a long time so I'm out of tune."

Jojo chuckled but still pressed, "You should come with Denny and me tonight." I watched as she tied yet another beaded bracelet, adding it to her collection. She stuck out her arm in front of her to study the stack. Seeming pleased, her gaze met mine. "It will be fun. Me and Denny are in show choir at school, so we can help you learn the songs you may not know."

Just thinking about it brought back a memory of singing with my mom in church. She and I were sitting in our pew, the sun beaming through the stained-glass windows, and a bright smile lit up her face. She had pointed to the hymnal in her lap, her finger pointing out the words to "Sweet By and By" to teach me how to sing the notes. Her voice was beautiful and melodic. Over time, I learned to harmonize with her, and our soprano voices blended well together.

"No pressure," Jojo carried on. "Even if you don't come to singing, you end up hearing it from almost anywhere on the grounds, so you might as well just come."

I leaned over the paint-stained table, eager to change the subject. "Are you ever going to tell him how you feel?"

Jojo's usual joyful demeanor crumbled. I witnessed her cheeks turning red and saw her drop the beads she was attempting to thread onto a new string.

"We, um, we're just friends."

"Jojo, what are you waiting for?" I eyed her. "If you guys talked, you might even have a date to the Banquet."

She sighed and I watched her eyes dart around the room just in case someone might overhear. Jojo leaned over the table, her voice a quiet whisper. "Denny is my best friend, and I would never want to jeopardize what we have."

As I observed Jojo's struggle, I felt gutted at the thought of hurting her. Jojo's eyes, normally bright with laughter, softened with a gentle sadness. I knew how it felt to lose friends and I could understand her reason for not starting anything with him, but I also knew how it felt to want something I couldn't have. The idea of a perfect family had long since eluded me, but no matter what, I found myself longing for it.

"I know how you feel," I told her. "I'm sorry, I shouldn't have said anything, that was out of line."

Jojo shrugged it off. "You're not the first person to say something."

"I'm not?"

Jojo's face flushed once more. "No, Lou actually asked me a while ago, too."

"Really?" I exclaimed. "What did she say?"

Jojo began speaking, but her eyes quickly darted to the right behind me, widening in shock. Her expression made me feel anxious, as if there was someone behind me. When I spun around, I saw Carter scoop up my crutches and scurry away.

"Carter, bring those back!" Jojo cried, throwing her hands to her face in shock. I was still watching him while he darted around the corner and disappeared.

"I can't believe him," I sighed. I found myself pushing off the table with a sudden urge to chase him down. I noticed other campers in the Craft Cabin pausing to stare at me. My wild outburst began to cause a scene, so I returned to my seat.

I felt my mind flash back to middle school. There was a pack of eighth-grade girls who made it their mission to single out the other eighth-grade girls who weren't cool enough to be their friends. The girls were scattered throughout the cafeteria, assigned to sit with either the seventh-grade or sixth-grade girls, which was even worse for them. Taylor Hayden, a girl I always thought to be beautiful and kind, would always reluctantly plop down at our lunch table and cry. All Taylor wanted was to sit with the cool girls who consistently singled her out.

Day after day, Taylor sauntered to the lunch table I shared with Lacey. She rarely talked to either of us, and got up as soon as she was finished. Glancing over at the other girls' table, they normally gossipped amongst each other and enjoyed themselves.

That went on for months until Lacey and I decided to start eating outside before school let out for the summer. One day, I felt a pang of guilt when walking outside for lunch. I spotted Taylor sitting at our normal table, but this time she was alone. A part of me wondered if I should invite her outside to sit with us but I never did. All the times she had wept at our lunch table were enough for me to know we were the last people she wanted to be friends with.

Now, I sat in the Craft Cabin feeling all eyes on me like I was some sort of pariah. This time, Carter was the source of my humiliation. I felt like we had finally started making some progress. *Had I been wrong about him?* The realization hit hard—I was exposed, and vulnerable, and the Craft Cabin that had once felt like a haven now seemed like a trap.

Jojo climbed to her feet, brushing the loose beads in front of her towards the center of the table so they wouldn't roll away. "I'm going to go find him and give him a piece of my mind."

I glared at her in disbelief. "What are you going to do if he doesn't give them back?"

She chuckled. "Carter isn't a thief, and I doubt he's going to let you hobble around with your legs."

"I wouldn't doubt it," I mumbled beneath my breath.

"Lena, he didn't steal them. But he can't just take your things, especially without asking," she tried to reason with me.

Before I could protest further, I saw Carter emerge from the stairs still holding my crutches in his arms. I could feel my face crinkle in confusion as he weaved between craft tables. His focused smile took me off-guard as he approached me with a spring in his step. With a slight bow, he presented my crutches to me.

"Here you go, Duchess."

I swiped them from his grasp and immediately noticed why he took them. On the arm pads, he had wrapped some sort of cushion beneath a tattered paisley fabric. I felt the cushion in my hand and couldn't help but smile.

"You can't just take people's things, Carter," Jojo scolded him.

Carter was too busy observing me check out the new look of my crutches. His topaz eyes narrowed as he worked to read my expression. I climbed back to my feet and placed the cushions beneath my arms.

"What do you think?" he asked, gazing expectantly at me.

"Two words," I sighed, gratefully, "instant relief."

Carter struggled to conceal his grin, but his dimples gave him away. Carter took a step forward and grabbed one of my crutches, revealing his clever solution: a large pad of wrapped styrofoam. "This should hold its shape well enough to relieve some of your soreness. Hopefully you won't need them for much longer, though."

As my eyes locked onto him, my stomach flip-flopped. "You didn't have to do this."

Carter rolled his eyes. "That's where you're wrong. You see, I'm on the Med Staff, and if I have a camper that's having pain or discomfort, it's up to me to solve it."

I felt a blush crawl over my cheeks. Thirty seconds ago, I was convinced that Carter was trying to pull one over on me. Now, here he was presenting me with cushioned crutches to help me navigate the camp terrain with more comfort.

"I don't know what to say."

Carter's eyes filled with amusement. "Honestly Dutch, a *thank you* will do just fine."

I rolled my eyes at him once again, replying in a mocking voice, "Thank you."

Carter tucked his hands in the pocket of his shorts. "On that note, I've got to get back to the family, but enjoy your new legs."

I grinned, leaning on my newly upgraded crutches until I heard Jojo clear her throat to my left. Jojo's mischievous gaze met mine as she propped her head in her hands.

"What?" I asked, dumbfounded by her expression..

"What on earth was that?"

Propping my crutches back down against the table, I decided to have a seat once again, and resumed making my headband.

"You have eyes, you saw Carter improve my crutches too, right?"

She narrowed her gaze. "You mean he was flirting with you?"

A bold laugh burst from my mouth. "Since when does someone doing something nice for someone else have to be flirting?"

Jojo heaved a deep sigh and gathered more beads into a pile in front of her. "I'm not buying it."

I frowned. "It's not like that with me and Carter."

"Whatever you say," she replied, keeping her eyes on her bracelet.

"Do you have a problem with Carter or something?"

The question dangled in the air between us for a moment as Jojo set her bracelet down, her gaze focusing on me.

"Are you telling me I haven't missed something going on between you two?"

There was no way for me to roll my eyes any harder. "There is *nothing* going on between us. We've talked a little since he's been driving me around camp, but that's it."

"Okay," Jojo said flatly, accepting this answer.

I couldn't help but glare at her, though, as she returned to her beading. "So what, that's it? Interrogation over? Come on, what's the big deal?"

Jojo locked eyes with me once more. "Riley is the big deal."

That was the last explanation I expected Jojo to give. Was Carter not allowed to have friends because of his ex-girlfriend? Suddenly, the thought of Lacey and Javier's on-and-off relationship flashed through my thoughts and I wondered if Carter and Riley were in the same situation.

"Just be careful," Jojo retorted. "There had been a lot of drama between the two of them and I just think that emotional distance around Carter is best."

A chuckle escaped me as she threw out the idea of emotional distance between us. I knew Jojo and I were just reacquainted, but she had yet to figure out that I was the queen of emotional distance.

"You don't have to worry about me," I replied. While Jojo seemed like someone who would become emotionally attached to others, my time at camp this summer was unlike anyone else's. The longer I kept everyone at a distance, the better it would be for all of us at the end of camp. While the others would go back to Meadowbrook, I would return to Freeport and likely never see any of them again.

15

Jojo went to find Denny and Theo after we both finished our crafts, leaving me with free time of my own. There were so many activities to try. Campers could do archery, go zip-lining, hike with a group, or use any of the sports equipment to play any number of games. The pool hosted different swim times for both girls and boys, and the lake had kayaking and paddle-boarding.

My plan had been to take a lengthy nap back in my bunk, but when I got back to my room, I saw my overflowing laundry bag and knew I needed to spend some of this time more wisely. I grabbed one of my few remaining clean shirts, a plain pink tee, and changed my top.

Thankfully, Lou had provided me with a nice-sized laundry bag during our pre-camp supply run. The bag had straps to make toting it on my back a breeze. I made my way down a private path from Girls Camp, past the large outdoor shelter to the pool house. Feeling the crunch of rocks beneath my crutches, I steadily pounded my way down the path under the afternoon summer sun. The light peeked below the heavy canopy of trees, creating a pleasant shade from the usual mountain heat.

Once the pool house came into view, I found the tiny sign marked LAUNDRY to my left. I stepped onto the sidewalk and opened the creaking door. The space was longer than it was wide and smelled of fresh cotton. To my left, there was a row of washing machines, and a row of dryers was on the right. The machines were worn out, rusty, and much older than any I had used before.

Releasing the bag on my back, I strode over to an empty top-load machine with the lid open. Placing my bag against the machine, I began emptying my clothes into the drum. Lou had tucked a small bottle of washing detergent and a pack of travel dryer sheets in the small pocket inside. Once again, guilt washed over me as I recalled how she had taken care of me while I had treated her poorly.

When I finished loading my clothes, I closed the lid and then paused, staring at the dials with too many options. There were the usual options to choose from, like Normal, Regular, Delicate, and Casual, but the lines in between were throwing me for a loop. Using my best guess, I grabbed the large knob to choose the Normal setting, but it didn't budge.

I tried once again, mustering all the strength I could from the awkward angle I was standing before giving up. Groaning in frustration, I glanced back around and saw no open machines aside from this one. *Of course I chose the washer that didn't work.* I gave the knob one last jiggle to see if that would help it, but it still wouldn't budge. Just as I was about to slam my fist down, I heard someone clear their throat behind me.

I jumped, feeling startled by the sudden noise, and whirled around to see Carter in the doorway. He stood with a laundry basket on his hip and an amused grin on his face.

"Oh, um, hi. I was just—"

"About to put that washing machine out of its misery?" he asked, moving towards me. He set his laundry basket on top of one of the closed dryers before approaching me.

Carter came so close to me that his forearm touched mine and I could smell his familiar scent of citrus and spice. I was torn between moving away to create some space or staying put to avoid making him uncomfortable. Staying in my place, I watched as Carter leaned over and rotated the knob to the left.

"Which setting do you need?"

"Normal is fine, but should I even use this one? I mean, the knob is supposed to turn the other way," I couldn't help but point out.

Carter chuckled while he closed the lid and added a small love tap. "This one just requires a special touch."

I raised an eyebrow and pointed to the machine rocking behind him. "Can your special touch stop that one from launching into space?"

He beamed at my joke, revealing his dimples. "I'm afraid you might need to take a crutch to this one. I'm pretty sure it's on its last leg."

"Washer and me both," I murmured. I heard Carter chuckle again as he turned his attention to one of the dryers and began unloading his laundry into the basket he carried in. I glanced away from him to give him some privacy.

"Speaking of last legs, how is your ankle?" he asked while he worked.

Using the line of washing machines as leverage, I hopped to grab the only chair in the room and slid it back to sit in front of the washer I occupied.

"The padding on these crutches has made all the difference, so thanks again for that."

Carter patted his laundry down into the basket and sat it on top of the now-unoccupied machine. "What about your ankle though?" His chocolate eyes gave his serious gaze an edge of concern. I watched as he motioned towards the floor where I had propped my boot out. "Have you tried to put any weight on it yet?"

Instinctively, I clasped my hands together to rest behind my upper thigh to take some of the weight off my lower leg. "I haven't yet. Normally, I don't willingly subject myself to additional pain or injury."

Carter took a few steps forward and crouched down in front of me. Reaching his hands out to my boot, he peered up at me. "Can I take a look?"

I nodded as he began to unstrap my splint. He carefully removed the velcro strips, revealing my ankle as he opened the shoe. Red indentations marked where the boot held my ankle in place.

With care, Carter lightly touched my foot and focused on twisting his upper body to get a better look at my ankle. His touch sent an electric current down my spine, igniting every nerve inside of me with the awareness of his closeness. Once he finished examining my foot, he put it back in the boot without fastening the straps. As he moved into a squat, he created some distance between us, allowing me to pull my leg back and fix my boot.

"I think it's starting to look good," he reported. "The bruising is subsiding and there isn't any swelling."

"Do you think I can put weight on it now?" I wondered, as I set the final velcro strap in place.

Carter met my gaze before saying, "I think you can check with Angie to see if she can determine if you're ready to put weight on it or not."

We locked eyes as a subtle curiosity danced between us.

"One week in and you're already tired of chaffeuring me around camp, huh?"

"That's not it," he answered before climbing to his feet. "I know crutches can be uncomfortable, so I imagine you would feel better the faster you can get both feet back under you."

His serious reply made me feel incredibly dumb. Of course, Carter wanted to see me improve. As a future health professional, having a crippled camper was probably a top priority for him to ensure I was healing well. If he just wanted me to heal, why did the thought of not riding around camp with him send an unpleasant ripple down my spine?

"Are you ever going to tell me how it happened?" he asked, as he slid back onto the dryer he just finished using. His eyes were locked on me, while the only sound in the room was the washing machine's gentle sloshing.

With the weight of Carter's anticipation, my fingers danced nervously, tracing invisible circles on my leg.

"There really isn't a lot to tell."

Carter scoffed. "You said you fell out of a tree, so I figured there was a good story behind that."

I nonchalantly shrugged, masking my true feelings. "Nope, no good story."

Carter tilted his head and wore a sly grin. "Come on, Dutch, you can tell me. Did you get chased by the cops or something?"

My eyes instantly darted to my feet and my heart was racing at the thought of him finding out about the type of person I was. I wasn't one of the nice girls he could expect to find here at camp. I was a girl who had walked away from church to party. I got into trouble at school and outside of school, and even lost my job for skipping work shifts. If he found out who I was, he would walk away, just like everyone else did.

"Did you?" he pressed further the longer I paused.

"Not exactly," I defended myself, while he eyed me curiously.

So far, all I knew about Carter was that he had a "colorful" past. I heard him confess he had broken the law, but I couldn't even picture him doing so. He was as straight-edge as a guy could be.

"How about this?" Carter proposed. "I'll tell you something I don't like to share with others, and then you can tell me how you found yourself up in a tree. Sound like a deal?"

Narrowing my eyes at him, I remained reluctant. "Maybe."

Carter's deep breath caught me off guard. *Was he nervous too? What kind of secret did he need to share?*

"The first time I was ever busted by the cops, it was for trying to outrun a police officer escaping a party my sophomore year," Carter confessed.

I pictured him wearing his soccer jersey, attempting to escape before getting tackled by a police officer. The occasional glimpses into his past painted a picture of him as a young criminal overlord, but I found it hard to believe.

"What happened when you got caught?"

Carter grinned at me, amused as he remembered the former version of himself. "I was hanging out at this girl's house and her parents were called. Well, everyone's parents were called. My parents didn't show up, though. I went back to their house in the back of a police car around one in the morning."

"What about your girlfriend?" I asked, interested in learning more about his partner in crime.

Carter smirked and pointed his finger at me, saying, "She wasn't my girlfriend, but after that, she stopped talking to me. For good reason."

"Wow," I mused. "I never would have taken you for a jailbird."

"Enough about me," Carter brushed off. "I want to know about you."

I winced and shifted my gaze back to my feet. It had been so long since I confided in anyone. The last person I let myself get close to ended up circling the drain of revenge, pulling me down with her. Before that, my best friend in the whole world couldn't even be there for me when I needed her most. Everyone I let myself get close to found it so easy to walk away. Why would Carter be any different?

"I really don't have anything to tell." Climbing to my feet, I put my weight on my crutches and began to saunter past him.

As I walked through the room, I could feel his eyes on me, yet I couldn't bring myself to face him.

Just as I was about to leave, I heard Carter's voice behind me. "Lena?"

The sun was streaming through the cracks in the door frame as I touched the warm doorknob. I didn't turn around to face him before he continued. "Whenever you're ready to talk, I'm here to listen."

His words were like an invisible string pulling me back towards him. I thought about Carter finding me trying to escape camp, begging me to turn around. In that moment, I thought he was just concerned about Lou and knew more about me than he had let on before. Now here we were once again, with Carter asking me to open up. But this time was different. Carter seemed to be slowly breaking down the walls I had built around myself. I let go of the doorknob and slowly turned back to face him.

"I was trying to get back at someone." Letting out a deep breath, I gripped the handles on my crutches as if hanging onto them for dear life. "I fell out of the tree outside her bedroom window while I was rolling her house with a, um, *friend*..."

Standing completely still, my voice faded as I glanced up to see Carter making his way towards me. The look on his face was one I had seen before, the day he found me trying to leave camp. That was the first time I felt as though we weren't at each other's throats. He had taken me by surprise with his immaculate ability to listen and the faith he so willingly confessed.

"I'm here," he murmured. Hearing his quiet support palpitated the air between us. Just like that, I felt the tension dissipate from my body as I let the truth pour out of me.

"Her name is Lacey and we were best friends," I told Carter, who stood still, taking in every bit of my truth. "When things got bad with my mom, she wasn't there when I needed her most. Eventually, we had a fight and decided we weren't friends anymore. After that, she became my worst nightmare."

"How so?" Carter wondered, his amber eyes solely focused on me.

"Lacey started rumors about me and turned my friends against me," I answered him.

Crossing his arms over his chest, Carter raised his eyebrows. "So, you decided it was time to get back at her?"

Sheepishly, I shrugged and said, "To sum it up, yes."

He wiped his hands down his face, processing the information. "What does any of this have to do with you being at camp?"

"My dad sent me here," I explained. The memory of my dad's face when he found me in the Lockharts' yard came rushing back, making my stomach sink. "That was kind of the last straw for him after everything I put him through."

A few moments of silence hung between us. I looked over at him as he took in everything I had just said. What I didn't expect was him to chuckle about it.

"What?" I asked, feeling a hint of embarrassment.

Carter's smile was so radiant that his dimples reappeared. "It's just ironic to me, I guess."

"What do you mean?" I wondered.

He ran another hand down his face, a move he made often. "It's just, I don't know. You make it seem like you're being punished by being here, but there are people I know that would give their left hand to be here."

Pushing away from the door, I decided to find my seat back in the chair once more. "You feel that way because you love it here. The truth is, I haven't been to church in years."

Carter's eyes softened again instead of casting judgment. "Why not?"

His eyes revealed his heart to me. Despite having many alternative places to go during free time, he inexplicably chose to spend it getting to know me in the laundry room.

"God just feels too far away from me," I whispered. More of my truth lingered in the air between us and I felt as if this might be the straw to break the camel's back. I couldn't look at Carter for fear of what he would think of me now that I had spoken those words. *Would he want to be friends with someone who had renounced her faith?*

A loud screech echoed in the air between us as the washing machine filled with my clothes came to a stop. I stood up, maneuvered around him, and opened the lid to retrieve my clothes and put them back in my laundry bag, ready to move them to an available dryer.

When I finished piling my clothes into the bag, I noticed Carter standing close again. "When you're done loading your things into the dryer, meet me outside."

I took a step back to gaze at him, but before I could, he grabbed his clothes basket and disappeared through the door. Within seconds, I had thrown my clothes into the dryer he had used. Without any trouble, I turned the knob and hurried to catch up with Carter outside.

***

"Trail mix?" Carter offered, holding out a small bag to me. Reaching out, I held my palm open as he dumped some of the contents into my hand.

He had driven us back to the lake where a group of campers were kayaking across. Dappled sunlight reflected over the surface of the water. The serene expanse mirrored the clear blue skies above, framed by shades of emerald greens from the forest surrounding us. The tranquil portrait of camp was much different than the hustle it held during the week.

"So," I wondered aloud. "What are we doing here?"

Beneath the steady blaze of the sun, Carter turned to me with his right eye closed as if the light from above was just too bright. The other eye squinted as he gestured to the scene before us.

"Tell me what you see."

Gawking, I decided to indulge him, "I see the lake, the sky, the woods." Still surveying the layout before us, I continued pointing out my observations. "There's a canoe over there that I wish I could be on." When I noticed a flock of birds flying overhead, I pointed to them too. "Oh yes, and looky there, it's a flying V."

When I peered back over to Carter, his expression was unreadable, and I found myself wondering if I gave him the answer he had been searching for. He kept devouring trail mix without even looking my way.

"Are you going to tell me if I passed your test, or is it your turn to answer?" I demanded.

Carter's expression didn't change. Instead, he gazed out, surveying the scene on his own. I had half a mind to ask him if he was feeling okay before he finally piped up. "I see the lake, the mountains, the sky, and even though I can't see the sun directly, I know it's right there." He explained. I noticed Carter leaning forward just slightly, continuing to point out what he spotted. "I hear the birds and the crickets, and I can hear and feel the breeze go by."

His posture changed suddenly and when he spoke again, there was a seriousness in his voice. "I know I can't see the breeze, but I know that it cools me off and gives me some relief when it's crazy hot out here."

I chuckled, silently agreeing with him while he continued, "I also know the breeze holds the oxygen I need to breathe." Squinting with both eyes now, he pointed up above us once more. "I know I can't stare directly into the sun or I'll go blind, but it's a reliable source of energy that helps sustain both me and every other life source on the planet."

While he spoke, I realized the answer I had given him wasn't wrong. I gave a shallow reply, only skimming the surface of what surrounded me.

"I also know I'm unable to feel the gravity or its direct pull to keep everything grounded," Carter told me. He swiveled in his seat, just slightly, to face me. "These are just tiny pieces of a natural order that exists all around us."

"I would agree," I nodded, finding myself squinting with him beneath the mid-afternoon sun.

With his hands clasped together, Carter spoke with the confidence of a speaker delivering a presentation. "Everything we've spotted together is just finite things we see every day. The difference is, I know that God has given me all of these things because they're all vital to my survival."

In that instant, I looked down at my hands again, knowing exactly where he was going with this. Not only did I feel called out, but I felt a pang deep in my chest. I knew exactly how he felt because I used to feel the same way.

"All of that seems so pretty and peaceful," Carter noted, "but let's consider the curveballs nature likes to throw us."

There was a noticeable change in his voice once more, this time reflecting his excitement. I noticed he began surveying me, as if trying to search my thoughts.

"There's hail that comes with rain or flooding, or mudslides even. Oh yeah, and hurricanes and typhoons, or even blizzards."

I laughed as his excitement grew with each type of precipitation he remembered. Instead of feeling called out, I felt like I was beginning to notice what I was lacking.

"All of those things can wreak havoc in our lives if we let them, right?" he asked. Unsure if he was being rhetorical, I simply nodded and listened attentively.

"But they're only temporary events," Carter almost preached. "Like seasons in our life, they're only temporary. Like the darkness or the nighttime, none of it lasts forever."

I found myself agreeing with him, a smile on my face, as his passion ignited a spark inside me that I thought was gone.

"I know I would rather have everything be super chill all the time," Carter confessed again. When his gaze met mine, I almost crumbled beneath the truth he delivered. "But that's not how life goes."

"Even when life starts to feel dark or tough to navigate," he continued, "I know God hasn't left me, but it's like He's giving me a chance to pause or refining me even if His plans make me uncomfortable."

I remained silent, taking in all he had said. Carter had this ability to take my secrets and bring light to them instead of making me feel shame. He not only heard me, but he had this extraordinary gift of making me feel truly seen, almost like he could read my heart.

"I'm sorry I went off on a tangent there," he apologized.

Feeling my throat stiffen, I just stared down at my hands as I shook my head. "Don't be."

I was unsure if he could hear my voice beginning to break or not. Carter slid closer to me and I could feel him peering down at me.

"Lena, that was a generic explanation, but I know with every fiber of my being that God brought me out of a difficult life."

Even though I nodded, I couldn't bring myself to face him. Tears welled up in my eyes, but I fought them back.

"You said you feel like God left you, but I don't think that's the case at all." Carter's voice came out as a whisper. "I guarantee He's been waiting for you to come back to Him."

As soon as he said that, I felt his hand on my shoulder, and I crumpled like a wet piece of paper in front of him. Tears fell from my eyes, each one representing the turmoil I felt. I felt Carter's comforting embrace without any hesitation as tears streamed down my face.

"It's okay," he repeated to me over and over. His hug felt like a steady solace as he whispered reassurances in my ear. "It's okay, Lena, I'm here."

As I cried and let myself be vulnerable, I sensed my emotional barriers crumbling. As we embraced each other, the world around us seemed to disappear momentarily.

"Everything just feels so hard all the time," I blurted out, finally pulling away from him. As I wiped the tears from my eyes through the sobs that escaped me, I felt Carter's hand moving up and down my arm while he listened to me.

"I get it, I really do," he spoke gently. "If you're up for it, we can do some trauma bonding."

I laughed at his joke and caught him smiling back at me. Using his crooked index finger, he gently wiped away a tear from my cheek. Taking a deep breath, I wiped my cheeks with the backs of my hands and actively shook my emotions away.

"I'm good now, I promise."

Carter's hand remained on my shoulder for a few extra seconds before returning to the driver's seat. He casually leaned over the steering wheel as he so often did while we chatted. I hated that I broke down almost every time I opened up about my family. I wished I could be more like Carter, who couldn't stop grinning once he began to share his story.

"My biological parents split when I was just a kid," Carter opened up further. "Trina, the woman who gave birth to me, was... Well, let's just say she wasn't as monogamous as Dan, my biological father."

I could read between the lines as he explained how Dan found out about Trina's cheating and filed for divorce.

"They fought all the time," Carter told me. He spoke about how open they were about getting divorced but how Trina begged Dan to stay and give her another chance. "He never did though. I think he just was so fed up with her that he left one day and never came back."

My stomach sank as he continued to share more about living with his biological mother after his father left.

"Trina started doing drugs and started up a relationship with Vincent, her dealer."

As I heard more, my stomach sank even deeper. Carter explained how Vincent became abusive towards his mother, and that he had children of his own that he wasn't allowed to see due to a restraining order from their mother.

"That never seemed to stop him though. He was always trying to worm his way into their life," Carter mentioned. "He would show up at their games and even snuck into his daughter's school play once.

"One day, he and Trina were screaming at each other." Carter's voice changed, turning more serious. "He hit her, and when I tried to stop him, he hit me too."

I felt frozen in place, a feeling of terror creeping up my spine as he went on. Carter shared how he fled to his grandmother's place, which was a few hours north.

"I hopped on a train with some money I took from Trina's wallet and decided I was never going back there."

When he got to his grandmother's house, he begged her not to contact Trina and told her Trina was in trouble. She ended up calling the cops, and Child Protective Services got involved.

"Vincent and Trina both went to jail, and they sent me to go live with Dan," Carter informed me. A glimmer of hope rose within me, but faded as I remembered his story continued. He had been adopted after all.

"We did not live happily ever after, though," he went on. As Carter shared how Dan had remarried and had another son, the situation seemed as bleak as living with Trina.

"I was not the son he wanted, Kimber was," Carter said. "I was the son he had hoped to leave behind and forget."

My situation was different, but I understood how he felt. My mother struggled with her own addictions, fighting a battle she couldn't win. In the past five years, I had seen her collapse under the weight of it all. Tears filled my eyes once more, and Carter did a double take when he saw.

"You don't have to keep listening, I'm sorry, I shouldn't have—"

"No," I protested, "I'm fine, it's just, I would have never guessed this was your story."

Carter's smile returned, as if he had regained his sense of contentment. "It gets better, I promise."

I chuckled, wiping lingering tears from my eyes. "I can't wait."

He turned, propping his leg at a ninety-degree angle in the seat to face me. "Long story short, Dan didn't love me. His wife didn't want me there and I was just this huge burden on their whole family."

Hearing him say *their family* sent another wave of shivers down my spine despite the warm afternoon. My father immediately came to mind, and I felt grateful for his unwavering love despite all of my poor decisions.

"Dan made this clear to me," Carter shared. "As a result, I stopped caring about everything: Trina, Dan and the Bryants, and even myself."

He delivered blow after blow as he spoke about how he gave up on his life. As just a freshman in high school, he had felt more alone than he ever had. Carter went to every party he was invited to and drank until he passed out.

"I'll spare you the exact details, but I found myself in several compromising situations with girls who I partied with."

This fact unexpectedly pummeled me. Carter carried on further as I decided I didn't want to think about what he meant. The feeling in my chest shocked me, as I acknowledged how long it had been since I'd felt this way.

"Anyways, I ended up getting into trouble with some friends who were dealing drugs," Carter confessed. Even though I was seated, his confession made me feel slightly unbalanced. I saw him hesitate briefly, as if he wanted to make sure I was okay.

"I wasn't arrested or charged, but they did take me in to the station," Carter mentioned, as if trying to reassure me he was not hopeless. "This little incident actually took a turn in the best direction."

Hope flickered back to life as he described his time at an Alternative School for troubled youth and his encounter with Amy Rose. While he talked about his rocky start with Amy, I saw his face light up with joy. Earlier in the day, I had witnessed the same light when he held his little sister Sadie, and my heart almost melted.

"My mom tried her best with me despite my best efforts to ward her off." Carter smirked. As he said the words *my mom*, I felt chills ripple down my arms again. "She never gave up on me."

I finally heard the emotion in his voice for the first time. Carter turned away from me and I knew then that he was choking back tears. I understood that it was my opportunity to console him, so I placed my hand on his shoulder, attempting to offer a small amount of relief.

"When I was finally showing progress with my grades, she introduced me to my dad and invited me to dinner at their house," he said, chuckling through a sob. "Eventually, I started spending more and more time with their family and started doing Bible study with them."

I breathed a quiet sigh of relief, hearing how his life finally turned around. Carter talked about joining them at church and meeting Denny, Theo, and the rest of the youth group. I recognized that by that time, I had fallen out of the picture. We stopped going to Meadowbrook around the time Carter must have started coming around. I felt a tiny wave of sadness at the thought of being able to meet him sooner had I not given up, too.

"Things got worse before they got better, though." Carter winced. "I had been spending so much time with the Roses that I hadn't been at home with Dan much to realize they were picking up their life and moving."

"What?" I gasped, removing my hand from his shoulder.

He was still smiling though. "Yeah, Dan and my stepmom ended up selling the house."

I was completely bewildered. "But how could you not have known?"

With a touch of sarcasm, he chuckled. "I was at a youth retreat, and they just picked up everything and moved."

My eyes filled with horror as he recounted coming home to find his empty house filled only with boxes of his clothes.

"I went to stay with a friend for a little while, but told my mom I had some family stuff going on and needed some time to sort through things. A few weeks went by, though, and she kept texting and calling to check on me and knew something was wrong.

"One day she called me and said she and Jack went to stop by my house and saw it had sold," Carter admitted. "Like I said, she never gave up on me."

"Is that when they adopted you?" I was in awe of all the things he had told me.

"Basically," Carter said. "I moved in with them and they contacted Child Protective Services. It wasn't a long battle though. Neither Dan nor Trina put up a fight and signed custody over to them."

I was amazed by him after learning about the ups and downs of his life. Despite everything, Carter remained unshaken. "I could have sat in the heartbreak I felt having parents that wanted nothing to do with me, but I couldn't. Not when I have God-given parents that fought so hard to choose me."

As soon as the words left his mouth, I felt my stomach sink again. I had been stuck in self-pity for a while, drowning in my own feelings of rejection. But then came Carter, with his own heartbreaking tale. He was healing and moving on from his past, not letting it consume him.

"Hindsight is twenty-twenty, Lena," he told me, his expression turning serious once more. "I couldn't see it when life was messy, but God was working. Like pieces on a chessboard, my pawn kept moving around the board, and even when I felt like I was in the middle of a bad move, I still found myself able to press forward. There were constant obstacles ahead, but God kept making moves for me. He kept putting all the right pieces in the right places. He kept showing up for me, and people like my family, and my friends, and even your Aunt Lou helped me realize I had a new home. I finally had a family that loved me."

Carter didn't have to say anything else, I had received his message loud and clear. *How could I not?* I had carried a heavy burden for a long time. The friends I had back home used the very weight as a weapon and my family was too busy carrying their own burdens to help bear mine. Here I was, seated next to Carter Rose, the person I least expected to connect with, as he opened up about his own struggles, willing to help carry mine as well.

I never thought I would be in this position, sitting next to him, feeling like he was the only person in the world who could come close to understanding what I had been through. A part of me still felt shocked to my core having found out so much about him. The other part of me was simply amazed by how far he had come since then. Never in a million years would I have imagined that his life would be so different from the life he led now.

"I don't want to put you on the spot, but do you want to talk about your mom?" he asked, pulling me from my thoughts. I remembered what he had said the other day, though and the skeptic in me triggered my suspicion switch.

"I'm not exactly sure what else there is to tell," I admitted, looking him in the eye. "I feel like you may know more than you're letting on."

Carter raised his hands in the air, feigning innocence, before dropping his left hand and raising his right. "I promise, all I know from what Lou told my mom is that your mom broke her heart and that she has struggled with drinking in the past."

Every time my mom's drinking became a topic of conversation, I could feel myself tense. Her problems were always the last topic of conversation I wanted to have, but after hearing about Carter's past and the fact that he already had a foot in the door to mine, I knew it was time.

"My mom is an alcoholic." I almost felt dirty saying the words. "She left right after school ended to get better, or at least that's what she said in a note she left. She never said goodbye."

"I'm so sorry, Lena," Carter responded. He shifted towards me, giving me his undivided attention. "That's tough."

Thinking about it made my heart break all over again. "My dad told me that he was able to catch her at the bus station before she left."

"Did he try to stop her?" Carter wondered.

I bit my lip nervously, reimagining the scene between them. "Dad said he tried at first, but she explained she was going to a treatment facility and that she had a friend she knew from Meadowbrook who was going to help her get back on track. Dad just says she was determined to get better and believes that she will."

"But you don't?' Carter eyed me curiously. I couldn't give him an answer, knowing how every attempt she had tried in the past never worked. After seeing her struggle and fall down time after time, I lost faith in her.

"So, if you know, does that mean the others know too?" I wondered. His eyes were chocolate pools boring into me as he held my gaze. He was sad for me. Not pitying, but sad.

"I wouldn't count on that," Carter tried to reassure me. "Lou is best friends with my mom, so it's a little different for them than with Jojo or Denny's parents."

I felt a wave of relief sweep over me, like a warm hug, as he offered me reassurance. Suddenly, an intrusive thought entered my mind that tumbled out of my mouth before I could consider if it was true.

"When we met and you knew who I was, why were you so rude to me?"

"Because you were being rude to me!" he admitted, as if the question was absurd. Carter nudged my arm as if to cheer me out of my sudden slump. "Let's get back to your mom. You're always so evasive about talking about her, why is that?"

I shrugged and set my focus back on the lake ahead of us. The sun was beginning to shift and so was the reflection over the waters.

"Freeport, where I'm from, is a really small town," I replied, trying to force back my wavering emotions. "News travels fast no matter how hard you try to hide it, and people talk."

"And what did they say?" he pressed.

Observing him once more, I could see that he was hanging onto my every word as if I were all that existed in that moment. The thing that I was beginning to notice about Carter, though, was that he wasn't being nosy. He seemed to have no ulterior motive here. The more he asked, the more I got the impression he was merely trying to get to know me.

"Everything you could possibly imagine," I answered him. "Everyone turned on me."

Carter watched me, the sadness leaving his eyes and being replaced by a discerning form of understanding. "I really do get it, Lena."

"Oh yeah?" I asked, wondering where his thoughts were. Carter reclined in his chair, gazing at the lake and appreciating the surrounding view. As the sun prepared to go down, the cascading effect over the lake was impossible to put into words. There was just something about a sunset, no matter where you were in the world, that held a tranquil beauty.

"It's not the same, I know, but I can understand how it feels when the people you think are in your corner are the first to disappear," he let on.

Knowing about Dan and Trina now, I knew he understood how I felt. The two people who were supposed to love him the most in the world were the very people who betrayed him. I realized that, for once, I was one of the lucky ones when I compared myself to him.

With the fading sun casting dark rays, Carter turned to me once more. "This is probably the last place you would expect to find friendship, but, trust me, if you let yourself, you can find it, and I would be willing to bet you already have."

16

As a new week began, the camp settled back into its usual routine, and I found myself waiting for Carter on the front porch after breakfast. The last forty-eight hours had been a whirlwind of emotions for me. In just over a week, I was reconnecting with old friends I thought I'd lost touch with. When I went to sleep, I found myself wondering when Jojo would be back if she was still out. Between daily activities, I relied on Carter to take me from place to place. I expected Theo to banter with me during team activities, and I counted on Denny and his crazy antics to make me laugh.

The more I let my guard down, the more I felt like myself again, the version I used to be, who enjoyed spending time with friends and relied on those I could trust. Though the nagging thought remained that these people could let me down, their actions were proving otherwise.

Camp was different because the people here were different. Something about yesterday's worship made me feel like things were changing. At first, I was nervous because I hadn't been to church in a long time, but the worship atmosphere completely drew me in. All eyes were on the guest speaker from the moment he addressed the crowd with how to speak to one another in love.

Speaking about Jesus should be as easy as talking to someone about your favorite hobby. The man's words kept swirling in my mind, one after the other.

Be someone who speaks the truth and speaks life into others.
The tongue holds the power of life and death.
Do not be ashamed of the Gospel of Christ.
God's word is a sword against evil, not against those who need it to hear the Gospel.

Truth after truth, his words pricked the hard edges of my heart. So much so that I asked Jojo for a piece of paper and pen to write down the scriptures he continued spewing off in his sermon. Before returning to the cabin, I grabbed one of the camp's worn-out Bibles, suddenly hungry to know more.

I had meant to read the verses Ephesians 4:15-16, Mark 8:34-38, and Second Corinthians 4:6-9 from the sermon notes I took, but I ended up reading through the whole passages instead. As I read, it hit me that I'd been stuck in this constant rejection mode, fighting with everyone around me, even friends and family.

The more I thought about how I had been using my own words as weapons, the clearer my situation in Freeport became. I thought I stayed true to myself while my closest friends betrayed me, but the truth was, I had changed.

When I took a moment to think about my day-to-day encounters at school over the past year, it became clear to me that I was living in a constant state of retaliation. I allowed the false opinions of others about me and my family to control me. As I clung to the belief that I was defending myself, I slowly realized that I had fallen into a much deeper pit than I could have imagined, and I had even blamed God for everything.

The door to the Dining Hall closed suddenly, bringing me back to reality. I instinctively shifted and spotted Lou standing there, holding a large tote. Her face reddened when she spotted me, and I knew exactly how she was feeling. The last time I had spoken with her was the night before I tried to run away, and the weight of my actions weighed heavily on my conscience as I replayed the conversation in my mind. *You have no idea what I've been through, Lou.* The words retraced their steps as I met her gaze. *I'm sick of being here!* I couldn't help but wonder if the conversation lingered in her mind as vividly as it did in mine.

"Good morning, Lena," she greeted me with a tiny grin that didn't quite reach her eyes. It had been days since I last saw her, and I had started to wonder if she was still around or if she was avoiding me. If she had, I couldn't blame her.

The tongue holds the power of life and death popped into my head again. Lou had tried to break through to me. I could still recall the words she spoke to me, filled with hope in a genuine attempt to reach me. *People will always hurt us or let us down, but Jesus doesn't.* In my moment of frustration, I had let my emotions take over and my words only added fuel to the fire.

"Lou," I started, "about the other night…" My voice trailed off as I tried my best to articulate what to say. Saying "I'm sorry" didn't sound sincere enough to make amends for the hurtful words I had said to her.

"It's okay," she tried to dismiss me.

"No, it's really not okay," I countered, not ready to let myself off the hook. Lou awkwardly adjusted the tote in her arms, and if I didn't have crutches, the least I could have done was offer to help her.

I stared at my feet, struggling to find the right words until they finally came to me. "The other night just stirred up a lot of emotions. I overreacted with everything I said—"

Lou set the tote down and moved closer to me before I could finish. She clasped her hands together as if kneading dough in her hands. There were so many tiny mannerisms she had in common with my mom that always made me think of her. The hand clasp was a nervous tic I thought only my mom had until now.

"Honey, I just want you to know that I really do understand where you're coming from—"

"And I'm sorry for saying that you didn't," I interrupted, hoping she could see just how sorry I felt.

She smiled shyly and said, "Please don't worry about how I'm feeling. Just trust me when I say that I'm here for you, anytime, anywhere. If you ever want to talk about things, just know that. Okay?"

The intensity in her gaze sent chills down my spine. I recognized that look all too well. She seemed wounded, wearing a silent plea for understanding, as if reaching out for a lifeline, even. It mirrored a haunting memory of my mother sharing her first relapse. She told me that Dad helped her find a rehab clinic nearby and promised me, *"No matter what I'm going through, just know that I'm still here for you."* The emotional moment I shared with my mom now collided with my present.

When I refocused on Lou, I only caught the last part of what she had been saying.

"... I will drop everything whenever you want to talk. That's how I've always felt, and that will never change."

I felt a storm of emotions when our eyes met.

"I'm so sorry." Even with two crutches to hold me up, I still felt more unsteady than before, and could only manage to apologize. After everything she did for me, I felt really bad about how I treated her. "I never thought about what you must have been going through, too."

I almost didn't recognize the Lou still standing before me. She wore a veil of uncertainty, and I sensed a heavy weight of unspoken words hanging in the air between us. Lou was about to say something, but she leaned over to look behind me. She waved her hand, and I watched her. In the blink of an eye, her expression shifted dramatically as a radiant smile spread across her face.

"Morning, Lou!" Carter called up to her.

I turned, using my crutches, and caught sight of Carter's casual smile just above the barely perceptible hum of the golf cart. The early sun's golden hues reflected off his sunglasses. Despite his caramel hair being tousled by the wind, his charm remained intact.

"You ready to go, Dutch?" he called out to me.

I spun back to Lou, who offered me a curious glance. Rolling my eyes, I shook my head.

"Don't ask."

She held up her hands in surrender while wearing a genuine smile. "I will contain my curiosity on that one."

Before turning to leave, I looked to her once more. "Can we talk soon?"

Her abashed smile returned. "Soon."

Knowing I could take Lou at her word, I made my way down the ramp to climb into my usual seat beside Carter. Without hesitation, he released the brake and we proceeded forward. The air was already warming outside, feeling dense with humidity despite our elevation. I noticed that Carter was wearing a simple charcoal t-shirt paired with white khaki shorts that stopped just above his knee. Most campers went for gym shorts, but Carter always looked sharp even when trying to be casual.

Sitting beside him, I felt a flutter of nerves dancing in the pit of my stomach. Any movement I made felt like a delicate balance on a tightrope. Each time I stole a glance at him, I could feel my nerves tremble. My heart raced with a mix of excitement and vulnerability whenever he was around, like a fireworks display of emotions.

"Did you sleep well?" he asked.

Peering over to him, I noticed how the wind gently tousled his hair, just as it always did. Carter seemed so light this morning, and I was quick to notice the change in him. A genuine smile played on his lips, much like before, but brighter somehow.

"I did, how about you?" I couldn't help but cringe as my voice sounded overly cheerful, making my face grow hot.

Carter only smiled brighter, and I wondered if he could tell how red my face probably was. "I always sleep well."

Small talk had never been my talent. In fact, I despised it. Yet, an infectious joy radiated from Carter, and I would not be the one to squash it. Trying my best to keep this momentum going, I said the only thing I could think of.

"What are you up to today?"

Carter raised his eyebrows, his smile turning more into one of curiosity. "The usual. Making my rounds, passing out medications and band-aids mostly, and, of course, driving you around, Dutch."

I let out a sigh, my cheeks burning with embarrassment. Inwardly, I was kicking myself for not being better at small talk.

"Okay, let me rephrase," I tried again. "How is today specifically looking for you?"

The gazebo came into sight, though I noticed only a few people had shown up so far. Adam was busy talking with another staff member, so I knew I had a moment to recover from this horrible excuse for a conversation.

Carter parked the cart and reached a hand behind the seat, appearing to fish for something. "I'm going to hang out at this session with you and then go do some rounds."

This stunned me, and my thoughts swirled. *Did he just say he was going to hang out with me? In this session? Right now?*

"Um, t–this session?" I stammered. "Like, right now?"

Carter fished his Bible out of his bag in the back and eyed me warily. "This one. Right now." He said the words slowly, as if to make sure I understood.

My thoughts were spinning and I had a million questions lingering in my mind. *Why was he coming to this session? Did he want to hang out with me? Were we friends now?*

He tapped my forehead with his index finger, releasing a laugh. "You in there, Dutch?"

I batted his hand away, chuckling. "I'm fine, but how are you able to get out of duty?"

Carter shrugged nonchalantly, as if his plan was foolproof. "I'm always on duty, for one." Counting with his hands, he held up his second finger. "And two, Denny and the guys are having a sports meeting this morning, so no imminent threats of injury are on the horizon for at least an hour."

Of all the places he could be this morning, like going for a run or hanging out with his other friends, he chose to come to the breakout session with me. *I couldn't believe it.*

While sliding out of the passenger's side, I watched him climb out of his seat and reach into the back to fetch his water bottle. I thought about what he said the other day about trying to put weight on my ankle, so I placed my foot flat on the ground. To my surprise, as I gradually put more weight on it, I felt no soreness.

When I peeked back up, Carter was studying me with my crutches in hand.

"How did that feel?"

I smiled. "Not bad at all, there's just pressure."

He nodded, like he saw it coming. "The pressure is probably just stiffness. That's normal, but like I said, we can go see Angie to see what she thinks about you taking things slow and putting some weight on it."

Carter motioned me forward, handing back my crutches. When my fingers grazed the top of his hand, I looked up at him, but he remained unfazed. As he fell in line beside me, I suddenly felt his soft touch on my shoulder, as though he was trying to guide me. It happened so quickly that I wondered if I had imagined it as he marched in front of me, leading us up the stairs to the gazebo.

Adam turned at once. "Hey guys! Come on in!"

I watched Carter shake Adam's hand before he moved to have a seat. For the tiniest moment, his eyes searched around until he spotted me, already seated, and took the spot to my left. Once the gazebo was packed with campers, Adam opened his Bible and got started.

"Welcome back, guys!" he greeted us. "Did everyone have a good weekend?" The crowd around me reacted with a few cheers, some grunts, and lots of nodding.

"How was your weekend?" Carter asked, bravely engaging in conversation with our teacher.

Adam pointed to Carter with his hand as if they were sharing an inside joke. "It was a blessed one," they said together in unison. I glanced from Adam to Carter as they both snickered.

"You know me too well, Rosie." Adam grinned.

As Adam instructed everyone to turn their Bibles back to the Book of Acts, I leaned in to Carter and whispered in his ear, "Rosie is it?"

Focused on flipping the pages in his Bible, Carter didn't look up at me as he murmured, "Don't you dare, Dutch."

Tossing a few ideas in my mind, I scrunched my face, teasing him further. "I think I'll have to keep Rosie in my back pocket, it's a little better than Scooter."

When I looked at him, he wore a sly smile, as if he dared me. At first, I was disappointed that he stopped our banter, but then I realized he was just trying to concentrate on the lesson. My heart filled with unexpected admiration as he focused on his Bible in his lap.

A little over a year ago, I had buried my nose in the pages of the Good Book as well, just for different reasons. I felt myself looking for answers on how to move forward, trying to bargain with God so that my life could go back to normal. I read through Psalm after Psalm trying to see examples of how David prayed to God in the darkest of times.

The more I tried to find answers and found none, the easier it was to throw in the towel. Just days ago, I had been on the verge of leaving. Yet, all it took was one person, the last person in the world I would have expected to stop me in my tracks. Carter saw me on the gravel road and reached out, not taking no for an answer.

Now, seeing him right beside me, I had no question about who he was. Seeing me at my wit's end that day, I truly believe he knew I needed someone. I just didn't think either of us could have guessed he would be the person to show up. *Was our budding friendship God's way of intervening in my life?*

"Let's recap," Adam instructed us. "To pick up where we last left off, you guys tell me the type of person Paul was. Just throw out what you know."

One by one, campers began answering his question.

Paul was a Roman who persecuted Christians before becoming a Christian.

His name was Saul until he was converted and became Paul.

Paul went on several missionary journeys.

He wrote thirteen letters in the New Testament.

"Very good, everyone!" Adam praised them. "Let's talk about what happened after Paul was baptized. Who can tell me?"

A moment of silence fell over the crowd before a guy to the far left spoke up.

"Paul began preaching about Jesus."

Adam pointed to the young man, acknowledging his good work. "Excellent job, Mateo. Who else?"

Another round of silence as Adam surveyed us, eager for someone to take their turn. "I really want to focus on the time frame here," Adam spoke, trying to pull the answer out of us.

Without a moment's hesitation, Carter took his turn. "Acts nine, verse twenty says 'immediately.'"

"Excellent, Rosie!" Adam cheered. "After encountering Jesus on the Road to Damascus, Saul stopped his mission to persecute Christians and was baptized and *immediately* began preaching about the Gospel."

The crowd grew silent as Adam's demeanor changed, growing more serious.

"If you were to see Jesus appearing before you right this very second, how do you think you would react?'

The thought of encountering Jesus right now filled me with an overwhelming sense of guilt. Jesus had been removed from my mind for so long that living for him had become a far-off thought for me. I had set foot in church enough times to know that encountering Jesus should be joyful for a Christian, not something to be afraid of. I also knew that not living a righteous life made me feel fearful. If I had to speak for my sins and shortcomings, today would not be the day I would want to meet the Lord.

"I wouldn't be able to stand or even look at Him," Carter spoke up.

Adam focused his attention on him once more. "Why do you think that is?"

Carter cleared his throat and spoke up louder. "For one, I really don't think any of us could truly stand to be in the presence of Jesus and feel the least bit worthy. And two, I think I'm going to be bowing and kissing His feet."

Laughter echoed around us, but as I caught a glimpse between Carter and Adam, I could sense the weight of their serious discussion. Adam stroked his again, narrowing his eyes.

"It's interesting that you say that you would react that way, Carter. When I study this, it seems like Paul didn't have to give much thought to what he should do. What does Paul's reaction teach us here?"

"Paul had no need to question who he was encountering," Carter said, his voice firm. "Miraculous events took place for Jesus to prove he was the Messiah. If I encountered Jesus in the flesh today, I would react the same way."

Continuing their discussion in the midst of the group, Adam grinned. "Can we encounter Jesus today?"

Holding up his Bible, Carter answered. "In God's Word we can."

"That's one of the many beautiful parts of being a Christian," Adam beamed. "No matter where we are, we have full access to hear the words of our God in the pages of the Word and to speak with Him through the avenue of prayer. What else does Paul's immediate reaction teach us?" Adam pressed further.

"That no one is too far out of God's reach to become a Christian," Mateo piped up from the corner again. He seemed younger than me but wise beyond his years. Much like Carter.

"Yes!" Adam exclaimed. "The Lord can help even the worst sinner turn around to live a faithful life."

Adam's eyes cut to me before turning away so quickly I wondered if he meant to or not.

"No one is ever too far from God," Carter added.

***

When the session ended, we all stood waiting to file out of the gazebo. Back when I was a churchgoer, the lessons always hit home. No matter what the preacher said, it always felt like they were talking directly to me. After this morning's session, I was beginning to feel the same way. I was dissecting portions of Paul's conversion story in my mind. This murderer encountered Jesus and immediately changed. As soon as he heard the Gospel, he obeyed and immediately started teaching and preaching it. Nothing about Paul's life was simple after that.

A man doesn't just change overnight and automatically become accepted by society or even other Christians. This struck me when I thought of my situation this summer. I thought I would stick out here like a sore thumb. Finding a friend in Carter was the last thing I ever expected, yet here we were. Slowly, I was beginning to think that there was more here for me than I had realized.

"Great job, my brother." Adam shook Carter's hand and pulled him into a one-armed hug. As we exited the gazebo, Carter whispered something to Adam before turning to trail behind me.

"I'll grab these," he said almost instinctively, helping me with my crutches. The more I got to know him, the more he took me by surprise. He had turned a complete one-eighty from the cold staff member I was first introduced to, and I wondered what else I had been wrong about.

Carter hopped in beside me and we jetted off. The wind rushed over me like a warm setting on a blow dryer and I instantly felt the heat from my hair on my neck. Taking the faithful hair bow off my wrist, I began working my hair into a ponytail when Carter leaned over to me.

"Sorry!"

"About what?" I asked, once I'd secured my ponytail up.

"I didn't mean to ruin your hair."

I chuckled, "You didn't. Did you?"

Carter laughed, seeing my expression, but shot me a side-long glance behind his sunglasses before facing the gravel path ahead of us.

"It looks great."

His compliment lingered in the rushing wind between us and I could feel an unexpected flutter dancing in the pit of my stomach. One look from him eased my self-consciousness. The more we interacted lately, the stronger the unspoken dynamic between us became.

The craziest thing about being with Carter was how spending more time with him made me feel an unusual sense of hope growing inside me. I began to question all the things I used to tell myself. *Had I been wrong about God this whole time? Could He forgive me for all the wrong I had done over the last year? Would I be able to go back to the person I used to be? Would my dad be able to forgive me? Could Lou and I work things out?*

My mind was racing with all of these possibilities, especially after hearing Adam and Carter discuss Paul's transformation. I couldn't stop thinking about just how quickly Paul changed his life just by encountering Jesus. He was so convinced that he was right and Christians were wrong. I didn't feel so different from Paul right now.

I remembered all the pain from school, the teasing and heartbreak. The more I got hurt, the more I thought I had to rely on myself. Rules didn't feel like they applied to me. I wanted to come and go whenever I pleased and do whatever I wanted to do. *But, at what cost?* I had driven away the one relationship that meant the most to me: my relationship with my dad.

I didn't want to be that girl anymore. I felt this renewed energy inside of me at the idea of shaking off the scales covering my own eyes just as Paul in the Bible had done. Here, at camp, I was beginning to see that I could forge a new path.

Carter took a left onto the gravel path, and when I realized the turn he made, I saw we were heading to the Med Cabin.

"What's going on?" I asked as we bobbed along the path.

A few campers were running around in front of us, chasing each other, and Carter had to slam on the brakes. I jutted forward in my seat as he laughed at me.

"I'm going to take you to see Angie to have your ankle looked at," he answered me.

Having caught myself from flying forward on the dash, I murmured, "I might need to see her for whiplash, too."

Carter flashed his coy smile. "Don't be dramatic, Dutch. I wasn't even going that fast."

Reaching the parking pad outside the Med Cabin, Carter threw the cart in park and hopped out. As I adjusted my crutches beneath my shoulders, I spotted him holding the door open for me. Before I let the butterflies in my stomach get the best of me, I decided it was time to take Carter up on the offer he had made known a few times now.

Hobbling forward, I reached him where he stood at the door and stopped. A nervous heat crept up the back of my neck as I peered up at him. Carter stood just a few inches above me. Tall but not too tall.

"Can we talk later?" I asked him. "About the session. You, um, have said some things to me lately that I'm curious about."

With a smile, Carter raised his sunglasses to meet my gaze.

"I'll find you after dinner."

All I could do was smile as he ushered me inside, where Angie was already waiting for me.

17

"Hey Theo, our cheerleader is here!" Asher alerted Theo, who was standing in the dugout. Our team was playing wiffle ball on the softball field, and it was our turn to bat.

"Better late than never, Mermaid!" Theo greeted me, as Carter put the cart in park. I heard him snicker beside me.

"What do you think you're laughing at?" I glared at him as I climbed out.

Carter innocently motioned to Theo, who was now swinging from the edge of the dugout like a teenage chimpanzee. "Come on, Mermaid is clever."

Rolling my eyes, I grabbed my crutches, even though I didn't plan on needing them for the rest of the day. Angie gave me permission to walk without them, but advised using them if I felt any discomfort or pain. The good thing was that I was already two weeks into a mild sprain. As long as I rested when needed and engaged in ankle exercises, I should be as good as new in no time.

"Not as clever as Rosie," I countered.

Before I could saunter off, Carter leaned over to me, lowering his voice to just above a whisper. "Remember, I'll come to find you after dinner, and hopefully we can have some time to talk before Devo tonight."

I hadn't forgotten that he told me we could talk after dinner, but the fact that he remembered sent me buzzing. "I'll see you then."

I took small, cautious steps to join the team in the dugout. Almost as if it were second nature, once I was out of sight, I turned to watch Carter jet off to his other staff duties.

"Oh wow!" Theo raised his voice. "Mermaid got her sea legs back!"

I rolled my eyes at him as a few others erupted in laughter. "Did I ever tell you I miss the version of you that didn't have a lot to say?"

He barely acknowledged this, rubbing his hands together as if he were devising some genius scheme.

"So what's the plan?" he asked me, bringing his focus back to the game. "Can you play now, or are you still going to be the world's worst cheerleader?"

If I could shoot laser beams out of my eyes, Theo would be the one I tested that superpower on. Without hesitation, I swiftly picked up the bat standing against the edge of the dugout.

"I'll bat, but I'm going to need your *sea legs* to run around the bases."

Eager to accept the challenge, Theo leaned down so we were at eye level. "You're on."

The team shuffled into a single-file line behind the dugout as Theo jogged out to the pitcher to let him know our plan. I slowly made my way to stand at home plate. There was a stiffness in my ankle, but a part of me also felt as I imagined a baby deer would after taking its first steps. I wasn't sure if the uncomfortable sensation was from actual pain or because I was finally using the joint. The crunch of dirt beneath me sounded with each step I took. With the wiffle bat in my hand, I found my spot next to home plate just as Theo came jogging towards me.

"Make it count, Mermaid," he said before taking his place by the pitcher to run the bases for me. "The Best Team trophy is at stake here, but no pressure."

I glared at Theo, feeling a mixture of nerves as the team in the field anticipated my hit. The Red Team in the dugout behind me eagerly cheered me on, adding to the pressure I already felt. I had dabbled in sports, playing basketball and softball for a year in middle school before I found my footing with cheerleading and dance at Freeport High. I had no hope of a future in athletics, but I could hold my own. A week had already gone by, and my team had to pull my weight. Now they would finally see what I was made of and the competitive spirit that coursed through me.

The boy on the mound pulled back to hurl an underhanded toss my way. I readied myself as the Swiss cheese-looking plastic ball sped towards me. I swung but missed as the ball whirled past me. The little girl who was acting as the catcher behind me leaped up in an attempt to catch the ball, but it ended up falling to the ground. As she shuffled around after the ball, I caught sight of Theo. Using two fingers, he gestured towards his eyes and then directed them towards me, urging me to concentrate.

There was no way I was going to stand here in front of Theo and swing and miss. I refocused on the pitcher as he released the ball again. This time, the small bat in my hands connected with a loud *thwack!*

On instinct, I dropped the bat and almost ran, but then I caught sight of Theo as he flew to first base like a bolt of lightning and landed safely, securing his position. Cheers erupted from the dugout as Asher made his way over to me, reaching for the bat.

"Good one, Lena!" he congratulated me.

I passed the bat to him and headed back to the dugout, but not before catching Theo's attention. He threw me a thumbs up, but I had the last say.

"You better make it home, Lockwood," I teased, throwing two fingers from my eyes to his in a gesture that mimicked his from before.

As we reached the final inning of the game, the scorching heat from the sun started to sap my energy, making my role as catcher even more challenging. There was no other position on the field where I could be stationary besides sitting out, and I was done being the Red Team benchwarmer. Wiping the sweat from my brow, I crouched down low, feeling the intensity in the air as Theo prepared to throw what we hoped would be the third strike. The current batter, a small blonde girl, held the bat tightly, her knuckles turning white.

Theo threw the pitch and the girl swung and made contact. I looked up as the ball flew straight up into the air. Everything happened so fast that it didn't register with me that I had caught the ball until the cheers on the field erupted. Before I had a chance to focus on the ball in my hand, Asher was running towards me from the in-field, and someone else was lifting me off the ground.

"You did it, Mermaid!" Theo shouted. When he gently placed me back on the ground, a twinge of pain shot through my ankle, but it was a far cry from the agony I had felt earlier. Still, I winced, pulling back from Theo and the others who had gathered around me.

"I would have never thought you would go from benchwarmer to the winning catch in a week!" Asher blurted.

I frowned and received an innocent shrug from him in return. Finished celebrating, I pushed through the crowd of teammates and over to the water cooler. I gulped down three cups until I was finally satisfied, then took a seat on the bench. From there,

I watched my team, still on the field, animatedly talking about our team's win. Over the last couple of years, I had forgotten what the camaraderie of teamwork felt like, having walked away from the cheer squad. Teamwork felt a lot like friendship, with everyone coming together for one common goal.

The last time I had felt even remotely similar to this had been when Freeport High won the football championship freshman year. That night, Lacey, Worthy, Camille, and I had found each other jumping up and down, hugging one another. It was the same night Lacey and Javier shared their first kiss.

"Hey, don't drink it all," Theo warned, pulling me back to the present.

"There's not enough water in there to fill your cup, bud," I teased.

Theo shook the jug and shrugged hopelessly. "You're right, there's barely enough here. I'll carry it up to the kitchen to fill."

"I'll go with you," I told him, grabbing my crutches from the bench. "I need to get ready for dinner."

Theo scrunched his face in disgust. "You should think about cleaning up before dinner."

I nudged him in the ribs with my elbow before leaning back on my crutches. "I should say the same to you."

He held up his hands, feigning innocence. "I've already had my weekly shower, thank you very much."

Now it was my turn to be disgusted. "So, that's what the smell was all afternoon."

"You mean the smell of rugged man and athleticism?"

I cackled before steering the conversation away from his ego. "So, what's new with you? You're not lurking in sandboxes to throw sand or living in fear of the cootie pandemic anymore?"

Theo furrowed his eyebrows. "I got my cootie shot and was cured a long time ago."

I sighed. Though I hated small talk, I was genuinely curious about him and his take on camp and Meadowbrook.

"For real though, Lockwood. What's your story?"

"Theo Lockwood," he began rattling off. "Seventeen, six-foot-one, left midfield for Valley View Varsity basketball team, upcoming senior, Kelsey Lockwood's younger brother, and the much more handsome sibling," he said with a wink. Continuing on, he shared, "Known ambivert, son of Meadowbrook's mayor, but most importantly, a Christian."

When he finished, he motioned with his hand and took a bow. "Alright, Mermaid, now it's your turn."

I continued to shuffle forward on my crutches beside him and tried to mimic his monologue. "Lena Harris. Five-foot-six. Former cheerleader for Freeport High."

"Introvert?" he asked, reminding me of one of the few responses I left out.

I shook my head. "I don't think so, but I also think it depends on the crowd I'm around."

"Any siblings?"

"I'm an only child," I answered.

"Are you not into the church camp scene?" he wondered.

I paused for a moment. The answer not as clear as it had been a week ago. When I looked up, he eyed me curiously before I replied, "It's growing on me."

Theo made a face as if he could relate. "I get that. And what about your parents?"

"What about them?" I countered, never eager to dive into the topic of my mother.

He shot me an obvious glance. "I will never forget your mom, and I was just curious if she's as scary as I remember her being that one time you tattle-taled on Denny and me."

I laughed, the memory of my mom lecturing them as fresh in my mind as the day it happened. "She's not scary."

When I saw the familiar gazebo where we had breakout sessions, I felt relieved that our long walk across camp was almost over. Theo hummed under his breath, as if contemplating an idea.

"I've always wondered about your mom and Lou."

"Why?" I eyed him suspiciously.

"My dad," Theo replied. "I've just always felt like there was this rift between our families or something."

We reached the open field by the Craft Cabin, and I came to a halt. He had my full attention now.

"What makes you think that?"

Theo didn't seem as fazed as I did. "Your grandpa used to be one of the elders at our church."

"I remember."

Theo shrugged. "I don't think he and my dad always saw eye-to-eye. Then, when you and your mom used to come up to visit, my parents just always seemed off. But my mom is the same way around Lou, too, so I've just always been curious, I guess."

Without giving an explanation, I began sifting through my memories for some recollection of Theo's dad, but came up short. I barely knew Theo or his family, but from what I was discovering, his sister Kelsey didn't have the best taste in friends and his parents clearly suffered from poor judgment. I had made up my mind a long time ago that anyone who had an issue with my Gramps was showing more of a reflection of themselves than of him. When measured against the rest of the Lockwoods, Theo appeared to be an apple that fell far from that family tree.

Theo motioned towards Girls Camp. "Looks like this is your stop, Mermaid."

I didn't even feel like I could laugh at his favorite little quip as I wondered about what he could have possibly meant about his father's grudge against my family. Before I could press further,

Theo saluted me and headed in the opposite direction to the Dining Hall.

Eagerly, my mind raced, desperate to uncover more details about the grudge Theo had just revealed. I was used to people having an issue with my mother, but not Lou or my grandparents. Taking a deep breath, I decided to do what I normally did, especially when it came to my mother: bury the thought into the corner of my mind where I locked away all the other things about her that I didn't want to know about.

***

After dinner, I slipped away as Jojo went to meet Theo and Denny at the canteen during free time. She seemed puzzled when I told her I couldn't go because I had other plans.

"Bible study," I told her. Jojo's face moved from shock to excitement within a matter of seconds before she disappeared to meet the boys.

I hadn't lied. Even though Carter and I wouldn't be conducting a Bible study, he would be answering my questions, and somehow the two didn't seem so different. Slowly, I followed the gravel path that led away from the bustling campsite, finding myself on the well-worn trail to the lake. Deciding to forego my crutches for the evening, I felt a dull ache in my ankle, but it was finally tolerable enough to endure.

Under the embrace of a warm summer night, the wooden trail unfolded like a secret pathway as dappled moonlight filtered through the thick canopy of leaves overhead. Crickets chirped nearby, their sound carried through the wind that swept around me, rustling the leaves on the trees as it breezed by. Once I approached the edge of the clearing where the path turned into sand, I could see a small bonfire going.

I noticed Carter adding more kindling to keep the flames lit. When I saw him, a sudden spark ignited inside me, making my heart race. As I crept closer, he looked up, his gaze meeting mine.

"Hey, Dutch!" he greeted me, a slow, easy smile spreading over his face. A shadow of flames danced over his cheeks. The light from the fire somehow made him seem older, brooding even, and I felt my stomach flip-flop. "No crutch?"

His awful attempt to rhyme made me laugh, and I took a seat beside him. "I'm trying to get back on both feet."

"I'm glad to see it," he said gently, as he continued to poke the fire. "As long as you're not in pain, that is."

Heat rose to my cheeks at the sound of concern in his voice. "Nothing I can't take."

With his elbows resting on his thighs, Carter leaned forward, taking the focus off the fire to face me. "I know we don't have a lot of time out here before Devo starts, but I'm dying to know what questions you have."

I couldn't resist placing my fingertips near the fire to experience its heat, even though I wasn't cold. "Dying to know, huh?"

Carter nodded, "I've been wondering what's been going on in that head of yours all day."

I felt another jolt of excitement. *Was everything he said to me now going to affect me like this?* Inhaling deeply, I let my anxiousness subside and allowed my lingering question to be set free.

"You said that you relate to Paul in the Bible because he was an enemy of God. So, what made you decide to become a Christian?"

Carter raised his eyebrows, surprised by the question. With his chin in his hand, he stared at the flickering flames in front of us, deep in thought, mulling over my words.

Seeing his reaction, I had the sudden urge to reel the question back in. "If you don't want to answer, you don't have to—"

"No, no, that's not it at all," Carter cut me off. He sat up then, his eyes narrowing. "It's just that it's kind of a long story."

Smiling, I asked, "Can you tell the short version for time's sake?"

Carter snickered, and I watched as his eyes grew serious. "It wasn't just about Paul being an enemy of God, but more about how the Lord made a way for him despite all the sins he had committed."

"Do you mean how Jesus stopped him when he was going to persecute Christians?" I tried to understand.

The smell of burning wood filled the air as Carter stoked the fire once again. "That was just the start. The more I read about Paul, the more I noticed God intervening in his life to use Paul for his glory."

"But doesn't he just get thrown in prison and persecuted in the same way he was persecuting Christians?" I asked.

I watched the corners of his mouth curve up into a grin. "That's a part of it, I guess. But for me, when I read about Paul's conversion and then his service to the early church, I see how he ran the race of faith without looking back because he knew the prize he would receive in the end. He was willing to endure the suffering because he knew what awaited him when his life was over."

"Heaven?" I asked, seeking to understand.

Carter nodded. "Let me explain it like this: I play soccer, and the only way to improve and get better is to stay disciplined, practice, and focus on my team. But it didn't start out like that for me."

"What do you mean?"

I watched as Carter's face fell slightly. "When I first went to live with my biological dad, I played soccer a little before I was kicked off the team for my bad grades. But I didn't play because I loved the game, I played because it was a means of escape from him and his new family that I didn't fit into."

"I'm so sorry Carter—"

"I'm not," he cut me off, dismissing my pity. "They made me appreciate having a chosen family. I endured a lot early on in my life, more than a kid should have had to. My life could have taken a totally different direction if I had gone down a different path. Like Paul received his intervention, I believe God placed Christians in my life to show me how to run the race of faith, too. I can endure anything else that comes my way. Paul knew this, and he endured whatever consequences he faced as a result because he met Jesus on that road and He changed Paul's life. Knowing that Jesus rewrites people's stories is why I decided to become a Christian."

The more I heard, the more convicted I felt. Since I stopped going to church, I had become so inwardly focused on my own shortcomings and family failures, I stopped believing God was there for me.

Carter faced me. "What else is going on in that head of yours?"

Carter's question was almost too big for me to answer. On the one hand, I could understand why he believed what he believed. On the other hand, there was still this nagging thought in the back of my mind: *Why would God allow my family to be torn apart?* I had always heard God would never leave me or forsake me, but isn't that what He had done by allowing my mom to get sick? Didn't He turn His back on me when He allowed my mom to leave us? Why would such a loving God allow so much pain?

"Lena?" Carter asked. I saw the concern in his eyes again as they searched mine.

"Sorry," I apologized. "I just feel like I have so many questions that it's hard to know where to start."

Without judgment, Carter accepted this. "It's okay to question things."

I raised an eyebrow in disbelief. He met my reaction with a small laugh.

"It is," he tried to affirm me. "In the Bible, there are several examples of people questioning God, even Jesus' disciples, and it made Him mad!" His voice came out a dramatic whisper at the last part, and his face contorted in a silly twist of anger. I couldn't help but laugh, and as soon as he heard my giggling, I saw him relax.

"But real talk, Lena." He sat back up, serious once more. "I can tell you all day what I believe, but what do you believe?"

Hesitating for a brief moment, I heaved a deep sigh and shrugged. "I don't know."

"Sure you do," Carter pressed, leaning into our conversation even more. "Do you believe in Jesus?"

I nodded, and before I could say it verbally, Carter continued.

"Do you believe the Bible is from God?"

I nodded again, feeling slightly amused as he started to get fired up.

"That's half the battle!" he exclaimed. "You know you believe in God, you know who Jesus is, and you know the Bible is God's Word. Now all you have to do is trust in that and move forward from there."

"You're right," I told him, peering back into the dancing flames in front of me. For some reason though, I still felt held back. Sure, it was easy for Carter to move past his own misconceptions, but for me, there was more to it. I had felt alone for so long that it was hard to believe God hadn't abandoned me.

"Here." Carter leaned backward slightly, reaching his hand into the front pocket of his shorts. He fished out his phone and slid over to me. Abruptly, I felt his shoulder press against my own as he moved closer to show me his screen.

"This is an app you can download to read the Bible," he said, his phone illuminating in front of our eyes as pages of text popped up on his screen. "You can search for keywords or topics and have the Bible in your pocket."

I couldn't help but feel nervous and giddy all at once. With Carter sitting so close, I felt excited, but even more than that, I felt drawn to him just by hearing about how much faith he had. There was a time in my life when I felt the same way, and the more I witnessed his passion, the more I longed for that same sense of hope.

"I don't have my phone with me, but I can download it when I get back to my cabin," I told him.

Carter shoved his phone at me, placing it in my hands. "Here, put your number in my contacts."

I felt my hands trembling as I took his phone and hoped he couldn't tell. Trying to play it cool, I tapped the warm phone screen, and under "Add New Contact," I typed in my name and number.

"Here you go," I smirked as I handed the device over.

"Now, I'm going to text you tonight with your Bible homework," he instructed me, sliding his phone back into his pocket. "Don't forget."

"I won't forget," I told him, playfully rolling my eyes.

Carter shook his head. "It's not really about you downloading the Bible app. I'm happy to help you get started with scriptures, but you should read it for yourself."

His words took me by surprise. Carter was so different from other boys I had known. Maybe that was it, though. They were boys. Carter seemed refined and wise beyond his years, as if he somehow had all the answers.

Yet, his words ricocheted through my mind. *Read it for yourself.* There was a freedom in those four little words. I didn't have to trust him or believe what *he* said. I had to decide for myself.

"I'll text you some passages to help you find a good starting place," Carter added. "Not because I'm trying to tell you what to read, but because it's where I started to study, and I know you'll be able to find your own answers."

I was silent for a moment, merely taking in all he had said. Some part of me was in awe of Carter, just being able to know him and hear more about his story. The other part of me was starting to feel something much deeper than awe. I suddenly wondered how different my life would be if I had known him a few years ago. Especially my spiritual life.

I wondered if getting to know him sooner would have grounded me. I thought of how different this summer would have been if I never left the church or lost touch with Lou. Had I not carried the weight of my shame to camp, I would have arrived with the same hopeful spirit as the rest of the campers—the same heart full of hope that Carter had.

Climbing to his feet, Carter began to kick sand into the small fire. I watched the flame grow dimmer and dimmer until it was just a tiny flare hanging onto a burnt, ashen limb. Eyeing the limb closely, I wondered if that's how God had seen me lately: a once dancing flame alight with faith that faded into nothingness. For the last few years, I thought my faith had extinguished, but now I knew it hadn't. My faith had merely lay dormant.

"Can I get a ride back to camp?" I asked Carter as he patted the lingering embers until they faded away.

"Of course," he told me, as if it should have been obvious. "We both have to get to Devo."

Smiling, I stood up and made my way over to the golf cart. The passenger side was so familiar to me now that it almost felt like my very own seat. Once he made sure the fire was out, Carter found his place beside me and drove us into the cloak of night.

18

"Hey!" Jojo called out, finding me in the crowd after Devo ended. "Me and the guys missed you during free time earlier. How did your studying go?"

"Good," I told her without missing a beat. "I got some questions answered."

"That's awesome!" Jojo cheered. "Let's walk back to the cabin and you can tell me all about it."

She hooked her arm through mine as if it were something we did every day. Initially, I didn't think much of Jojo's friendship, but as time went on, our laughter filled the air and a warm feeling engulfed me, as if I had discovered a part of myself that was missing. I would always remember her as the girl who stood up for me on the playground. This summer, it seemed as though nothing had changed between us—Jojo was still standing by my side, even though years had passed.

"I've just had some Paul-related questions from my breakout sessions," I replied, trying to remain inconspicuous.

Tonight's Devo had been about the importance of obeying God and the necessity of rules. Adam used the example of David and Bathsheba. During the lesson, it occurred to me that Carter and I had broken camp rules by meeting alone together. Though nothing had happened, I worried someone may have seen us. The more I thought about it, I wondered if we really had broken any rules. After all, our conversation was centered around faith, which is what we were here for in the first place.

"Paul's example has always inspired me. Despite all that he faced in his life, he remained steadfast and obedient to God. I hope to be half the servant he was," Jojo shared. "One of my favorite verses he wrote was, *'Imitate me as I imitate Christ.'*"

My face lit up with a big smile, even though it was too dark to see. Jojo was the second camper I had met who connected to Paul's example of living life for Jesus. I'm not sure why it had never occurred to me before to actually open the Bible and search for answers instead of just closing it up and blaming God.

"Have you always believed in God?" I asked her.

Beneath the moonlight, I could make out a sliver of her face as she eyed me. Her voice was full of amusement.

"Do I breathe oxygen? Of course, I've always believed!"

We both laughed.

"Okay, okay, but what made you decide to act on it?"

Jojo didn't miss a beat. "I've gone to church my whole life, but it wasn't until my dad was diagnosed with multiple sclerosis that my faith felt solid."

Not expecting this, I frowned. "Your dad getting diagnosed with a disease helped you believe?"

She chuckled. "No, that came out wrong. My dad had struggled with his health for a while and no one could tell us what was wrong. Me and my parents prayed for a long time for Dad's health to improve, but instead of him being healed, we at least found out his diagnosis."

Still confused, I asked, "But your dad wasn't healed, how did that help your faith?"

"Even though we haven't had our prayers answered, there is a comfort in knowing what disease he has. My family worried for so long that when we finally figured it out, there was a plan of treatment and a way forward," Jojo confided. "Sometimes God doesn't answer our prayers in the way we want him to, and I learned that when His answer is no, it's not because He doesn't want to help me, it's just that God's plans are far better than any of mine."

Her words struck a chord with me as I thought about how I had done the very opposite. When I felt like God wasn't answering my prayers, I turned my back on Him in the way I assumed He was turning His back on me.

"'For my thoughts are not your thoughts, nor are your ways my ways, says the Lord,'" Jojo quoted. "Even though my prayers weren't answered how I hoped they would be, every day with my dad feels like a gift, and that's enough for me."

Her perspective was so pure and humbling. Though I didn't know her whole story, I could imagine just how painful it would be to wonder what's wrong with a sick loved one. Especially when I knew how painful it was to see a sick loved one struggle *knowing* what was wrong.

"I know how precious time can be," I replied. All I had left of my mom now were the memories we had made. The only thing I didn't know now is if I would ever see her again.

The lights from Girls Camp began to illuminate our path the closer we approached. As we made our forward, I could hear faint chatter coming from the cabins as campers prepared for bed.

I felt Jojo give my arm a gentle squeeze. "It's hard to know you have a sick parent, but in time, it gets easier, and I trust that God is working even though I can't see him. Dad's illness reminded our family just how precious and short our time here on earth is and that we need to make the most of it. God doesn't allow pain without allowing something good to come from it."

My heart swelled the more she shared her story with me. Jojo was so firm in her faith and didn't allow doubt or disbelief to creep in, no matter how hard things got. Her story both inspired and convicted me.

When we reached our cabin, I followed Jojo inside and into our room. She plopped down on her bunk and began collecting her bathroom bag as I sat across from her and removed my ankle boot. I flexed my foot, trying to alleviate the stiffness as Jojo drifted out to the bathroom.

Beside me, a buzzing sound caught my attention, and I looked over to see my phone light up right where I left it in my bunk. The screen showed it was just past ten o'clock, and to my surprise, I had several unread messages.

I opened the first and smiled.

> Daddy-O: Hey kiddo, remember I love U. Don't text back, I know U have rules 2 follow. Just missing U.

Between what Jojo had just shared about her dad and the fact that it had been over a week since I had seen mine, I was not going to leave him on read.

> Me: I love you. I'll call you when I can.

Opening the next, I knew exactly who it was from. My smile grew as I felt those butterflies fluttering in my stomach once more upon receiving a text from Carter. I selected the Add Contact button in the right-hand corner of the screen, entered *"Rosie"* into the Last Name line, and clicked Save. I opened the conversation and read:

> Rosie: Hey Dutch, here's your homework.

> Rosie: Read Luke 15:11-3 BC God wants YOU to come back to Him.
>
> Rosie: Matthew 26:53-54 BC Jesus could've called for 12K angels to destroy the world but He chose the cross for YOU.
>
> Rosie: Mark 15:17-20 BC Jesus died for YOU.
>
> Rosie: Matthew 27:46 BC Jesus bore all of OUR sins & felt alone & rejected - but He wasn't. It was part of God's plan for Jesus to defeat sin once & for all. ;-)
>
> Rosie: Read these verses & know how much God loves YOU.
>
> Rosie: #sorrynotsorry for blowing up your phone.

Hitting the Power button on the side of my phone, I watched the screen go black and then hurried to the bathroom to shower and get to bed. Jojo was brushing her teeth when I finished showering. She was already dressed in her matching kitten pajamas with her long, damp hair braided into the usual pigtails she wore.

"Do you think it will bother you if I read on my phone tonight?" I asked, squirting toothpaste on my toothbrush beside her.

She spit the last of her toothpaste out and wiped her mouth with the back of her hand, flashing me a quick, pearly-white smile. "Not a bit, I'll just roll over to face the wall."

"Thanks," I garbled through a mouthful of toothpaste foam.

"More Bible study?" she wondered, reloading her bathroom bag.

I nodded and Jojo smiled. There was something in her eye that caused me to pause. She caught me off-guard, gazing at me like a proud parent.

"What's up?" I asked, letting out a muddled chuckle.

Without a word, Jojo just grinned before tiptoeing back to our room. When I finished brushing my teeth, I threw on my pajamas and crept quietly back to my bunk. Jojo had been gracious enough to leave the light on for me, though she was tucked in for the night with her back to my bunk as she said she would be.

I hit the light switch off and slowly maneuvered myself into my sleeping bag until I was lying on my stomach. I turned my phone back on and searched the App Store to find the Bible app that Carter showed me earlier.

"I said a prayer for you tonight," Jojo's voice drifted over to me in the darkness. "I hope your study goes well. Good night."

"Good night," I whispered back. Knowing that someone was praying for me felt like being engulfed in a hug. I stopped praying a long time ago when I decided God likely wasn't listening to me anymore. After hearing Jojo talk about her dad earlier, I was beginning to feel catapulted towards change. I felt inspired by her faith but ashamed at myself by how easily I turned from God when it seemed like things weren't going the way I wanted. The more I thought about it, the more I wanted to make up my mind once and for all. That's when Carter's earlier comment returned to me.

Read it for yourself.

Following his advice, I opened the newly installed Bible app on my phone and began reading the scriptures he shared with me.

The very first heading in the Book of Luke sucked me into the story immediately as I began reading the *Parable of the Prodigal Son*. The parable described how a father's youngest son had been given a portion of goods, though he went off into a foreign country and wasted them. He was then impacted by a famine that spread throughout the land and had nothing left of his father's gift. Though he began to work feeding pigs, he was still suffering. He quickly became homesick, even to be a simple servant in his father's house.

The son became sorrowful, knowing he had sinned, and vowed to return to his father's house as a servant. Yet, when the son returned, his father welcomed him, wrapping him in the best clothes and serving up a feast to celebrate him coming home. As they celebrated the prodigal son, the older brother became jealous. He had remained with his father and been obedient to him. His father gave him reassurance that what he had done was right, but because his brother had been lost and was now found, reminded the son that this was a time of celebration.

I thought about what Carter had said about God waiting for me to turn back to him. *Would I be like the prodigal son in this case?* If I imagined it was me in the story, I pictured myself being welcomed back by God instead of being rejected. He would celebrate my return to him. The idea made my thoughts spin with joy as I hurried to the next section.

In Matthew chapter twenty-six, Jesus was betrayed by Judas, one of his apostles, who brought a mob to arrest Jesus. When another apostle, Peter, struck one of the men from the crowd with his sword, Jesus stopped him. Jesus commanded Peter to put his sword away and reminded him that He could easily pray to God to send for more than 12,000 angels to stop this. Yet, Jesus told Peter He had to go to fulfill the scriptures.

When I realized how Jesus so willingly went to the cross, knowing what He would endure, my heart sank. I hadn't been to church in a long time, but I knew Jesus died as a sacrifice for sins. Since I had never really studied the Bible on my own before, this was just one of the many aspects of Jesus' life I had never heard about.

Eager to keep going, I flipped to Mark chapter fifteen and felt a pang in my chest as I read. In this passage, the crowd mocked Jesus, clothing Him with a purple robe and placing a crown of thorns on His head. Then they beat and spat on Him before He was led to be crucified.

I didn't need to read on to know about the nails that had held Jesus to the cross. I could already feel the hot tears growing behind my eyes, knowing He had chosen that death so I could be forgiven of my sins.

Suppressing my tears, I scrolled to the last section of verses in Matthew chapter twenty-seven. I was surprised to read about Jesus asking why God had forsaken Him. I had never read this before, either. Carter had mentioned this was part of God's plan, but what did it mean? As I kept on reading through the end of the book, Jesus' question became obvious. Jesus' death fulfilled scripture, and those who witnessed His death realized Jesus truly was the Son of God. Jesus rose again and received God's promise that He would rule by His side in Heaven.

When I finished reading, the truth was staring me in the face. Jesus knew how it had felt to be rejected by those around Him, even those He loved and trusted the most. He obeyed and followed God's plan even though it led to His death on the cross. Jesus made the way for all of us to join Him in Heaven one day.

While I processed everything, I began to understand how both Carter and Jojo held onto their faith even when they faced their own difficulties. They had been through so much, but they trusted in God to keep His promises. They trusted because God had sent His only son to die for them, for everyone. *Even for me.*

When the realization hit me, the tears I had been holding back slid down my face. I opened up my texts to reply to Carter but paused. It was almost midnight now, and I didn't want to wake him. Considering the whirlwind of emotions within me, I knew I had to tell him I had read the verses he sent. Even more, I needed him to know how much they meant to me.

> Me: Hey Rosie, I finished my homework but you were wrong about one thing. I don't think I can ever understand God's love for me. It's more than I could ever imagine.

19

The next few days went by in a blur. When I wasn't on duty or between activities, I was reading my Bible. Using the notebook I received in my camp grab bag, I had filled it halfway full of notes in just a few days. With each book I finished, I rediscovered my love for learning. Growing up, I had always given my all in school. If there was a topic or subject I didn't fully grasp, I would dig until I understood. All the straight-A's I had earned in school truly were because of the work I put in. I just wished I had never let all my hard work fall by the wayside.

So far, I had read through the first four books of the New Testament and was making my way through the Book of Acts. I had never truly picked up the Bible to read through it like this. As I delved deeper into Jesus' mission on earth and the challenges He faced, my curiosity grew. Why would anyone choose to go through all He experienced on earth if He didn't love those He died for? Jesus didn't just say He loves us, He not only showed it, but He proved it by laying down His life to save the whole world.

While moving through the Book of Acts, I realized the first-century church Jesus had died to establish began. His disciples continued to face persecution as they worked to spread the Gospel. Though the work meant risking their lives, they never let up and were unashamed. As the Gospel began to move in those times, more and more people believed. I read about so many people who heard—Lydia, an Ethiopian Eunuch, a Philippian Jailer, just to name a few. Then I started reading about Paul's conversion myself. Everything was coming full circle for me.

As I read, I scribbled down questions and notes to refer back to later. Even though I went to church my whole life and heard a lot of what I was studying, I never really knew why I believed. I didn't know where my faith started or if I had ever truly developed a faith of my own. It was as if I had been wearing blinders all along and simply following the path that was laid out for me.

The problem with that was that I knew that wasn't enough. I couldn't ride someone else's coattails to get to Heaven. For most of my life, I had listened to my mom and followed her, but I was beginning to realize I needed to have my own faith. The more I connected my faith and belief in God to her, the more I wanted to leave it behind. After all, that's what she had done to me. But as I studied for myself, I realized just how wrong I had been in doing so. God had never abandoned me, it was me who turned my back on Him.

One of the accounts from the four Gospels that impacted me most was the story of Peter. I really connected with him. Peter was an emotionally reactive man. He was abrasive with a strong opinion and not afraid to get angry and lash out. When I read about Jesus inviting him to walk on the water and Peter sinking, it hit me how much I related to Peter.

For the last few years, my faith had tanked. In the end, I had been sinking deeper and deeper below the waves while Jesus waited for me to take His hand and come back.

After Peter denied Jesus, just as the Lord had told him he would, Peter repented and returned to serve Jesus. Not only had Jesus forgiven Peter, He had restored him, too.

One of the major Bible characters we had studied at camp was Paul, and I knew so many related to his example, but as I read about Peter, I felt like I was seeing his life come right off the page. I could understand his emotions, his questions, his fears, and even his confusion. What struck me most was how, despite everything Peter experienced, he still had faith big enough to drop everything to follow Jesus.

Peter's life was an example that I didn't have to be perfect. I didn't have to be the smartest person or say all the right things. I just had to be willing to stand back up when I was wrong. I had to have the iron willpower to keep going and never give up no matter how tough things became or how others tried to hurt me. Through all of this, Jesus loved him regardless of all his flaws.

Night after night, everything started to click for me, until I finally understood what Lou had told me the night I stormed out of Devo and what Carter had been saying this whole time. *It was never too late for me to turn back.*

When Friday night rolled around, I was in my bunk studying again when Jojo burst into our room.

"There you are!" she declared. "I've been looking for you!"

She startled me, and I jumped.

"I've been studying here all week during free time. What's going on?"

"You have to come with me. Right. Now," Jojo commanded as she attempted to catch her breath. *What was the hurry?*

The edge in her voice made me throw everything aside and follow her. Together, we bounded out of the cabin, hurrying down the path leading to the pool. We made our way up the ramp just past the women's locker room and rounded the corner, where a large crowd had gathered around the pool. A young girl was in the water with Adam while everyone watched them.

"Bridget has decided that it is time to make a change in her life!" Adam declared before the crowd. "She is done living a life for herself and is ready to follow Jesus!"

Bridget was a young girl, a few years younger than me, with short hair tied back in two small pigtails. Wearing a homemade tie-dye shirt from the Craft Cabin, she looked up at Adam with a heart full of joy.

"Bridget, I have one question for you." Adam grinned down at her. "Do you believe that Jesus is the son of God?"

Her smile only brightened as she declared, "I do believe."

Adam, without a second thought, reached out and took her shoulder, maintaining his radiant smile.

"Bridget, with your confession I now baptize you in the name of the Son, the Father, and the Holy Spirit for the remission of your sins."

In one fell swoop, Bridget closed her eyes and covered her nose as Adam quickly immersed her whole body beneath the surface of the water. Bridget resurfaced, drenched from head to toe, while Adam embraced her in a watery hug. As they made their way over to the ladder on the other side of the pool, Theo stepped out of the crowd and began to lead a song. Voices reverberated around me singing the words, "I have decided to follow Jesus."

As Bridget climbed out of the pool, the crowd transformed into a line to congratulate her for her decision. Lou emerged from the line with a large beach towel in hand to wrap around the young girl's shoulders. One by one, people lined up to embrace Bridget for her new life, unfazed by her being soaked from head to toe. As the song ended, the crowd parted, revealing Bridget's tear-streaked, tomato-red face.

Following that, Jojo stepped forward and joined the line to give Bridget a hug. Seeing the joy in the heavy night air brought tears to my eyes, but I held them back. All week, I studied how lives in the Bible were radically changed by following Jesus. Now, I was seeing it firsthand.

I didn't know Bridget, but I admired her for her decision. It was just a few minutes past nine and she made the decision to turn her life around. Seeing her be immersed in the water, I felt a sudden yearning to do the same.

As I watched Bridget and Jojo hug each other, Jojo whispered something to her and gave her another quick squeeze before traipsing back over to me. Jojo's bright pink shirt was damp from her hug, but she didn't seem one bit fazed by it.

"I'm so proud of her," Jojo gushed, returning to my side. "She's been studying with Hannah all week."

I scanned the crowd again and found Hannah standing by Lou, who surprisingly had her eyes on me. Lou waved and, despite the tears in her eyes, didn't miss a beat. She must have been close to Bridget too.

"Do you want to walk down to Devo with me?" Jojo asked, staring down at the watch on her wrist. "I think we're going to be starting a bit late tonight."

The crowd had thinned, but I still recognized other campers who hadn't yet made their way to the amphitheater. I glanced back at Jojo and her damp shirt.

"Are you sure you don't want to change first?" I asked, pointing to her front.

Jojo shrugged it off. "It's just a little water. Besides, I'm wearing someone's decision to follow Jesus and there is nothing wrong with that."

I smiled to myself, feeling another yearning pull from the water as Jojo and I marched across camp.

***

As always, Jojo found Denny in the small crowd of teenagers that had assembled for Teen Devo. Only a third of the expected crowd had arrived, and the atmosphere was lively with campers chatting.

Jojo sat beside Denny, who was too absorbed in arguing with Josh to notice her. From across the crowd, I saw Theo cheesing beside a girl with long mahogany hair. I chuckled. Two weeks ago, he was a loner at a bonfire; now he was openly flirting with a pretty girl.

"That's Katie," Jojo pointed out, following my gaze. "Theo's been head over heels for her for like three summers now."

"Really?" I asked in disbelief.

Jojo giggled. "He's never acted on his crush because Katie is one of Kelsey's best friends, but this summer might be different."

I glanced back at Denny, who was trying to disengage from Josh's conversation now that he knew Jojo was beside him. There seemed to be a common thread among the members of this friend group. Almost every one of them was carrying a torch for someone they had feelings for but didn't want to act on. A part of me wanted to just say something to Jojo and Denny right now, but I continued to bite my tongue. If Jojo was too scared of losing Denny's friendship, it wasn't up to me to push her.

"Sounds familiar," I discreetly whispered.

Jojo's head whipped back to me, curiosity flashing on her face. But before she could speak, someone jostled my arm.

Carter joined us, sitting down beside me, his gray shirt still damp from the hug he'd shared with Bridget. Jojo held up her hand to high-five him.

"My fellow hugger!"

Carter smiled, his expression skeptical, before returning her high-five.

Jojo sighed, "It was the only thing I could come up with to say that didn't sound weird."

Carter chuckled, pulling his shirt away from his chest to examine it. "You know, it's actually refreshing. I've been so hot all day. Maybe I'll just wear wet shirts from now on," he joked.

"Better not, my friend, take my word for it," Denny chimed in. He wore a weary expression on his face and Jojo chuckled at him.

"Nice to see you're alive, Dutch," Carter teased, leaning his shoulder into mine. "I feel like I've barely seen you this week. Still studying hard?"

"You already know that." I eyed him playfully. "I've been texting you all about it."

Before he could reply, Denny leaned over Jojo, his eyes fixed on Carter in bewilderment. "What did you call, Lena?"

Carter's laugh made me all flustered and embarrassed. It was a weird mix of emotions—I wanted to hide, but also secretly felt proud that people knew his nickname for me.

"It's just a name I gave Her Majesty for needing my chauffeuring services," Carter joked.

"Awwww," Denny teased as Carter waved him off.

"Don't worry, I'll take care of that for you," Josh whispered to Carter before punching Denny in the arm. Before I knew what was going on, Denny's teasing turned into groaning. Denny whipped his head up, glaring at Josh, who instantly broke into a sprint, running away from his payback.

Carter laughed, but Denny pointed his finger in warning, a small grin pulling at the corner of his mouth.

"I know where you sleep, man."

"I'll be waiting" Carter egged him on.

Just as their conversation heated up, a voice called out Carter's name from the left, and I noticed Riley with her friends waving him over.

"Come sit with us!" she beckoned. Beside her, I noticed Kelsey—Theo's sister—and another girl to her right waving him over, too. "We made a vintage paper fortune teller game, come play!"

Carter slumped beside me, his arms wrapped around his knees in a tense, self-protective pose. I couldn't read his mood—was he seeking comfort or hiding from something? The thought of him getting up to join Riley made my heart sink. Hadn't he been trying to avoid her?

"Come on!" Riley waved again. "You have to come try it!"

Just then, more campers began to stream in, having left the pool to make their way over. The crowd's louder chatter created an invisible wall, interrupting Riley's conversation attempt.

Carter struggled to catch her eye, his gaze repeatedly darting towards her as campers jostled around us. Meanwhile, Adam made his way to the front, sporting a dry change of clothes. But it was Carter's tortured expression, as he tried to engage with Riley across the crowd, that really caught my attention and held me captive.

A gap in the crowd opened and Carter motioned to where he was seated. "I'm going to sit here with Lena and the guys, I'll catch you later!"

At the sound of my name, I felt chills crawl up my arms. *Had he really just told her he was sitting with me?*

Riley tilted her head and squinted as if she hadn't heard him. He called out again, but she still looked puzzled. I glanced away, my face heating up in embarrassment. The more Carter tried to explain, the more awkward I felt.

Unable to take it any longer, Denny cupped his hands around his mouth and shouted, "HE SAID HE'S SITTING WITH LENA!"

I dropped my chin, trying to hide my face and shrink away. As Carter sat back down, his face matched the redness of my own. He shot Denny a warning glance, but Denny just shrugged before sitting back down beside Jojo.

"She couldn't hear you, so I was trying to help out," Denny defended himself.

My heart began to race as I grew more mortified by the minute. To my left, Carter tensed.

When Adam started the lesson, I breathed a sigh of relief, but my gaze snagged on Carter, still tense and stiff. I glanced back over at Riley, now slumped in the same spot with her head hung in defeat. Feeling a surge of empathy, my stomach twisted in response, and I swiftly moved away, careful not to draw any unwanted attention to myself.

I caught Jojo staring at me, and when I met her gaze, her raised eyebrow said it all. The unspoken question on her face was clear: *"What's going on?"*

In an effort to ease the tension, I shrugged and deliberately turned my attention back to Adam. Unable to focus on the lesson, I found myself stealing glances at Carter. As the evening wore on, I noticed Carter's shoulders loosen when he finally focused on Adam's preaching.

As Carter relaxed, I felt a sense of relief, though the tension between us was still palpable, fueled by Denny's outburst. At first, I was thrilled to be the one Carter chose to sit by, but seeing his reaction now had me reeling. I had no idea what was bothering him, especially since he'd tried to tell Riley the same thing Denny had. The rest of the evening passed by in a hazy blur, my mind filled with confusion as I sat in silence, anxiously waiting for the lesson to be over.

20

My second weekend at camp arrived faster than I had hoped. Friday night had seemed endless as I tossed and turned in my bunk. The more I wondered what I had missed between Carter and Riley, the harder it was for me to fall asleep. I was so embarrassed when Denny yelled at Riley, and I'm sure Carter felt the same way. What I didn't understand was why it had affected him so badly. *Had I done something?* I had never been this girl who obsessed over what other people thought, especially Carter. *So why was this bothering me so much?*

Just after five a.m. on Saturday morning, I heard my phone buzz from the bunk rail above my head where I kept it at night. When I opened the notification, a text from my dad became a welcome distraction.

> *Daddy-O: Hey kiddo! It's been 2 wks w/out U. Remember I love U and I'll C U soon.*

Reading my dad's message brought me back down to earth. Even though things between us had been tense before I left, I knew he loved me unconditionally. One of the things I loved most about Dad was his ability to show up for me, especially when I needed him most. After moving to Freeport, my dad would take me on his boat for "daddy-daughter dates." We'd have sandwiches, catch up, and just enjoy each other's company. It was simple, but those boat rides had meant everything to me.

I sent back a quick text to let him know I loved him back and then tried, once again, to doze off. When that plan failed, I sighed and stared up at the bottom of the top bunk above me. The last thing I wanted was to get out of bed early on my day off, but I knew there was one place that could make me feel more grounded and help me clear my head.

Just shy of six a.m., I ventured down the gravel path, the cool blades of grass still moist with morning dew beneath my feet. It was still early enough to see the moon and the sun making their silent exchange in the sky.

I tucked my phone into the back pocket of my jean shorts and buttoned the thin plaid long-sleeve I wore as the morning air sent a chill up my bare legs. The gravel path gave way to the lakeshore, where I slipped off my sandals and let the sand crunch beneath my feet. As I trudged along, my feet didn't sink into the sand as they did on the coast back home. Instead, the sand felt firmer and more rigid, with tiny rocks embedded that lacked the welcoming texture I remembered from the Carolina Coast.

I carefully made my way over to the dock, climbing up and then tiptoeing to the edge to sit down. As I balanced on the end, I dangled my legs over the side to gaze out at the water below. Though I was too high to dip my toes in the water, I was struck by the sight of my own reflection waving back at me from the surface.

My long, sandy hair cascaded down my shoulders, veiling my face as I stared. As I let out a yawn, the vast expanse of water before me had its usual profound effect, instantly calming my spirit and bringing me peace. I sat in silence, taking in the breathtaking view as the sun rose above the tree line. The sky transformed into a kaleidoscope of burnt orange, purple, and pink hues, a stunning display of nature's beauty. I wondered if God ever gazed down from Heaven, admiring the world He created.

When my stomach started growling, I got up and was about to head back to the cabin to see if Jojo wanted to grab breakfast together, but then I saw a runner coming through the woods. The closer he came to shore, the easier it became to recognize him.

Carter.

He slowed to a jog, then veered off his path, heading towards me. The usual butterflies in my stomach were replaced by a sudden jolt of electricity, leaving me feeling wide awake.

"Hey Dutch!" he called out to me, pulling out his earbuds. His sweat-drenched hair clung to his forehead, while the top of his t-shirt was soaked and clinging to his neck. As he approached, he used his shirt sleeve to wipe his forehead, then squinted at me beneath the sun's glare. "What are you doing all alone out here?"

Grimacing, I said, "I couldn't sleep."

Mirroring my expression, Carter wiped his forehead on his sleeve again. "I hate it when that happens."

"Me too," I agreed and settled back down on the dock's edge.

"Anything on your mind?" he pried, taking a seat beside me. I noticed he seemed like himself this morning, relaxed and at ease, his shoulders weightless as he waited for my response.

After seeing him so tense last night, I hesitated to answer him. I had a lot on my mind, but should I just unload it all on him? I imagined what it would be like to share my stewing thoughts with him.

Hey Carter, I've been thinking about my faith lately and missing my dad. I'm starting to think he was right about camp. Oh yeah, and last night was awkward... I'm still trying to figure out what happened. Did you feel embarrassed by me or is there something going on with you and Riley that no one knows about?

I stopped spiraling when his hand touched my shoulder. When I turned to face him, his eyes locked onto mine with a curious expression.

"Everything okay?" he asked, releasing his hand from my shoulder. I could still feel the warmth through my sleeve.

I didn't want to revisit last night, so I changed the subject. Crossing my legs, I forced a bright smile.

"Do you think Denny and Jojo will ever tell each other how they feel?"

Carter let out a deep sigh, throwing his head back in laughter. He stretched out his left leg, his smile growing as he squinted beneath the sun's rising rays.

"With those two, there's no telling. I've asked Denny about it but he insists they're *just* friends."

I cringed, thinking about how much it would hurt Jojo if she found out. Growing up, I admired my parents' love and longed for a similar relationship. Despite my mom's mistakes, I knew my dad still loved her and would wait for her no matter what. Jojo had the same tenacity I saw in my dad. My dad's broken heart lingered for years, a pain I wouldn't wish on anyone. I didn't want Jojo to suffer the same, especially since she deserved Denny's love. If only they could let go and lean into it.

"Has he ever said anything to you about her?" I asked him.

Carter flashed a coy smile. "Dutch, what kind of friend would I be if I shared Denny's secrets?"

I rolled my eyes and stared back out at the lake. "Secrets don't make friends, you know."

Carter laughed, releasing one leg as he switched to begin stretching the other. "I can't share Denny's business, but I really don't think I need to tell you the feeling is mutual for him."

My jaw dropped, and I released a groan. "Why can't they just get over their fear and be together already?"

Carter shrugged, switching to stretch out his arms. "They just haven't figured it out yet. I mean, when you think about it, they must really love each other to choose to be *just friends*. They never risk losing each other that way."

As he spoke, the flutter in my stomach returned. His eyes met mine, and I could feel his attempt to read my mind. Carter could read people without even trying, even me. That talent was a rare gift for someone so young.

"I hope they can get past their fear," I admitted. "We're all rooting for them."

Carter smirked, releasing his arm as he finished his stretch. "So, what about you? Any guys back home?"

"No!" I blurted out, my face suddenly burned with heat. Carter gave me a funny look, raising his eyebrows in surprise. Lowering my voice, I explained, "I just mean, I haven't dated in a long time. My last relationship kind of ended with my ex-boyfriend dumping me for one of my best friends."

"Ouch!" Carter flinched. "I'm sorry."

I shrugged and leaned back, casually stretching my arms. "I'm not, it was hard at first but I'm glad it happened."

Carter leaned over the dock, rubbing his arms, his eyes fixed on the water. I sensed a change in him, like last night but less intense.

"Just so you know, whoever this ex of yours is, choosing someone else over you is his loss."

My heart began to race as Carter's words hung between us, wrapping me in a surprising warmth.

"You don't have to say that." I tried to remain casual despite the fireworks exploding inside my chest. "I'm over it now. Everything happens for a reason, right?"

Carter nodded, and I noticed his smile tilt to one side.

"I think it does."

The air was tense as we sat in silence, and I couldn't help but feel as though there was some magnetic pull between us. Holding my gaze, Carter placed his hands below his thighs.

"I like spending time with you, Lena."

I gulped and felt my face flush as I heard him use my actual name. "You do?"

Carter nodded, his expression serious. "I don't know what it is, but now that all the baggage is out of the way, things just feel easy between us. I feel like I can be myself around you."

"Really?" I managed, my voice coming out a whisper.

Carter chuckled, but I detected a tremor in his voice as he nervously ran his hands through his hair.

"It's one of the reasons I think camp has been so much better this summer. I even want to spend more time with you, it's just..."

The hesitation in his voice hinted at the unsaid words that had kept me up last night. I could tell things were still awkward between us and I had a feeling I was right to be worried.

"It's Riley, isn't it?" I asked, trying to brace myself.

With a sigh, Carter avoided making eye contact and ran his hands down his face, a gesture I had come to recognize. "Riley and I were never serious. Even though we didn't go out for long, we had a bad breakup a few months ago and she's not over it. I just want to avoid any Riley-related drama this summer."

"I totally get it," I said, though my voice fell flat. My stomach churned when he admitted she was holding him back. I understood though, especially after seeing Chase and Camille go behind my back. Their betrayal felt like a knife to my heart. It wasn't just that I liked Chase and he chose someone else, but he picked my best friend and she never even said anything.

I turned to face him, trying my best to be brave though I felt anything but. "I know how hard and uncomfortable bad breakups are. Everything just feels covered in ick."

Carter laughed and began rubbing his hands through his hair.

"You should know that I enjoy spending time with you, too," I confessed, summoning all my courage to get the words out. "Even if it means we only see each other right here on the lake. I hope nothing changes."

A genuine smile spread across Carter's face, now shining with a mischievous twinkle. "Then we won't let it."

I extended my pinky, presenting him with a solemn vow on the tip of my finger.

"I promise to spend time with you, just like this, and it can be our little secret."

As our fingers intertwined, a warm smile spread across Carter's face, his eyes never leaving mine. "I promise. It'll be our secret."

I tried to pull back, but he held tighter, his expression appalled.

"Wait a second, Dutch." Carter kissed his fist after pulling our hands to his face, then pushed them back to me.

"You can't be serious," I laughed.

Carter's jaw dropped and he looked stricken. "I'm dead serious. A pinky promise is void unless you kiss and seal it. Come on, Dutch, everyone knows this."

I couldn't meet his gaze as butterflies fluttered wildly in my stomach. I kissed my hand and hastily pulled away. Turning back to the lake, I felt Carter's shoulder nudge mine. In an instant, I faced him and met his charming gaze. It was impossible not to notice the playful grin that appeared on his face and the faint blush that tinged his cheeks.

"What?" I asked, my voice still brimming with amusement.

Carter shook his head, though I saw him struggling to hide his smile as he gazed out at the water.

"I think the lake just became my new favorite place."

21

With each passing day at camp, I began to realize that time was slipping through my fingers. Carter's weekend was cut short when he got sick on Saturday evening. I hadn't seen him since he had been sent home. By Tuesday afternoon, I hadn't heard from him and decided to ask Denny if he had any news. I didn't want to bother Carter while he wasn't feeling well, but I also wanted to know how he was doing. I had seen him every day since arriving at New Hope, and the last few days had me worried.

"Must have been all those early morning runs," Denny joked as I followed him and Jojo to the canteen for snacks. "I told him he didn't have to train so hard for soccer this summer, but does he listen to me? No."

"He isn't contagious, right?" Jojo wondered.

Denny gave her a bemused grin. "He was dehydrated, not sick. As disciplined as Carter is, you would think he would remember to drink fluids like he's always preaching to the campers."

Jojo nudged him in the ribs, and I was thankful for her silent gesture to stick up for Carter when he wasn't here.

Denny let out a low moan and stared down at her, rubbing his side. "What? I'm just saying."

I chuckled quietly to myself. With the afternoon stretching out before me, I was determined to make the most of every minute I had to myself.

"Hey guys, I'll catch you later."

Jojo spun to face me as she stood with Denny in the growing canteen line. "Are you going to study?"

I nodded. "So much to learn, so little time."

Denny and Jojo began discussing which flavor popsicle they were going to get while I snuck to a shaded picnic table by the Dining Hall. The sun peeked through the branches above, rustling my hair with a gentle mountain breeze. I tucked loose strands behind my ear and used my shirt as a makeshift barrier to shield my phone. Since I worked in the kitchen, I wasn't too worried about using my phone openly, but I didn't want to attract attention since there were younger campers around.

Now that I knew what was going on with him, I decided to send Carter a text.

> Me: Can you confirm you're alive please?

I didn't know if he would see the message right away, so I was surprised when I sat my phone on the picnic table in front of me and it buzzed almost immediately. I felt a flutter in my chest and swiped the device back up to see one new message from him.

> Rosie: Please? Are you using manners with me, Dutch?

I grinned at his retort and sent a quick response back.

> Me: I know you're not feeling well so I can't tease you too much or you won't come back.

As I waited, my excitement built as three dots appeared on the screen as he replied.

> Rosie: Trust me, Dutch. When my mom decides to let me, I'll be back as soon as I can.

> Me: Feel better fast.

> Rosie: Keep my seat at our spot warm for me.

When I saw the phrase "our spot," I melted and imagined his smile, just like when he declared the lake as his new favorite place. I had been replaying that moment in my head since I last saw Carter. His smile. The way he looked at me. The sun shining on the water. Carter was right, the lake was becoming my favorite place, too.

"You're going to need to be a bit more inconspicuous with that phone if you want to actually hide it," a voice called above me. Seeing a shadow blocking the sun, I whipped my head up to see Lou.

"I'm just reading my Bible." I held up the phone to show her the open app I had yet to dig into.

Her eyes fell on the screen, registering her silent surprise. Lou said nothing but took a seat across from me. "How has that been going?"

I snorted. "Three weeks ago this was the last thing I would have imagined doing this summer."

Lou offered a sheepish smile, though she had a look in her eyes. "What changed?"

A memory struck me as I studied her. Just before her first rehab attempt, my mother sat at our kitchen table, her head bowed and hands fidgeting, to announce she'd be away for two weeks. The same haunted expression I'd once seen in my mother's eyes now gazed back at me from Lou's. I knew exactly what she was feeling.

Regret.

"I think maybe I just needed a different perspective," I finally answered Lou, recalling Carter's advice for me to hear her out.

"What have you studied so far?" she asked with genuine interest.

"I started out with just a few verses from the four Gospels before moving on to the crucifixion," I replied, trying to retrace my steps through the scriptures. "I learned a lot about Paul and Peter, and the other apostles. It turns out they were all just ordinary guys."

Lou grinned, though her eyes didn't quite hold their usual light. "They were quite the fallible followers, weren't they?"

I placed my phone on the table and leaned forward, folding my arms across my chest. "Imperfect, uneducated, completely unqualified, but Jesus still chose them to be the ones to build His church. It's been kind of impossible for me to not realize the truth..."

My voice faltered once I saw Lou's eyes well up. She gripped her hands together, her chin resting on them while her gaze drifted away.

"Lou, what's the matter?" I asked, wondering what I could have said.

She wiped at her eyes before turning back to face me. I watched again as she fought to choke back tears. "I'm just so incredibly happy to hear this."

"You are?" I asked bewilderedly. For someone crying happy tears, she looked anything but. "Lou, you don't have to cry. I still have a long way to go, but I'm trying to figure things out."

Lou pinched the bridge of her nose before she peered back up at me. "After all you've been through with your mom, I wasn't sure how this summer would impact you. But now, hearing that you're studying, I just..."

She choked up again as tears streamed down her cheek. After taking a deep breath, she regained control. After all she'd done for me this summer and all she'd likely endured all on her own, I couldn't sit and watch her break down. I climbed swiftly around the table and sat on the bench beside her. As I placed a steady hand on her shoulder, I said, "We can talk about it."

The moment I spoke, Lou's gaze snapped to mine. Her eyes were red from holding back tears, showing how much she was struggling.

"I owe you an explanation."

"Lou, it's okay—" I tried to empathize, but she motioned for me to stop.

I watched her take a deep breath and gather herself before her eyes met mine again.

"I've blamed your mom for a lot of things—"

"That makes two of us," I interjected, eyeing her as I owned my faults.

She winced and continued, "But you should know that I deserve some of that blame, too."

I released my hold on her shoulder and leaned against the table while Lou shared.

"The last time we all saw each other at the funeral, I lashed out at your mom."

"I remember," I frowned. The memory of their fight was still fresh in my mind. Witnessing their argument changed how I saw Lou for a long time, though I never imagined I would hear her side.

She frowned and looked down at her hands. "I had been so mad at her for years and I just unleashed everything that day. I wish you had never seen that side of me or heard me say all those horrible things to her."

Once more, Lou's regretful gaze met mine. Her vulnerability stood out in sharp contrast to her typical strength. She seemed so much like my mother in this moment, it was hard to see her like this.

"I was so mad at her for not being there when I needed her after our mom died and then everything with our dad happened so suddenly..." Lou's voice trailed off and her chin began to quiver. "I knew she had fallen away and stopped going to church, but I didn't know about the drinking until I saw her that day at the funeral."

"What is falling away?" I wondered, confused by the phrase. "How could my mom do that?"

Lou swiped at her runny nose. "That's a term used in church to describe people who turn from God."

It stung to hear her say that about my mom, but mostly because she wasn't wrong. My mom, a mere echo of her former self, was absent from everything, including church, as her addiction took over. Suddenly, it dawned on me that I had stopped showing up, too. *Did this mean I had fallen away?*

"Mom gave up on everything." My voice came out flat as I turned her words over.

Lou sighed and wiped at her eyes. "I know it can feel that way, Lena, but she's sick and has a long road ahead of her."

The impact of her words was immediate, causing tears to pool in my eyes and a single tear to silently stream down my face. In an instant, Lou's comforting touch swiftly wiped it away.

"Your mom was my best friend, and she broke my heart, too," Lou confessed, struggling against her emotion. "I'm so sorry for how much your heart has been hurting."

My voice cracked and I stared down at my hands in my lap, only to see Lou reach over to place her fingers in mine. It felt as though my vulnerability somehow empowered her to find her own strength.

"I'm so sorry that I've blamed you without knowing how much you were hurting."

"Oh, honey," Lou cried as she drew me in her arms, "you have nothing to be sorry about."

I sobbed against her neck, whispering, "I'm so sorry for all the pain mom caused."

Lou released me and took my quivering chin in her palm. "Don't be sorry, Lena. Nothing that happened between any of us is your fault." Our embrace tightened, a burst of warmth enveloping us, as her words brought a radiant smile to my lips and a surge of happiness in my chest.

"I just wish I hadn't lost so much time." Another sob escaped me. "I've spent so much time being mad at her, but where has it gotten me?"

Lou shushed me, trying to calm me down. She tucked my hair behind my ear and pulled me back against her, and I sank into her embrace.

"You're not alone anymore, Lena," she whispered against my ear as she slid her comforting hand over my hair. We sat there holding each other for a long moment before her words penetrated my heart. "The Lord has brought you exactly where you need to be."

22

After dinner, Jojo and I were back in line at the canteen with a craving for cotton candy, but when it was finally our turn, the woman at the window abruptly shut down the line and instructed us to immediately make our way to the pool. With wide eyes, Jojo gasped and did exactly as she was told. I was thankful to no longer be using my crutches as I hurried behind Jojo making a mad dash to the pool. The moment we entered through the gate, we were met with a bustling crowd, forcing us to push our way through to get a clear view of the watery scene below.

"Do we do this every time there is a baptism?" I leaned over to Jojo on my right. She nodded and joined in singing the lyrics to "I Surrender All" with everyone that had gathered around. Asher was leading the crowd in one hymn after another. The area was filled with the resonating echoes of singing campers as the setting sun cast a stunning glow of violet, orange, and magenta behind the trees.

"If you can imagine, this is exactly how the angels in Heaven rejoice when someone gives their life to Jesus. Why would we celebrate any differently?" Jojo pointed out in between songs.

The crowd parted suddenly, and I instantly recognized the girl entering the pool with Adam behind her. She was the girl I saw Theo sitting with at Devo one night. Katie.

Before she was immersed in the water, Katie made her confession that she believed Jesus was the Son of God. As she rose through the surface of the waters, she was no longer the person she used to be. Over the past week, I had studied the Bible, going over countless examples of people who decided to follow Jesus. The first sermon delivered by Peter in the Book of Acts resulted in an incredible response, with a crowd of three thousand choosing to be baptized and committing themselves to following Jesus. Katie, too, had followed the same pattern to leave her old life behind.

I watched as she climbed the ladder to exit the pool and found that Riley was there to meet Katie with a towel. For once, I felt my heart warm towards her as she embraced her friend. Behind Riley, I watched Theo emerge, pushing through the remaining campers to reach Katie. Theo cradled her head in his hands and cupped her face, smiling down while they talked excitedly to each other. The sight of the two of them almost distracted me from another camper who was climbing into the pool where he, too, was baptized.

One by one, other campers followed until a total of four teens had made their way into the pool to become Christians. They fearlessly and proudly proclaimed their devotion to Jesus, ready to surrender everything to Him. Each person exited the pool, and I witnessed the heartfelt reception they received from those who were proud of them.

The last girl who came out of the water caught my attention. She was climbing out of the pool when I noticed that her mother, father, and two younger siblings were present. It suddenly occurred to me that her entire family had made the conscious choice to travel all the way to the camp just to witness her baptism. They took turns hugging her, and a rush of emotions engulfed me like a tidal wave.

Tears welled up in my eyes as I watched the camper's mom lovingly kiss her forehead and put a warm towel around her shoulders. I tried my hardest to fight the tears back as the crowd began to disperse to congratulate the four new brothers and sisters in Christ. It caught my attention that a small group of people had gathered around Katie and Theo, who remained in each other's arms. Despite the ongoing celebration, time seemed to slow down for me. My knees buckled beneath me, and a heavy lump lodged itself in my throat.

"Hey, let's go get in line," Jojo started to pull me forward but stopped once she gazed at me. "Lena, are you okay?"

I forced myself to hold the tears back and smile so she wouldn't worry. "You should go, I'll be right there."

Jojo eyed me warily, her eyes still searching mine. Though she seemed uncertain, she quickly gave in. "Okay, come over when you're ready."

Once she had joined the others, I quickly made my way out of the pool area and managed to slip through the gate without drawing any attention. The moment my feet made contact with the gravel path, a wave of pent-up tears broke loose. For the last few days, I had felt so ready to make the same decision I witnessed those four campers make tonight. Yet, seeing the family that had come together at the pool tonight just made my heart break all over again.

In a rush to distance myself from everyone, I quickly made my way up the path that led back to my cabin. I sprinted up the stairs and through the front door, where I collapsed onto my bunk and unleashed a torrent of uncontrollable sobs. For several minutes, I remained still on my sleeping bag before mustering the strength to pull myself up to walk to the bathroom. I couldn't risk Jojo coming in and seeing me like this.

I pulled a few paper towels loose from the dispenser by the bathroom sink and blew my nose. As I glanced at my reflection in the mirror, all I could see was my red, tear-stained face. Though the sight made me want to cry more, from a distance, I heard the familiar creak of the front door opening and instinctively ran into the first bathroom stall to hide. I locked the door, then sat down on the toilet, just as I heard footsteps echoing across the cold floor.

"Lena? Are you in here?" Jojo called out.

Trying my best to clear my throat, I replied, "In here!"

At once, I heard her footsteps tap across the floor until she was just outside the stall. "I just wanted to make sure you're okay."

The concern in her voice made it harder to hold in my tears. Jojo cared about me, I knew that without question in the way she looked out for me by covering my kitchen duties and staying at camp on the weekends so I wouldn't be alone. But right now I wasn't okay, and the only way I knew how to pull myself together was to just be alone.

"I'm fine," I croaked. Thinking quickly for an excuse, I added, "My stomach just started to hurt all of a sudden."

"Oh." I heard her voice fall. "Is there something I can get you?"

"No," I objected. "I'll be okay, I think I'll just need to lie down."

"Okay," Jojo said. Despite the lingering worry in her voice, I could tell she believed my story. "If you change your mind and do need anything, just send me a text and I'll be right back."

"Thanks, Jojo."

Her sudden turn on her heel caused her shoe to squeak on the tile, and I listened while her footsteps faded away. Once I heard the front door close, I leaned back against the stall and allowed my tears to flow freely once more.

***

The next morning, I opted out of the breakout session and hid at the lake. I pulled the zipper of my hoodie all the way up and leaned over the edge of the dock, relishing the sensation of the crisp morning breeze against my skin. As I gazed out at the water, I attempted to shake off the lingering thoughts that were still haunting me.

Last night, I tossed and turned in a restless sleep before finally waking up for breakfast duty. The entire morning was spent going through the motions, as I was feeling deflated and out of sorts. Just when I thought I was making real progress, the sight of one happy family instantly brought back all the pain that I had been struggling to bury for over a year.

For the first time, last night I felt the weight of being lost. After watching four other campers make their confessions before the entire camp and God Himself, I walked away feeling more broken than I ever had. The truth was right there in front of me. I had studied the scriptures and I knew what I had to do, but all it had taken was a single moment to set me back off course.

What kind of Christian could I even be if the sight of a happy family caused me to doubt myself? How could I focus on living a life for God when all I could think about was how much my heart hurt? God deserved my whole heart, not a broken one.

The sound of fast footsteps on the dock behind me pulled me to attention. As Carter approached, I couldn't help but notice the visible relief on his face. The last time we had seen each other, I had been in a completely different head space. Even though I was thrilled to lay eyes on him again after the last few days apart, I felt like a mess and I didn't want him to see me like this.

"I found you!" he exhaled, taking a seat on the edge of the dock beside me. As I watched him sweep his windblown hair out of his eyes, I couldn't help but feel my stomach do somersaults, just like it always did when he was near.

"You're back," I greeted, putting on a brave smile. I sensed Carter's gaze on me as I looked out at the lake and felt the pressure to make small talk. "Are you feeling better?"

Brushing the blowing hair from my face, I caught his eye, and in that instant, I could tell he was onto me.

"I'm feeling better, but I think there's something bothering you."

I gulped, and though I wanted to change the subject, I knew it was no use. For the short amount of time I had known Carter, he had figured out how to read me like a book.

"Is it that obvious?"

Carter slid over so his left thigh was touching my right one and stared down at me. "It's obvious when you've skipped the breakout session where I thought I would find you."

Beneath my long curtain of hair, I met his gaze. I wasn't up to talking or being interrogated for skipping this morning's breakout session but, a part of me felt guilty for breaking camp rules. "Is Adam upset?"

Carter shrugged, keeping his eyes on me. "I don't know. I drove by but didn't see you, so I came straight here hoping to find you, and voilà."

My stomach sank as I imagined just how much trouble I would be in when Lou found out I had decided to skip this morning's class. The conversation we had shared had left me feeling incredibly fragile, and I didn't want her to see just how much it affected me, how my shame and guilt from the past were slowly but surely crushing me. I didn't want anyone to know that the hurt in my own heart was causing me to doubt if I could truly follow God for good this time. The fear of failing all over again was holding me back. When I thought of how much trouble I would get into for skipping the breakout session, a lecture was the last thing I needed with everything on my mind.

"What's going on, Lena?" Carter pressed, his eyes focused on me.

At the mention of my name, I felt the heat behind my eyes again. *Could I even cry anymore?* I was confident my tear ducts were empty after last night, but the more I tried to hold them back, the larger the lump in my throat grew. While I fought to keep my emotions at bay, without pause, Carter slid closer and threw his arms around me. I let him hold me as he cradled my head against his chest.

"Talk to me," he whispered, his voice a soothing hum. "Tell me what's going on, Lena."

I shook my head against his shirt, feeling the soft material beneath my tear-stained face. All that made him do was hold me even tighter, and we sat there for several moments until I found the strength to compose myself.

Carter broke away first, but made sure to keep a steady hand on my back. "Whatever is going on, you can tell me."

Wiping at my nose, I peered up at him and felt his soft thumb brush away the tears from my chin. His chocolate eyes filled with tenderness.

"E-everything just feels wrong again," I cried, and when I looked into his eyes, the truth tumbled out of my mouth. "My mom really hurt a lot of people and I've been trying to do better but it's always one step forward and four steps back."

"Whoa, whoa, whoa, hang on. What happened after I went home this weekend?" Carter's gaze was filled with confusion and concern.

With a deep breath, I sighed and explained how Lou and I had talked. I opened up about hearing her side of things, and how she had been so angry with my mom at my grandfather's funeral that they had their blow-up.

"All I could think about was how guilty I've been feeling over everything," I confided in him. "I blamed Lou for my mom's addiction because I thought it had been from their fight, but how could I have been so blind?"

Carter remained silent, unwavering as I continued. "When my mom got sick, everything seemed to unravel from there. All I had to do was reach out to Lou, but I didn't. I just fell down into this dark abyss and just let myself keep sinking."

He touched my back again, as if transferring his strength to me while I wiped at my tears.

"You know what the worst part of it all is though?"

Carter raised his eyebrows, waiting for me to share.

Staring out at the waters in front of us I shook my head, the feeling of disappointment hitting me again. "Because of this whole misunderstanding, I drifted away from Lou and destroyed my relationship with God."

I felt his hand slip from my back while he straightened, and Carter narrowed his eyes. "You can't say that, Lena."

"How can I not?" I protested, my brows furrowing. "You don't get it, Carter. Even though Lou was hurting, she went to God. My family basically abandoned her, but she never turned her back on Him, and what did I do? I completely turned away from Him, and the more I want to run back, the more I feel like I'm just going to fail all over again."

Carter leaned in close, and I was surprised to hear an edge of amusement in his voice. "Have you not figured it out yet?"

"What?" I asked, brushing the back of my hand across my wet face.

Carter's eyes softened and he grinned. "You are never too far from God."

I stared into his eyes, feeling his words come over me like a warm blanket.

"What's the most famous verse of the Bible?" Carter asked, as if he were onto some great idea.

"John 3:16?" I asked, unsure of my answer.

Grinning, Carter nodded. "What does it say?"

"For God so loved the world that He gave His only begotten Son, so that whoever should believe in Him should not perish but have everlasting life," I answered.

"Exactly!" Carter exclaimed. "Lena, don't you get it yet? God gave His only Son because He loves you and wants you to choose Him. That's how simple the Gospel is. You don't have to complicate things, you just have to make the choice."

Deep down, I still couldn't shake my doubts. There was this thought stuck in my head that I just wasn't enough and didn't have what it takes to be who God wanted me to be.

"What's holding you back, Dutch?" Carter questioned. When my eyes met his, the look he gave me signaled a plea for me to reach out and grab the lifeline he was holding.

"My heart just hurts and I know I'm just going to fail," I whispered, shame filling me once again.

"Is that it?" he asked, still sounding amused. "God doesn't expect you to be perfect. We all fall short sometimes, Lena."

"You don't understand," I cried, still pushing against the idea. "I can't fully give God my heart. It's too broken right now. He deserves my full heart and someone who can fully surrender and dedicate their life to Him."

Carter slid closer and reached over to take my chin in his hands. He leaned in, slowly inching towards me, causing my heart to start beating so rapidly I thought it would jump from my chest. "Give God the broken pieces of your heart, Lena, and *He* will put it back together."

As soon as he said the words, he let go. I didn't even feel the disappointment of an almost kiss as his words finally struck a chord within me.

"You think it's that easy?" I wondered.

Carter scoffed and threw up his hands. "Yes! I know you've been studying, and if your fear of pain and disappointment is all that's holding you back, then that's all the more reason to make your decision."

I sighed, "I just don't think I'm ever going to feel good enough to follow God."

Carter laughed incredulously. "Who does?"

I could see the care in his eyes, and it made me want to reach out and throw my arms around him.

"Do you think Paul felt good enough to follow the Lord after killing and persecuting Christians?" he asked. "What about Judas? Jesus knew Judas would betray Him, but he still allowed Judas to serve with Him."

As he gave me more examples, I began to realize the point he was trying so hard to make. God didn't need perfect disciples. He just needed those with an open and willing heart to choose him and carry out his mission to tell others the Gospel.

"You know that Jesus took the most unlikely men to follow Him to build His church." Carter preached. "Then God allowed Jesus' blood to be shed for all of us, but he had you in mind, Lena. Don't you think God knows what you've done?"

Without hesitation, I agreed with him, feeling my spirit rise with the truth he spoke to me.

"God knows what you've done, Lena," Carter pleaded with me. "He knew you would fail and fall short and he made a way so that you can overcome your mistakes. All God wants is your love and obedience so you can be with Him in Heaven one day. Do you believe that?"

I gulped, knowing just how much weight my words carried. "I do."

After I confessed, Carter's face lit up with relief. "Then if you believe that God loves you and wants you to choose and obey Him, what are you waiting for?"

As soon as he asked me that, I realized I had no confusion and no more doubts. I didn't have to complicate things with my excuses or feelings. All I knew was I wanted to be rid of the guilt and the pain I had carried for so long. I wanted to know the joy that others knew when they made the decision to follow Jesus. It was time for me to be free of my past and allow God to give me the fresh new start I desperately needed.

Seeing the steady reassurance in Carter's eyes, I knew exactly what I needed to do and realized it was finally time. He stared back at me expectantly, and I knew I was tired of waiting.

I climbed to my feet and motioned for him to stand and follow me.

"I'm ready, let's go."

23

"Throw this on," Jojo instructed, as she offered me one of her tie-dye shirts. "You need a top that isn't see-through."

I took the shirt from her without protest and began to change. She and Denny had been on their way to run an errand when Carter and I found them outside our cabin, climbing on the four-wheeler. As soon as Carter told them about my decision to be baptized, Jojo jumped off the ATV and flung herself into my arms. Denny immediately left to spread the word while Jojo ushered me back to our room to help me get ready.

As I finished changing into gym shorts and Jojo's shirt, I kept thinking about the examples I had read in the Bible of those who had made the same decision that I was about to. None of them had hesitated. Once they heard the good news, they went and obeyed immediately. Those stories made me realize just how much time I had wasted following my own thoughts and feelings, and I didn't want to keep waiting. All I had needed was someone to share the truth with me and give me a gentle nudge in the right direction.

"I'm all set," I told Jojo, sliding my feet into my flip flops. She was grinning from ear to ear and released an excited squeal before embracing me for the millionth time.

"I can't believe you're really doing this!" she exclaimed, wriggling me back and forth in her tight grip.

I returned her hug and chuckled excitedly. "I don't want to wait anymore."

Jojo pulled back suddenly with wide eyes, still gripping my arms, and announced, "We have to go tell Lou."

She didn't allow me to answer before she dragged me back outside. Carter was still sitting on the golf cart, waiting exactly where we left him. He grinned when he saw me and I felt my cheeks flush.

"Are you finally ready?" he asked eagerly, sitting up where he was seated.

I didn't get to answer before Jojo interjected, "We have to find Lou first."

Carter glanced from Jojo to me before he agreed, "Yeah, we should go get her."

"I'm okay if it's just us," I protested, eager to get to the pool. Every second that ticked by felt like time slipping away through my fingers. I didn't need a show or a large crowd around me, I just wanted to be a Christian.

"Lena," Carter peered at me from his seated position. Leaning in, he spoke with a serious and inquisitive tone. "Don't you think Lou wants to be there to support you? Considering everything you two have been through?"

As Carter offered up the idea, I could feel the conviction in his voice, and I knew he was right. The last time Lou and I saw each other, we held each other tightly, crying and holding on, as if trying to make up for all of our lost time. She knew my heartbreak because it had been her own. If there was anyone I needed there to stand beside me while I gave my life to the Lord, it was Lou. Putting aside our shared hurt, Lou had helped make a way for me to come to camp and find my way back to God. Considering how God used different people in the Bible to fulfill His plans, I wondered if Lou played a similar role in helping me get to camp this summer.

Without bothering to argue further, I hurried around the golf cart and climbed into the passenger's seat. I reached over to turn the key for him while Jojo slid into the back seat at full force. Carter stared back at me as if I had lost my senses.

"What are we waiting for?" I demanded, staring back at him. "Let's go find Lou."

***

Luckily, we didn't have to go far before we found Lou in the Dining Hall. Jojo and I burst through the front doors and stopped once we realized there was some sort of meeting going on with a few of the camp directors.

"Hey girls," Lou waved when she spotted us entering the front door. "Is everything okay?"

"Can we borrow you please?" Jojo waved her over.

Lou looked back at the man leading their meeting and held up her index finger for him to give her a minute. She hurriedly crossed the room and stared from me to Jojo and back.

"What's up, girls?"

I opened my mouth to answer, but Jojo squealed over me, "Lena wants to get baptized!"

Though she stole my chance to share my news, I couldn't be mad at Jojo. She was so excited for me. Lou's gasp made us both turn our heads, and I watched her hands fly to her face in disbelief before she wrapped her arms around me. Lou suddenly pulled back to look me in the eyes.

"Lena, are you sure?"

"I promise, I'm so sure about this," I replied without question, holding her forearms in my hands.

She grinned as she let me go. "I'm so proud of you! Do you mind if we go out on the porch for a few minutes and just chat about this?"

For a moment I felt my heart sink at the further delay, but I imagined if I argued, making it to the pool may take even longer. I agreed and pushed back through the front door as Lou quickly tip-toed back to the group of directors. Jojo followed me onto the porch as we found Carter still waiting with the golf cart running.

"Is she in there?" he asked us, squinting beneath the afternoon sun.

"We found her," I informed him. "Lou and I are going to talk for a few minutes though."

The door opened again as Lou met us outside. When she found Jojo, Carter, and me waiting, Lou marched to the edge of the porch and held out a key ring to Carter.

"Do you mind going to the pool to get things ready for us?"

Not missing a beat, Carter climbed out of the golf cart and took her keys before offering an obedient salute. He hopped back in the seat and backed the cart up.

"I'll see you in a bit!" he vowed, glancing over at me. I offered him a small wave as he raced up the gravel drive to the pool.

"Come sit," Lou offered, patting one of the Adirondack chairs on the porch. Jojo took a seat on the arm of Lou's chair as I took the empty chair beside them. "I just want to talk through your decision with you."

"Okay," I answered, my voice suddenly shaky. "Where should I start?"

Leaning forward with her elbows on her knees, Lou began. "I know you and I had a talk the other day, and it wasn't an easy one."

"No, it was not," I agreed, remembering our tearful conversation.

Lou's eyes softened. "But you mentioned you had been studying, and all I want to talk about is what you've learned and how you came to your decision."

Jojo looked at me with an encouraging smile. "We want to support you and see if you have any lingering questions, this is a big decision."

When I met her gaze, I felt this wave of nostalgia hit me, and I felt overcome with gratitude for her. As children, she offered me support on the playground when we were being bullied by boys, and now, in one of the most crucial moments of my life, she was by my side once again. I couldn't believe I had ever thought I was alone.

"I started reading last week about Jesus' sacrifice on the cross," I shared with them. I explained that I read about how Jesus was betrayed and left alone on the cross to die for the sins of the world to offer us hope. Then, I explained how the Apostles built the church and dedicated their lives to spreading the Gospel.

"There are so many examples of people who heard the Gospel and chose to follow Jesus," I finished. "I'm ready to do the same."

Lou beamed. "I love that, it sounds like you've read your Bible."

I looked from Lou to Jojo and couldn't shake the feeling that I was missing something.

"Do you know what it means to become a Christian?" Lou asked me, point blank.

Pursing my lips, I tilted my head and stared at her curiously. "Are you asking if I know what it means to follow Jesus?"

Lou turned to face me more directly. "I mean, do you understand the commitment you're about to make?"

Still feeling unsure, I asked, "That I'm going to commit to follow Jesus for the rest of my life?"

"Yes!" Jojo cheered. Lou cut her eyes to her and smiled sheepishly before turning back to me. "When you make your confession, you're declaring that Jesus is the Son of God and that you believe that with your whole heart."

"I do, I do believe that," I replied, eagerly, not fully understanding her obvious hesitation.

"I'm glad you do, Lena. When you're in the water, it's like burying your old self. The old you is put to death, which is symbolic of Jesus' death on the cross," Lou explained further. "When you rise up, you'll be a Christian, which is symbolic of when Jesus rose from death. Your old life will be gone and you'll have a fresh, clean slate."

As she explained, I felt a sense of peace but even more eager. I had no desire to continue living the way I was. The more I realized why Jesus had been crucified, the more I understood that the things that led Him to the cross could never satisfy me.

"I understand," I spoke sincerely. "I'm ready to live a life in service to God because it's the least I can do for all He's done for me."

"This is a lifelong commitment, Lena," Lou told me. "You won't live it perfectly, but think of the Lord as a shepherd, and you are one of His sheep. If you start to wander off, remember that He is always there to bring you back to His flock."

I looked from Jojo to Lou. "I know life is hard sometimes, but I have faith that God will see me through. I can't prove it, but I don't think coming here this summer was a coincidence."

Just then, Jojo reached out to take my hand in hers, smiling through misty eyes. I squeezed her hand back and continued to pour out my heart. "God sacrificed His only Son to die for me. Jesus could have asked for God to destroy the world, but instead, the love He has for me kept Him on that cross. Not the nails. How can I not give my life back to Him? It's the very least I could do."

I paused and watched Lou's chin quiver as she fought back more tears. Jojo's hand suddenly dropped from mine as Lou closed the distance between us and pulled me into a tight embrace. When she pulled back, I felt her lips on the side of my head as she whispered, "I love you, Lena. I love you, I love you, I love you."

"I love you, too," I cried. Jojo quickly joined in, throwing her arms around me, and the three of us sat in one large hug. We stayed that way for a few moments before I felt the tightness of their hold on me. "Okay guys, it's getting hard to breathe."

Hearing my wheeze, they released me and we all climbed to our feet. Jojo wiped her eyes and took my hand again.

"Is it time?"

With a smile, I nodded. "Let's go."

Lou took my other hand as we finally made our way to the pool.

***

I heard the singing before we reached the pool's gate. My footsteps slowed to a stop as the voices began to harmonize.

Tho' none go with me, I still will follow... The song lyrics drifted towards me. All at once, it hit me, and I gasped, causing the others to turn.

Jojo was the first to spot my reaction. "Come on, Lena."

I looked to Lou, who eyed me curiously, and pointed. "Do you guys hear that?"

Jojo chuckled. "Do you mean the singing?"

My eyes grew wide. "Is that for me?"

Lou stepped forward and stretched out her hand to me. "Everyone is here for you."

As soon as she said it, I felt as if I were having my first out-of-body experience. Everything that came next just felt like one huge blur. Lou led me and Jojo through the pool gate, and the sight of the singing crowd took my breath away.

My cross I'll carry, 'til I see Jesus.

As I made my way around the pool, I spotted Theo and Katie in the large group, the two of them smiling while they sang along.

No turning back, no turning back.

When I reached the ladder, Denny stretched out a hand to help me into the pool, and then I saw him. Carter was standing in the water as the sunlight glowed around him. He grinned at the sight of me and lifted his left hand to usher me to come in. I kicked off my flip flops as Denny kept a hand on my arm. When I lowered myself into the water, I felt its warmth envelop me as my toes slipped beneath the surface. Under the summer sun, the water felt like a warm bath as I waded out to Carter.

The world behind me, the cross before me.

I was so nervous as the chorus around me came to a halt and Carter reached out a wet hand to pull me towards him. He held a hand on my upper back and began speaking to the crowd surrounding us. I tried my best to focus on his words, but everything felt so surreal.

The crowd around me fell silent as I gazed into Carter's rich brown eyes staring back into mine.

"Lena, do you believe that Jesus Christ is the Son of God?"

I smiled as I remembered our earlier conversation on the dock. I recalled just how easy declaring the truth seemed then. Now, I felt a pitter-patter in my heart while he waited for my answer. Not because of Carter, but because I knew that once I made my confession, I wouldn't be alone anymore. I knew I would never be forsaken, unloved, or left behind. I knew if I lived for Jesus, I could meet Him one day, and He'd greet me with open arms.

Without letting one more moment pass me by, I declared my faith.

"I do."

Carter's eyes shone as the sunlight reflected off the waves dancing around us. "Lena, upon your confession, I baptize you in the name of the Father, the Son, and the Holy Spirit for the remission of your sins."

He instructed me to hold my nose as he gathered me in his arms. I took a deep breath as he immersed me fully beneath the water. Beneath the surface, I felt the warm waters embrace me, momentarily becoming weightless as I buried the girl I had once been.

No turning back, no turning back.

I heard the roar of water in my ears and the singing beginning again as Carter lifted me up through the surface. I gasped, taking the first breath of my new life. Before I could wipe the hair from my face, I felt Carter pull me into a soaking wet embrace. All I felt was joy coursing through my body as I realized everything had changed. The life I once knew was over. I was mine no more.

As Carter locked me in his embrace, I heard him whisper in my ear, "You did it, Lena. You did it."

He clung to me, his hand on the back of my head pressing me into his shoulder as the waters lapped around us. I heard him continue whispering, "You did it, I'm so happy for you."

Before he pulled away, I felt his warm mouth against my ear as his lips left the gentlest kiss on the side of my head. Carter finally released me, and I met his gaze once more. He was beaming with pride, completely unreactive to the kiss he just gave me. Taking my wet hand in his, he led me back up through the waters to the ladder where Denny still waited for me.

When I took Denny's hand, he practically pulled me back up the ladder into a bear hug. The water soaked me, dripping into a puddle around me as my wet clothes clung heavily against me. When Lou found me, she wrapped a warm beach towel around my shoulders before pulling me into her arms.

"I'm so so proud of you, honey," she said. "I could never be more proud of you."

I felt the weight of her words more profoundly than I had before. When she pulled back, I realized we both felt the freedom we now shared. She wasn't just my Aunt Lou, but also my sister in Christ.

The rest of the day was met with a joy I had never known before. I knew how it felt to have a small group of friends, but this was different. I had never known what it was like to belong. Everywhere I went, I was met with congratulations from others and embraced by campers I had never met before.

During dinner, Theo came into the kitchen to find me. "It was almost impossible to get through to you back at the pool, so I figured I would wait until now."

Before I could prepare myself, Theo pulled me into a small side hug before he disappeared to have dinner with Katie. The two of them seemed cozier than before and I wondered if he finally told her how he felt. I would bet that Theo was well on his way to asking Katie to be his date to the Banquet.

Later, when I was headed to the amphitheater for Devo, Lou intercepted me. "I have something for you, come with me."

I followed her to her SUV, where she retrieved a small black box from the backseat. She handed it to me, and as I looked down at the box, I noticed the words HOLY BIBLE on the front. When I lifted the lid, I discovered a leather-bound Bible. On the cover, in the bottom right corner, I gently ran my fingers over my name engraved in gold letters: LENA HARRIS.

"Lou, I can't believe you did this!" I exclaimed.

Her eyes danced as she looked at the book in my hands. "Everyone should have a Bible of their own."

I dropped the box back into the seat and threw my arms around her. "I can't thank you enough for all you've done for me."

Releasing me, she brushed her hand over my hair. "I can't even begin to describe how much having you here this summer has meant to me."

"I know how you feel," I agreed.

Lou gave me a gentle nudge, shaking off our emotional moment. "Alright, well get down to Devo before I start crying again."

I gave her hand a gentle squeeze and picked my new Bible back up. As I found my way across the field to the amphitheater, I smiled when I spotted my friends. For the first time all summer, I finally felt like one of them.

Before I took a seat, I spotted Carter lingering near the back with his feet propped up on the dash of the golf cart. I noticed he wore a dry white Vikings soccer jersey and black gym shorts as I made my way over. His hair, sun-kissed and tousled, stood up in the front as he greeted me with a wide, toothy smile. The look in his eyes caught me off-guard, it was as if he were seeing me for the first time.

"There she is," he called out to me.

I grinned, tucking my Bible to my chest. "Here I am."

He eyed me curiously, pointing to the book in my hands. "What have you got there?"

I offered the box to Carter, and he reached out and took it. Lifting the lid to see inside, I watched as his eyebrows flew up and his jaw dropped like mine had.

"This is so nice!" he exclaimed, smoothing his fingers over the cover. "Where did you get this?"

"Lou just gave it to me," I answered, beaming excitedly for the millionth time today.

Carter handed it over as he peered back at me. "So, how do you feel?"

I could barely contain the joy inside me. "I don't think I can describe it."

Carter patted the empty seat beside him. "Come sit with me and you can try."

I paused, thinking about him kissing me. The adrenaline rush I felt earlier made me question if it was all in my head, but now, seeing him right in front of me, I knew it wasn't.

"What is it?" he cocked his head, zeroing in on me.

I sucked in my lower lip, biting it gently, feeling my nerves shoot to the tips of my fingers. Why was I suddenly so nervous? This was Carter, after all, the person I had been able to open up to unlike anyone else.

"Earth to Lena!" He snapped his fingers in front of my face.

"Sorry," I snapped out of my thoughts, feeling bashful suddenly. "I just, um, earlier I thought that there was…"

My voice trailed off before I could even get the words out. Carter's eyes searched my face.

"You thought?"

When I met his gaze again, I chuckled, feeling ridiculous. I grabbed the bridge of my nose and pinched to get the words out. "When I came up out of the water, I just… I thought we had a moment."

Once the words left my mouth, I wanted to curl up in a ball and hide. But when I found the courage to glimpse back at him, I was surprised to find him trying not to laugh.

"You mean when I kissed you?" he asked me point blank.

I gulped, feeling like my heart would leap out of my chest. "So, I didn't imagine it?"

Carter ran his hands through his hair before looking back up at me, his smile fading a little. "You did not imagine it."

I had only seen him make this move when he felt on edge, and I suddenly felt the urge to protect myself. "You don't have to explain, I mean, you were happy for me and probably just got swept up in the moment."

Carter's brows instantly furrowed, creating a huge wrinkle on his forehead. He uncrossed his arms and rotated to face me. He had my complete attention when I saw that he was no longer joking, but instead was being just as sincere as he was on the dock when we talked about my soul.

"I kissed you because I have feelings for you. When you came up out of the water and I realized you were going to Heaven with me, it was all I could do to obey the rules and not give you a real kiss."

I stared blankly, feeling my heart melt into a puddle at my feet. The butterflies in my stomach began fluttering like crazy. Unable to look into Carter's eyes, I stared down at my feet, trying to hide the emotion stirring within me.

"Can you maybe say something now?" he asked, chuckling. "Like maybe you like me too?"

My cheeks heated as I stole a glance at him. "Isn't it obvious?"

Carter scoffed and fell back into his seat as if I had wounded him.

Holding up my hands defensively, I chuckled, "I'm just glad to hear that it wasn't a mistake."

Carter shook his head as if I were driving him crazy. His warm brown eyes settled on mine as he leaned forward and whispered, "The only mistake I've made was not telling you sooner."

24

During breakfast the next few days, we had some unexpected visitors. I noticed Denny began hovering by Jojo, sneaking bites of food she prepared. Carter began sneaking into the kitchen while I was on duty to deliver his own dirty dishes to me, though he always washed them himself.

"You know you don't have to do that," I scolded him on Thursday morning.

Leaning over the sink, he flashed a coy smile and whispered, "But when else will I see you?"

My stomach flipped and I couldn't contain the smile creeping across my face. "You can always come to my breakout session."

Carter drew in a long breath, stacking his clean, wet dishes on the drying rack. He stood so close I could feel his breath on my cheek. "I know, it's just... this summer has gone by faster than I would have liked..."

As his voice trailed off, I offered what little reassurance I could muster, knowing the days were quickly ticking away. "We'll just have to make the most of the time we have left."

And that's exactly what we did.

That afternoon, the two of us were able to sneak away to the lake, each with an ice cream cone in hand. We sat in our usual spot on the dock, watching a group of campers as they rowed together, two in matching kayaks, two more in a canoe.

"If you could be anywhere in the world right now, where would you want to be?" Carter asked me between taking bites of his ice cream.

I smirked, staring at the water before me. "Right here."

Carter flashed his eyes at me. "Why is that?"

I took a bite from the cone in my hand and felt the cold cream melt on my tongue. "Because this is the happiest I've been in a long time."

Squinting beneath the sun, Carter asked, "What's made you so happy?"

"All of it," I replied, taking another small bite from my dessert.

Seeming exasperated, Carter's face grew serious. "But if you had to choose, name one thing."

I pretended to think hard for a moment as I stared out at the moving water. The wind whipping around us stirred up the surface of the lake. I had to squint beneath the sun's rays to look Carter in the eye.

"Getting my ankle boot off," I answered, trying to hide my grin.

As soon as I said it, Carter's face fell, and I fought the laughter trying to escape me.

"Really, Dutch?" he asked, clearly disappointed.

Lifting my leg up, I pointed down at my foot. "I can wear actual shoes again and walk! How can I not be happy about that?"

Carter sighed, taking another bite of his ice cream, and glanced over to where the others were getting further and further from the shore. I reached out, taking my ice cream cone in my right hand and bringing it right beside Carter's face when he wasn't looking.

"Hey Rosie?" I called. Without delay, Carter turned his face, and his nose fell right into my ice cream cone. I burst out laughing as my breath caught in my throat. Carter's eyes widened in shock and I watched as he swiped at his face, now covered in ice cream, and glared at me.

"You know you're in for a treat too," he warned me. I laughed as he lunged to attack with his ice cream cone, though I dodged his attempt to splatter me. Carter seized my arm and spun me around, rendering me unable to snake out of his grasp. He smeared his melting ice cream cone across my face and down my chin.

I gasped. "No, you didn't!"

Carter cackled, still holding me, as ice cream dripped from his nose and down his face. Once again, I tried to smear him with my cone, but he skillfully dodged my attack, resulting in the scoop falling off the cone and landing on the dock.

"You missed!" he snorted. We were laughing so hard in our mini-food fight that it took me a moment to notice when Carter had stopped. His smile faltered as he drew near, our vanilla-covered noses almost touching.

Under the summer sun, the world seemed to shrink around us. Carter's brown eyes locked onto mine, warm with anticipation. I felt his nose touch mine as he leaned in closer and closer. As I drew in a breath, a sudden splash echoed behind us. Carter released me and turned. I glanced over his shoulder to see a kayaker go over, splashing into the lake.

"Wait here," he instructed as he raced down to the shore. As the camper swam back to the kayak, the others in the canoe rushed to help him flip the vessel over. Carter waded into the lake quickly to ensure everyone's safety.

Though I was thankful when everyone got back to shore, our missed kiss was all I could think about for the rest of the day.

***

The summer's most eventful day, Field Day, arrived on Friday, unleashing a frenzy of activity around camp. We rotated through stations, while my team focused on preparing for Capture the Flag, the game that would make or break us.

During our final round against Katie's Yellow Team, Theo had applied so much pressure that we all felt his insane desire to win. In our final moments, Asher tossed the ball to Mateo as Theo shouted at him to run across the field. All the shouting from the field caused Mateo to freeze with the ball in his hands. When he finally broke into a sprint, it was too late. Katie had gained on him so quickly that she managed to grab his flag right out from under him. We watched as Katie waved the red flag, prancing our team's defeat right in Theo's face. Though I expected him to be upset over our loss, Theo was too busy flirting to care.

After lunch, the Yellow Team was in the lead, and I noticed Theo celebrating with Katie despite our team's loss. After a sun-soaked day, I was eager for the refreshing air conditioning that came with dinner duty.

Tonight's menu included hot dogs, crinkle fries, fruit, and a salad bar. I noticed pickles were brought out while I scarfed down my dinner hurriedly before the campers arrived. The sight brought back memories of the nickname Lacey had given me, making my stomach lurch. I forced down the rest of my hot dog and then settled into my dishwashing routine as the Dining Hall filled with campers.

When Denny came in to snag a cookie from Jojo, I peered through the window by the sink but saw no sign of Carter at the Med Table. Denny and Jojo's quiet laughter left me feeling a twinge of unease, as I half-expected Carter to appear.

Trying to distract myself, I snatched the trash bag in front of me and dragged it outside to get some air. I pushed open the creaking door and marched across the gravel to dump the trash in the dumpster. Brushing off my hands, I leisurely made my way around the back of the Dining Hall to the front porch. Before I could climb the stairs, I froze.

Carter stood with his arms around a girl on the deck, his eyes fixed on her. I didn't recognize her until she looked up to meet his gaze.

Riley.

The scene before me sent a shiver of discomfort down my spine. The last time he had mentioned Riley to me, he had been set on avoiding any drama and seemed eager to steer clear of her. Yet, from the look of their embrace, it seemed much more than a friendly hug.

I spun on my heel, quickly returning to the kitchen the way I had come. Just days ago, he admitted his feelings for me. We'd been inseparable since then, and I had started to dread the thought of leaving and not seeing him every day. There were so many thoughts I had been considering of how we could try to make long distance work. Yet, the sight of the two of them together knocked my plans off course.

Taking a deep breath, I opened the back door, and the eruption of chatter from the Dining Hall filled my ears. I retreated to the sink, trying to drown out the noise of clanging pans and my own turbulent thoughts. My mind raced to every worst-case scenario as I scrubbed dish after dish. I worked that way until I decided that I would find Carter and ask if we could talk. The last thing I wanted with just a week left of camp was to not know where we stood.

"Hey, do you want to come to the lake when you're finished?" Jojo asked, bringing a large mixing bowl over to the sink. Denny appeared behind her, chowing down on a cookie.

"I think I need to go to the Med Cabin, but maybe after," I offered.

Jojo's expression filled with concern. "Is everything okay with your ankle?"

I nodded. Of course, that's why she would think I needed to go down there. "Yeah, I'm fine, I just need to check on something."

She patted my shoulder reassuringly. "I totally understand, especially after Field Day. Just know I want to spend as much time with you as I can before we have to leave."

Jojo's eyes softened and I offered her a smile. The thought of leaving felt so daunting as the day crept closer and closer, the very least I could give Jojo was time.

"I'll meet you down there as soon as I can."

Jojo grinned, her excitement returning as she wheeled around and shuffled Denny back to her table. I finished cleaning up and rushed out of the kitchen, only to stop short as I almost collided with two girls standing outside the door. I felt a jolt flow through me once I saw Riley looming in front of me.

"Hey, you go ahead, I'll be right there," she mentioned to Kelsey.

Riley spun to face me as Kelsey crept away. She reached out to touch my arm and I felt the urge to recoil.

"I just wanted to say congratulations on your decision!" she exclaimed. "It's always awesome when someone decides to become a Christian. I'm so happy for you!"

"Thank you," I said, feeling apprehensive.

"Of course." She took a step closer to me and lowered her voice. "Carter told me that he had been helping a friend study, but I had no idea it was you."

I didn't say anything as I felt the knot in my stomach return. Though she wore an excited smile on her painted red lips, it didn't reach her eyes.

"Carter's great like that," Riley continued, "He's always thinking of others and is there whenever anyone needs him."

Trying my best to maintain my composure, I forced a smile.

Riley's gaze dropped to her feet, as if she was suddenly too self-conscious to meet my gaze. "After hearing about your study, I realized just how much I missed him."

The words felt like a gut punch, leaving me frozen and defenseless. She looked back up at me with her same smile and forced sincerity. "I don't know if you heard, but we recently broke up. Just seeing him around the last couple of weeks made me realize just how good I think we are together."

I suddenly felt like every nerve in my body was on fire, and she whispered, "I decided to ask him to the End of Summer Banquet as my date."

Those last three words hit me, and I felt my pulse quicken and my blood boil. I could only stare at her. *What did she expect me to say to that?*

"That's okay though, right?" she asked, her eyes searching my face. "Aren't you two just friends?"

Had Carter said these things to her? How could he confess his feelings to me one day and then get back together with his ex? A storm of confusion and hurt seized me, and I wanted nothing more than to get away from her. Summoning all the self-control I could at that moment, I choked out, "You two have fun. I've got to get going."

As I pressed past her, I heard Riley call, "Congrats again, Lena!"

When I made my way onto the front porch, I let the door to the Dining Hall slam behind me. I felt so confused. I wanted answers from Carter, but after seeing the two of them earlier and then hearing from Riley, maybe that was all the explanation I really needed. On impulse, I decided to make my way down to the lake as the sun began to set.

When Jojo spotted me as my feet hit the sand, she waved me over to where she was sitting on the back of the four-wheeler, as the guys were skipping rocks. "That was a quick trip to the Med Cabin."

"Yeah..." I murmured, my voice trailing off as I stood beside her.

"So, how is everything?" she asked.

I took a deep breath, still trying my best to settle the turmoil within me. "My ankle's fine."

"Are you sure?" she pressed, eyeing me curiously. I drew in a slow, steady breath, willing myself to calm down.

I nodded as Jojo began to say something, but I couldn't stop my racing thoughts. If Carter had liked me as much as he said he did, why had he never mentioned the Banquet to me? There was a part of me that questioned whether I was just a person he relied on to steer clear of ex-girlfriend complications, or his summer camp project. On the other hand, it's possible that I was just his responsibility and he felt obligated to spend time with me until my ankle started to heal. Maybe this whole time I had just been a summer distraction for him.

"Lena?" Jojo waved her hand in front of my face. "What do you think? Should I just keep waiting for him or do you think I should tell Denny how I feel? The banquet is just around the corner."

This took me off guard, considering my own situation, and I realized I completely missed what she had been telling me. Everyone knew Denny and Jojo liked each other, and I knew her honesty could only work out for her. I just wished Carter had been honest with me.

"You should tell him the truth," I confessed. "Everyone deserves honesty."

Her face revealed a mix of worry and hesitation before she finally accepted my response. "You're right, it's time I told him the truth."

"Atta girl." I gave her a pat on the shoulder, forcing a smile.

Jojo took a deep breath and slid her hands nervously down the top of her thighs. "Well, here goes nothing."

I watched as she leaped off the four-wheeler and made her way down the shore to speak with Denny. I felt a mix of happiness for her and worry over the slim chance he could break her heart. Not only did I know how it felt to have my heart broken and betrayed by a friend, I now knew how it felt to feel humiliated by someone I trusted. Jojo had warned me to steer clear of Carter, and now I wished I had listened to her.

25

Jojo woke me up, shuffling around our room to get ready. I had no idea what time it was, but the throbbing headache I had was making it hard to open my eyes. With a groan, I shifted my body and rolled back over, not ready to face the day just yet.

"Good morning, sleepyhead," Jojo greeted me as she nudged my shoulder. I was thankful she kept her cheerful voice to a minimum.

"Don't tell me it's morning already." I groaned once more. As the morning light peeked through the window, I had to squint to shield my eyes against it.

Jojo giggled, and I noticed her long dark hair was a tangled web at the back of her head as she rummaged through her bag in search of her glasses. "Was it a rough night?"

"Something like that," I admitted. My voice came out ragged as I tried to blink away my grogginess. Despite my careful movements, as I gingerly sat up, the pounding in my head intensified.

Jojo's eyes flashed with concern as she turned her attention towards me. "Are you feeling okay?"

I let out a deep sigh and forcefully threw myself back onto my pillow, using my forearm to shield my eyes. "No, my head is killing me."

My mattress sank down as Jojo had a seat on the edge. "I'm going to go get ready and head down for breakfast. Do you want me to bring you something before duty?"

I slid my arm away from my eyes and nodded as I looked up at her. "I need some kind of pain reliever and probably a bucket of water."

"Did you drink enough during Field Day?" she asked, sliding her glasses on.

I rubbed my eyes once more, trying to wipe away the pain behind them. With each move I made, the throbbing in my head grew worse. "I don't know, but if this is how dehydration feels, I'm a goner."

The mattress rose as Jojo climbed to her feet. She picked up her bathroom bag, casting another worried glance at me. "Should I bring Carter by to check on you?"

Despite the pounding pain behind my eyes, I shot her a fierce glare. "No!"

"But Lena, if you're sick..."

"Don't!" I interjected. My outburst caught Jojo off guard, and I could see the surprise on her face. "I just don't want to put any of us in a weird situation by asking him to come to Girls Camp. You can just tell Angie or Lou."

Jojo remained silent but sat back down beside me, staring down inquisitively. "Lena, did something happen between you and Carter?"

I sighed and rested my arm back over my eyes. Suddenly, I remembered the look on Riley's face when she told me about their Banquet plans. "You warned me to keep an *emotional distance* from him."

"I know, but it doesn't seem like you listened," Jojo replied with an edge in her voice.

"I meant to," I tried to explain, as I stared up at her hovering on the edge of my bunk.

Jojo reached out and ruffled my bedhead and exhaled an exasperated sigh. "Lena, Carter drove you around camp most of the summer. You guys obviously became friends, I mean, he *baptized* you. It's obvious there's more to the story there."

Hearing the reminder, I thought about how much time we had spent together. We had so many memories between us, from our long talks on the lake to the time spent in our breakout sessions, and every moment in between. Carter had been by my side this whole time, even with my baptism. All it had taken me was a few weeks to fall for him, and one word from Riley had ruined everything.

"There's nothing more to tell," I confessed. "I should have listened and stayed away from him. Last night Riley said they're starting things up again."

Jojo instinctively grimaced before her expression softened as her eyes met mine. "It was probably only a matter of time, after they've been at camp all summer together."

She didn't mean to, but her words wounded me and made me wonder if he had been spending time with her when we weren't together. If they had really had such an awful breakup, maybe it was because they had unfinished business. Regardless of my feelings, there was no way I would come between them.

"I just don't want to be in the middle of any drama," I admitted. "I had enough to deal with before I got here."

"Consider it forgotten," Jojo tried to reassure me.

I slowly sat back up, squinting to try and relieve the intensifying throbbing feeling in my head. "Can you go find Lou for me? We can just keep the Med Staff out of it."

"You got it," she vowed, launching to her feet.

Jojo kept her word, but Lou insisted on me leaving to recover at her house. Though I was reluctant at first, unwilling to leave Jojo, I agreed. Lou had been right, though, and I felt grateful to have the opportunity to get out of my bunk, take a nice long shower, and rest. Lou had bought a few different sports drinks fueled with electrolytes to rehydrate my body that I alternated with water throughout the day. She made chicken noodle soup to keep the juices flowing and help with the nausea from my headache.

Though I spent most of the day napping, my headache had only dulled. Lou kept reminding me just how important staying hydrated was, especially with all the recent activities at camp. Some time had gone by since I had been on any sort of sports team, and I was kicking myself for not taking better care of myself during camp Field Day.

Sleeping seemed the only way to escape the throbbing in my head, so that evening I tried to tuck in early, but when I climbed into bed, my phone buzzed on the nightstand. I felt my heart sink as I read the message.

> *Rosie: Hey Dutch! I'm sorry you're not feeling well. Let me know if you need anything.*

I set the phone back on the nightstand after swiping away the message. There was no way I could reply to him. Even though I was still processing everything, I knew I needed to make a decision for when I returned to camp. It seemed like my only option was to actually take Jojo's advice and steer clear of Carter and Riley. I had come too far this summer to let someone else's relationship drama mess up my progress.

Suddenly, my phone began to ring, and I plopped a pillow over my face to stifle a loud groan. *Why was Carter trying to get in touch with me?* Sighing, I picked up my phone, but once I saw the name, I knew I had to answer.

"Hey Dad!" I greeted, relieved it was him on the other line.

"Hey kiddo!" he called out. "Lou called and said you weren't feeling well."

"I'm okay," I explained, picking up on the edge in his voice. "I've just had a pounding headache all day."

I could hear the concern in his voice. "Just make sure you're drinking plenty of water and try to keep the sun off of you. Dehydration is no joke."

"I'm working on it," I admitted. "I've just been resting at Lou's today. How are you?"

"Missing you, of course," Dad replied. "It feels like it's been ages since I've seen you. We haven't been apart this long since my last deployment."

"I know," I said, as the fact dawned on me. Even though I missed him, too, it felt like so much had changed this summer. When I realized the short time I had left at camp, the thought made my heart ache.

As upset as I felt about Carter, I knew I would miss Jojo, Denny, and even Theo a little. On top of that, I hardly spent any time with Lou this summer. Four weeks had felt like a lifetime at first, but now that they were almost gone, the days were passing by like sand in an hourglass. I didn't feel ready to go back home just yet.

"I know you aren't feeling well, but you sound better than you did the last time we talked," Dad pointed out.

He was right. The last time we saw each other, I had dreaded the thought of spending the summer away. Now, camp was the place I felt like I belonged.

"I am doing a lot better," I said, unable to put the last few weeks into words. "This summer surprised me."

I could practically hear his happiness from the other line. "I'm glad to hear it, honey. Listen, I've got to run, but I will see you soon and we'll catch up. We can even go out for a ride in the boat, just like old times."

"I can't wait." I tried my best to sound cheerful. "I love you, Dad."

"I love you, Lenny," Dad said.

We said our goodbyes and I rolled over to see the view of the moonlight pouring through the opaque curtains. With a real mattress beneath me, I drifted off and slept my first full night in weeks.

On Sunday, I woke up feeling improved, with only a dull ache in the back of my head. When I went down the stairs to search for Lou, I found a note beneath a River Ridge Realty mug.

> *Good morning, my favorite niece,*
> *Hopefully, you feel better. I've got to run by camp this morning for worship, but I'll be back to check on you soon. Make yourself at home.*
>
> *Love, Lou*

Not only did her note bring a smile to my face, but it also served as a gentle reminder of the importance of worshiping on the first day of the week. I made myself a cup of coffee and waltzed back up the stairs to grab my new Bible. I sipped my coffee and opened my Bible on the back deck while I continued to recover. The warm morning sun bathed me in its golden glow, and its rays danced upon the surface of the pond.

When I last visited Lou's, before camp, I had felt like a stranger. Now that we had cleared the air between us, I leaned into the view and felt the familiarity of my surroundings. Growing up, Lou's house was where our family always came together. Now, I knew I had a second chance with Lou to move forward and rebuild our relationship. We could finally be there for each other, walking in faith together.

Feeling overwhelmed with gratitude, I bowed my head to pray and thanked God for the new life I had. But more importantly, I thanked him for my new beginning and the hope I now carried with me. Finally, I asked him to help me focus on my faith and to take away anything or anyone that would distract me. I knew how it felt to be lost and I had found my way back. There was no way I was going to lose myself again.

***

There was a bounce in my step again as I left Tuesday's morning breakout session. Having made up my mind to leave any negativity behind me, I just wanted to focus on enjoying my final days at camp before returning home. I had spotted Jojo and Denny in the Canteen line and began making my way over to join them. As I crossed the field, I froze when I heard the sound of tires quickly moving over the gravel path behind me.

My heart began to pitter-patter in my chest. So far, I successfully dodged Carter when I made it back to camp first thing yesterday morning. The more I thought about it, the sillier I felt for making a big deal out of things. Riley and Carter's relationship was none of my business. He and I could be friends if that's what he wanted. With my faith restored, that had to be my main focus right now. I didn't have time for boys or any other distractions.

"Lena!" I heard Carter's voice ring out.

Forcing a friendly smile, I turned to him and waved. The golf cart puttered to a halt a few feet from me, and he hopped off and jogged over. "How are you feeling?"

"Better," I replied, clasping my Bible in front of me like a shield. "I spent the weekend at Lou's. Dehydration is the worst."

"You don't have to tell me," Carter noted. The curve of his smile faded a little and I watched while he ran his hands through his hair. He stared down at his feet, and I felt my stomach lurch. "I texted you the other day. When I didn't hear from you, I started to worry, until Jojo told me you had gone to Lou's."

"Yeah, sorry about that," I apologized. Feeling my pulse quicken, I tried to keep my cool. "I just needed to rest."

Carter scrunched up his face as his chocolate eyes searched my face. "I just got the feeling you were avoiding me."

My face flamed instantly once he called me out. I knew I would be having this conversation sometime this week, I had just imagined it going much differently.

I flashed him a nervous smile. "I'm sorry if it felt that way. I should have replied to you and let you know I was okay."

The way he stared at me was like he was reading my thoughts. His intense stare made me clutch my Bible tighter to my chest.

"So, we're okay then?"

I nodded as a lump formed in my throat as I forced the words out. "Of course. We're friends, right?"

He narrowed his eyes. "Friends?"

"Aren't we?" I asked incredulously. "I heard you and Riley are going to the banquet together, and if that's what you both want, then I'm happy for you."

Carter's face fell, making me wonder if he wanted to be the one to confess the truth to me himself. "Where did you hear that?"

"Riley told me a few days ago," I confirmed. Though I was trying to remain calm, I could feel my hands begin to tremble. I watched as he shifted his weight from one leg to another and released a deep breath.

"Lena," Carter began to explain, "you should know that whatever you heard from her... it's not like that."

"Not like what?" I asked, trying to hold my cheerful façade.

I watched as he grappled for the right words. "Riley and I—we aren't... I mean, she asked me to go to the banquet with her but I—"

"Look, Carter, it's fine really," I tried to console him, as pain ripped through my chest. "I know you said you liked me, but I know you guys have a history and I can't compete with that. There's a reason you came into my life, and I couldn't be more grateful for you helping me find my way back to God this summer."

Carter put his hands on his hips as his mouth formed a flat line. Silently, he slid his hand down his stubbly face. I glanced back to the Canteen where Jojo and Denny were now up at the window to order. I needed a way out of this horrible conversation and decided to seize my opportunity.

"Carter, I've got to run, but I'll see you, okay?"

He offered me a small, almost unrecognizable nod and I felt my stomach sink as I turned and left him standing there dejected.

Our talk had been so much more painful than I imagined. In just a few short weeks, Carter had become the person I counted on and one of my newest, closest friends. I owed it to him to step aside so he could be happy, even if that meant breaking my own heart.

26

"Look at all the mud you just tracked in!" Jojo groaned. It had rained all night and well into Thursday morning. My final fun day at camp had turned into a disappointment, with me spending most of lunch mopping the Dining Hall. The campers' dirty shoes left mud scattered everywhere.

Denny stood behind Jojo, his gaze fixed on the dirty footprints from the kitchen doors to where he now stood. With a wince and a charming expression, he effortlessly won Jojo over in an instant. Despite spending more time together, I had yet to ask her if they had talked.

Crossing the kitchen, I placed a hand on Denny's shoulder. "I'll clean it up, but you should probably go wipe your feet off in the back."

I pointed to a rug in front of the back door. Denny gave me a gentle pat with his huge hand, showing his gratitude. I walked behind him and grabbed the mop bucket that was already filled. Then, I dipped the mop in the dirty water while he wiped off his shoes. I bent down and mopped over Denny's muddy footsteps, scrubbing all the way out of the kitchen and to the front door.

As I gazed out of the front window, I noticed that the rain had finally transformed into a soothing, gentle drizzle. Once the door swung open, I wasted no time in moving out of the way, and to my surprise, I immediately met Riley's distressed gaze.

In a matter of seconds, she swept her gaze across the room, only to divert her eyes to the floor when they connected with mine. She briskly made her way to her usual table, pushing past me. Out of the corner of my eye, I spotted movement outside the front window as Carter made his way past. In a feeble attempt to hide, I pushed back through the double doors and took my place in the kitchen by the sink.

When Carter sat down with Angie at the Med Table, I quickly glanced out the window near the sink and noticed something about him seemed off. I felt a growing sense of unease as I looked at Riley, who was sitting slumped at the table with Kelsey's arm around her. *Had something happened between the two of them?*

I took a step back and leaned against the sink as my thoughts raced. I didn't want to think about Carter or Riley anymore. He had chosen her, and if they already had issues again, that had nothing to do with me.

While I worked to finish mopping, Lou found me.

"How's my niece feeling?"

"Never better," I answered as I wrung out the mop in the bucket again. Cleaning the muddy floor was giving me a welcome distraction from Carter, and I was happy to lean into the task. "How are you?"

Lou's eyes lit up, and she tucked her straight locks behind one ear. "I'm great, but I promise today is about to get a lot better."

"Oh?" I asked, my eyes widening as I paused my mopping to look at her. "What's going on?"

Bending her index finger, she motioned for me to follow her. Leading me through the kitchen to the back door, Lou held it open for me as we both stepped out to clear skies opening up overhead.

"Follow me," Lou instructed, practically skipping over the wet gravel. She pulled me along, and I quickly fell into step beside her. The air was heavy with the scent of rain-soaked earth and pine. Just outside of Girls Camp, I immediately recognized the worn old truck I'd ridden in countless times before. The driver's door creaked open, releasing a loud screech, and a man climbed out, slamming it shut behind him.

I gasped and broke into a full sprint. "Dad!"

Dad turned, his face lighting up with a warm smile as he spotted me, his eyes shining with pride. "Hey, honey!"

"What are you doing here?" I shrieked, throwing myself into his arms. "I still have one more day!"

When he released me, I stared up at him. He seemed a little lighter than the last time I had seen him, as if some of his worry had diminished. His facial hair had grown to a scruffy length, but he pulled it off. Pointing behind me to Lou, he mentioned, "Your aunt called me and said something about a Family Day."

Lou caught my eye, her eyes shimmering with excitement. "I thought you could use a date at the banquet tomorrow night."

I gave her a quick side hug while rolling my eyes. "I didn't need a date, but thank you for inviting Dad."

"Of course." She smiled and motioned to the Dining Hall. "I should get back, but you two have fun. Lena, remember that your guest comes above duties today."

My eyes widened. "You mean, I'm done?"

Lou tilted her head, as if weighing the option. "We'll have plenty of help, but if not, Tommy, feel free to pitch in."

Dad's eyes softened. "For all you've done for Lena this summer, just let me know. Otherwise, I'll find you before I head out later."

"I would do anything for my favorite niece," Lou winked at me. "But you're right, find me before you leave."

Dad gave her a thumbs-up before turning back to me and placing his hands on my shoulders. "Look at you. I honestly think you may have gotten a little taller since I saw you last."

I rolled my eyes, chuckling. "I doubt it, but it's probably just because I'm back on both legs."

Dad's eyes softened as he took me in. "Honestly Lenny, you look different, happier maybe."

His eyes searched mine as he looked for a reaction before I agreed.

"I am happier than the last time you saw me, and since you're here for the day, I can tell you all about it. But maybe we can start with a tour."

Dad's grin faltered only slightly, and I knew he was thinking about me being unhappy. Yet, when I held out my hand to him, he placed his palm in mine firmly, as if he would never let me go again. "Lead the way, kiddo."

***

Before dinner, Dad and I finished the tour around camp. After meeting Jojo and Denny on the way to the kitchen, I grabbed some leftovers being cleaned out of the refrigerators. With our salads in takeout containers, I led Dad to the Craft Cabin, where we could find some dry picnic tables to enjoy our lunch outside the noisy Dining Hall.

"I can't believe how much this place has changed," Dad commented, taking a bite of lettuce.

I stared curiously across the table at him. "You've been here before?"

Dad nodded, gulping down the mouthful. "A long time ago. It was during your mom's last summer here. I came for a visit when we first started dating. They've done a lot of expanding. The larger buildings are the same, just a bit updated, but the lodge is new. Oh, and the cabins too. There are more of them."

"So, you knew more about this place than you let on?" I shot him a skeptical look.

Dad averted my gaze and stabbed at his salad. "I did. I know a lot about this place, actually."

"Why didn't you tell me?"

Setting his fork down, Dad sighed as he peered back up at me. "I thought that if I told you about your mom's and my experiences, you might have done something rash, like running away with Ronni."

Hearing the words tumble out of his words stung me, but Dad had every right to feel that way. I had never given him a reason to think differently, with all the choices I made last school year. With my time at camp coming to a close, I felt so far from the person I arrived as, the girl I promised I would never be again.

"I'm sorry about the things I said to you before I brought you to Lou's, but I don't think I can apologize for the time you've spent here," Dad confessed. "You finally seem like yourself again, Lena. You deserve to be happy."

My heart swelled inside my chest and I reached out to take his hand in mine. "So do you, Dad. I'm really sorry for everything I've put you through this year. I was just so angry."

Dad squeezed my hand, and I watch his lips form a tight line. "Nothing that has happened with your mother was fair to you. This summer wasn't about sending you away. I wanted to help you get away so you could remember what a normal life feels like."

Keeping my eyes downcast, I felt my chin quiver. "What are we going to do if she never comes back?"

I felt him tighten his hold on my hand, but I couldn't look at him. The concept of a normal life seemed far off for us, but maybe he was right. Maybe our life now was our new normal.

"Lena, your mom left to get help because she's sick. I know it's been difficult, but she did what she thought was best so she could get better."

With a sidelong glance, I asked. "So, are you saying you think she did the right thing?"

He released my hand and stroked his stubbly chin thoughtfully. "I didn't say that. I hate the way your mother left, but she's not herself. Addicts don't think rationally. My job is to support you both and try to give you a stable life. Your job is to be a kid."

I knew this summer didn't heal all of my wounds, but I rediscovered the Great Physician who could. Returning back to Freeport would be challenging, but hearing the truth of how my dad disagreed with my mom's decision brought me some form of comfort. I was still mad at her, but when I considered what Dad said, I just felt sorry for her. With a long road of recovery ahead, I wondered how possible her recovery would even be without God.

"So, Lou has been keeping me in the loop," Dad said, changing the subject. He picked up his fork again, and I realized avoiding tough subjects was a trait I had inherited from him. "She said you've decided to recommit to your faith again."

I searched his face, trying to read him. Knowing my dad's past and how he never quite came around to following the Lord himself, I wondered how he felt about hearing my news. I recalled watching campers get baptized, surrounded by their families. Finding out that Lou informed him about my decision after it had already happened relieved the pain I once felt about him missing out.

"I did," I told him, sitting straighter, watching him carefully.

"I'm proud of you, Lenny," he said, casually taking another bite of salad.

"You are?"

Dad nodded, his expression skeptical. "Of course I am. Your faith is part of who you are."

Hearing this, I picked up my fork and began nervously stabbing at my salad. "Dad, do you think you'll ever decide to follow God?"

Still chewing, he didn't seem fazed by the question. "God and I are still working things out. But I never want that to affect you and your faith. I'm here to support you no matter what."

Though this wasn't exactly the news I wanted to hear, I could understand it. Having found my way back to the Lord this summer, I realized everyone had their own choice to make. The sooner the better, but the choice was still one's own. I felt hopeful that when we went home, I could do my best to plant seeds and leave the rest to God to work on Dad's heart.

His eyes still lingered on me, flashing from me to my salad. "Are you going to eat, kiddo?"

I looked down at my salad before smiling sheepishly back up at him. "I want to say grace first."

Dad paused mid-chew and laid down his fork. "Well, what are we waiting for?"

We both bowed and prayed for the blessing of our food and our time together. I grinned when Dad murmured, "Amen" and dug in alongside him. Though there was still a lot about our life that was far from perfect, a peace settled over us. I trusted that no matter what came next, everything would be okay.

***

Dad and I spent the rest of the evening at the rope course. With all of his former Coast Guard training, Dad did even better than most of the campers who ended up competing. We ended the afternoon at the archery range before I led him back across camp to the parking lot.

"I've just got a few things to get accomplished around Lou's place," he said, as we made our way to his truck, "just to say thank you to her for taking you on this summer."

He nudged me teasingly, and I fake laughed. "Hilarious."

I noticed Theo coming around the back of a large white truck close by that was worth more than my father's annual salary.

"Hey, Mer—" he started, but his eyes flashed at my dad and he changed his tune. "Hey Lena!"

I chuckled, "Hey, Theo!"

He cradled clothes in his arms, as a tall man loomed behind him. He had neatly styled salt-and-pepper hair, and he wore a crisp dress shirt and khaki pants. He resembled a clean-shaven, older Theo.

Motioning between the two of them, I introduced Theo and my father. "Dad, this is Theo. Theo, this is my dad."

When Theo extended his hand for a handshake, Dad responded by firmly grasping it, his smile tight-lipped yet polite. "Hey there."

"Nice to meet you, Mr..." Theo forgot my last name momentarily, but his dad intervened, placing his hands on Theo's shoulders.

"Tommy Harris," the man, obviously Theo's father, stepped in to finish. As tall as Theo was, his father stood at least two inches over him. It was odd that he called Dad by a nickname only my mom and close family used. Surveying our fathers, I felt the tension in the air grow so thick I could have cut it with a knife.

"Grant Lockwood." Dad called his name with a slight tic of his mouth. "It's been a long time."

"Too long," Grant proposed with an edge in his voice. Confusion filled Theo's eyes as he quickly shifted his gaze between the two of them. He looked at me, his brow furrowing as if seeking answers.

"My dad just brought me some clothes for the banquet tomorrow." He held up his pants and shirt in his hands innocently.

"My dad is in town for the banquet," I replied, trying to offer my own explanation. "And to take me home tomorrow night, obviously."

I was grateful when my dad faced me once again and gave me a gentle side hug. "Well, speaking of tomorrow, I'll see you then, hun. I've got to run."

"It's a date," I joked.

"Gentlemen." Dad tipped his head down, still wearing a polite façade. Without sparing another second, Dad climbed into his truck and turned the key over, and it sputtered and rumbled to life.

"We better run too, son," Grant told Theo. Before Theo could say anything, I noticed his father gave him a gentle shove forward. "Nice to see you, Natalie."

I felt my jaw drop as the two of them stalked past me. Turning, I watched them walk away, and the mystery of the Lockwood family grew heavier in my mind. Earlier this summer, Theo had mentioned that our families knew each other. Now, watching the tense introduction between our fathers, I sensed there was more to the story than I knew. Especially hearing Grant call me by my mother's first name.

27

"So we were in the canoe," Jojo explained, curling her midnight hair into ringlets. She had been beaming all day, and promised to recount her discussion with Denny from last night while we got ready for the Banquet together.

"He rowed us out into the middle of the lake before he said it," she mused. "Denny said that he had rowed us out into the middle of the lake so neither of us could run away from our feelings anymore."

I gasped with excitement as I finished braiding my hair and putting on mascara. "That sounds like him."

Jojo all but melted where she stood. "Then he said he's been crazy about me for a long time, and thought I felt the same."

"To which you said?" I asked, gawking at her.

"Nothing," Jojo giggled, as she finished her half-up hairstyle. "It felt so surreal, Lena. I couldn't believe it! I was speechless!"

"So, did he ask you to the banquet?" I asked, admiring her completed look. Jojo created a chic half-updo that turned her curls into bouncy waves and rocked a flawless cat-eye and pouty pink lips. She completed her look with a cute pink dress covered in tiny red hearts, and funky red shoes. Jojo embraced her uniqueness without apology, and those who knew her loved her for it.

"No." Her expression turned serious as she spun to face me, but before I could respond, her eyes sparkled with mischief. "He asked me to be his girlfriend!"

We both squealed, and I hugged her tightly. "I can't believe it!"

"Me either!" she shrieked. "Denny is my boyfriend!"

I laughed, then rolled my eyes. "It's about time, now we can all stop talking about you two behind your backs."

Jojo's jaw dropped in disbelief. "What are you talking about? Not everyone knew."

I eyeballed her, unable to take her seriously. "You're kidding, right? You guys have been so obvious."

She glared and picked up a scrunchie from the counter to throw at me. "Stop, no we weren't!"

"I'm serious," I countered. "Everyone knew. Deep down, the two of you knew the truth too, you were just too scared to admit it."

She shrugged and checked her reflection again. I finished my mascara and then did a once-over myself. The only nice outfit I had brought with me was a plain black skater dress, which paired well with the high-top sneakers I sported. Compared to Jojo, I didn't look as fancy, but I felt like myself, and that was all that mattered to me.

"I just wish everyone could be as happy as Denny and I are," Jojo opened up, eyeing me expectantly.

"I'm not unhappy," I started, but the look on Jojo's face made me pause.

Puzzled by my reaction, she tilted her head. "I didn't mean you, I just meant Carter. When Denny and I were getting out of the canoe, he was sitting on the dock all by himself."

"Did he say something?" I asked, studying her.

Jojo's eyes softened. "He was just talking about how this summer started out going so well and then went downhill."

I could feel my heart beating rapidly in my chest. There were so many times the two of us sat on the dock together, that had been our spot. Or so I thought.

"Denny sat with him for a while, and I know you said he and Riley were getting back together, but he said they weren't," she broke the news to me.

Confusion blurred my mind and instantly faded when I felt a small glimmer of hope that he and Riley weren't back on. "What else did he say?"

Jojo shrugged. "I left to give the two of them privacy, but when Denny and I talked this morning, he said Carter's heartbroken."

Dread washed over me as she spoke. I'd thought I'd made the right choice by getting out of the way so he could be with Riley. I resisted the urge to act on my feelings, trying to make him happy. I didn't realize doing so had broken his heart, too.

"I have to go," I told Jojo abruptly.

Her eyes grew wide. "Go where?"

"I'll explain later," I told her. I sprinted to the front door and hopped down the front stairs of the cabin two at a time. Feeling thankful for the shoes I had on, I hurried down the gravel path to make my way to the Med Cabin. I had to act quickly before I ran out of time with Carter. Before I left Girls Camp, though, I heard my name shouted behind me.

I looked in the direction of the voice and saw my dad getting out of his truck, just in time for the banquet. Though I was happy to see him, his timing was terrible. I felt a pang in my gut, feeling torn between trying to find Carter and having to explain things to my dad.

"Where are you off to in such a hurry?" he called. My dad had carefully chosen to wear his nicest jeans and a striped polo shirt, which I knew he only wore on special occasions.

"Um, coming to find you," I fibbed. The gravel crunched beneath my feet as I strode towards him. I would have to find Carter at the banquet and hopefully talk to him then.

"You look..." Dad's voice trailed off as he took me in. I did a little twirl, trying my best to act natural, and he laughed. "Very you."

"I'm sure there's a compliment in there somewhere," I joked.

He grinned and threw an arm around my shoulders. "I know we're early, but do you think there's any chance appetizers will be served? I'm starving. Lou had me on maintenance this morning."

"And didn't feed you?" I guffawed. "Let's go see what I can swipe from the kitchen. They're cleaning things out since tonight is the last night anyway."

Dad trekked beside me, recounting his visit to Lou's. He spoke about how it was strange to be there without Mom. I could relate—it had been a long time since we'd all been together in Meadowbrook. After the last few weeks, we seemed to slowly be putting the pieces of our family puzzle back together.

We ambled up to the Dining Hall when Lou suddenly appeared. Sweat-drenched and dressed in a New Hope Bible Camp t-shirt, she looked out of place for the banquet, though I knew tonight was the night the adults served the campers.

Lou's expression caught me off guard, her eyes filled with concern. "I need to speak to you."

I watched as she narrowed her eyes and flicked her gaze over to Dad. "You should come, too."

Bewildered, I stared from Lou to my Dad. "What's going on?"

Her nostrils flared. "I feel like I should be asking you the same thing."

I didn't ask any further questions as she strode off across the front yard. Dad looked at me, equally perplexed. I gestured for him to follow us, sighing in frustration. We followed as Lou headed down the field. The faster we marched along, the faster I realized where we were going. The Med Cabin.

Why was she so upset? I wondered as we crossed the yard in swift strides, darting under the pavilion and through the Med Cabin's front door. The bell on the door chimed, and within seconds, Carter appeared.

He was still rolling up the sleeves on his dress shirt when he saw us. His eyes widened with curiosity as they landed on Lou, then me.

"Hey guys," he greeted us, with a hint of confusion. "Is there something I can do for you?"

"Let's have a seat." Lou pointed to the row of chairs where campers waited in the foyer before being seen. As I claimed the first chair, Carter opted for the third chair, which happened to be the one farthest away from where I sat. I had no idea if he wanted to put distance between us or if he was just trying to save my dad a seat. Dad opted not to sit, though. Instead, he chose to stand with arms crossed.

"What's going on, Lou?" Dad scrutinized.

Lou swiftly handed me her phone, pulling it from her back pocket. "I should be asking the two of you that question."

Peering at the photo on Lou's phone screen, my stomach sank. In the picture, Carter and I were seated close with his arm around me, our faces inches apart.

"You can swipe to the right, too," she offered. "There's more to see."

I swiped right, and the next photo showed us together, seemingly alone on the dock. The photos didn't show the other campers that had been around, but they made us look guilty of breaking the camp rules. I watched Carter's face fall when I passed the phone to him, next.

"Let me see," My dad held out his hand, demanding the phone from Carter. I looked away, unable to bear disappointing him.

"I'm not sure what you two have to say for yourselves, but you've broken camp rules by the looks of these," Lou explained.

I felt my face flame.

"Lena, you were nominated for an award this summer, but this disqualifies you," she informed me.

"Where did you even get these?" Carter asked, sounding hurt. "We weren't even alone out there if someone was able to take pictures of us."

"Tone, young man," Lou chided Carter. "Where the photo came from is for me to know. What were the two of you thinking?"

"If the pictures came from another camper, are they going to be in trouble for breaking camp rules, too?" I pushed back.

"Lena, that's enough," Dad scolded. I winced, hearing the frustration in his tone. I had promised him I would change, and now this situation made me seem like a liar.

Sighing, Carter pinched the bridge of his nose. "This was my mistake, Lou. I'm sorry."

As he spoke, his words felt like a gut punch. Was that all I was to him? *A mistake?*

"You are both on staff," Lou went on. "The two of you should have been setting an example."

I glanced up at my dad, who stood silently, shaking his head in disappointment. Everything looked so bad, but Dad had no idea what had really happened.

"Would either of you care to explain?" Lou interrogated us.

I'd faced hurt and shame before, but this heartbreak was uniquely brutal. Not only did he think I was a mistake, but Carter's indifference towards me was devastating. He offered no explanation, no apology for his feelings. It was as if everything had changed overnight. *Again.*

I stood up, refusing to hear another word, and glared at Lou as I tried to keep my voice from shaking. "You heard Carter, nothing happened, it was just a mistake."

I pushed past Lou and my dad and yanked open the front door as Carter called out, "Lena, wait!"

Not stopping or looking back, I climbed the stairs, storming the top deck and dodging scattered Adirondack chairs. It was impossible to know who had taken the photos and sent them to Lou, but I had a gut feeling Riley was behind this.

Why would she do this to me? To Carter? This summer was supposed to be my fresh start, but now, because of this, Lou and my dad would never believe I had changed. I collapsed onto the deck bench, my head in my hands.

This was my last night at camp, and it was turning into a disaster. I should've been celebrating with Jojo, Denny, and Theo, but instead, I was ending camp just like I started it: *on my own.*

Footsteps echoed up the deck, and I spun to see my dad rushing towards me. His face was stern, and I buried my hands in my face again. "Dad, I just need a minute."

My dad sat down beside me, his tone firm but softer than before. "I'm not here to lecture you, Lena."

Shocked, I stared up at him. "You're not?"

"No." He shook his head, eyeing me skeptically. "I left that young man downstairs to talk to Lou, but I didn't want to hear his version of the story. I want the truth from you."

Defensively, I clasped my hands in my lap. "Dad, I know what those pictures showed but it's not what it looked like."

"I don't want excuses, Lena," he countered, narrowing his eyes at me. "Why did you break camp rules? Lou stuck her neck out to get you here."

"It's not what you think!" I cried. "Why do you always have to believe the worst in me? Why can't you just see for once that I'm trying my best here?"

Dad's expression faltered. "Stop shouting and just tell me the truth."

"Okay," I gave in, leveling with him. "The truth is that I hated it here. I even tried to hitchhike to the bus stop in Meadowbrook—on crutches, I might add."

To my surprise, Dad remained unfazed.

"But Carter was there for me," I carried on. "He stopped me and he listened and he studied with me. He was there when I decided to become a Christian—"

"So why all the sneaking around?" Dad interjected.

I grappled with how to tell him, but I knew it was best for me to just come right out and say it. "His ex-girlfriend is here, and they had a bad breakup, and we were trying to just keep things to ourselves."

Dad's sudden laughter caught me off guard.

"What's so funny?"

"You just remind me of me when I was your age," he confessed. "I can see where you're coming from."

"You can?" I choked out.

He nodded, bemused by my truth. "Honey, I don't believe the worst in you. If I did, I would have never sent you up here this summer. I have always seen your big heart, even when you're hurting. I just wanted my little girl back, and though you couldn't see it at the time, I believed this place was what your heart needed to get back on track."

As the conversation turned around, I wrapped my arms around his shoulders. He hugged me close, chuckling softly into my ear. Pulling back, he brushed a stray hair out of my face. "I believe you, and I think this young man is genuine. But I think someone else needs your apology right now."

Dad was right. I didn't have a moment to waste, and I didn't want to leave any words unsaid.

"I should find Lou."

***

As Dad and I headed into the Dining Hall, the ceremony was already starting. Hannah was onstage announcing Craft Cabin art winners, handing ribbons out to the campers she called to the stage. Colorful plastic tablecloths and clear plates adorned the tables, a departure from the worn dishes we'd reused all year. Campers, dressed in their best, stood out in stark contrast to their casual summer attire.

Out of the corner of my eye, I caught sight of Denny and Jojo. Jojo looked just as beautiful as ever, and Denny—well he looked like Denny. He wore a neon floral Hawaiian shirt and had styled his hair, clearly making an effort to impress her. When she spotted me, she waved me over.

"Hey, Jojo is over there, can you go grab a seat?" I directed dad. "I'm going to find Lou."

I managed to catch a glimpse of Lou hurrying back into the kitchen as Dad quietly slipped between the tables, making his way towards Jojo.

In a swift manner, I hurriedly trailed behind Lou and entered the kitchen, only to be met with the noisy summer farewell of the clanging pots and pans. As I entered, she spun to face me, surprisingly calm. "Lena, what are you—"

"You deserve an explanation," I pleaded. "I'm so sorry, I know what Carter and I did was against the rules, but I can't apologize for spending time with him."

Her eyes widened in surprise and embarrassment as others stared. I saw her neck flush, but I needed her to listen.

"I mean, I am sorry for breaking the rules," I apologized. "But I was really struggling when I got here."

"I know," she confirmed her eyes softening.

"Carter helped me though, Lou," I explained, lowering my voice. "We weren't always alone, but I know that's beside the point. He helped me find my way back to God and I can't apologize for that."

"I hear you," she sighed. "I can't condone what you both did, but I am proud of you. Well, proud of you both."

"You are?" I asked, feeling relieved.

She nodded frantically. "Getting to see you this summer and the growth you've made here has helped me, too. I've missed you so much, Lena. I've missed all of you."

Feeling heat prickle behind my eyes, I threw my arms around her. "Thank you, Lou. Thank you for everything."

She held me tightly before pulling back. "Now you have to go to dinner. Those are the rules and I have hungry campers to feed."

Lou didn't have to tell me twice. Ducking out of the way, I crept over and found my seat beside my dad. I looked to the stage where Denny was standing proudly with a trophy in his hands.

"What have I missed?" I wondered, leaning over to Dad.

He shrugged, his expression puzzled, but Jojo caught me up. "They're calling out Mister and Miss NHBC."

I beamed in surprise. "Denny won?"

Jojo nodded in elation. From the stage, Hannah leaned back into the microphone. "And this year's Miss NHBC is... Jojo Wright!"

Cheering wildly, I joined the hall's thunderous applause. Jojo and Denny shared a triumphant hug when she reached the stage, and together they held their trophies to the sky.

As the cheers faded, Hannah grabbed a ribbon just as I noticed Lou slip off the stage, zooming around the Dining Hall like The Flash. "This next award is for the camper who has shown the most growth since arriving at camp. When you come to camp, it's not about where you begin, but about where you end up before you leave. This camper showed tremendous growth, and I personally cannot wait to see what the Lord has in store for this person."

The hall grew silent as Hannah paused before she announced, "Without further ado, this year's award for Most Improved Camper goes to Lena Harris!"

I was frozen in place until Dad's gentle tug brought me back to reality. I stood up, and the surreal moment washed over me as I made my way to the stage. Hannah pulled me into a quick embrace before handing the ribbon to me.

Placing her hand over the mic, she whispered, "I'm so proud of you, Lena. Great job this summer!"

Those words held deep meaning, coming from a girl I'd admired for her inner and outer beauty since I was a little kid. As I gazed out at the cheering crowd, my eyes drank in the surreal scene. What struck me most were the cheers erupting from the small table by the fireplace. I turned to find Carter standing, shouting from the top of his lungs, "GO LENA!"

Carter raised his hands, clapping wildly, his eyes a mix of joy and sorrow. I stood frozen, my gaze fixed on his until Hannah's voice interrupted the moment, moving on to the next award. I was stunned to win, thinking I had been disqualified, but seeing Carter cheer me on after everything that had happened between us proved to be the biggest surprise of all.

28

"Are you sure you want to stay for Devo?" I asked Dad.

"Of course, now stop worrying about me."

We sat down beside Jojo and Denny, still clutching their trophies, settling in at the amphitheater for the final Devo of the summer. I startled when Theo sat down next to me with Katie in tow, trying to discreetly hold hands.

"Congratulations on the award, Mermaid," Theo commended quietly, so only I could hear.

I grinned, finally receiving a compliment from him. "Thanks, Theo."

"It would have been nice to see that improvement on the field, but we'll chalk it up to that pesky ankle of yours."

I scoffed, knowing he was incapable of giving too high a compliment. Theo flashed me a sly smile before returning to Katie. With all of the past week's drama, I had missed out on Theo's good news. I knew he had waited a long time for his shot with Katie, and I was happy for him.

I nudged him, throwing him a subtle double thumbs-up, silently mouthing, "Good job!"

He brushed me off with a dismissive hand, as if I were an annoying sibling. I grinned to myself, noticing his sideways grin before Katie grabbed his full attention. With Theo and Katie and Denny and Jojo, all of my friends seemed to get their summer shot at happiness. I tried not to dwell on my missed opportunity with Carter.

Adam took his place at the front of the crowd to start the lesson, and I glanced over at Dad, who appeared tense but focused. I wasn't sure if it was Theo's presence or the rarity of Dad hearing sermons, but I decided not to take this moment for granted. Bowing my head ever so slightly, I silently thanked God.

"This summer, you have all heard several devotionals," Adam declared at the front of the crowd. "Tonight, on our final evening, I'm not going to preach to you. These fleeting moments of fellowship together are just as meaningful as any lesson I can share tonight."

"I want to leave you all with this advice," Adam continued. "Treat the messages you have heard this summer as fuel. When you go back out into the world, back to your homes, back to school, back to your jobs, remember that no matter where you are, there is always someone there in need of the Gospel."

As I listened to Adam for the last time, emotion swelled in my chest, knowing tomorrow I would leave and all of this would be over.

"You all carry the sword of Truth," Adam shared, holding up the Bible in his hand. "You can tackle anything that comes your way with the Lord by your side. But each of you has a light inside of you, so don't be afraid to let it shine so others can see Jesus in each of you."

As Adam spoke, a lump formed in my throat, moved by his inspiring words.

"Before we leave here tonight," Adam finished, scanning the crowd. "I hope that none of you leave without a clear conscience before God. If there is anyone here tonight who has a need, please come forward as we stand together and sing."

With Adam's invitation, we rose to our feet in unison. Lyrics flashed on the projector behind him, and the crowd joined in the song on display.

Love one another for love is of God
He who loves is born of God and knows God
He who does not love does not know God
For God is love, God is love

I struggled to hold back tears as the lyrics swept over me. Nearby, Theo and Katie held hands, while Denny wrapped his arm around Jojo on the other side of my dad. In a few minutes, I would be climbing into my dad's truck and leaving all of them and the summer we spent together behind.

Swallowing my tears, I saw a figure emerge from the left edge of the crowd as the song ended. My stomach leaped into my chest when I noticed Carter was standing beside Adam. The two of them were whispering together, Adam holding the mic behind his back.

When they were finished, Adam clapped Carter on the back, facing the crowd once again. "My brother Carter here comes before us tonight with a broken and contrite heart."

I grasped my hands in my lap, my palms growing clammy as I listened.

"Would you like to have a word, brother?" Adam passed the mic to Carter.

Carter tapped the microphone, sending a piercing beep through the sound system, causing groans to erupt among the throng of campers. I winced, covering my ears as others squirmed.

"Sorry about that," Carter spoke into the mic. "I, um, have done some things this summer that I need to apologize to all of you for."

My stomach twisted as I braced for the truth. I couldn't believe he was apologizing publicly.

"I'm sorry for breaking camp rules this summer and setting a bad example. I'm not perfect, and I've made mistakes that hurt people," Carter confessed, as he stood bravely before the crowd, his eyes downcast. "I want to do better and ask for forgiveness. If anyone wants to talk, I'll be down at the lake tonight before we leave."

He handed the microphone back to Adam, and I watched as Carter walked away, disappearing over the hill and heading for our spot. Adam dismissed us, and I suddenly felt eyes on me.

"What?" I asked, staring back at my dad, Denny, Theo, Jojo, and a shy Katie.

To my surprise, Dad was the one to break the silence. "I haven't been around this summer, but even I knew that apology was for you."

My jaw dropped, and Jojo moved to stand beside me. "Lena, I had no idea what happened between you two until Denny filled me in at dinner. I'm not sure what you're thinking, but if there's one thing I know about Carter Rose, it's that you can trust him to stand by his word."

"I'm just glad it wasn't someone else," my dad interrupted, his gaze drifting to Theo. I shot him a suspicious look, wondering again what his problem was with the Lockwoods.

"Look," Denny offered, "I've never seen Carter broken up over anyone like he's been broken up over you, Lena. He would kill me if he knew I told you that, but there is no greater love than when one helps out a friend."

"That's not even how the verse goes, *Dennis*," Theo interjected, returning to the conversation.

"I wasn't quoting scripture, *Theodore*," Denny retorted.

"Obviously," Theo rolled his eyes.

I scanned the eyes of those staring back at me before crossing my arms defensively. "So, I'm guessing you all think I need to go find Carter?"

"Yes," they chirped in unison, including my dad.

"You guys don't know what's happened," I objected, still feeling hesitant.

"So?" Theo asked, re-engaged in the conversation. "The guy went up before the whole camp and God Himself to apologize and repent. The least you can do is hear him out."

I was shocked to see my dad chuckling at Theo. "He's right, honey."

"Dad!" I shouted, appalled.

Dad shrugged, "Camp is over Lena. You're not breaking any rules now."

I realized they were right. After all Carter and I had been through this summer, I couldn't just leave things unresolved between us. Carter had been there for me, especially when I felt all alone. If we had any shot at moving forward, even as friends, I knew what I had to do.

"Okay, okay!" I exclaimed. "I'm going."

***

As I had done several times before, I made my way down the gravel path towards the lake. Under the moonlit canopy of trees, the crunch of rocks beneath my feet harmonized with the crickets' chirping. As I reached the shore, the rocks' gentle rhythm blended with the soft sand. A tiny bonfire crackled beside Carter, its firelight dancing across his face. Standing with his hands in his pockets, Carter had loosened his shirt. He didn't move until I drew near, his eyes meeting mine.

"Hi," he greeted me, with notes of uncertainty in his voice. "Thanks for coming."

"Hi," I spoke flatly, approaching him until we were close enough to talk, but keeping my distance. We stood in silence for a long moment before he took a step closer to me. As I kept my gaze fixed on the crackling fire, I attempted to ready myself, but I had no idea what to expect.

"The other day when you were telling me about Riley," Carter began, "you said that I was going to the banquet with her. Did she tell you that?"

I kept my eyes lowered and nodded silently in response.

"I want you to know there was more to that conversation." He edged closer to me. "But only if you want to hear it."

I gazed up at Carter, his face inches from mine, the fire's shadows dancing across his features. "I'm listening."

Standing still, he spoke slowly. "She saw me going to the kitchen the other day and confronted me about you."

I frowned. "She did?"

Carter nodded. "She saw me kiss you in the pool but wanted to know where she and I stood."

"Where you stood?" I asked, repeating after him, trying to process his story.

He ran his hands through his hair. "She asked if I was interested in going to the banquet with her, and I didn't really give her an answer, which was *my mistake*. That's what I tried to tell you and Lou tonight, but you ran out."

"I was upset," I told him, sounding annoyed, my eyes flicking back to the fire.

"I know." Carter crept closer. "I didn't want Riley to get upset, so I told her I had to be on duty for the banquet. I thought I was doing the right thing, trying to keep the peace, so I made a dumb joke and told her if I was just a camper for the summer we could go as friends."

Casting another glance at him, I couldn't help but notice the unmistakable expression of regret in his eyes.

"But I saw you hug her too, that day, the two of you were on the porch in front of the Dining Hall." I whispered, the hurt clear in my voice. "It seemed like you two were having a moment."

The disappointment shone clear in his eyes. "There was no moment. I was only trying to be kind to her, I promise. Now I know that I shouldn't have hugged her and I hate that you thought what you saw was anything other than me trying to be a friend to Riley and nothing more."

Unable to find the words, I stared down at the flames in front of us as I processed his truth.

"I'm sorry for whatever she said to you to make you believe we were getting back together, Lena," he apologized again. "I've been so focused on keeping the peace with Riley that I may have given her false hope and, in the process, ruined what you and I have. Or, maybe I should say, *had*."

I sighed, feeling foolish for believing Riley. If only I'd spoken to Carter sooner, we could have avoided this huge mess and spent more time together.

"The other day, I saw her come into the Dining Hall, and she looked upset."

Carter raised his eyebrows, recalling the moment. "She was really upset. I reminded her that our relationship was over, and so was any chance of having a friendship."

"Wow." I eyed him. "I can't believe that."

"Believe it," Carter said, his voice firm. "I'm not some guy that goes around trying to play the field, Lena. I meant what I said earlier this week. I have feelings for you, and I'm not ready to let you leave without making sure you know that."

Our eyes locked, and he drew closer, the distance between us shrinking in the flickering firelight.

Peering nervously down at my feet suddenly, I chuckled. "When I first got to camp this summer, this was the last place on earth where I thought I would find happiness."

"And you feel differently now?" he asked, towering right above me.

I nodded, keeping my head down as I spoke. "I never thought I would be leaving so much behind."

"What are you leaving behind, Lena?"

"You," I spoke, our faces inches apart. If I moved any closer, there was no going back. "And Lou, and Jojo, and this whole amazing summer."

His eyes met mine, a sad smile scrawling over his face. "I don't want you to leave."

"Me either," I agreed.

Carter took a small step back and held out his pinky to me. I looked down at his hand, and a small smile spread across my face. "What are you doing?"

"Give me your pinky and let's make a promise," he said. Taking his little finger, I interlaced it with mine.

"What are we promising?" I wondered, holding his hand with mine.

"No matter where we are or where life takes us, we will talk every day. We'll always be honest with each other and we'll always tell each other the truth, even if it hurts."

"I promise," I vowed without pause.

With a satisfied grin, Carter nudged our joined fists towards me. "You have to kiss it to seal it."

I chuckled and kissed my balled-up fist. With a gentle movement, Carter leaned in, bringing his face close to our entwined fingers, before he carefully let go of our hands. As his warm and tender lips gently brushed against mine, I felt a wave of shivers coursing down my spine.

When he pulled back, he smiled, gazing down at me. "You can't break our promise."

I grinned up as he pulled me to his chest. "I won't."

"I know Freeport is far, but I'm willing to try to make things work if you are," Carter offered, his chocolate eyes staring into mine, dancing with firelight.

I pulled back to look up at him. "Like, make our relationship official?"

He laughed, nodding. "That's exactly what I mean."

"Okay," I agreed. Before I could say anything else, he pulled me to him once more. "You know, this summer turned out far better than I could have ever imagined."

"How so, Dutch?" he questioned, his chin resting on top of my head as we held each other beneath the night sky.

"Because no matter where I look, good or bad, God's hand is all over it," I replied.

He drew back, his smile plastered to his handsome face. "I told you."

Releasing me, Carter stepped back, withdrew a beaded bracelet from his pocket, and handed it to me. "I've been trying to give you this all week. Not just to remember me by, but to remember *whose* you truly are."

My jaw dropped as I stared down at the colorful beaded bracelet that read *July twenty-fourth*. The day I became a Christian.

"Carter, I love it," I gasped, as I slid the piece onto my left wrist.

Carefully, he patted out the fire before reaching for my hand. "Shall we?"

I took his hand as we walked side by side up the shore and back to camp to say our goodbyes. Neither of us knew what tomorrow held, but I had faith that God would be guiding us, no matter what happened next.

Acknowledgements

This book has been in the making since COVID consumed the world in 2020. Telling others about Jesus has always been important to me and at the forefront of my Christian walk. I had been reading a lot but felt unsatisfied by the books I picked up. I craved a certain story that seemed impossible to find and I wondered if others were feeling the same. While I felt lonely and isolated in that season of life, Lena's story began to take shape and was eventually born.

There are so many people to thank for helping me create this story. I first have to thank my Heavenly Father, in short, for everything. I hope Lena's story is able to reach many more people than I ever could, but more than that, I hope the gospel packed in these pages pricks the heart of all those who need to hear and know the truth. Mark 16:15 says, *"And He said to them, 'Go into all the world and preach the gospel to every creature. He who believes and is baptized will be saved, but he who does not believe will be condemned.'"* I gave my life to the Lord years ago and this verse was pivotal in my decision to write this book and share the Gospel. The Lord loves each and every one of us and no matter where we are in life, we are never too far or too late to give our lives back to Him.

Next, I have to thank my husband, Homer. Fourteen years ago you walked into chemistry class and changed my life. Thank you for choosing to love me and for daring to be a man to challenge me and push me out of my comfort zone. When I begin to dream, question myself or wonder if my aspirations are even possible, you keep me grounded and always help make my dreams a reality. Every time you tell me, "I'm here for you," I feel your unwavering support. I love you and our life together.

To my mom and dad, you both always supported me in everything I wanted to try, even if I failed. Mom, you have always been the best listener and advice giver. You have always been in my corner encouraging me to do anything I set my mind to. Thank you for everything you have done and will do for me.

Dad, every hour you spent in our backyard helping me improve in playing softball, basketball, tennis, and every other sport I tried; and also for the hours you spent teaching me math at the kitchen table. None of it ever went unnoticed. I will forever hear your cheers from the sidelines, no matter what I'm trying to conquer in my life. I love you and I'm so thankful to you and mom for the simple life you gave me. Growing up in our tiny, humble home, I never had to doubt that I was loved, which is more than many people can say.

To my sister, thank you for your input and feedback when I needed your help. Your blunt honesty has become one of your most endearing qualities. It is a rare gift that I count on, and as I've said a million times before, I hope to be just like you when I grow up.

To John and MAA, thank you for being two of the best people I know and for welcoming me into your family with open arms. Your ability to help me find Bible answers is a blessing to me. You both live your lives as a ministry to the Lord that inspires all who know you. Thank you for all you do, for all you have done, and for all you will do for me. Because of your continued encouragement, this book became a possibility for me. I love you guys.

To Sara, you were willing to take on my initial manuscript and help me develop Lena's story from the other side of the world. I can't thank you enough for your dedication and helping me make this book a reality. I could write an essay on how grateful I am to you, but I hope a simple thank you will do.

To Jackie, thank you for seeing my vision and creating the book cover of my dreams. One of the greatest blessings of the military is the community it brings into our lives. Your talent is unmatched and I'm so grateful you volunteered as tribute to take this project on.

To Sandy, thank you for your encouragement when I've shared my dreams with you and for the writing dice you gifted me to fight writer's block. You are a treasure and I'm grateful for your leadership.

To my dear friends, Casey, Kyla, Kate, Amber, Pam and all who have cheered me on in this process, I'm so grateful for you. Also, to my ARC readers for all the honest feedback you gave me. Because of all of you, I felt confident to push forward when doubt or insecurity would set in. I hope you all love this story, I couldn't have written this book without you.

To Susan and Robin, thank you for taking my mess of a document and beautifying the pages so this book can be out in the world. I appreciate your hard work so much. Thank you for your help in my publishing journey and helping make my dreams come true.

Finally, to you, the reader, I hope this book resonates with you in some way, and helps you, *wherever you are*, in your walk with the Lord. I know what it's like to struggle with my faith and oftentimes, I wish I had a book or character I could relate to. A book that didn't shy away from tough topics but still showed me God's love. A book that demonstrates the struggles and hardships of the Christian walk, but also shows Christian love. A book that not only inspires but also shows how important it is to not take mine or anyone else's word as gospel, but God's. Lastly, a book that inspires you to pick up your Bible and read it for yourself.

My dream is to help bridge the gap in young adult Christian fiction and give you a book you love. This passion project is for you. Thank you for picking up this book and for taking this journey with me. I hope you are blessed by this story and find this book worth sharing with others who are deserving of the message within.

HYMNS

Albert E. Brumley. "I'll Fly Away" Hartford Music Company, 1932.

Simon Marak. "I Have Decided to Follow Jesus"

Geoff Moore and Steven Curtis Chapman. "Listen to Our Hearts" *Listen to Our Hearts, Vol. 2* Phil Naish & Brown Bannister, 1998.

Judson W. Van DeVenter. "I Surrender All" *Gospel Songs of Grace and Glory*, 1896.

Janice Detweiler. "The Greatest Commands" *Maranatha!*, 1973.

Bob Hudson. "Humble Yourself in the Sight of the Lord" *Maranatha!* 1978.

Scripture References

"Greater love has no one than this, than to lay down one's life for his friends."

John 15:13 NKJV

"When He had called the people to Himself, with His disciples also, He said to them, Whoever desires to come after Me, let him deny himself, and take up his cross, and follow Me. For whoever desires to save his life will lose it, but whoever loses his life for My sake and the gospel's will save it. For what will it profit a man if he gains the whole world, and loses his own soul? Or what will a man give in exchange for his soul? For whoever is ashamed of Me and My words in this adulterous and sinful generation, of him the Son of Man also will be ashamed when He comes in the glory of His Father with the holy angels."

Mark 8:34-38 NKJV

"For it is the God who commanded light to shine out of darkness, who has shone in our hearts to give the light of the knowledge of the glory of God in the face of Jesus Christ. But we have this treasure in earthen vessels, that the excellence of the power may be of God and not of us. We are hard-pressed on every side, yet not crushed; we are perplexed, but not in despair; persecuted, but not forsaken; struck down, but not destroyed—"

2 Corinthians 4:6-9 NKJV

"But, speaking the truth in love, may grow up in all things into Him who is the head—Christ—from whom the whole body, joined and knit together by what every joint supplies, according to the effective working by which every part does its share, causes growth of the body for the edifying of itself in love."
Ephesians 4:15-16 NKJV

"Death and life are in the power of the tongue, And those who love it will eat its fruit."
Proverbs 18:21 NKJV

"Imitate me, just as I also imitate Christ."
1 Corinthians 11:1 NKJV

"Then He said: 'A certain man had two sons. And the younger of them said to his father, 'Father, give me the portion of goods that falls to me.' So he divided to them his livelihood. And not many days after, the younger son gathered all together, journeyed to a far country, and there wasted his possessions with prodigal living. But when he had spent all, there arose a severe famine in that land, and he began to be in want. Then he went and joined himself to a citizen of that country, and he sent him into his fields to feed swine. And he would gladly have filled his stomach with the [b]pods that the swine ate, and no one gave him anything."

But when he came to himself, he said, 'How many of my father's hired servants have bread enough and to spare, and I perish with hunger! I will arise and go to my father, and will say to him, "Father, I have sinned against heaven and before you, and I am no longer worthy to be called your son. Make me like one of your hired servants.'

And he arose and came to his father. But when he was still a great way off, his father saw him and had compassion, and ran and fell on his neck and kissed him. And the son said to him, 'Father, I have sinned against heaven and in your sight, and am no longer worthy to be called your son.'

"But the father said to his servants, 'Bring out the best robe and put it on him, and put a ring on his hand and sandals on his feet. And bring the fatted calf here and kill it, and let us eat and be merry; for this my son was dead and is alive again; he was lost and is found.' And they began to be merry.

Now his older son was in the field. And as he came and drew near to the house, he heard music and dancing. So he called one of the servants and asked what these things meant. And he said to him, 'Your brother has come, and because he has received him safe and sound, your father has killed the fatted calf.'

But he was angry and would not go in. Therefore his father came out and pleaded with him. So he answered and said to his father, 'Lo, these many years I have been serving you; I never transgressed your commandment at any time; and yet you never gave me a young goat, that I might make merry with my friends. But as soon as this son of yours came, who has devoured your livelihood with harlots, you killed the fatted calf for him.

And he said to him, 'Son, you are always with me, and all that I have is yours."

Luke 15:11-31 NKJV

"Or do you think that I cannot now pray to My Father, and He will provide Me with more than twelve legions of angels? How then could the Scriptures be fulfilled, that it must happen thus?"

Matthew 26:53-54 NKJV

"And they clothed Him with purple; and they twisted a crown of thorns, put it on His head, and began to salute Him, "Hail,

King of the Jews!" Then they struck Him on the head with a reed and spat on Him; and bowing the knee, they worshiped Him. And when they had mocked Him, they took the purple off Him, put His own clothes on Him, and led Him out to crucify Him."

Mark 15:17-20 NKJV

"And about the ninth hour Jesus cried out with a loud voice, saying, "Eli, Eli, lama sabachthani?" that is, "My God, My God, why have You forsaken Me?"

Matthew 27:46 NKJV

"For My thoughts are not your thoughts, Nor are your ways My ways," says the Lord."

Isaiah 55:8 NKJV

DISCUSSION QUESTIONS

1. Lena arrives at camp feeling disconnected and uncertain about her faith. How do her experiences at camp challenge her perspective about God?

2. Lena reconnects with old acquaintances and forms strong friendships at camp. How do her friends help guide and support her through her struggles?

3. How does Lena's faith transform over the course of the story? Have you ever had a moment where your faith was challenged or tested?

4. What role does Christian community play in Lena's transformation? How important is community in your own faith journey? What does scripture tell us about fellowship with one another?

5. Carter encourages Lena to read the Bible for herself. Why do you think he gives her this advice? Why is it important to study scripture for yourself rather than what others say about salvation?

6. As Lena studies the Bible for herself, she feels convicted by God's Word. Have you ever felt convicted of your need for salvation? If so, what held you back from taking

the next step?

7. Lena reads the Parable of the Prodigal Son. What do we learn about God's love and forgiveness from the story of the prodigal son? How does this reflect His desire for a relationship with us?

8. Jesus' betrayal, suffering, and death convicts Lena. Why do you think Jesus endured these events? What does this reveal about His purpose and the price of sin?

9. Lena reads about how Peter denied Jesus three times, yet Jesus restored him. What does this teach us about grace, second chances, and our own failures?

10. Lena learns how Paul went from persecuting Christians to preaching the gospel. What does his transformation show about the power of Jesus to change lives?

11. Lena discovers that salvation is a gift from God. What does the Bible say about how we should respond to it? How does faith and obedience work together?

12. In her study, Lena discovers that many people in the Bible followed Jesus after hearing the gospel. What do you think made them take that step? Have you ever considered what your response should be?

13. Lena witnesses others at camp become Christians after hearing the gospel and then reads how the Apostle Peter shared the gospel with others. If you heard Paul preaching as he did in Acts Chapter 2, how do you think you would have responded to his sermon? What does their reaction teach us about the urgency of salvation?

14. What moments in Lena's journey stood out to you as

pivotal in her decision to become a Christian? Why?

15. Lena learns that no matter our circumstances, Jesus invites everyone to follow Him, but He also calls for faithfulness. What do you think it means to truly surrender your life to Christ, and if you have not, what might be holding you back?

About the Author

Aiessa Holland is an Enneagram two, fur-mom, and avid reader. She was born in Bangor, Maine, and raised in the small town of East Bend, North Carolina. Aiessa graduated Summa Cum Laude from American Military University with a Bachelor's of Business Management. She is married to her high school sweetheart and is an active duty military spouse. Wherever the Air Force sends her family is where she calls home.

As a lifelong reader with a fervent desire to serve God, Aiessa decided to step out in faith to write her debut novel, The Summer Away. Her hope is that the story helps readers to find an inspirational book that also serves as a compass, pointing them to the Lord.

When Aiessa isn't reading or writing, you can find her serving the military through non-profit work, volunteering in her local community, spending time with her family and enjoying the great outdoors.

CONNECT WITH AIESSA

Website: https://aiessaholland.wixsite.com/aiessaholland

Instagram: https://www.instagram.com/iesuh000/

iesuh's inside circle official Facebook group:
https://www.facebook.com/groups/1702121220531467